Dorothea in the Mirror

Other Books by Lois Santalo

The Wind Dies at Sunrise

Oops, I Lost My Sense of Humor

The House of Music

The Women of Stormland

Petoskey Stones

I'll Meet You in Syracuse

Dorothea in the Mirror

A Jill Szekely Mystery

Lois Wells Santalo

iUniverse, Inc.

New York   Bloomington

iUniverse books may be ordered through booksellers or by contacting:

iUniverse
1663 Liberty Drive
Bloomington, IN 47403
www.iuniverse.com
1-800-Authors (1-800-288-4677)

Because of the dynamic nature of the Internet, any Web addresses or links contained in this book may have changed since publication and may no longer be valid. The views expressed in this work are solely those of the author and do not necessarily reflect the views of the publisher, and the publisher hereby disclaims any responsibility for them.

ISBN: 978-1-4401-9091-9 (sc)
ISBN: 978-1-4401-9093-3 (dj)
ISBN: 978-1-4401-9092-6 (ebook)

Printed in the United States of America

iUniverse rev. date: 11/25/2009

For Megan and Grace

Acknowledgments

My thanks to the writers' group at Summit UU Fellowship for their help and suggestions in the writing of this book. And a special thanks to Carol Straubinger and my daughter Melanie for proofreading the manuscript.

Introduction

In the 1930s, a wave of immigration different from earlier ones tumbled refugees like the Szekelys onto American shores.

The new arrivals were not steerage immigrants. The Szekely family traveled second class aboard the big liner only to guard what little wealth they were allowed to take with them in their flight from Europe. They dreamed of no mythical streets paved with gold; they were no part of those huddled masses welcomed by the Statue of Liberty. On the contrary, they were the crème de la crème, Europe's best educated and most creative. In this family alone, father Janos had invented a television tube crucial to the development of the new technology, and mother Annika had achieved fame as a concert pianist. Their gifted musician son, Zoltan, had already at age ten performed with the Budapest Philharmonic, while six-year-old Katya had won a school prize for linguistic excellence in Spanish and English.

In Budapest, in the late 1920s, the parents had watched as a tidal wave of anti-Semitism rolled toward them, with a pogrom to forewarn them of Kristallnacht. For young Zoltan's sake, not to mention that of his little sister, Katya, they resolved to flee a homeland where, after traveling the high road to success, they now saw little hope for the future.

The decision meant abandoning not only their life savings but also job, family, friends, house, furniture, inherited Pleyel piano, everything they treasured except for the few heirlooms packed in their trunks. Yet when rumors circulated that Jews were being forced to wear armbands and herded back into ghettos, they knew that, whatever they might encounter in the New World, it had to be better than the Old.

They clung to this belief as, after the long torment of applications, appeals, and uncertainty, the dream came true and they at last stood on deck watching the harbor of the French city of Cherbourg recede into the distance.

They couldn't have guessed what the New World had in store for the children they'd hoped to guard from disaster.

CHAPTER 1

⟶◦⟵

Shocking News

—1948

THE CALL CAME AN HOUR before quitting time. My boss at Columbia University's Butler Library waved me to the phone, saying, "For you, Mrs. Szekely." Puzzling as to who would bother me at work, I concealed my annoyance and tried not to bark out my hello.

In a sepulchral voice, my estranged husband, Zoltan, said, "Jill, Dorothea has been murdered." Before I could do more than gasp in surprise, he added, "The police seem to think I had something to do with it. I'm being held for questioning."

I didn't believe it; it was too improbable. "But, Zoltan," I sputtered, "you're not … I mean, Dorothea is—" He and Dorothea had something going long ago, one of those youthful romances never meant for permanence, but that was ancient history now. "It's been eons, hasn't it?"

He persisted, giving no clue that my question had even registered. "I need you to get in touch with my parents, Jill, and also contact Cousin Nadya. Would you do that for me, please?"

I hung up convinced he'd call back, laughing at his prank. Yet I was puzzled, disturbed. Zoltan wasn't given to practical jokes. When it struck me he wouldn't kid around with me at my job—my spouse took all sources of income seriously—I called his apartment. A roomer who shared the place informed me, "Sorry to scare you, but it's true. Our boy has been carted off by the police."

Could he be in on the foolishness? "Come on, George, quit your kidding. This is not funny. I'm at work and—"

"I'm not kidding. I didn't believe it either. A concert pianist—these things don't happen to people like him. I debated whether to call you, but being that you and Zoltan are separated … well, I didn't know what to do."

I sighed and hung up. Shaken, I took a break, went out to the corner drugstore equipped with change to cover long distance charges, and headed for the pay phone.

With some hesitation, I called my father-in-law, Janos, at his workplace in Schenectady. It hadn't been easy for me to talk to him since I'd left my husband. As I'd anticipated, Janos's tone grew cool and dismissive when he recognized my voice. Still, I somehow managed to convince him I had news. When I finished imparting it, he answered dubiously, "Someone's pulling your leg. My son knows better than to involve himself again with Dorothea."

"It was Zoltan's voice."

"Pranksters can be good vocal imitators," he reminded me.

I agreed but still felt uneasy. I bit my lip. "Janos, it can't hurt to check."

"All right, I'll contact the NYPD." He told me not to worry, that it couldn't be true. He added a promise to handle everything, including getting in touch with his New York cousins if it should prove necessary. "Which it won't," he added with a finality that ended the conversation.

I spent the final minutes of the workday assuring myself that misguided friends had created a scene to arouse my sympathy for my spouse. They'd all been pushing for us to get back together, and they clearly hoped to set me worrying about him—not without success. I clock-watched, clicking fingernail against tooth as the minute hand made its slow climb to the top of the hour.

When I arrived home after work, my housemate, Frieda Fishbein, informed me I'd had a return call from my father-in-law. "He said to tell you your in-laws are en route to New York. They couldn't learn anything; the police won't answer questions over the phone."

I winced. "Tell me I didn't send Zoltan's folks on a wild-goose chase." We'd never had a warm relationship to begin with, but this craziness could finish me off in their eyes.

Frieda wanted to know what was going on. I told her about the phone call that had left me nervous and alarmed. Hands behind my back, I paced the small Greenwich Village apartment I'd recently, after leaving Zoltan, begun sharing with my one-time college roommate. I peered out the window for a moment before flinging myself onto an overstuffed chair and hugging my knees. I tried to think what might have happened. "Could Zoltan possibly be involved?" He did have a complex history with Dorothea. Yet I answered my own question with an emphatic, "Of course not." And then, "But the police may think—"

"It's easy enough to look into it," Frieda said. "A ten-minute subway ride should provide answers. If we knock on Dorothea's door and she opens it to welcome us, she's okay and this is someone's idea of a joke."

"Frieda, it's rush hour."

"We'll be going the other way." She grabbed her sweater. "Come on, Jill. One quick trip and you'll have your answer."

I hesitated. I didn't want to fall for a trick. "I'm not some naive midwesterner anymore." My New York friends used to kid that I'd buy the Brooklyn Bridge. *I've wised up, pals*, I silently told them.

Admittedly, I wouldn't be satisfied until I checked. Yet I felt wary of testing my hoax theory. The last thing I ever anticipated was that I, or any relative of mine, might be involved in a murder investigation. I mean, I come from a family that's all Gandhi types. Even while we supported the recent war, even while we believed passionately in the need to eliminate Nazism, we Unitarians, Quakers, and Mennonites mourned the killing. "I'd have said," I told Frieda, "that, raised as I was in a church leaning toward conscientious objections, it's impossible for me to be attracted to the type of man who could physically attack a woman. Zoltan, of all people? The idea is ludicrous."

Frieda frowned and tossed me a skeptical look.

Nothing in my experience had prepared me for the possibility that the spouse I'd been married to for more than five years, even granting he was about to become an ex, might be involved in a murder. My impulse was to scream that he wasn't the type. He was a musician for God's sake, and the mildest of men. He'd never shown a capacity for violence. Even under extreme provocation, he wouldn't fight back. Despite all these things that I knew to be true of my husband, I forced myself to face the fact that not even a wife can look deep into the soul of another human being.

"Who the hell is Zoltan Szekely anyway?" Flinging her sweater around her shoulders, Frieda stood by the window and folded her arms. In silhouette, I saw the soft curls I'd long envied and a protruding elbow. "He's a soldier you met and married during the war without knowing a damn thing about him."

"But since then I've had time to find out."

I'm a Szekely at the moment, but my maiden name was Gillian Foster, an anonymous sort of name. I was unique only because I managed to graduate from the university in prewar days, when few women went to college—I was the only female in my high school class who did so—and, right after graduation, contrived to meet this glamorous and gifted Hungarian concert pianist.

"Not Zoltan, not Zoltan!" I repeated it over and over. In honesty, I didn't want the news to be true. I felt no burning jealousy: Dorothea had been before my time. Money shortages, not lack of love, drove us apart. I still loved him. Though ours was a wartime marriage, it wasn't the conventional tale of two incompatible people driven together in the face of a long, perhaps endless, separation.

"What's so special about Zoltan?" Frieda demanded. "He can't crack like other human beings?" She swung around to peer out the window. "I grant he was special for you—I support intermarriages. It's romantic to see a couple so deeply in love that they'll turn away from their own people and embrace another's. But, like the rest of us, Zoltan can reach a breaking point."

I leaned back against the upholstery, ran my hands through my short-cropped red hair, and tried the yoga trick of concentrating on my breathing. *How could this situation come about? Did Zoltan crack because I left him?* Guilt feelings, already close to the surface, flooded through me.

Frieda proffered my sweater and grabbed my arm. "Come on, Jill, up, up. You'll never be satisfied until you check."

"I guess you're right." Rising, I smoothed my coppery hair and my kelly green dress—my favorite color, which I'd worn in mistaken expectation of a lovely spring day. I took the sweater and followed her out the door and down three flights of stairs.

As she'd anticipated, the downtown express wasn't jam-packed. After two stations we got a seat. In a short time, we were in the Village, where my spouse's former girlfriend, Dorothea, rented a room from an Italian family named Falucci. I'd visited her there once, and I led Frieda past neat red brick row houses, each with its own concrete steps, its own green doorway and green shutters.

When we approached Dorothea's place, we saw that the front door stood open and a police car sat parked at the curb. Pangs of apprehension shot through me. I didn't want to know what had happened there.

We paused and waited until the police drove away. With Frieda pulling me, we inched on. No sooner had we reached the steps when a slim, neatly dressed woman appeared in the doorway. She wore a gray business suit, her hair severely drawn back in a bun. Carrying an overnight bag and briefcase, she stared down at us, her expression curious and uneasy.

"We came to visit Dorothea Granger." At the foot of the steps, I forced myself to act casual, pretending I knew nothing.

She brightened and looked us over, her eyes and hair black against a maroon scarf. "Are you a relative of Dotty?" She snapped out the question eagerly, as if she couldn't wait to place her problems in other hands.

I shook my head. "Just a friend. I brought my housemate to meet her. Is she home?"

The woman sighed, slumped, set her bags down, and unbuttoned her jacket. "Dorothea," she announced, "was murdered this morning." *It's true; she is dead! Zoltan? Is it possible?*

A sharp stab of fear went through me.

I straightened and expressed the horror I felt. "Oh, that couldn't be." I floundered. No answer seemed appropriate. "I mean, she wasn't young enough or glamorous enough to inspire murderous jealousy, and she certainly wasn't rich. Who'd bother—?"

"There are other motives besides money and passion." The woman grasped her bags again and gestured toward the door. "Why don't you come in and I'll tell you about it."

I offered up a polite lie. "We don't want to interrupt your plans." Actually, I very much wanted to do exactly that. By now I was overcome with curiosity as well as flooded with jitters. It seemed my spouse really might have wandered into something over his head.

"I'm in no rush." While we climbed the steps, she added, "I'm Maria Bini. I rent the third-floor apartment. The homeowners, the Faluccis, have the second floor, and Dorothea had a room on the first floor." She set the suitcase inside and shut and latched the door behind us. "Mrs. Falucci is in the hospital. Her teenage daughter, Leila, and I were in the house alone when the murder happened. The child's terrified and went to spend the night with friends. I'm about to do the same."

A lingering odor of spicy Italian sauces hung in the air. We stepped into a living room with a large, bare window. As we sidestepped the flowered draperies spread on the floor, Maria explained. "He took the drapes down so he could get the cord he used to strangle her. I found the body slumped over the desk. It was awful."

"He?" I asked.

"The murderer. He'd been visiting Dorothea. A foreigner, name of Zoltan Sake … Sakey … something. The police arrested him. I know we're safe here now, but," she shrugged, "I don't feel safe. It's the shock, I suppose."

She gestured toward the couch. "I can't show you the murder site; the officers locked it up. But they didn't seal off this room."

We sat. I crossed my legs and grasped my knees to stop my hands from shaking. I introduced myself and Frieda, but only by our first names so as not to alert our hostess to my identity. She might not be honest with us if she heard the name Szekely.

She offered tea, which we declined, and asked if we knew Dorothea well. I claimed to be a longtime acquaintance. That wasn't strictly true; I'd only recently learned of her. But I wanted to keep the woman talking, and indeed she relaxed and began her story. "It was just luck that I happened to come home early today. I'm a bookkeeper, and my firm held a sales conference this morning. There were sales reps in town from all over the area—Pennsylvania, New Jersey, Upstate New York. It was chaos. With all the noise and confusion, I couldn't concentrate. I fancied that here I'd find peace and quiet. Ha, I couldn't have been more wrong."

She let a shudder go through her whole body. Then she plumped a pillow and leaned back against it in a gesture of collapse. "I planned to make cookies—you know, to munch while I worked. I came down here to borrow sugar. The Falucci girl, Leila, was in the shower. I heard the water running. When I passed Dorothea's door, I looked in and saw the woman slumped over her desk. I asked if she was all right. She didn't answer."

"Poor Dorothea," I said. Remembering my manners through the fog of dread that had now struck me, I added, "And what a nightmare experience for you."

She shivered again. "It was spooky. She was so still. I knew something was wrong. Then I spotted that cord around her neck … the splotchy red spots, face blue around the edges, protruding tongue. Ooh, terrible." Her shivering grew more dramatic as she recalled the scene of her gruesome discovery. "I screamed. Leila came running, wet and wrapped in a towel. The poor girl went crazy with yelling. She feared the man was still in the house. I had a terrible time calming her down—and then I had a struggle dialing the police. My fingers shook. They're still shaking." She held up trembling hands to show us.

"But Zoltan?" I said. "Are you sure?"

"Oh, it was him all right," she insisted. "I saw him clearly. He left as I entered, and then started back. If only I'd slammed and locked the door right then, Dorothea would be alive now—but who knew? I went on upstairs. Dotty was writing in her diary when he brought the cord and flung it around her neck. She all but named her killer."

"But why on earth would he do such a thing? It's been years since he and Dorothea—." I caught my breath, fearing I'd given away my identity. Luckily, my informant failed to notice my slip of tongue.

"It was because of the kid," she said.

"The kid? What kid?"

"Dorothea, you see, wanted to talk to him about—well, he fathered one of her children."

"He fathered—?" I choked on the word. Now we were beyond impossible; we'd moved into the realm of the grotesque.

"Didn't you know?" she asked. "She has three children. Zoltan fathered the youngest, Marce, who's almost six. The man's been away in the army, so she couldn't get in touch. When she contacted him, he must have become really, really angry. I mean furious. Zany. Out of control."

She couldn't possibly be talking about my Zoltan. My Zoltan had no child. He'd have told me if he did. He couldn't have concealed such a thing, even had he wanted to—and he wasn't the type of man to want to. Not to mention that the army would have used part of his allotment for child support during those war years. I'd have known.

Either this was a major misunderstanding or someone contrived a masterful frame-up. In any case, my sympathies were all with Zoltan. I shouldn't have left him. I tried to think how I could help. There must be something I could do.

CHAPTER 2

―⁓―

Cody

—1948

EARLIER IN THE DAY, WHEN they first learned of the murder of Dorothea Granger, Cyril Cody had listened as the lieutenant let out a stream of curses. Not that he knew the deceased or agonized over her death; he simply had too much on his plate.

"Well, it's the full moon, sir." The Yanks called Lieutenant Brent Johnson by his initials, B.J., but Cody, being a Brit, felt compelled to speak respectfully to superior officers. Rejected for the British army because one leg was shorter than the other, and wishing to make himself useful, he'd come to New York bringing a group of English children to safety from the bombing. When America joined the war, he found himself stranded, unable to get home. He'd had no trouble getting hired for the NYPD. During wartime, if you were breathing, you qualified for a job.

By now he had married and settled down. Even after nearly a decade on the force, he wasn't what the Yanks called hard-boiled, at least not to a degree to render him a stone-faced New York cop, and he still forgot and dropped his aitches now and then. But his wife wanted to live close to her family, and he had no one back home, so it looked like he'd be staying on

"There's no sign of the moon this time of the day," B.J. growled. "So what in hell's their rush to get a head start on murder? Is there some kind of competition among killers this month?"

Cody shrugged. "The death squad could have bloody waited for the moon to appear." This was a bad time, with the homicide team shorthanded, one detective on vacation, another off to a family funeral.

"Go check it out and see what we've got. Family named Falucci. Seems the Granger woman lived with them." B.J. sighed. "Give me a call and let me know what you find."

"Right, sir."

Cody headed for Greenwich Village. Hotheaded Italians! Their normal conversation would qualify as a catfight in polite-and-proper Britain, so it hardly seemed surprising when their quarrels escalated out of control. He limped along past three-story row houses, many now divided into apartments. When he spotted the right house, he realized he'd beaten the coroner this time. The familiar tan Nash station wagon was nowhere to be seen.

He noticed that the front window was bare of draperies. The door stood open, and two women awaited him on the stoop—or rather, a woman and a girl of about seventeen or eighteen. The woman, neatly dressed in a gray suit, had an arm draped consolingly around the skinny, trembling teenager. The kid's long, dark hair hung awry. Wet, it clung against her shoulder as if she'd just stepped out of the shower. She'd apparently thrown on her pale green dress—to an Englishman, her frock—in haste without first drying herself. He could see water spots here and there on the material.

Cody climbed the steps and held out his ID. "Detective Cyril Cody, NYPD."

"Oh, thank God you've come." The woman breathed a sigh of relief. "There's been a murder, and this child is terrified. We're both terrified."

"I need to see the crime scene, please." Cody spoke calmly, hoping to soothe the trembling pair.

The woman stepped aside. The girl said, "You show him, Maria. I don't want to look at that … thing … again." She covered her eyes.

"It's the first time Leila ever saw a corpse," the woman called Maria explained to Cody. "Hard on young people, you know; they don't take it in that we're all mortal." She added, "I'm Mrs. Bini, and I rent the top-floor flat. Leila is the daughter of the homeowner." Though her voice shook, she clearly struggled to remain calm, probably for the teenager's benefit. "The two of us are the only ones living here—well, Dorothea, of course, and her kid, Marcie. He's in preschool this morning, didn't witness anything. Thank God for that."

Voice barely audible, the girl identified herself. "Leila Falucci." She added, more forcefully, "I need to call my boyfriend. I have no one—my mom's in the hospital."

Cody grasped her shoulder. "'Ere now, don't get your knickers in a twist. You're okay."

"Unless the killer's still in there," she said.

"I'll check out the rest of the house. Which of you found the body?"

"I did." Maria fingered her neck and made a face.

"You didn't touch anything?"

"Well, her shoulder and wrist." She freed herself from the teenager's grasp and raised a hand. "I undid the cord and I … I shook her hoping she wasn't dead. I felt for her pulse. Nothing." She rubbed her cheeks. "I can't believe this—and almost on her wedding day."

"Her wedding day? Who was she marrying?"

"A man named Reggie Jackson. He'll be devastated. Oh, dear, this is such a tragedy."

She led the way indoors. On stepping inside, Cody smelled the pervasive odors of garlic and Italian spices. The Bini woman paused in the front hall and pointed to flowered draperies spread out on the living room floor. "Those weren't like that this morning. He—the visitor—pulled them down so he could use the cord to strangle Dot."

While Leila slid downward to seat herself on the stairs, Maria Bini moved along a narrow hall preceded by a white cat that scuttled into the farthest room. Following, Cody saw that the house had been modified from the original railroad style, with rooms made smaller in order to add a hall. He'd often seen that done with these row houses, allowing for space to be rented out. The room beside the kitchen, no doubt the original dining room, had here been separately enclosed.

With the door flung open, Cody stepped into a sunny studio with a large window looking onto the rear of the house, its postage-stamp yard just big enough to accommodate trash cans, a few red hollyhocks, and straggling morning glories against the fence. A bed piled with pillows doubled as a couch by day. Toys arranged on a shelf under the window, and a truck and blocks on the floor in one corner, indicated a child had played here. A woman—or the remains of one—sat slumped at a desk. He touched her gingerly. Still warm.

Cody hated strangled corpses almost more than the bloody, battered kind, but he made himself inspect the body, red-faced and red-eyed from multiple broken capillaries caused by the pressure of trapped blood. She'd clearly been writing in a book—a diary, he noted—before her death. One hand all but clutched the pen, which had fallen close by. A once good-looking woman, slim, late thirties, well preserved, only the faintest of lines around the eyes and mouth—but ugly now, with discolored face and abrasions on the neck. She'd kicked and fought hard enough to lose a shoe; he saw scrape marks on the desk legs. The cord, fine but strong, clearly the pull-cord for those newly removed draperies in the living room and a perfect murder weapon, had been flung onto the floor beside her. There'd be no fingerprints on a thing like that.

Just when he began mourning the problems this would cause, Maria announced, "We can identify the man who did it, Sergeant."

He looked up. "This visitor bloke?"

"Yes. I understand he was the father of her third child. Dot was excited about getting in touch with him again. Little did she know. When he decided on murder, he must have sneaked into the living room and taken down the draperies to get—"

"You can confirm all this for sure?"

"Well, as I say, you can see … in the living room—"

"I mean, about the bloke?" In a quick glance at the diary, he'd spotted the name *Zoltan Szekely*.

"I saw him go out and then heard the door open again." She leaned against the wall and narrowed her eyes as if trying to visualize the scene. She swallowed hard and clearly sought to organize her story. "I looked back from the stairway when I felt the breeze, and there he stood, on the stoop, frowning. No doubt you'll find his prints on the doorknob."

"You haven't touched it?"

"The door stood ajar when we went out."

"So, after entering, you went on upstairs?"

"Yes, but Leila heard this guy come in and walk down the hall. She was showering when he clomped past the bathroom. He didn't even try to be quiet."

Leila confirmed the story from the stairs. "That's true, officer."

"It took him only minutes to do the killing," Maria said. "Poor Dot didn't even have a chance to scream. Later, I came down to borrow sugar and found the corpse like this."

"How much later?"

"Four or five minutes. I'd only just removed my hat and washed my hands. Leila was still in the shower."

"And who's this 'he'?"

"He's Dot's former lover. A foreign sounding name—Leila knows it. She saw him. She even let him in."

Cody soon phoned the lieutenant. "Seems we won't have to worry about a lengthy investigation with this one, sir. There are two witnesses who claim to have seen the murderer enter the place—foreigner named Zoltan Szekely—plus the woman's diary describes their disagreement. Miss Granger had just informed the bloke he'd fathered her youngster. Learning he had a kid would mean he'd be liable for child support. He appears to have been too angry to discuss the matter. He left but then apparently had second thoughts and returned. Miss Granger heard his footsteps behind her and noted the fact in her diary. The Falucci girl heard them, too, from the bathroom. It's kind of spooky, sir—the victim practically recorded her own murder. She thought the bloke was teasing her."

"I can't believe this. Nobody'd be dumb enough to commit murder with witnesses so close. Who is this Zoltan Szekely?"

"I understand he's a music student, Juilliard graduate, former lover of Miss Granger. No previous arrests, nothing on him—but I have his address. Found it in the victim's desk."

A deep sigh breathed across the phone wires. "Juilliard students don't generally turn violent. They're a motivated bunch—takes years of practice to become a musician. Are you sure about this, Cody?"

"Well, sir, I have no evidence yet. I mean, you can't get fingerprints from a drapery cord, and there are no priors—we don't have prints on record. But we have the witnesses, the diary—and the doorknob."

As if determined to prick Cody's balloon, B.J. pointed out, "Your witnesses, Cody, are the gals who found the body. They were already in the house; that puts them at the top of the suspect list. Don't be too quick to believe—"

"I admit I haven't interviewed the birds extensively. They're pretty shaken. One's just a kid, and the other is a renter, moved in recently, no apparent involvement with the family. They believe Szekely came here seeking consolation for a broken marriage and got more than he bargained for when he learned of the boy. Also, the Granger woman was soon to be married, so there might be jealousy there."

"Married? Might the fiancé be involved?"

"It was Szekely who came here. We have witnesses, and the diary."

"Who knows, the deceased may have helped events along," the lieutenant speculated. "Taunting, you know. Victims don't always know when to shut up."

"I'd say we have sufficient cause to pick up our man for questioning and a lineup."

The lieutenant sighed again. "Maybe you're onto something. High time we got a break on a case. We've had corpses coming at us hot and heavy of late."

"You're so right, sir."

"You'll have to take on this one, Cody. Don't let the women off the hook without further investigation. But go ahead, haul the guy in and grill him—and rope in those women for a lineup. If they finger him, book him. Also try to get his permission to search his apartment. If he balks, get a warrant—and use his fingerprints for comparison with any you find at the murder scene. You'll need to interview the estranged wife, too. I'll send Yonkers along to help you." Yonkers was Detective Joe Larramie, newly moved to the city from the northerly town.

"Yes, sir." Vaguely irritated at being told how to do his job, Cody concealed his annoyance and hung up the phone. At least he was in charge for once. Turning back as the coroner arrived, he waved the elderly man toward the crime scene. "Down the hall, Wilkins—the room before the kitchen. I'm off to check out the rest of the house. Send Yonkers to me when he comes."

CHAPTER 3

∽

Who Was Dorothea?

—*1948*

Despite the evidence against Szekely, Cody chose not to rush in with an arrest until he knew more. Having secured the house, he left the forensics crew to work on the crime scene and set out to learn about both victim and suspect.

When he flipped open the diary, labeled volume two, he found in front a list of names, addresses, and phone numbers of friends, along with notations about each. From these he made his own list. He could get little information from the quivering teenager, so, accompanied by Yonkers, he settled down to talk to Mrs. Bini, a prim widow who dressed severely, as if to signal to the world her lack of interest in replacing her deceased spouse. She perched on the couch opposite him with a cup of herb tea she'd made to "soothe her nerves," as she explained.

Mrs. Bini claimed she'd moved in only recently and didn't know all that much about her housemates. "Poor Dorothea, she had it rough and didn't deserve this. I heard she came to New York as a runaway. Her Virginia coal miner father died in a mine accident, and her mother married a first-class louse. The guy tended—you know—to paw, fondle, and worse. Luckily, Dotty could be a wildcat if she chose."

She paused as if reassessing her statement and fumbled with her hair. Having neatened what was already neat, she added that she'd never personally seen this wild side of her housemate. "She was always nice to me. Mind you, I'm not suggesting she had a temper or asked for what happened to her. Poor darling, she didn't always make the wisest decisions, but she wasn't *bad.*"

With three children out of wedlock, each by a different man, that might be arguable. Still, Cody nodded. "You never saw her become violent?"

"Never. I can't imagine it. I guess you want to know if your suspect can claim self-defense. I mean, I listen to the radio police reports, and I know you look for that sort of thing. I'd say absolutely not. Not with Dorothea. She'd fight back, but she wouldn't start a battle.

"Anyhow, her mother was furious. She blamed her daughter, called her a temptress, and even accused her of deliberately making a play for her stepfather."

It seemed Dorothea had escaped her tormenter, Carr Follinger, by quitting school and heading to New York. Life in the big city proved less easy than she'd hoped. "She was a tall, awkward girl," Mrs. Bini affirmed, "and she told me she lost several different waitress jobs before she got the hang of the work. She had trouble remembering orders and couldn't carry multiple plates of food without dropping them."

Maria's brown-eyed gaze focused on the window as though, where Cody saw a scraggly tree branch, she saw Dorothea's life unrolling. Unfortunately, the tale focused on irrelevancies such as trips to the beauty parlor—or, in this case, a longing for them. He heard about how a bony Dorothea bemoaned her gauntness and complained of the fact that she, a dishwater blonde, lacked money for rinses and dyes. Yet she was blessed with natural curls, which, when kept short, twined charmingly around her face. She prided herself on a pert, upturned nose that appealed to boys. In school, as she'd reported, she'd been considered a "looker." The independent type, she trusted herself to manage on her own.

"After fighting off that stepfather, she assumed she possessed the street smarts of city dwellers. She claimed she knew what men were all about, knew how to handle them." The woman smiled grimly. "Well, I guess that proved not to be true, didn't it?"

Dorothea had finally, with the help of roommate Norma Ray, who took pity on her and taught her tricks of the trade, become a successful waitress. Having learned at last how to put herself together so she looked like a New Yorker rather than a hick from Appalachia, she began to attract men. This, according to Mrs. Bini, was the moment when her troubles started. "Those awful guys, you wouldn't believe them. From what I hear, she faced one betrayal after another. Not a decent joe in the crowd. But that Zoltan Szekely was the worst; he presented himself as such a sweetheart. Of course, they all do in the beginning."

Cody moved his feet restlessly He'd heard enough. Perhaps he should interview Norma Ray herself. He added her name to his list.

"I need to know," he said, "if you got a good look at the man."

"I certainly did. I passed him on the stoop out there."

"You could identify him?"

"I believe so. I hope you get him right away. We don't need him wandering about the neighborhood." She waved dramatically.

He rose and thanked her. With a promise to get back to her, and a signal to Yonkers, he left her still sipping her tea.

Checking again on young Leila Falucci in the front hall, he found her still too shaken and incoherent to be interviewed. He traveled uptown with Yonkers, where he stopped off at Juilliard. He was in luck; one of the pianist's instructors, having not yet departed for summer vacation, was available.

Upon questioning, the man, Dr. Jacobs, insisted Szekely could not possibly have committed a murder. He was not the type. A gifted musician with a promising future, he'd performed with symphony orchestras both here and abroad. He wouldn't compromise his career. Dr. Jacobs claimed to know him well and to feel sure he was not given to impulsive anger. "We're talking dedication. I watched him work steadily, patiently, toward his goal of becoming a concert pianist. Even during army duty, he hung in there, seeking out pianos in USO halls where he might practice in free time."

"Split personality," Yonkers sighed when they left. "The sweetheart croaker. Sounds like something for the tabloids."

"Oh, I've no doubt the tabloids will latch onto this one," Cody speculated. "'Musician Turned Killer: From Concert Halls to Prison Walls.' Who could resist headlines like that?"

On learning that Miss Ray, who lived not far from Juilliard, would arrive home from work shortly after 1:00 PM, the detectives lunched while waiting for her. At 1:15, they rang the bell at her apartment, and she buzzed them in.

Miss Ray turned out to be a tall but graceful bird; when she opened her door, Cody met her eye to eye, as he rarely did with women. She wore a blue and white print dress, neither subdued nor flamboyant, but a confident statement of her personal taste in clothing. She seemed a person who put herself together properly in the morning and gave little further thought to her appearance throughout her day. She didn't seem the type to hover in the powder room.

He introduced himself and his companion. Followed by Yonkers, he stepped into a living room that struck him as busy, with ceramic doodads on shelves along the walls, so many that he felt claustrophobic. Miss Ray explained that she'd just come home from her waitress job. "I was so shocked when you called. I can't believe this yet. Dotty murdered?" She offered the detectives seats on the couch and asked them to wait while she changed her shoes. "My feet hurt at the end of the day."

She click-clacked away in Cuban heels and slip-slapped back in go-aheads. She sat opposite him—or rather, she slid into a chair, moving in a slinky, film actress sort of way. She asserted, "I'm … that is, I *was* Dorothea's best friend in New York."

He admitted to knowing she'd taught Dorothea the waitress trade. She promptly picked up the threads of his previous informant's story. Dorothea, she said, had arrived in New York alone and naive. In time she'd latched onto a tall, darkly handsome guy named Joel Fisk, who promised to marry her. "But it was—you know—just talk. He kept procrastinating, wouldn't set the date. I hate to say it, but Dot was a genius at finding foot-draggers. When she became pregnant, the good-for-nothing moved out denying the kid was his. He accused Dot of cheating on him. It wasn't true, not for a minute. Her friends and colleagues could testify to that; we'd watched her hurry home after work with never a stop-off anywhere."

Cody hoped to hear about Zoltan, but Miss Ray talked about his predecessor, Joel. The accusations of Dot's unfaithfulness, she declared, were not only untrue but unfair. "We all told the guy that Dorothea was the loyal type—but you can't talk to Joel Fisk. He knows what he knows. He's stubborn as a—I won't say a mule, because that's trite, but you know what I mean."

Cody nodded; he knew exactly what she meant. He wanted to get on to what he didn't know, the facts about Szekely.

"Dorothea made bad choices in men," Norma theorized. "I hear that's a problem with women who've been abused by fathers or stepfathers. They keep seeking out abusive men, hoping to win with them." She flung hand to chest and gazed at the detectives uneasily. "Not that Zoltan was in that category. Well, he wouldn't have been but for his father getting involved." She took a deep breath. "Don't get me wrong. I told you about Joel so you'd understand. After these forays into Rotten Row, Dorothea saw the error of her ways and made a conscious effort to find a better sort of guy. Things would have worked out for her with Zoltan if Daddy Szekely had minded his own damn business."

As soon as his informants began to second-guess themselves, Cody tended to give up on them. People blurted things out and then, on second thought, tried to repair the damage. After that, it was hard to get straight answers.

He thanked her, shuffled his feet, and signaled to Yonkers to leave. When Norma rattled on, he relaxed and urged her to tell the story in a straightforward way, without editorializing. Yonkers again flipped his notebook open.

"When young Randy was four, Joel the Viper vanished completely. Dorothea then formed a relationship with another man who also made promises but in the end abandoned her, leaving her with two children, Randy, five, and Denny, an infant. The second man—I've forgotten his name—finally admitted he'd planned all along to return eventually to his wife in Peoria. I mean, come on. That was a low blow for Dotty, after two years and a child. How can men do things like that?"

Cody thought, but didn't say, that women were equally good at tricking their partners when they chose.

Struggling on her waitress salary to care for two children, Dorothea found a nine-year-old baby sitter, who ditched school to mind the youngsters. When a social worker learned of it, the children were taken from her and placed in foster care.

While he watched Yonkers jot a note about that, Cody asked, "Did she get them back?"

Norma declared that, though heartbroken, Dorothea made the hard decision not to fight the court order. "If she got the kids back, she'd have to go on relief—or do they now call it welfare? Her mother would hate that. Poor Dot, she worried over her mom's anger. The woman saw the New Deal giveaways as the end of mankind's hope of sturdy independence." Norma sighed and shook her head. "They were a family that really needed help. Funny, isn't it? Often it was the very people whose lives were saved by the New Deal who most objected to what they called Roosevelt's socialist measures. WPA workers hated the WPA program—as if it weren't putting food on their tables and a roof over their heads. Not to mention building our roads and bridges and—"

Cody's impatient shuffle must have reminded his informant she was off the subject again. She quickly reverted to her story. "Foster care gave Dot freedom to work extra shifts at the restaurant and save for a decent apartment and better help when—if—she could retrieve her children."

By now, according to Norma, Dorothea had grown cautious and seemed resigned to settling for any good man she could get. She'd learned that people viewed unwed mothers as no better than prostitutes, no matter that she'd been faithful and loving. So, no more of those suave, smooth guys for her. Having decided that the glamorous types tended to be unfaithful, she vowed, in the future, to seek a man with scruples about the treatment of women. "She felt she needed to find someone more, you know, malleable—like the piano student down the hall." That would be Zoltan Szekely. Cody perked up. At last they were getting to it.

"Zoltan was younger than her—I mean than she—but he seemed mature for his age. He had a charming accent and a warm smile, and—most appealing—he treated women with respect. She'd rarely won respect from guys, so she reveled in his treatment of her. She used to speak with awe of his lovely manners."

"So they had an ongoing relationship?" Cody asked.

"Oh, yes—three years. If not for his parents, he would have married her.

God, Zoltan's folks were heartless. Makes you wonder how they produced such a nice son."

"That sheds a different light on things."

Norma looked uncomfortable. "This stuff's all in the past. Dot and Zoltan separated before the war. I don't want you to think—"

"Feelings can linger," Cody said. "What can you tell me about this guy Szekely, Miss Ray? It is Miss, isn't it?"

"It's Miss." She smiled grimly. "I have the opposite problem from Dorothea's. She adored her men, tried to keep them, yet they took off. My guys stick around until they get on my nerves and I dump them. Dorothea used to accuse me of a fear of commitment—no doubt true." Choosing her words, she reached out to pluck a dead leaf off a plant on the end table beside her. "Let's see, Zoltan—well, I can tell you he's a talented musician and he works hard at it. There's no question in my mind he'll make it to the top. And he seemed good-hearted; he just couldn't cope with his crazy dad. Still, I doubt he was right for Dorothea. She liked her men to be present and in attendance. Zoltan dreamed of traveling the world on concert tours."

"But they had a child. What about that?

"She's been wonderful about the child. She carried the whole burden by herself. It was a failed abortion, you know. Zoltan's parents—oh, well, I suppose they were just acting like parents, but still you'd think … their grandchild … Anyway, Dorothea didn't want them controlling her life so she stayed away from Zoltan after Marcie's birth. As far as I know, Zoltan never even heard about the kid."

Cody decided he didn't need to listen to further tales of Dorothea's love life. He could now put the facts together for himself. He planted his feet firmly on the carpet, hoisted himself out of his chair, and nodded to Yonkers, who snapped his notebook shut and stood. They thanked Norma for her help.

"I couldn't make heads or tails out of all that," Yonkers complained when they'd left the building.

Cody said, "Boils down to the fact that the Granger woman lived with two blokes who abandoned her, and then she met this sweetheart who ended by killing her on learning of the kid. No surprise there. The sweethearts are under great pressure, always having to be Mr. Nice Guy."

"That's the truth. Escape artists know how to look after number one. But for the Szekelys of the world … there's only one way out for guys like him."

"I'd say we have enough to take Szekely in for questioning. Maybe we'll learn from him the details of their relationship. We won't have to hear any more of that girly stuff about Mr. Nice Guy and Mr. Stinker." He sighed.

"I never thought my first case of my own would be a *True Confessions*–style murder."

"You should talk. You only had to listen. I had to write it down."

From 125th Street they hadn't far to go. Szekely lived on Manhattan Avenue at 106th Street in an impressive stone building with rounded corners sporting large windows. As they parked at the curb, a cascade of piano notes spilled from the second floor. Clearly, their Juilliard graduate was at home and at work. Cody knew nothing of classical music, but to him the performance sounded professional. It did seem unlikely a man like that would get involved in a murder. He had to remind himself of the words he'd just spoken, that sweethearts could crack under strain.

They rode the elevator to the second floor and knocked. The music stopped, and a moment later the door opened. Cody felt certain that before them stood Szekely himself. He was as described—a stocky man of above medium height with wavy hair touching his shoulders. There was a vaguely East European look about him, emphasized by slightly slanted eyes. Exotic. Women would go for that.

Cody held up his ID. "Sergeant Cyril Cody of NYPD. This is my assistant, Yonk—uh, Joe Larramie."

Szekely looked puzzled. "Yes?" No sign of uneasiness or guilt. *Is he an actor as well as a musician?* Cody wondered.

"Are you Zoltan Szekely?"

"I am."

"We'd like to ask you some questions regarding the death of Dorothea Granger."

His eyebrows shot up in a look registering amazement. "Dot's not dead. I saw her this morning." Cody noticed a lingering Hungarian accent.

"She died right after you left. As the last person to see her alive, you may have information."

He seemed genuinely astonished. He protested, "I don't know anything. I didn't even know she—uh—I can't believe this. How in the world did it happen so suddenly?"

Yonkers added, "We'd also like permission to search your apartment."

Cody could scarcely conceal his surprise at their suspect's openness. He waved an arm. "Feel free. I have nothing to hide."

He led them into the kitchen, where a tallish, skinny young man sat at the table drinking coffee. He said, "This is my tenant, Clarence Hoffman." While Clarence rumpled his own fuzzy hair and gazed at them in puzzlement, Szekely added, "Most of the rooms are rented out. I only have the one at the end of the hall. We all share the living room and kitchen."

Szekely followed as the two officers walked down the hall to the designated room, a bedroom off the living room, with a dresser and a desk. On the desk, in plain sight, they found two treasures—an invitation Dorothea had written to Zoltan the previous night, urging him to visit her, and volume one of her diary. It seemed almost too good to be true, but there they both were, in handwriting already familiar to Cody from volume two.

"How did you come to have this?" Cody held the book up.

Szekely shook his head in puzzlement. "I have no idea. My wife found it among the things I'd stored when I went into the army. Dorothea must have put it there. I do seem to recall that she came for a visit before I left and offered to help me pack. Can't you tell me what happened and what this is about?"

"We don't know what happened. That's why we're investigating." Cody flipped through the book. He'd skimmed only a few pages before he realized it was time to arrange that lineup. He had more than enough evidence in hand to remove any worry that he was rushing things. He pocketed the note and diary and gave Szekely the bad news. "I have to take you in for questioning."

The musician looked more puzzled than frightened. With a shrug and a repeated "I have nothing to hide," he accompanied them willingly.

CHAPTER 4

Jill, the Smiling Wallflower

—1948 and 1943

My world was in chaos. Stomach churning with apprehension over my spouse's predicament, I paced the floor and spoke compulsively to Frieda about how we'd met, Zoltan and I, how we'd worked our way through our two very different backgrounds and learned to know one another. Though much of it was old news to her, she indulged my need to talk.

Unlike Dorothea, I had a happy childhood with loving parents. My problems started in the middle of my senior year at the university, early in the war. With savings depleted, I'd taken a job doing housework for room and board. Despite inevitable time shortages, I managed somehow to stay in the top 10 percent of my class and hoped to graduate with honors.

Not that I was the scholarly type, mind you. I was merely shy. To my father's disappointment—he loved vaudeville, dreamed of raising a Ginger Rogers who might dance with a new Fred Astaire, and provided lessons throughout my childhood—I didn't practice my dancing and instead buried myself in books. The good grades came as part of the package.

In April, the battle to juggle study time with work time overwhelmed me. I appealed to my father for funds to see me through. Busy with term papers and finals, I could no longer meet the demands of a job.

Since Dad wasn't hot on college for women, not to mention that he opposed the idea of parents supporting adult children, I'd worked in a cherry canning factory to save money for my university studies. Now, with that money gone, Dad compromised his principles and sent me a check—for the exact price of rent and food to tide me over until graduation day. He announced there'd be no more financial aid. "You're twenty-three, you've graduated, you're on your own," he wrote. "We do our children no favor when we continue to support them into adulthood."

I sensed his dismay. Not only did I show no sign of becoming the new Ginger Rogers, in his opinion I'd chosen a foolish major—psychiatric social work, who'd ever heard of such a thing?—which required a master's degree. As I've said, he wasn't firm on higher education for women, especially after enduring four years of jeering from colleagues, not to mention his own sister, my Aunt Lorna, over his uselessly educated girl child. Beaten down by scoffers who proclaimed him crazy to educate a female, he was not up for financing me through graduate school.

He offered, if I could find no work, to send me a bus ticket to come home to California. In his letter, he said, "Jill Foster (when Mom and Dad used my last name, it meant they were seriously annoyed with me), you must learn to manage your money better." I didn't take him up on this because I felt humiliated. I well knew my high school friends were living on their own, earning an income or married to men who did so. And here was I, college educated, failing at that most basic of life's undertakings and requiring parental help.

Dad's ill humor was not unjustified. I'd treated myself to more coffee and sweet rolls at the Women's League cafeteria than my budget allowed for, joining my classmates in what we laughingly called bull sessions. I remember yet those silly college-girl arguments over questions like whether Wordsworth was a pagan who worshipped nature directly (my opinion) or a Christian seeking God through nature (theirs). We actually grew tearful over them, my more conventional friends hotly insisting on their hero's ties to orthodox religion.

Having failed to guard my money, I ended up too broke even to rent a cap and gown. At graduation I had to sit in the audience rather than onstage with suitably garbed honor students.

Dad wasn't mean. He was just an old-line Unitarian, a descendant of puritans who, like Emerson, believed passionately in self-reliance. We all had to stand on our own feet and accept no help—not from relatives, government, or friends. Though I knew that about him, I felt discarded and alone. Other graduates had family members waiting to hug and congratulate them. Around me after the ceremony stood young men and women in robes holding bouquets of flowers while proud loved ones pointed cameras at them and took snapshots. My parents in Pasadena hadn't even wired congratulations.

Fellow graduates had been purchasing expensive, quality clothing—what they could buy of it in wartime—designed to impress employers at job interviews. Since I was in no position to manage that, I planned to move to Ypsilanti for war work at Willow Run while saving for graduate school.

On checking, I learned that housing in Ypsilanti was in short supply, and anything decent, if found, would prove exorbitant. Lacking cash for even a week's rent, I grabbed instead a local job as secretary at the Congregational Church and stayed put with a landlady who knew me and extended credit. Though my pay was minimal, I'd have a roof over my head, three meals a day, and a university nearby for graduate work. Dad's letter had upset me and I hungered for security.

It was in this condition, alone and scared, that I met this glamorous Hungarian Jewish refugee, a concert pianist improbably wearing an army uniform. I'd paused to listen to his practicing on the League piano. Looking up while his hands wavered, he smiled and asked if I was a music lover. I ventured to request Chopin's Ballade no. 1 in G Minor. He promptly played it—beautifully, professionally. He confessed, "It's one of my favorites, too." With a diffidence surprising in one so accomplished, he suggested I join him for a snack in the League cafeteria.

Over coffee and sweet rolls, we chatted. He told me he'd grown up in Budapest, performing with the orchestra at the age of eight, before his parents fled the country. He talked of his recent studies at Juilliard and his summers at music camp in the Berkshires. At closing time—college women faced deadlines of 10:30—he walked me home and invited me to go canoeing with him on Sunday.

No doubt I should have asked early on how a pianist planned to support a wife, but I was too excited to think of such questions. I found his interest in me downright miraculous. I wasn't high on most men's glamour lists. Growing up in a family that moved often, and blessed with neither siblings nor close friends to relate to, I never learned the finer social arts of how to make small talk or how to kid people along. When I complained to my mother that I lacked friends, she accused me of being standoffish. She said, "If you'd turn on the charm, people would like you."

I worked at it. I became a smiling wallflower, wearing at parties a Kewpie doll happy face, as if I found sideline-sitting my ultimate joy in life.

When suddenly I found myself dating a concert pianist, I was as surprised as was the unnamed heroine of the novel *Rebecca* on attracting attention from the wealthy scion of Manderley. I'd done nothing to win love; I hadn't even gone to the beauty salon for a hair styling as my housemates had urged. Whatever appeal I had was strictly that of nature. Later, when my in-laws would accuse me of setting my cap for Zoltan, I could assure myself I wasn't guilty. My budget didn't stretch to glamorous clothing or even sufficient makeup to cover the numerous freckles on my upturned nose. My rent was still unpaid, and my landlady awaited my first paycheck as eagerly as I did.

I theorized that maybe Zoltan just enjoyed hero worship, since that was all I had to offer. Certainly I stood in awe of his musical gifts and felt I could listen forever to the G Minor Ballade as he performed it on the League piano. Pretending that I'd been transformed into the glamorous Bette Davis in the company of Paul Henreid, I settled in to enjoy a new and exciting experience.

I soon found myself in over my head. I'd never before met people like the Szekelys. Their life experience was as far from mine as it was possible to be. I'd fancied all immigrants were greenhorns eager to become Americans. The songs, stories, and movies of the day told me so. No one had ever suggested there might be other, more sophisticated and disenchanted types.

CHAPTER 5

Tea and Sympathy

—1939–1942

CODY'S QUESTIONING OF SZEKELY IN the small, bare interrogation room, while it provided abundant background material about the refugee experience, shed little light on the murder. The pianist continued to insist that Dorothea was alive and well when he left her. When asked about their past relationship, he stated they'd had one once, but it had ended long ago. "I'm still not sure it's true there's a child, or that he's mine." Of his feelings about the boy, he said, "I didn't even know about him until yesterday, so how could I feel anything? When someone announces of a five-year-old, 'He's yours,' a man doesn't form an instant bond." He shook his head thoughtfully. "I'm not hard of heart, officer, but these things take time. I've never met the boy. Never knew of him. Never saw him."

When pressed, he added that he liked children, enjoyed their company, and would no doubt in time come to love the boy. Cody couldn't break the pianist down and coax a murder confession from him. Luckily, he possessed that treasure from the Manhattan Avenue apartment, volume one of Dorothea's diary, dating back to her meeting with Szekely in prewar days. He felt confident he'd find there a developing source of conflict. Meanwhile, he planned to keep Szekely in custody.

Late that night, having forewarned his wife that he was busy on a case, Cody poured himself a cup of coffee and settled down at his desk with volume one. Dorothea proved a surprisingly fluent writer for one who dropped out of high school early on. He suspected she must have taken night school classes to improve her skills. This was no sophomoric theme about "My Summer Vacation." She told the story well and even recorded conversations.

It seemed that before the war Dorothea had lived in one of the many six-room apartments in New York that had been divided into what the English called bed-sitters, studios with a common kitchen. Located on 124th Street near Juilliard, it was shared, with the exception of a female switchboard operator and herself, among Juilliard students. She described them in detail. One was a married singer whose wife worked out of town while he warbled away at opera arias and visited him on weekends. Another, a violinist, welcomed a shocking and tragic—shocking because she'd never heard of guys loving guys, and tragic because the guys were handsome yet unresponsive to her feminine charms—stream of young men in and out of his room. That left the pianist, Zoltan Szekely, whose name she'd learned one evening when the two were preparing a meal. He was nice looking, though not, despite his brown curls, as handsome as her first lover, Joel. To her his face looked foreign, pushed together, asymmetrical, and vaguely Asian. Yet he was polite, friendly, and interested in the opposite sex. Several times he'd lingered in the kitchen, talking to her while she made dinner.

She cautioned herself to be clever this time, to proceed slowly. At her age, almost thirty, she couldn't afford to lose any more husband candidates. This one had to be for keeps.

One evening when Zoltan appeared in the kitchen, she offered to share the tuna casserole she'd just baked. Lifting his head to sniff the warm and tempting aromas, fishy and cheesy from extra cheddar, he smiled and gratefully accepted.

"This is a rare treat," he said. "I haven't had a home-cooked meal in months. I can't afford trips to Kentucky, where my parents live."

She made a mental note of the fact he was on his own, probably lonesome, and in need of someone to cook for him. She told him, "Casseroles are easy. In the future, I'll make enough to share with you."

He protested. "I wouldn't want you to go to extra trouble."

"Hey, I love to cook. It's what I do—like piano-playing for you."

While they ate, he talked, in his charming Hungarian accent, about Freud's theories of sex. To her it all sounded highfalutin, beyond her understanding—but she saw her opportunity and grabbed it. She noted in her diary that when she suggested they go to her room and try out the theories, Zoltan reacted like a kid who has just seen Santa Claus come down the chimney. Thrilled yet disbelieving, he eagerly followed her down the hall.

He also proved, for all his Freud talk, shy, inept, and inexperienced. He fumbled as he helped her remove her slip and bra. Hesitant about shedding his trousers, he turned his back as if he feared embarrassing her. She almost giggled.

Once in bed she had to guide him every step of the way; she had to explain that men could use their hands on a woman's body, that it was all right for his fingers to explore below the waist. "Don't be afraid, I like your touch," she said.

Obviously he hadn't spoken much with other guys about women and sex. He admitted he had few friends. "Guys discuss sports—and with my music keeping me busy, I haven't had time to catch up with that stuff." Abashed, he confessed, "I never know what to say when the fellows ask me what I think of the Yankees. Fact is, I don't think of them."

She welcomed that. Her former lovers had been glued to the couch by the radio, beer bottle in hand, when a game was on.

Looking sheepish, Zoltan admitted he owned no condoms. She supplied him with one.

Once past his embarrassment, he proved a quick learner, even more gentle and caring than Joel. She was careful not to seem too bold, too knowledgeable. To avoid shocking him by appearing earthy, she didn't thrust open her thighs or pile pillows beneath her as she'd normally have done. She just offered hints and let him experiment on his own. In taking the young pianist to her bed, she opened a new world to him.

During their subsequent nights together, she began to talk about her past experiences. "I really loved the men I lived with, both of them. I cooked, I cleaned, and I ironed. I responded eagerly in bed. I avoided nagging and complaining. I tried to seem a promising wife. Yet they both took off when I got pregnant."

Zoltan whistled and shook his head. "I can't believe a man would treat a woman that way." She congratulated herself; she'd at last found a family man. Her dream of a home where she might raise her two children—and of course a third, of Zoltan's—would finally come true.

She offered to share his room, but he insisted she retain a room of her own. She found it touching that he seemed to care about her reputation. She did worry sometimes, however, that his concern might be rooted in something deeper. Despite their increasing involvement, Zoltan remained unwilling to inform his parents of their relationship. In fact, he sent her packing—gently, of course, with a regretful, "I can't see you for a few days, Dotty, and if we meet in the hall, I need you to pretend you don't know me"—when his folks visited. She assured herself that would change. It was early yet. True, she hungered for an offer of marriage, but she knew better than to press. Zoltan faced two more years of undergraduate work. He'd been promised a teaching fellowship and an income after graduation. Until then, she'd need to hang onto her waitress job, leave her children in foster care, and resign herself to the occasional brief visit with them.

The diary enthused over how much she loved her guy and how great he'd become in bed. Cody squirmed with embarrassment, rubbed his eyes, and turned pages, skimming. He gathered that Zoltan liked Dorothea's children and was good about letting her bring them along on weekend outings to Central Park and Coney Island. He even pushed the stroller for little Denny. She pretended they were married and he'd already become a dad. She prided herself that she'd picked well this time; she'd finally gotten it right. She even fantasized that she'd one day discuss child-rearing problems with mother-in-law Annie. She claimed she'd welcome guidance from a caring older woman. She still couldn't get along with her own mother, who, incredibly, seemed jealous of that nightmare relationship she'd had with her stepdad.

Meanwhile, she went along with Zoltan in his insistence on birth control and obtained a diaphragm. He was right; they didn't need to have a child while he was still a student. Vowing to be sensible this time, she used the diaphragm faithfully—for now. It was only a matter of time until things would develop toward marriage. She felt so sure of this fact that she even arranged to get her children for a weekend trip for all of them to her home in Pennsylvania. She told Zoltan she needed his help with the youngsters on the train, but she wrote her mother that she was bringing her future husband to meet his in-laws.

She recorded, on her return to New York, that "the children loved the train ride, and Zoltan acted like a youngster himself, taking the kids through the train to the dining car and club car. He played games with them. I think he was having more fun than they were.

"Unfortunately, the visit itself didn't go well. I thought Mom would be won over when she met Zoltan and the boys. I mean, how could she not love them? They were all so cute, and the kids were so happy to meet their grandmother. Grandmother Iceberg, alas. She served us dinner but hardly said a word. I had to talk to that scum, Carr Follinger, whom I'd hoped never to see again. He nauseates me; he's still an octopus with extra arms that flip out and touch you in the wrong places. Can he possibly fancy that he attracts women that way?

"I felt *so* relieved when it was time to go back to the train station. We couldn't afford a sleeper and had to sit up all night with the kids sprawled over our laps, but anything was better than staying on in that house. I remember now why I was so anxious to make my getaway years ago.

"I hope in time Mama Annie will learn to love me, because my own mom remains, alas, a giant zero."

The story went into erotic passages about Dorothea's love for Zoltan. Cody flipped through, trying to move on. The tale picked up as, the following year, Dorothea began pressing, ever more urgently as time went on, for Zoltan to tell his parents about her. "At least introduce me when they come." She wanted desperately to be part of the family; she could hardly bear her role as outsider.

Zoltan stood firm in his refusal. "I can't risk getting into a fight with my folks before I graduate. I'd be in big trouble if they balked about supporting me. If I'm no longer a student, I'll lose my military exemption—for me, a catastrophe. Pianists can't afford years without practice. If I lose fluency in my fingers, it will be all over for my concert career."

She suspected the military was just an excuse. The truth, as she'd sensed from different things he said, was that Zoltan feared his father's disapproval. "I'm not asking you to say I'm your girlfriend," she argued. "I just want your folks to know I'm around so that the news won't come as a shock. When you graduate, you can tell them we're going together—work up to the big announcement gradually."

As time went by, and after constant pressure and not a few tears from her, he finally, in his senior year, complied, dropping her name into his letters, referring to her as "the girl down the hall." Suspecting she was rather more than that, his parents asked probing questions. Finally, in the face of their insistent curiosity, he poured out the whole truth. By then his graduation was only weeks away, and he admitted the couple had been living together for three years.

"All hell broke loose," the diary recorded. Father Janos wrote urging Zoltan to break off the relationship at once, before the "disaster" of a pregnancy occurred. Janos also wrote to Dorothea, explaining that his son was not good husband material, that even if he avoided the draft, he faced many years of hard work, practicing, memorizing concert pieces, before he could hope for success in his field. "You'd be well advised," he warned, "not to waste time on him, but to seek an established working man with a steady income as a father for your children."

A heartbroken Dorothea reassured herself she could ignore the letter. Zoltan was a caring and loyal young man who agreed that was no way to treat the girl he'd lived with for so long. She believed she could rely on him. He had that teaching fellowship for next year, and, by giving piano lessons on the side, he'd support her—minimally, it was true, but they'd get by.

Given his poor eyesight, she believed him unlikely to be called for military duty. The only dark spot on the horizon was the coming summer, which he planned to spend in Kentucky playing recitals. She dreaded his parents' influence on him. Even now he was wasting time justifying this relationship, writing explanatory letters—as if a grown man needed to play Mother, May I!

When America joined the war, she pleaded that he needed the status of "married father," if only to ensure his continued exemption from military duty. Fathers were not then subject to the draft. He responded, "If I'm drafted, I'll do my duty. I won't plunge into one crisis just to escape another."

"Would marriage to me be that bad?" she asked in a voice trembling with emotion. "Bad enough to count as a crisis?"

He ignored her bid for sympathy. "It would break my parents' hearts. They've lived and breathed for my concert career. They've spent a fortune on me."

As his parents continued their campaign to split the couple up, Zoltan finally confessed it was only his unwillingness to hurt Dorothea that kept him with her. She knew he'd reached the point of capitulation; he'd begun hinting that his dad might be right after all. "I've been naive," he confessed. "I thought of us as involved in a great love affair like that of Chopin and George Sand, but I now realize it's not like that at all. Those were two successful people who didn't care to own each other. With us, you want marriage, I can't afford it, and if I continue to see you, I'm just using you. That's wrong, and something I never want to do to anyone."

She decided it was time for all-out war. She held the power; she controlled the diaphragm. She plotted her menstrual cycles and chose the night she must withhold the object. It was now or never, she told herself.

Cody squirmed and bit his lip. He hated this part of his job; it compared to participating in an autopsy and finding semen in the vagina of the corpse or an unannounced fetus in the womb. Prying into such personal aspects of people's lives left him feeling as if he'd violated them somehow. He had to force his gaze over the page.

Terrified as she crawled into bed beside her lover, naked as a baby, Dorothea wondered, would he feel the lack? Would he suspect? But he said nothing.

For two weeks, worrying, hoping, she chewed her nails. When her menstrual cycle failed to come, she took a day off to check with the doctor and then celebrated alone, treating herself to a lunch of her favorite beef pie from the Automat. She was pregnant; they would have to marry.

That night she broke the news to Zoltan. His agony was terrible. He seemed about to lose his mind, pounding the table and clutching his forehead so hard he pulled out hair. He went for a lone walk and was gone all night. The next day he missed his classes. Instead he sat on an embankment overlooking the Hudson River, staring at nothing, refusing to answer when she spoke to him.

She'd anticipated his shock but hadn't supposed it would continue for so long. Night after night he paced, sleepless with worry. He couldn't walk out on a pregnant woman, yet he couldn't abandon a promising career his parents had sacrificed so much for. "They gave up everything in Hungary and came to America just for Kitty and me," he said. "Just so we'd never have to worry about anti-Semitism, just so we'd be free to have educations and successful careers. Now I'm about to destroy their hopes. Saddled with a wife and children to support, I can't possibly pursue my concert career." He clutched his head. "God, how could this happen?"

Dorothea didn't confess how it happened. She almost regretted what she'd done. Almost, but not quite. Her own dream of having a home was stronger than her compassion for Zoltan.

They argued. Annie, on learning of the pregnancy, suffered a breakdown and had to be taken to the hospital. Her husband was torn between caring for his wife and his son. When Zoltan talked of suicide, Janos rushed to New York. Sending Zoltan off to perform in a contest in Albany, Janos sat in the communal kitchen all night drinking coffee and counseling Dorothea. While she tearfully pleaded her case, he insisted this situation could not go on. "I'll find a good doctor; I'll even give you money so you can move elsewhere and start over on your own." Zoltan, his father argued, had many lean years ahead of him while preparing for concert work. "There's no way he can support a family for years to come. You must terminate this pregnancy. Your relationship is bad for him and for you. A baby at this time is unthinkable."

Facing the end of her dreams, she wept. "Zoltan promised he wouldn't abandon me in my delicate condition—and he certainly won't abandon his child. I know him; I'm sure of how he feels."

Janos assured her there would be no abandonment. "We'll stand by and see you through, and later we'll help you find another job and a place to live. But this relationship must be broken off, and this pregnancy must end. The situation is impossible. The marriage wouldn't last a year, and the breakup would be hard on everyone, not to mention disastrous for the child." He repeated, lamely, his promise. "We'll set you up so you're okay on your own."

Dorothea sobbed. She'd been so sure she could win this battle. When Zoltan returned, she clung to him while her tears flowed. He wavered, smoothing her hair and consoling her as she leaned against him. He promised to talk to his father and try to find a better solution.

In the end his parents' distress overwhelmed him. He claimed he knew too well what the couple had gone through in escaping the Nazis and adjusting to a new society. He insisted he couldn't add to their burdens by marrying at this time. Embarrassed, he confessed that colleagues at Juilliard had long been asking why he was with a woman who didn't know Beethoven from Gershwin.

She argued, "So I quit school early, but I'm still a good person."

"You're a very good person, and you deserve better than to be the secret girlfriend of a penniless musician. I shouldn't have let you go on this way for so long."

"You could make it up to me by marrying me."

"You wouldn't be happy with me."

"Of course I would. Haven't we been happy all these years?"

As gently as possible, holding her hand, he confessed. "I'm not in love with you, Dorothea. I never have been. It wouldn't be a good marriage. I already feel trapped."

Though well aware of the truth of those words—she'd certainly sensed, by his refusal to introduce her to parents and sister, that he was not in love, and indeed he'd never claimed to be—she responded in fury. "Not in love? You mean you've been using me? You too, like the others? I was just your sex slave?"

"Come on, you know that isn't true. You enjoy sex. You even admitted that women as well as men need the release."

And so she had—to show him she'd make a good wife. To that end she'd have agreed to anything.

They argued for hours, and through it all Zoltan was kind enough not to remind her she was older than he. Though she suspected that fact had something to do with the problem, he never said so.

She considered refusing the abortion and raising the child on her own, but rejected the plan because of her two boys in foster homes. She needed to put them first.

The next day she followed an implacable Janos, her eyes teary yet focused on the bald spot in his graying hair, along a gray street full of papers and debris, and into a dreary entryway with a narrow stairway leading upward two flights. She knew that for years to come she would see in her mind that partly bald head moving ahead of her along the sunless walkway and up those stairs.

Their climb took them to a dimly lit hallway, where gray walls and worn carpets led to an equally gray, bare room that appeared none too sanitary, its unwashed window opaque with dust. The bearded, white-coated man who moved toward them offered no smile, no handshake, and no consolation. He simply rubbed his hands impatiently.

Janos was sent to wait in a chair in the hall, and, given nothing to cover herself with, Dorothea was told to step behind a screen and strip below the waist. She shuddered as a gurney was wheeled over and, half-naked, she was shoved onto it. As her legs were folded up and spread apart, she sobbed in protest over the new life being flushed out of her body—all her years of waiting, all her careful planning, lost in one quick moment.

Placed in a tiny, bare room, she was told to lie still for two hours to control the bleeding. Janos went out for coffee and then came back in a taxi to get her. When the doctor said, "Your father's here," she sobbed because Janos would never become her father. She wept the entire way home.

In the days that followed, Janos helped her find a small flat near Greenwich Village, where he paid three months' rent and laid in a supply of groceries. He told her, "Take time to rest and recover; you needn't rush right out to find a job."

Father and son both tried to be kind. They even brought her children to visit her, but she pleaded a migraine and sent them all away. Three years of her life were gone, down the tubes like they'd meant nothing. She was past thirty now and struggling to accept that she might never have a home for her youngsters. She felt convinced Zoltan on his own wouldn't have done this to her. Their breakup was his father's fault. It was that terrible European philosophy about educated folks being better than others. Clearly Janos neither understood America—how everyone's as good as everyone else in this country—nor valued her loyalty and devotion to his son.

There were pages upon pages of personal confessions detailing how much she'd loved Zoltan and how great their sex had been. She wallowed in recollections of desire, passion, ecstasy—to the point where Cody lost all capacity to believe. *No man is that good in bed*, he told himself.

He skipped and skimmed over passages of pure fiction until he came upon the statement that, feeling abandoned and alone, she'd begun contemplating suicide. Luckily, she met Mama Falucci, who offered her a home. Her immediate problem solved, she went again into erotica of past happiness with her pianist lover.

Cody felt he had the story of Zoltan and Dorothea. He rubbed his burning eyes, poured himself another cup of coffee, and debated whether to turn further pages. The decision was made for him when he was interrupted by late-night arrivals—eerily, two of the very people he'd just been reading about, Janos Szekely and his wife, Annika.

CHAPTER 6

Wartime Marriage

—*Ann Arbor, 1943*

MIRACULOUSLY, ZOLTAN'S INTEREST IN ME survived and flourished.
Me, Jill Foster, the smiling wallflower—and this in wartime when there
were almost no men on campus, when any man could have his pick of
females, when women claimed they'd marry anything in pants. I reveled in
my astounding good fortune.

With sandwiches and bags of peaches, we went canoeing on weekends
and picnicked as we floated, along with other women students and uniformed
army guys, down the Huron River. While we passed sunny, green meadows
where cows grazed, Zoltan talked about Europe, about the anti-Semitism his
family had fled from. "They threatened to make us wear armbands labeling
us as Jews. They talked of putting us back in ghettos." He shuddered just
speaking the words. "They meant it, too. Even that early on, we heard awful
rumors. Our parents tried to shield us, but word gets through. Children have
a way of sensing what's going on."

I nodded and told him the rumors had reached America. We'd heard
them; we just couldn't believe the German and Austro-Hungarian people
would do such things. Even as I tried to imagine the horrors, I fought my
mind's tendency to focus on his almond-shaped brown eyes, his strong pianist
fingers grasping the paddle, his wavy brown hair and exotic looks. I couldn't
stop daydreaming that he'd propose. I pictured him on his knees telling me
what a great wife I'd make, how much he loved me, how he couldn't live
without me.

Instead, the thing I dreaded occurred. He asked if I'd like to go to a hotel
during his few hours of weekend leave. I panicked. In those wartime days,
women were often left alone, unmarried and pregnant, their men overseas.

One heard rumors of back-alley abortion clinics where women were made sterile or even died. I didn't need that disaster. Mom and Dad would disown me. What would I do? How would I manage with no help from my family?

After biting my lip in indecision, I shook my head and blurted, "I don't plan to have sex before marriage." At once I chastised myself for this frank stance. Expecting his request to be repeated with more pressure—I'd heard from housemates that men grew more demanding as time went on—I sought words to communicate less harshly that the hotel adventure was out of the question. "I can't risk being left behind in a compromised position when you ship out."

I felt sure that I'd now be history and Zoltan would go looking for a more compliant freckle-faced midwestern girl.

Instead, he reacted with embarrassment, as if he knew he ought not to have suggested such a thing. He apologized. "I can't get married at this time, Jill. I have two more years of study at Juilliard ahead of me, and then a year of practice for a Town Hall recital, before I can launch my career and support a wife."

Was this the prelude to further pressure or a hint of the end? I worried for a whole week. Neither outcome would be good; neither was what I wanted.

He startled me next time we saw each other by saying, "I know you don't care to risk sex before marriage, Jill, so we should get married as soon as possible. I could be sent overseas and we'd lose our chance to be together."

I was speechless with surprise. "But, Zoltan, you said—"

"I changed my mind. I've been too grim about the future."

So, the dream had become reality, but in such an offhand way that I hadn't even been asked if I wanted to marry him.

It hit me how little I knew Zoltan—how little we knew each other. He thought I was a Congregationalist because I worked for that church, and I hadn't even had a chance to tell him I was really Unitarian. Shouldn't married people know such things about one another? There'd be children someday, presumably, and these details would matter. He hadn't ever asked about my background. I sensed he pictured me as the typical American girl, though I didn't feel particularly typical—there weren't a lot of women working their way through college in prewar days when I set off to do so. If their families lacked the money to see them through, they stayed home. Women didn't expect or even long for careers; they anticipated that their future husbands would support them. College, for coeds, was mostly about meeting men who would one day become doctors, lawyers, or engineers, and hence make desirable husbands.

In describing the anti-Semitism in Europe, Zoltan had spoken very little about his own family and their personal tribulations. I knew he'd attended

Juilliard, but I had no idea if he still had a girlfriend in New York. *Of course he must have*, I assured myself. *No man makes it to age twenty-four without girlfriends*. What baggage, what ties had been left? Was someone waiting for him? Surely, after four years, there must be a lonely heart somewhere pining for this talented musician. What promises had he made to her? He hadn't given me even a hint of his past involvements.

He stopped paddling the canoe and studied my face. Baffled, he said, "You're hesitating. You think it's too soon?"

I panicked. I wasn't ready for this decision. I didn't even know if I wanted to get married. Busy with studies, I'd fantasized often but never faced the reality of marriage. I'd certainly anticipated—and looked forward to—a period of romance beforehand.

Yet I knew for sure I didn't want to let this handsome, glamorous man get away. A concert pianist! Visions danced before my eyes of my beautifully garbed self attending my husband's performances, of his peering up from the stage to smile at me in the foremost box, resplendent in my new gown, just as in movies about musicians.

I sputtered, "It's only … you took me by surprise."

He chuckled and admitted he'd taken himself by surprise. "I'm not usually prone to impulsiveness. It must be the pressure of wartime. Fleeing Hitler, getting an education, joining the military, all the while trying to hang onto my fluency at the piano—I've had no chance to think about personal happiness. Now I need to catch up."

I confessed it was the same with me. I'd worked my way through school: babysitting at age ten, picking fruit at thirteen, waitressing at sixteen. In Depression times, with families hurting financially, young people were expected to help out. Everyone I knew had a job of some sort. Girls began babysitting around age eight. Older girls scrubbed floors or did laundry and ironing for elderly neighbors. Boys bagged and delivered groceries. We all picked fruit in season.

I stalled; I told him marriage was a serious step and we needed to talk it over. I had no idea what my parents would think. He admitted he hadn't yet worked up the courage to tell his parents about me. "With their worries over the developing nightmare in Europe, there just hasn't been a good time to bring it up. They've gone through so much for my sister and me, and all we've done is disappoint them. Kitty's dating a factory worker, and before the war I was dating a high school dropout—neither one would fit into our family. I fear the folks have grown wary." He frowned, stroked his chin where brown bristles had begun to show, and added, "I'll notify them after the fact. It'll be easier for them to handle a *fait accompli*, and it'll spare us additional pressure and stress."

Zoltan didn't wait for my answer. He took it for granted I wanted this wedding—not without reason. I'd implied willingness. When he'd made that suggestion about visiting a hotel, I'd responded, "Not until after marriage." I could still hear my own voice echoing those words.

He started planning, saying the military allowed half days for weddings, noon to midnight. He would report to his commanding officer, request permission to marry, and hopefully be granted the brief leave. "It won't be a fancy wedding," he warned. "I don't know just when the leave will come through—and besides, I don't have much money. It'll be spur of the moment."

I'd paid weddings so little attention that I didn't even realize the bride's family was supposed to finance the event. It didn't occur to me to ask my parents for funds. I let Zoltan take charge. He bought me a fake diamond engagement ring, promising that the real thing would be forthcoming as soon as he could save up for it. At the moment his military allotment went to support his sister Kitty in college. "Even a fake should give you premarital status with the university so you can get birth control information from the health center," he said.

I gasped; I'd forgotten about that, too.

He walked me home, gave me a passionate, movie-star kiss, which, because of the bristles, made me wince, and didn't again press for sex. He merely reminded me that soon we'd no longer have to separate at the door like this. Everything seemed right and proper except my feelings. Though I longed to remain in his arms, I didn't feel blissful about the forthcoming marriage. I felt frightened. Perhaps in time the bliss would steal over me.

She's engaged! She's lovely! She uses Pond's! proclaimed the ads of the day. Every young woman looked forward to the great moment of her engagement. I knew I was supposed to be thrilled. The unthinkable had happened; Zoltan had capitulated. I would be the wife of a famous concert pianist. He'd promised that my career would be taken seriously in our home; he insisted he wanted me to go on with graduate work. So what on earth was the matter with me? Why this panic?

For one thing, I worried over the fact he'd changed his mind so quickly. "You sounded very positive last Sunday when you told me marriage was out of the question until after you finish your studies," I reminded him.

"I'm promised a teaching fellowship. Things will be tight, but we'll manage."

"And didn't you say marriage would be too much of a shock for your parents after all they've been through?"

"It struck me their hopes for me are unrealistic," he confessed. "The girl they've envisioned for me doesn't exist. Times have changed. You and

I can't be celibate forever waiting for their approval; we may have only this moment now. Who knows what the future holds for a soldier overseas. It's true I'm unlikely to be assigned to the infantry, but there are bombs dropping everywhere in war zones. Anything could happen."

On the front porch of my rooming house, he hugged me and again gave me a passionate kiss. Then, like a virtuous alter ego Don Jose scorning the naughty gypsy, Carmen, in favor of a more righteous love, he dutifully returned to his army quarters.

I went into the house and showed off my ring, which, fake though it was, glittered enough to announce my new status. In time, if not replaced, it would turn my finger green, but right now it made me the center of attention among my housemates. The coed from California had pulled off a great coup, and all the women in the house gathered round to grasp my fingers with envious oohs and ahs. The symbolism was what counted. Clearly, in that single-sex society, with men dying overseas and women facing spinsterhood, there wasn't one of my housemates who wouldn't have traded places with me. I stilled my inner butterflies and assured myself I'd done the right thing.

I wrote my parents that night to tell them I'd become engaged to the concert pianist I'd been dating and would be married soon. Three days later I received a telegram—something they hadn't been willing to spring for even at my graduation—from my mother. Seemed she was ecstatic about the news and wanted Zoltan's address so she could write welcoming him into the family. I sent it at once, aware I might expect no such welcoming letter from the Szekely family. I added that Zoltan had a six-hour marriage leave for the following Wednesday, one week away, and that I was searching for a room where we could be together after the ceremony.

Meanwhile, I coped with the painful process of getting fitted for a diaphragm. The unpleasant experience consisted of the doctor breaking my hymen—suddenly and without warning, eliciting a scream from his hapless, naive patient who, having been told nothing about her own body, had no idea what was coming. Then, despite the resulting blood and pain, I was made to practice, over and over, the insertion of the rubber dam. It felt, to my inexperienced fingers, as if I were reaching inside my body to fiddle with inner organs. What was that weird lump? Did it belong there?

The gesture was a kindness, really. Doc wanted to make sure I knew what I was doing and wouldn't be stuck with a baby in the event that my spouse went overseas. All the same, it added greatly to the stress of the occasion.

A friend living in a loft on State Street decided to move into a real apartment and turn the loft over to us. And so, in my best dress, which was tan rather than white, and with my roommate, Frieda, as my sole attendant and an army friend of Zoltan's as best man, we stood, three Jews and a Unitarian, before the altar of the Congregational Church. The ceremony seemed stagy and unreal. The only reality was our two wedding rings. No cheap imitation here; Zoltan had bought gold.

Afterward, Zoltan's buddy snapped shots of us. Then, with a farewell to our two attendants, we took off for a meal at the Corner House Restaurant, an eatery beyond our means, where we treated ourselves to an expensive rarity not normally available to civilians, filet mignon. Served with fresh peas and mashed potatoes, it tasted doubly good after wartime years of deprivation. From there we went to the loft, bare except for bed, dresser, and desk, and not yet furnished with my belongings. There, we experimented with the sex Zoltan had hungered for. Still sore and shaken from the diaphragm fitting, I was more apprehensive than eager, and I'm sure I came across as dutiful rather than loving. However, Zoltan proved patient; he consoled and assured me things would improve.

Just before midnight Zoltan went off to muster, and the next day I awoke alone, with swollen eyelids and itchy eyes, in that semifurnished loft. My Sunday dress lay crumbled on the floor nearby, as if to remind me of yesterday. I stared at it and told myself I was married. It wasn't a dream; there'd really been a wedding. Zoltan and I had become a couple. And I hardly knew him. I'd spent a great deal of time trying to impress him—and very little time getting acquainted.

Who was that miner's daughter he'd spoken of as his former girlfriend? Dorothy something? And wasn't there a girl named Betty Ann, back in Kentucky? He'd never told me anything about either of them. That fact began to seem ominous, especially in view of his reluctance to inform his parents about our marriage. Surely he retained ties to the past that I would eventually have to cope with. I began to wonder what I'd gotten myself involved in.

CHAPTER 7

⌒

Cody's Late-Night Visitors

—1948

THOUGH NOT A TALL MAN, Janos Szekely managed, as he followed his wife into the interview area, to convey to Cody a sense of height. Perhaps it was his straight back and almost military posture. He wore a dark brown suit and brown and white striped tie that looked expensive. Cody had read in the diary that the man was an electronic engineer, a profession that would undoubtedly provide a decent salary and account for the quality clothing.

Szekely seemed less East European than his son. He also seemed nervous and upset, running his hands through salt-and-pepper hair until he messed it badly. Points of it stood up on his head. His wife was pale and withdrawn, but neatly attired in an oatmeal-colored tweed suit, her brown hair drawn back though not so severely as to compromise its soft wave.

Cody shook hands with the Szekelys and offered them seats.

"Officer, I came to tell you, you really have the wrong suspect," Mr. Szekely burst out. "In recent years, my son has had nothing whatever to do with Miss Granger. I can testify to that. He was away in the army, and he married someone else." The man even spoke like a Londoner. *His English is better than mine*, Cody thought. *Maybe a bit bookish, but still, he sounds like a toff.*

"How can you be sure he hasn't seen her?" Cody asked. "Do you get to the city regularly?"

"No, but I know my son. I know … we know he's incapable of violence." Beside him, his wife nodded.

"Your son hasn't been charged," Cody said. "However, we have evidence he was there on the premises. We have his fingerprints, and we have witnesses. Unfortunately, your faith in him can't be used in court."

"I'm here to find the opposing evidence." As if remembering about his hair, the man tried to smooth it. He frowned again, clasping his hands together. In the light of the diary narrative, he came across as almost obsessed. He'd created a concert pianist, and he meant to make sure the musician was available to perform for the public, even if he had to … to what? Might he hope to get his son off the hook by confessing his own involvement in the murder? The diary had hinted at his willingness to do anything necessary to help his son avoid difficulties.

Cody toyed with that thought while Mrs. Szekely peered at him with bright brown eyes. "You sound English," she remarked. "How do you happen to be working in New York?"

"Got stranded here in the war and couldn't get back," he explained.

"Then perhaps you know how we feel. We came here from Hungary and felt so lucky to escape Hitler—believe me, we wouldn't do anything to get in trouble with the law. I mean, none of us would. Not our children, either."

Some people, Cody had discovered, clam up when worried, while others become talkative. Mrs. Szekely appeared to be one of the latter. She seemed ready to blurt out almost anything he wanted to know. He leaned back and listened. She spoke with nervous energy, as if feeling an urgent need to communicate. Hoping to hear something important, he let her run on.

She described her first impression of New York. "We had a terrible time with an official at Ellis Island. It was terrifying. Afterward, I had a headache and couldn't wait to get to our hotel and lie down. We taxied to this massive building that flung itself into the sky, and then had to walk miles across vast lobbies to the elevator, where we were scooped upward at a heart-stopping rate. It was all so confusing; everything seemed to be happening so fast. You must know what it's like, Officer, coming here from Europe for the first time. You want to flee the chaos and go home, but you have no home."

While he nodded, she went on to complain that their cousins had rented an apartment for them on West End Avenue, but it lacked furniture. Until they could buy a few pieces, she had to stay in the hotel room, alone with the children, for days while Janos went off to the job the cousins had found for him. "It was … how you say in English? … traumatic. It made us all timid. We don't … we wouldn't—"

"I don't think the officer wants to hear about our first days in New York, Annie." Mr. Szekely spoke gently but firmly.

"I don't mind hearing this," Cody said. "Had pretty much the same reaction to New York myself when I first came. It's noisy and confusing."

"It was a nightmare," Mrs. Szekely said. "Before things got bad for us in Budapest, we'd always—well, perhaps you're not greatly interested in the arts, Officer Cody, but in Hungary, where I was a concert pianist, we artists and musicians pretty much lived in a world of our own. I mean, my husband's an engineer, so we had money and servants. I didn't do housework. When the anti-Semitism got bad and we had to emigrate, we were forced to leave our bank account behind. I had to get used to a new world of poverty. I didn't know how to cook; I'd never made a bed." She spread her hands helplessly. "I had no idea how people here felt about Jews. Since I couldn't guess where my children would be safe, I kept them close to me. I made sure I always knew where they were and what they were up to. I can tell you … I can guarantee … I know my son and what he'll do."

"It must have been rough," Cody admitted. Yet it struck him that the family lived in a pressure cooker that might well have exploded into violence.

"America is so confusing and even … even hostile," she went on. "No one is elite here. Waiters, doormen, taxi drivers—they all believe they can be president someday. They feel free to talk back and snap at you. They're impatient. They curse the government. They don't respect or defer to anyone. They don't even feel a need to be polite. If you turn to them for help, they'll tell you it's not their job to worry about your problem."

And so we become desperate and murder a bothersome ex-mistress, Cody added to himself. *Or support our son in doing it.*

To keep the woman talking, Cody offered coffee. The couple declined. Mrs. Szekely complained that even the American Jews she encountered were not friendly. They seemed resentful of the high intellectual level of the refugees and actually boasted of their own forebears' poverty and ignorance. They spoke proudly of their parents' desolate journey to America by steerage in the bowels of ships, of how they'd fled the pogroms of Europe and, on arrival here, been forced to live in squalor, packed into tiny tenement apartments on the Lower East Side. They wanted everyone to know that those forebears slaved for long hours at low-paying jobs in garment factories just to survive and educate their children, as if it were a badge of honor. To the new refugees the American Jews were generous with money but withheld love and caring. She didn't know who to trust as she tried to guide her children through this minefield.

Then, as things grew worse in Europe, those terrible rumors of concentration camps and gas chambers began to surface. Realizing the family might never be able to return, she'd had no choice but to remain aloof, to send her children to private schools, to make sure they were carefully nurtured. "I'm not complaining, Officer Cody; I'm saying it would be impossible for Zoltan to … to—"

"What my wife is trying to tell you," Mr. Szekely said, "is that we're not the type to get involved in crime. We've learned to conform. We don't even cling to our Jewish background anymore. When we moved to Kentucky, we Americanized our daughter's name to Kitty and sent her to the Presbyterian Sunday school. Our children learned to identify themselves as Christians, not Jews."

"You live in Kentucky now?" If they'd come all the way from Kentucky, there seemed a definite possibility they'd traveled here for the purpose of helping their son once again escape the clutches of a predatory female. Cody felt he was gaining insight into a growing crisis in their family.

"No, we live in Schenectady," Szekely said. "But Zoltan grew up in Kentucky, in a peaceful town where no one commits murder. He hasn't had the kind of background you'd need for … this."

"We don't have much in common with neighbors who drink beer and listen to football games on the radio," his wife added, "but we were determined to fit in. We rented a pleasant home among a row of houses with fenced backyards, bought a dog, and sent our children to summer camp along with the neighbor youngsters. Zoltan preferred to stay home and practice on his piano, but we wanted him not to seem … well, different."

"American boys love sports," Janos added, "and since Zoltan showed no interest in baseball or football, we made sure he at least learned archery and canoeing and other skills taught at camp. We felt he needed to get away from the piano occasionally and become an outdoorsman."

Cody was forming a picture of a boy who grew up feeling different, isolated, yet subjected to pressure from his family to hide his difference. No wonder, on moving to New York, he was vulnerable to the blandishments of an older, more sophisticated woman. And no wonder his parents felt protective of him.

"How did you get to New York so quickly if you live in Schenectady?" he asked.

Mr. Szekely explained. "Immediately after we got word of what was happening, we caught the train."

"This afternoon?" Cody asked.

"Yes, we came straight here."

"Where's your luggage?"

"We had it sent on to the hotel."

"Can you prove you just arrived?"

"Of course. I have the train tickets." Janos Szekely fished two tickets from his pocket and handed them over. Cody saw the day's date on them. He stifled a sigh; there went his theory that these parents had aided their son in his ongoing battle with Dorothea. He hated to let go of it. It had seemed to fit so beautifully with their frantic denials.

Since it was after midnight when the Szekelys left, Cody went home. He reported the encounter to B.J. the next morning. "For one brief moment I thought I had new suspects. If ever I saw people act guilty, the Szekelys were the ones. But I guess they were just upset."

"I'm convinced there has to be another suspect somewhere," B.J. said. "This has the earmarks of a frame-up."

"I agree, but so far I can't place another person at the scene."

"Better check on who really used those train tickets," the lieutenant said. "From what you tell me, daddy sounds almost more devoted to that prospective concert career than Zoltan himself."

"He certainly comes across that way," Cody agreed.

He took out the diary, recalled with distaste those racy pages, and shoved the book back into the drawer. He knew what had happened; he didn't need to wade through verbiage about it. What happened was that Dorothea learned Zoltan had separated from his wife and promptly got in touch with him—and Zoltan couldn't endure the stress of going through a second round with a woman who'd become his nemesis. It was a straightforward scenario. Dorothea sought to recapture him by demanding a father for her child, and he wanted no part of her or the youngster. He was a man in a pressure cooker, trying to mend a broken marriage and also please parents who'd devoted their lives to him.

It seemed certain he took the obvious way out: he saw a cord, unloosed it from the draperies, and dropped it over Dorothea's head. He'd found the right guy; now Cody had only to squeeze a confession from him.

CHAPTER 8

―○―

Arrival

―1930

Annika Szekely's memoirs;

Midnight—I can't sleep. I'm sitting here watching Jan thrash in our hotel bed, and I know he's worrying, as am I, about our son in jail. Wondering how I'll get through this night, I recall that a psychiatrist friend once told me that a good plan when under stress is to write one's memoirs. The effort focuses the mind and clarifies life's problems. Luckily the hotel provided stationery. So, starting with our arrival in America, a moment burned forever into my memory, here goes.

The crossing was rocky, but after rough days in which only Tanni managed to run around enjoying himself, the ship docked at last. His sister, Katya, along with myself and most other passengers, had suffered queasiness, and Janos had been stuck in the cabin caring for us—not that there was much he could do. Our seasickness ended only on the last day, when the waters calmed.

On disembarking at Ellis Island, I rejoiced to feel solid ground beneath my feet. The worst seemed behind us now, the rolling ship and the rampant anti-Semitism. Just one hurdle remained. At U.S. ports of entry, everyone had to talk, even the children—to prove they were not idiots. Any child over five who failed to speak would be put on the returning ship and sent back— and obviously a parent would have to go along. That involved a grim choice: either split up the family or deny one and all the opportunity to escape the nightmare brewing for Jews in Europe.

We anticipated no problems from our intelligent offspring. We couldn't have been more wrong. Intimidated by a boy who'd taunted her with the epithet "dirty Jew," our linguistically gifted six-year-old clammed up and refused to speak a word in either English or Hungarian. Though in moments free of seasickness she'd chatted amiably with American and English children on board, she now seemed to have forgotten all she knew. She glared in silence at the official.

Trying to be kind, the man spoke a few words of Hungarian, quietly, encouragingly. He coaxed in vain; her mouth remained shut. Frightened, I pleaded with her to tell the inspector about her American friends from the ship, about her home in Hungary—about anything she chose to speak of. She clutched her teddy bear and remained obstinately silent.

"Don't you want to go to the big city? Don't you want to see New York?" asked the man. No answer, not even a nod. He persisted. "We have a place called Coney Island where you can ride the carousel. You'd like that, wouldn't you?" Silence. He tried questions. "Do you like traveling on a ship? Did you get seasick? I bet you were sick at mealtime and couldn't eat those good dinners." Still nothing. Not even a flick of her shoulder-length golden hair.

Frowning, her father took a turn at urging. "Kat, tell about leaving Europe. Tell about how you waved to your cousins on the dock until they became little specks."

Silence. I tried again. "Tell about the sea gulls following the ship and how you tossed crumbs to them, and how some caught the bread in midair. Tell how you cried at leaving Grandmother, and hugged her and clung to her."

Again, silence. Our desperation grew.

Even Tanni urged and pleaded. "Tell about the boy who called you a dirty Jew, and how you said, 'I'm not a Jew, and I had a bath this morning.'"

Mute and mutinous, Katya frowned, her lower lip protruding in a pout. She'd never before been the center of attention; big brother was the entertainer in the family. She obviously resented the requirement that she switch instantly into the performer.

After several minutes of patient encouragement, the inspector sighed and announced, "I don't have time for this. There are hundreds of other people waiting to be interviewed."

My throat went tight with terror. I pleaded, "Leave us alone with her for just a few minutes."

The man, who was young and probably new to this sort of thing, agreed to take a coffee break and give the child time to relax and plan her answers. When he was gone, Janos and I pleaded until I was reduced to tears. Silent, Katya hung her head until her blonde hair covered her face.

Returning to try again, with no more luck than before, the inspector sighed and shook his head. He spoke the words that knelled our death sentence. "Sorry, I can't okay this child for entry. I'll allow one adult to take the boy and go on to New York, but one of you will have to return to Europe with the girl."

I wrung my hands. I could see young Tanni biting his lip and clenching his fists. He knew what we'd gone through to get here. All the frantic letters to relatives in New York, the pleading for them to sponsor the family, the forms to fill out, the people to see, the visits to the embassy, the standing in long lines, the many officials stamping the many necessary approvals— he'd watched it all. He had to be wondering, as were we, was it for nothing? Would the family not escape the ominous and escalating anti-Semitism of Europe after all? Though we adults had tried not to speak of it, Tanni had to sense that something terrible was in store for us in Europe. He'd seen me in tears over the postponements and denials that flooded in before permission to emigrate was finally granted.

Once again we pleaded with the silent child. Please, please, why wouldn't she speak? Couldn't she understand that our lives depended on it? With me running trembling fingers through my hair, my husband clenching his fists with suppressed anger, my son fingernail-clicking with nervousness, and even the young inspector, obviously unhappy about his role, moving his fingers as if tempted to wring his hands, we discussed our options. Katya clamped her lips shut.

The inspector finally shook his head, apologized, and moved on to the group at the next booth, leaving us to decide among ourselves: Should an adult remain here with Tanni, to ensure the safety of one child at least? Or should we all return to face the developing catastrophe in Europe and hang together as a family? Frantically, tearfully, I rejected the unthinkable idea of separation but then found myself forced to reconsider. It seemed best for two at least to escape the nightmare. But which adult would stay, which would go? Janos wanted to be the one to return, alone with Kat, so he would at least know his wife and son were safe. I argued that a little girl needed her mother, and that *I* should be elected to take Katya back. Besides, Janos had a job. He must remain here and go to work.

We argued, but I insisted that I be the one to go back. I had relatives in Budapest; I would stay with my sister and hope for a chance to come again when Kat was older. Jan's protests proved futile. I pointed out that he was being unrealistic. He would be away at work all day; he couldn't possibly care for a child of six. Even a ten-year-old would be a problem. Despite his promises to be good, to look after himself, Tanni was not old enough to be left on his own and would require after-school supervision. That would cost money. We'd need Jan's job.

Grimly, we made the unthinkable choice: Janos and Zoltan would stay, and Katya and I would return. We braced ourselves to proclaim the decision to the official. Yet when the door opened, we choked on the words and couldn't speak. I desperately held myself together; I feared I would give way to the urge to throw myself on the man, dissolve into tears, and indulge in frantic and useless pleas.

Then Kat pointed to the door and announced in clear English, "Mama, the mean inspector is here again! I won't talk to him! I won't, I won't!"

Pausing in the doorway, the man chuckled. "Well, those weren't the words I hoped to hear, but they'll do. I see she talks. I'll stamp the passport, and you can all go on through."

With tears streaming down my face, heart pounding, and overwrought imagination still envisioning the ship sailing back across that writhing sea with Kat and me aboard to a country ready to round us up for who knew what horrors, I grasped the child's hand and stumbled, near to collapse, through the gate. Jan and Tanni gathered up the luggage and followed. The inspector handed over the passport, and I could finally breathe again. I felt I'd returned to life after a brief death.

If I were superstitious, which luckily I'm not, I'd surely have seen this incident as a foreshadowing of our destiny in America. Instead, I smiled bravely at the two children and led them aboard the tender to the mainland, where New York, with its skyscrapers, waited in the slanting sunlight of late afternoon.

CHAPTER 9

∽◯∽

Jill's Honeymoon

—Ann Arbor, 1943

THE DAY AFTER OUR WEDDING, Zoltan developed a bad case of bursitis, while I suffered from conjunctivitis. On encountering us, Zoltan with his arm in a sling, me with eyes almost swollen shut, friends laughed, saying we must have had a wild wedding night. The stress of the marriage decision told on us both; we worried especially about Zoltan's parents. Zoltan continued to insist on waiting to break the news to them in person.

Our health problems soon cleared up, and I learned to look forward to Zoltan's brief moments of leave. Married men were allowed three hours with their wives each evening between dinner and bedtime. Zoltan often managed to bring me a slice of roast beef, hidden in a sandwich and accompanied by a piece of cake, both great treats in a time when civilians were allotted little sugar or meat. After I ate, we would settle down in our studio. Zoltan, the avid reader of Freud, proved an apt and gentle teacher in bed. I felt lucky and grew to love those evenings with him. Former housemates had told horror tales of newly married young people fumbling about in ignorance, the woman assuming she was meant to endure rather than enjoy the experience, the guy having no idea how to please a woman and often not even knowing he was supposed to do so. Thanks to Zoltan's sophistication along sexual lines, we faced no such problems.

We had one happy month, shadowed only by uneasiness over the visit to his parents' home, scheduled for January. Zoltan had completed his language course and expected soon to be shipped out, so he anticipated receiving a five-day leave, which would be spent with his parents in Kentucky. He wrote to notify them that they were to play host to the "fiancée" he would bring to meet them. I felt tempted to chew my already-bitten nails with worry over this encounter and their reaction to our startling news.

The leave just four weeks after our wedding, our one opportunity for time alone together, should have been our honeymoon. Instead, for two reasons, it had to be spent with Zoltan's family: one, because he was soon to go overseas and they might never see him again, and two, because they, who were unalterably opposed to their son's marrying, now must be informed of it.

Zoltan shared with me letters in which they'd sought to argue him out of marriage, and in reading them I'd generated my own feelings of apprehension. An incurable optimist, Zoltan insisted he knew just how to handle the situation. His parents, he assured me, on encountering the inevitable, would come to terms with it. They were strong in that regard, and realistic. Look how they'd faced up to conditions in Europe, escaping long before other Jews had done so. We would simply pretend still to be engaged, and at some point during our visit—"I'll know the right moment when I sense their attitude, their newfound approval of you"—he would announce his news, and they would happily embrace me as their daughter-in-law.

"What if that moment doesn't come?" I asked.

He remained euphoric. "Jill, they'll want you in the family just as I did. Our marriage is so *right*. They'll have to see that."

Their letters pointed out that people in wartime, limited to hasty meetings and brief leaves of absence, couldn't get to know one another well enough for marriage. But their true objection, Zoltan claimed, lay in the fact they wanted their son to finish his education and develop a concert career before tying himself down to a wife and family. "Personally," he said, "I've quit worrying about the future. After all, I'll have that teaching fellowship from Juilliard, and I'll give private lessons." He theorized that, once registered and known to the faculty, I'd probably land a teaching assistantship for graduate work at nearby Columbia. That way, we'd make out all right. "I trust you to be very careful in using the diaphragm, dear, because I know you value your future career—and mine."

The parents, it seemed, had been living a life of pretense in Kentucky—attending but not joining the Presbyterian Church, accepting social invitations from people they had little in common with, struggling to fit into an alien society. Though they'd never yet admitted to themselves that this new life was forever, that their Europe was extinct, he felt sure they would in time come to terms with the fact. Also, on getting to know me, they'd love me as he did. He could announce our news and all would be well.

Worried, I kept badgering him about how I should dress. Should I wear my best clothes? No, he thought they'd consider that foolish on an overnight bus ride where clothing would get wrinkled. "Just be yourself," he said. "Choose whatever you'd normally wear. My folks are not picky that way."

Not suspecting that I couldn't please them no matter what I wore, I tried to look my best. I bought a dramatic, wide-brimmed, brown and white Bette Davis hat, matching spectator pumps, and a dress which appeared an exact replica of the actress's spectacular *Now, Voyager* outfit. I believed I looked better in it than she did, since I was tall and willowy. I fished out my last pair of hoarded nylons from the bottom drawer of my dresser. For this special occasion, I did something I hadn't even managed at my wedding: For the first time in my life, I had my hair done in a beauty salon. I even polished my fingernails.

I packed my finery into a suitcase and hatbox, and wore my student clothing for the bus trip. I took off both rings, the wedding ring for obvious reasons and the engagement ring because Zoltan feared the fake diamond might seem to his parents too cheap and blatant. I hid them in my suitcase, assuming they could be restored to my finger once the announcement was made.

On the overnight trip, despite my best efforts, I fell asleep scrunched up in the seat. I awoke in the morning to discover that I'd messed my hair and chipped my nail polish. I hastily repaired the hairdo at the last rest stop, and as we traveled on, I removed my nail polish and asked Zoltan to hold the bottle while I replaced it. The bus jiggled; I kept wiping away polish and starting over. He insisted, "There's no need of this, dear. My parents don't judge people by the polish on their nails. They're not superficial like that."

His reassurance failed to calm my fears. I felt as if I were about to take a major exam for which I hadn't read the textbook. Butterflies flitted in my midriff. We were already in the outskirts of town when I heard with dismay the driver's announcement, "Station stop in five minutes." While I blew on my fingers, Zoltan put away the polish and urged me to relax. "You look fine. They'll love you as I do."

When we stepped off the bus, I spotted at once the handsome European-looking couple standing at the rear of the crowd, the woman wearing English tweeds in subdued brown and tan colors, the man in a well-cut suit. Their faces brightened when they saw Zoltan but then fell when they eyed me. Perhaps they hadn't received the letter telling them he was bringing me. When we reached the couple, I immediately set my bags down and touched my hair. Zoltan beamed. "Mother, Father, this is Jill Foster, my fiancée."

They looked me over. Their expressions plainly expressed their dismay at seeing their Hungarian concert pianist son arriving in the company of this American Betty Coed. I waited uneasily through the "brief shock" Zoltan had warned of. After a long moment of silence, Zoltan's mother said, "We thought you'd choose someone short and dark, not tall and blonde."

My pride in my willowy height vanished. I instinctively slumped in an attempt to make myself shorter. I grew painfully aware I matched Zoltan in feet and inches; indeed, when wearing high heels, I'd loom over him. And worse, I was taller than either Janos or Annika. I felt gigantic, awkward. My mother, who labeled me "Juno-esque," always urged me to revel in my height, but now I suddenly longed to shrink and turn brunette.

Yet, since slouching wasn't becoming and it was too late to dye my permed curls, I apologized for those things I could change. "I'm afraid I got mussed on the trip. It's hard to stay neat on the bus. If you loan me an iron, I'll press my clothes as soon as …" My voice trailed off when I realized they weren't listening to me. They'd focused on Zoltan and were inspecting him approvingly, fondly.

"Well, come along." Like one making the best of a bad situation, Zoltan's father sighed and picked up my hatbox. "We're parked over beyond the station."

As we walked, with me trying to compress myself to look shorter, Annika told Zoltan she'd arranged a recital for him. "It'll mean practicing hard for the next few days, dear, to prepare for it." To me, she added, "You need to dress well in this town, Jill. Zoltan is known and liked here; he's performed at many local concerts."

I looked down at my clothes and cringed at having worn, for this important meeting, the then-conventional student costume of a plaid skirt and a sweater, accompanied by a single strand of fake pearls—not to mention those ungainly saddle shoes. I should have arrived here resplendent in my best outfit. But I'd feared spotting my good dress while eating and drinking on the bus, and besides, as I vividly recalled, Zoltan had promised I wouldn't be judged in this way.

We got our luggage from the baggage check and carried it to the car. As we drove, Annika talked at length to Zoltan about recent musical events in town. It seemed that he had a girlfriend here named Betty Ann, with whom he'd often played two-piano recitals, and that this young woman looked forward to many musical sessions during his visit. I had to bite my tongue not to protest. I reminded myself my wedding ring was stowed in my purse and Annika had no idea she was arranging this musical twosome for a married man.

With Kitty away at college, I was assigned her room. It sported a sewing machine under the window, and Annie claimed Kitty made all her own clothes. I felt intimidated; I'd never made anything beyond, at age eight, a few outfits for my Kewpie dolls. In home ec class, I'd opted for cooking rather than sewing; with my mother being a gifted seamstress who loved making my clothes, I'd felt no need to learn. While the sewing machine swashbuckled there to remind me of my negligence in learning to operate it, I unpacked my sparse collection of clothes, hung everything in the closet, and assessed my wardrobe. Nothing appeared suitable for wear at that upcoming recital. The new hat and shoes seemed Hollywood flamboyant.

We gathered in the living room, and, while I fidgeted, miserable in the conviction I'd failed to impress my hosts, Zoltan played Bach on his parents' beautiful concert grand piano. He sounded great to me, but his mother shook her head and severely critiqued his performance. "It's not crisp. You haven't worked hard enough on it."

He admitted his technique had slipped. "I don't have time to practice properly." I felt guilty because I knew why he'd failed. I'd been taking up his time. Those canoe trips and those romps in bed were to blame.

I'd supposed that, as Zoltan's intended, I'd be subjected to intensive queries about my background, my religious beliefs, my feelings about children, all those things important in marriage. I'd looked forward to telling stories of my family, of my Unitarian grandfathers who were so different from one another, one a follower of atheist Robert Ingersoll, the other a former pillar of the Congregational Church who spoke grace before meals and duly thanked God for each good thing that happened to him. Then there were my two Christian grandmothers who "put up with" the weird beliefs—or lack of belief—of their husbands. And parents who'd designed and built their home in California.

I'd planned to describe my own struggle to work my way through college, how I'd spent a year in a cherry canning plant to save up for the university and then had to take a housework job for my senior year, and how I'd once fallen asleep in class after a late night of party cleanup and almost gotten myself expelled by the insulted instructor. Disastrous at the time but humorous later, I perceived it to be a good subject for conversation. I'd given careful thought to the best way of describing my career dreams of becoming a social worker. I wanted to sound excited, hopeful, undefeated by money shortages.

With all these tales on the tip of my tongue, I found no opportunity to offer up any of them. Annie, when not talking of Zoltan's upcoming performance and the urgency of working hard to perfect his technique, talked of the two-piano girl and the need for him to find time for sessions with her. "Poor child, she'd be heartbroken," Annie told him, "if she didn't get to play with you. She's looked forward to it all year." She went on to tell of all the things Two-Piano, apparently her star pupil, had done during this lengthy wait for Zoltan's visit, of the recitals she'd played and the accolades she'd won for her music.

No one looked in my direction; no one talked to me or paid me any attention. I suspected I could go for a long walk and not be missed. After dinner I cleared the table and brought the dishes to Annie, who scraped and stacked them. On filling the sink with soapy water, she turned to me and said, "You can do the dishes." Left alone in the kitchen, not knowing where the towels were kept, I stood with dripping, soapy hands looking around, hesitating to open drawers in someone else's house.

At night, no nightlight was provided, and after midnight I stumbled my way to the bathroom, setting the dog to barking. A door snapped open, and the faces of my in-laws stared at me in the sudden glare of the bedroom light. I cringed in embarrassment and apologized.

I went back to bed and shed a few tears onto my pillow. Clearly I was being given a message: You're not acceptable. We prefer Two-Piano.

In time I abandoned hope of becoming the cherished daughter-in-law and just tried to think how to escape the situation. Tempted to demand that Zoltan give me my bus ticket so I could return home alone, I squelched that impulse, reminding myself we were married. To rush away would make things worse. My role, right now, was that of the tolerated. Once the family learned the truth, it was likely to become that of the unwanted. I decided I must hang in there and face whatever blow might come.

This was not a traditional Jewish household. Zoltan had explained to me that lingering memories of pogroms prevented his parents from displaying a menorah or any object sporting a Star of David. Their books, expensive, scholarly studies of politics and history, I found more intimidating than inviting. I hesitated to take them down from the shelves; they seemed part of the decor. Also, the highly polished Steinway grand, occupying half the living room, seemed not the sort of piano one sat down at to enhance limited skills. I dared not touch that awesome instrument. I scarcely dared to touch anything in that house.

Zoltan's upcoming recital and his necessary course of practice continued to be the focus of conversation. Once I mentioned to Janos that our family home in Michigan was nearly a hundred years old. I'd meant the remark as a prelude to speaking of my parents, my grandparents, my childhood. He responded, "That would be a new house in Europe." Hearing the scorn in his voice, I abandoned my feeble attempt at conversation. Clearly, the man wasn't interested. I bit my lip in bafflement. Why would he not want to know the background of his son's intended?

I washed the dishes and kept my room neat. Every evening I offered to walk the dog, just for respite from the pressure of trying to please. A friendly dog, a terrier named Spooky, he always accepted my offer, and with him as my guide, we explored the town.

Three days into our visit, on the evening after Two-Piano's music session with Zoltan, at which I'd sat like a log, saying nothing, Janos waved us over. He indicated chairs for the two of us, and while Zoltan and I perched before him like obedient children, he solemnly introduced his subject. "We need to talk about this plan you have for getting married. I want to urge you to rethink the idea. It's simply no good at this wartime moment, not fair to either of you." He turned an intense, brown-eyed gaze on me. "As you know, Zoltan is about to go overseas, Jill. When—if—he returns, he'll have many years of study and practice ahead before he can support a wife. It isn't practical or sensible for you to talk of marriage at this time. You both need to postpone your plans until after the war."

Here it comes, I thought. *Now Zoltan has to make his announcement.*

Fisting his hands, Zoltan spoke up, but not dramatically as I'd anticipated. He lowered his head and seemed apologetic. He said, "We have considered it, Father, but we want to be together now."

"Of course you do, but let me remind you—if a baby arrives, you'll have no way to support it. Unknown musicians can't earn money. You could perhaps give lessons to children at a dollar or two per lesson. As you well know, you need to finish your education, hold a Town Hall recital, get reviews and credits, and then find a topnotch agent and promoter. I'm sure you realize this will take years after the war—assuming we win the war and all goes well."

"We plan to be careful with birth control," Zoltan said.

His father shook his head. "I understand your feelings, but you *must* put them aside for now. A marriage without children is a mere legalized affair. Believe me, once you're wed, you'll want home and children. It's natural. You'll find that marriage alone solves nothing."

Zoltan persisted. "We love each other, and we want to be together now. We want to share our lives for the few brief moments before I go overseas."

Janos frowned and shook his head more emphatically. "I'm telling you, you need to rethink. This idea is folly. You're exchanging brief moments of happiness for a lifetime of problems."

Zoltan said no more. The great revelation didn't come. In view of his father's closed attitude, I could understand his silence.

That night I went to bed very depressed. I realized now why the elder Szekelys had made no effort to get to know me, had asked no questions about my family and background. They viewed me as someone to get rid of.

The rest of the visit focused on preparations for the recital. Zoltan did not make his wedding announcement; I did not fish my rings out of my suitcase and slip them on my finger; I did not talk of my family or my background. I saw that there would be no happy ending in which we all embraced and accepted one another. Zoltan told me, in our few moments alone together during a trek around the neighborhood with the dog, that he'd decided to wait until after we returned to Michigan and then write a letter. This would spare us the upset of an explosion over the news. For better or worse, his parents would have to accept what we'd done.

The recital went well. Zoltan was congratulated by audience members afterward, and his mother made sure that Two-Piano stood near him and was introduced. The next morning, Two-Piano was invited to breakfast to say good-bye to Zoltan, and both Annie and Janos treated her with warmth and friendliness, behaving for all the world as if she were the cherished daughter-in-law.

To do her justice, she acted embarrassed and uncomfortable, finding herself the center of attention while I was pushed to the sidelines. She tried to talk to me, but Janos kept interrupting to ask her about her future plans in music. Annie promised to provide a glowing recommendation if her pupil decided to apply to Juilliard. Clearly they were hinting to Zoltan that there would be other women in his future if he chose to dump me.

At the station, as we stood ready to board the bus, Janos repeated his earlier urging. "Remember what I said. You must postpone those wedding plans. Wartime marriages are not fair to either the man or the woman."

It was his only farewell. When I thanked him and Annie for having me, I heard no "We enjoyed visiting with you," no "We were happy to meet you." Annie turned to Zoltan, reminding him to write regularly when he went overseas. Janos said to me as I climbed aboard the bus, "Think about what I told you, Jill. It's for your benefit as well as my son's."

Just as the bus pulled out, I collapsed my seat to lean back, taking what small measure of refuge it offered. The visit had been a disaster. It would have been better if we hadn't come, hadn't been given those orders which it was too late for us to obey. Mentally exhausted from the ordeal, I finally broke down and wailed. "Why wouldn't they like me? Is it because I'm not Jewish?"

Zoltan was quick to reassure me on that score. "Oh, no, they believe in intermarriage. They've often said that wars will only end when people intermarry and learn to understand each other's culture."

Brave words, yet even Zoltan seemed depressed. He spent his time on the bus trying out and tearing up different drafts of the letter he would send. By the time we reached Michigan, he'd settled on a way to announce the facts, and the moment we were back in our loft room, he wrote out his final draft, to be mailed on his way back to the base. "It's all I can do now." He kissed me and then brought my left hand to his lips and gently kissed my ring finger.

"Don't worry; they'll come to terms with the situation once they realize it's a done deal."

"I hope so." I didn't confess my newfound fear that we'd made a mistake in marrying.

We watched hopefully for the mailman but received no response to the letter. Zoltan tried hard to justify their viewpoint. "Our wedding," he pointed out to me, "has slammed shut the prison gates for them, uniting them with an American family and future American grandchildren who will anchor them in this country. Clearly it'll take time for them to deal with the fact they won't be going home again. We must be patient." He squeezed my hand consolingly. "Things will work out, dear."

CHAPTER 10

Disaster for the Szekelys

—1944

Annika's memoir:

As I stood on the porch near the mailbox and opened my son's letter, I couldn't help smiling in anticipation. If I knew my Tanni, he'd be writing to thank us for the visit and for entertaining the girl, Jill, and for our good advice about postponing marriage.

At first, as I read, the words swam. My mind didn't take in what my eyes were seeing. I struggled to focus, at first disbelieving, then panicky, and finally faint. I clung to the porch post. After a while I staggered into the house and collapsed in a chair. Jan looked up in concern and demanded to know what was wrong.

"It's Zoltan." My hand massaged my chest. I lost my English and reverted to Hungarian. "He claims he married that girl."

"That's impossible." Jan responded in the same language but more calmly. "You're probably reading it wrong. You never were good in English." He thought about it and added, "They haven't been gone from here long enough to arrange a wedding." He held out his hand for the letter.

"He says they were already married when they came here. They'd been married for five weeks. He didn't tell us because he wanted us to meet Jill first." I passed the letter over to him and then slumped deep into the overstuffed chair. While he scanned the offending page, I reached for a fan on the coffee table and, frantic for cool air on this stuffy-warm morning, fanned myself. I commented, "This is not my Tanni. He wouldn't do this to us."

"God, I can't believe he really … and without telling us?" Janos scanned the paper, frowned, and bit his lip. "What on earth does he see in the girl?

61

She seemed ordinary, no special talents or anything. She doesn't even know how to dress well. Those awful saddle shoes."

I fought tears. "Just a big, awkward, ungainly girl—one of the touristy types who used to visit Europe, buy fake artifacts from street vendors, and boast they'd acquired collectors' items from Pompeii or somewhere." I grasped the chair arm for support but then gave up, leaned back, and flung a hand over my eyes. "Oh God, there's Betty Ann. All this time, poor child, so hopeful, working so hard at her piano studies so she could match Tanni's abilities and play two pianos with him—and to think I encouraged her. Jan, this is awful. How will I tell her? I'll die of embarrassment."

Janos shook his head gloomily. "I don't know how we'll get Tanni out of this one. I had my hands full extricating him from his first sexual adventure."

"It's the price we pay for having a gifted son. Every girl is out to get him."

"For the life of me, I can't see why this one succeeded," Jan said. "Her attractions are well hidden. She's every bit as gaunt and gauche as Dorothea."

My ever-ready impulse to defend my son sprang to life. I said, "Well, he's young, the sex-drive is strong—and he faces overseas assignment. That has to be scary, and no doubt it got the better of him." I forced a courageous smile. "We may not have to do anything. Once this Jill is alone, she'll rethink her situation. She may seek a divorce on her own."

"She'll do nothing of the sort. She'll revel in the allotment check."

"Oh, Lord! I'd forgotten about that!"

Janos voiced the concern I cringed over in silence. "This means his income will no longer go to help Kitty with college expenses. We'll have to support the child out of our savings."

I realized that of course Jill would now be receiving the allotment checks directly. I moaned. How could things have gone so wrong? "Tanni promised us that if we put him through school, he'd put Kitty through. He knows we have no money to spare for her college expenses. He saw how we left everything behind in Europe."

"Tanni apologizes for that here in his letter. He claims Jill has not asked to receive his allotment, but the government will probably send it to her automatically."

"Of course they'll do it automatically. A man has to support his wife. There goes our retirement fund, what little we have!" I wanted to weep. "And she's such an ungainly girl, so inept. She can't even carry on a conversation. How will she manage as the wife of a concert pianist? All she seems to know how to do is smile and say nothing—which is probably lucky because one feels that if she spoke, she'd put her foot in her mouth."

"I'm afraid we failed badly in teaching our children how to judge people." Janos again shook his head. "There's Kitty, our linguistics professor-to-be, in love with an uneducated factory worker. How can Barry Flannigan possibly be the husband of a college professor? How can those two find enough in common to carry them through life? And there's Tanni, living for years with a waitress—and now he marries this nonentity. To think, he might have had Betty Ann with her Swiss finishing school background!"

I echoed his bafflement. "How could he do this? And not even tell us?" Suddenly chagrin swept over me. I reviewed the visit in my mind and admitted, "We weren't very nice to her, I'm afraid."

"We have to be nice to a woman just because she sets her cap for our son? We never felt compelled to be nice to Barry Flannigan."

"At least, if I'd known, I wouldn't have insisted on including Betty Ann in all our social affairs. I was trying so hard to show Tanni how a proper wife would behave. I … I'm afraid I botched that."

"You did fine; you were a perfectly gracious hostess. This Jill person wasn't a gracious guest. She sat here like a country bumpkin. She was only nice to the dog."

My eyes filled with tears as I swallowed the lump in my throat. "I can't cope with this, Jan. Now we have to notify everyone—Kitty and all the cousins—that there was a wedding to which they weren't invited. I can't imagine how they'll react. There'll be hard feelings all around."

"We can only explain that we weren't invited either, and that it wasn't our idea." Jan sighed and put the offending paper aside. "I'll write to the relatives if you feel you can't do it. I'll remind them that wartime changes people. I'll tell them we have to be patient with Tanni because he's about to go into harm's way overseas."

"Yes, you do it. You're so much more diplomatic than I am."

"We'll have to write to the girl, too, and manage some sort of welcome—for Tanni's sake."

"I can't imagine what we'll say. Maybe we could just send a printed card. Then we needn't include anything personal."

"Well, we don't have to do it right away. Give it time; we'll think of something."

This was the worst thing that had happened since the awful time of Dorothea's abortion. I still recalled how, right after that event, as if in retribution, we received the fateful notice from Uncle Sam that Zoltan must report for army duty.

Within days, Zoltan went off to face the horrors of war. Meanwhile,

Kitty had fallen in love with a factory worker—and a Catholic, at that. I began to see myself as Job's wife, struggling desperately to keep my children's lives together in the face of impossible odds. I tried to console myself with reminders that I was lucky compared to Jews in concentration camps, Jews sent off jammed in cattle trains to unknown destinations where they disappeared, never to be heard from again.

Life had become an ongoing nightmare, with incredible horror stories pouring out of Europe, and people guessing but not really knowing what might be happening to relatives hauled mysteriously away. In America, no one listened; everyone claimed that stuff was just Communist propaganda. The German people, they insisted, wouldn't do such terrible things. Little did they know. They never saw those European pogroms.

I knew I must pull myself together and face the realities of the times. With limited eyesight, Zoltan was unlikely to be assigned to the infantry. Maybe, now that the Americans had joined the fight, the madness in Europe would be stopped and these disasters would end.

I tried hard to be hopeful, but I felt despairing. The news from Europe was becoming grimmer by the day. My mother had died, but the rest of my family—my sister, my nephew, my aunt and cousins—were still over there, coping with it, hiding out in attics. There was no way I could remain uninvolved.

This marriage seemed just one thing too many for fate to ask of me. How bad could things get? When would it ever end?

People are dying in droves, I reminded myself. *Living means problems. So deal with it. Tanni's a grown man now, and if he loves this girl, it's because she proved herself lovable.*

Just three days before Tanni was to ship out, I bought a card with a single tulip pictured on it, and though I couldn't bring myself to say, "Dear Jill," I wrote a brief note. "It was nice to meet you, my dear. I hope we may get together while Tanni is overseas and get to know one another better." I sealed the envelope and then hesitated a long time. To spare myself the impulse to snatch it back, I waited until the moment I saw the postman arriving before putting it out.

CHAPTER 11

War's End

—Camp Crowder and Ann Arbor, 1944–1946

DESPITE IN-LAW COOLNESS, I BELIEVED mine was a good marriage. Zoltan acted eager to be with me, a man in love, and I happily responded. When he was sent to Camp Crowder, I traveled to Missouri so that we could be together until the last possible moment.

We had six ecstatic weeks during which his hours and days of leave allowed us to share our evenings and Sundays. To support myself, I took a job as nanny to a lieutenant's children and fell in love with his two darling toddlers. Zoltan and I talked of the far-off future when we would begin raising our own children. We finally found the time to explore our mutual religious orientations. Would the children be raised as Unitarians or Jews? We agreed that we would expose them to both sides of their background and let them choose.

Eventually, Zoltan was transferred to Seattle for assignment in the Pacific theater, and I headed back north.

On returning to the university, I decided against doing war work, since I knew I'd need to be ready to embark on my career when we went to New York. I settled down to resume my church secretary position and my interrupted graduate studies. To save pennies, I cooked my meals on the hot plate. I figured the savings would finance a honeymoon trip for the two of us when Zoltan received his discharge.

By early spring I began to feel hopeful of seeing my spouse soon. Having won, just before Christmas, the Battle of the Bulge, the Allies marched through Europe, reclaiming countries. The war seemed to wind down, and indeed, VE day soon arrived with much celebrating. The men from the European theater began coming home. Jukeboxes everywhere blasted out the popular song of the moment: "Kiss me once, and kiss me twice, and kiss me once again; it's been a long, long time."

Each time I heard the song, I felt a nostalgic longing for Zoltan. I dreamed of his return, of our happy nights together, of our chance to cement our marriage by taking that belated honeymoon trip.

Kitty's beloved Barry came home from Italy, and without waiting for him to be discharged, Kitty traveled to his base in South Carolina, along with two of her sorority sisters whose men had also come home, for a multiple wedding. My mother-in-law wrote to me bewailing the fact that her grandchildren would be raised Catholic. I wrote back assuring her I doubted Kitty would allow the children to grow up unaware of the Jewish side of their heritage. "I don't know Kitty very well," I said, "but I know how much Zoltan and I look forward to raising children who'll value both cultures. No doubt Kitty will feel the same."

It seemed Japan must capitulate soon. The great moment we military wives dreamed of, shopping with our men for civilian clothes, wasn't far off for me now. Since the men were not then permitted to appear in public out of uniform, most of us had never seen our spouses in civilian garb. Our excitement grew as we pondered incessantly, "What will he look like in civvies?" We window-shopped, not for suits, which couldn't be bought during the war, but for shirts, trousers, and jackets. We pointed out to one another our favorites. "I can't wait to see him in those slacks! He'll be smashing in dark blue." We all had our eye on outfits we'd picked out for our men to try on. Kitty wrote me that, for her, the experience of shopping with her new husband proved almost more exciting than the wedding itself. "Barry looked great in uniform, but you should see him in his new civvies!"

In August, the United States dropped the atom bomb. Japan surrendered. This time the celebration was muted, tempered by guilt over how we'd won, unleashing on the world a weapon which put the very existence of the human race in question. Many Americans joined the Japanese in vowing an end to all war.

Zoltan, who'd been assigned to Special Services and sent to give concerts for the troops in India, was among the last to be demobilized. As long as there were men overseas, there remained a need of entertainers for them. I'd half-finished my graduate work by the time he arrived in the States. Even then we faced a wait. Time seemed to drag on interminably.

Finally, in early summer of '46, he received his discharge papers. Excitement overwhelmed me. He headed straight to Ann Arbor, and I paced the loft, watching the clock. When it came time to meet him, I rushed off, my midriff flitting with butterflies.

I'd almost forgotten what he looked like. As he hurried toward me,

I paused and studied his exotic, slant-eyed face. I noticed he'd lost a few pounds, and I wondered if I too looked different. I'm sure that for both of us, the first moment felt like an encounter with a stranger. It had been nearly two years. We hesitated, self-conscious and uneasy. We stood in the entryway of the building that had once been his base and eyed one another. Then suddenly we laughed, rushed into one another's arms, and hugged and hugged. We clung to each other as if we could never let go. I felt the warmth of him; I smelled his aftershave; I longed for the stirring sensation created by his closeness to last forever. We kissed passionately, over and over, barely pausing for breath between kisses.

I suggested we go at once to our loft, where I'd managed, by first cooking each ingredient separately, an incredible feat: preparing on the hot plate beef stroganoff complete with a long-simmering sauce. Our snug bed also waited, and though I struggled with embarrassment at the thought of shedding my clothes in front of him after so long a time, I looked forward to those remembered romps. Zoltan seemed all eagerness. He clasped my hand and we started off.

While I blinked and squinted against the bright morning sun, having forgotten my sunglasses in my excitement, Zoltan said, "I hope you've given your notice to the landlord and the church." I smiled and nodded. He squeezed my hand and then added a startling announcement. "We'll need to leave for Kentucky at dawn tomorrow. I promised my parents we'd come to them right away."

My smile fled. I withdrew my hand. Thunderstruck, I gasped, "Tomorrow? But … but surely we're to have a couple of weeks to ourselves! I mean, to … to shop for civvies and all that."

"My father plans to take me shopping for civvies." Obviously not guessing what this meant to me, Zoltan tossed off the announcement. "Dad's so knowledgeable about quality clothing and where to shop for it. You must have noticed how well my parents dress on a limited income."

His words were like ice water in my face. That great shared shopping moment I'd dreamed of and saved for was never to happen—and Zoltan didn't even seem to regret the loss. I protested vociferously. "You're all grown up now. You don't need your father to take you shopping."

"Dad's counted on it," Zoltan countered. "He's been writing to me all year about the bargains he picked out—shoes at Thom McAn, clothing at Sears and Montgomery Ward. He says suits are coming back on the market now, if you know where to look."

"But I've picked out civvies, too!"

His dad, Zoltan argued, knew how to find that one truly expensive-looking suit in a modestly priced store. "After all, I'll need to dress well to attract students. I plan to supplement my income with private piano lessons."

"I didn't think piano teachers were judged by the quality of their clothing," I said. "I thought long hair and a scruffy appearance went with the profession."

"In Europe maybe. In America, everyone is judged by their clothes. Dad harps at me about that."

In that long and lonely period while he was overseas, it hadn't once occurred to me that the coming shopping trip wouldn't involve Zoltan and me together. Yet clearly Janos's wishes took first priority. Father knew best.

What right, I wanted to demand, had Janos to look forward to, to preempt, an event so special, so sacred, to husband and wife? An event every military wife dreamed of? Among my friends, not one returning husband had been subjected to the indignity of having daddy take him shopping.

I swallowed the words lest I start a fight right here on State Street en route to our loft. I ventured the opinion that we shouldn't even go to Kentucky until we'd had time by ourselves to get reacquainted.

Zoltan bit his lip uneasily. "My parents feel they have a right to see their son after all this time. My absence has been harrowing for them. They've worried about me."

"And I haven't?"

His brown eyes troubled, he gazed at me in distress. "I know you have, dear, but we'll be together in the future. I can't disappoint my dad again. I haven't been a very good son to him after he's made so many sacrifices for me."

Yet he could disappoint his wife. I didn't speak, but he must have sensed my dismay. "You and I have our whole lives ahead, and my parents won't see much of me when I'm in New York." He tried to counter my disappointment by explaining further. "Seeing what happened to the Jews in Europe, including one of our own relatives, I just … well, it made me feel that family is important. We have to stay close, we have to care for one another."

That was true, and I had to admit it. I'd gazed in horror at those photographs of gaunt, starving Jews in the captured concentration camps—but somehow I hadn't associated them with my in-laws, who'd after all escaped, as had most of their family. Annie's sister had gone to South America, while her cousins had hidden out in attics in Holland. I seemed to have heard that one cousin fighting in the underground had been caught and murdered by the Nazis, but the others were safe. Still, one was enough to bring the Holocaust home to them—that plus the fear and apprehension they'd endured.

I swallowed my disappointment. That great shopping trip awaiting Zoltan in Kentucky was not to include his unsophisticated wife. He offered further consolation. "I've written to Juilliard to notify them of my return," he said. "I'll soon take up my teaching fellowship. We'll be together—for all time." He squeezed my hand again as we walked. When I couldn't manage a responding smile, I felt guilty over my own reaction. Here was Zoltan being so brave about our lack of time together, and I was sulking like a child.

He went on to confess the rest of his news: "I promised your parents the second half of the summer."

This announcement brought me again to attention. I gaped. "Zoltan, my parents' guest room is just off the kitchen, and my mom is a light sleeper. She wanders out for snacks in the night. We won't have any privacy at all!"

Zoltan frowned uneasily. "It's only for a month."

"A month!"

He nodded. "Your mom is dying to have us visit. I gave her my word we'd spend a month there. She said she needed at least a month, as she plans to rent a piano so I can practice. Seems pianos rent by the month." He managed a consoling smile, which struck me as forced. "She and I have exchanged wonderful letters, Jill. She's been ever so friendly. She suggested they might drive to Kentucky to meet my folks and bring us back to San Diego in their car. That way we can stop off at interesting sights en route— Carlsbad Caverns, the Grand Canyon, the cliff dwellings. It sounds super, don't you think?"

And all this had been planned without my knowledge! My future was all arranged—by others. My father-in-law would pick out Zoltan's civvies; my parents would show my spouse the sights of the West. All the wondrous twosome things I'd looked forward to would be preempted by family.

"I've saved all the allotment checks so you and I can go by ourselves to see the West," I ventured. "It'd be a sort of belated honeymoon, a chance to be alone together for once without you having to muster."

"We have to keep our parents happy." He squeezed my hand. "We want them to accept our marriage and rejoice in it, don't we? They'll only do that if we include them in our plans." Again he smiled consolingly.

I wasn't consoled. The frabjous day had turned unfrabjous very quickly. I could agree to visiting parents for a few days, but not for all summer. I felt angry and yet, at the same time, guilty about my anger, as if Zoltan were more loving than I and knew how to care more deeply for relatives. Was this what it meant to be married, this conflicted uneasiness?

Feeling upstaged and overwhelmed by family, I lost my enthusiasm for this reunion. The dinner and bed that awaited us in the loft began to seem more duty than treat. I tried to see Zoltan's side of it, but I couldn't help viewing us as two adults behaving like obedient children and placating our caregivers.

I let out a sigh; I couldn't interfere with Zoltan's relationship with his parents. It struck me those horrific pictures of the concentration camps must have shocked Jews everywhere into feeling they must close ranks and support one another. Since I'd chosen to marry a Jew, I had to accept and participate in their experiences. Until Zoltan was ready, all on his own, to loosen the ties, I must be patient.

I managed somehow to return his hand squeeze. "Kentucky, here we come."

CHAPTER 12

Cody Hits Snags

—1948

IF DAY ONE PROVED TOO easy, smelling of a frame-up as Lieutenant Brent Johnson claimed, day two proved too difficult, with snags everywhere. First Cody looked into the travel records. He learned that Janos Szekely and his wife had indeed arrived in New York the previous evening. His hunch about the couple had misfired.

At the train station, Cody checked out other recent arrivals and found that one Carr Follinger had also come to town the previous day. The name struck a familiar cord. Cody knew he'd heard it—recently and in connection with this case. He searched his memory. Yes, Carr Follinger was the pawing stepfather of Dorothea. His presence in New York at this moment seemed suspicious, and Cody made inquiries, located Follinger and, accompanied by Yonkers, went off to interview him.

They found him breakfasting alone in the coffee shop of his hotel. At moments like this, Cody was very aware of his short leg. Limping across the room compromised his ability to present a commanding stance in confronting his suspect. He damned the childhood polio that had done this to him.

The two officers displayed their ID. Cody asked, "Mind if we join you?"

Follinger shrugged. A tall, lean, clean-shaven man with a rugged face and dark hair plastered shiny with Vaseline, he waved them into the opposite seat at the booth. There was something oily about him. Cody wondered if he might charge the man with child molestation on the basis of Dorothea's diary entries. Probably not, he thought, since the accuser herself was no longer available to back up her claims.

"So what's up?" he asked. "Why am I of interest to the NYPD?"

"We're wondering how you happened to come to town at this precise moment."

"Hell, I'm in town once a month. I work for Penn-Wellington Lumber, and I come here to order supplies. No big deal. Why do you ask?"

"Actually, we need to notify you," Cody told him, "you have a relative who died yesterday."

The man stared. His surprise seemed genuine. "I have a relative—?" Suddenly he laughed. "God, I hope it's a rich uncle I don't know about, and he left me a fortune. Tell me that's what you've come to—"

"That would be nice," Cody agreed, "but I'm afraid you won't glean a fortune out of this one. The deceased was a woman so hard up she placed her children in foster care."

"A woman, related to me?" He frowned, looking baffled. Then suddenly his eyes widened. "Dorothea?" He shook his head. "Oh, no, she's too young to die."

"No one's too young to die if they're murdered," Cody asserted.

"Murdered? Hell, you're kidding me. Who'd want to murder Dorothea? I heard she planned to marry some well-off guy, a fellow by the name of Reggie Jackson, but it hasn't happened yet, so she doesn't … didn't have money." He started to chuckle and then, as if recalling his audience, stifled it. "Did her future husband get tired of her already? Or was there a jilted lover?"

"We don't know who murdered her, but we intend to find out," Cody said. "We were hoping you might offer suggestions, you being her stepfather and all."

"Hey, don't put me on your suspect list," Mr. Oily said. "I ain't seen the girl in years. She and her mom don't get along too well, so we don't visit back and forth. I tried once or twice to get 'em together, but it didn't work out."

"And what, in your opinion, is the source of this estrangement?" Cody asked.

Follinger rubbed his face. "Hell, who can figure women? Her mom got the idea Dotty was making a play for me and threw her out of the house. I found the whole ruckus silly. After all, I'd have something to say about that, wouldn't I? I mean, if she ever done such a thing—which of course she didn't. Dot wasn't that kind of girl."

"So you hadn't seen Dorothea in years?"

"Nah. Last time's when she visited us before the war, when the kids was still little. At that time she planned to marry someone else, a guy with a foreign name I've forgotten—German? Hungarian?—and she wanted us to meet him. Dot's always about to marry somebody, but it don't ever seem to come off. I can't say why. She's a pretty-enough girl—or she was. Hard to think of her as dead. I'm still expecting to hear about her marriage."

"Could you tell me what you did after you arrived yesterday?"

"Better, I can prove it." He reached in his pocket. "Got the receipts right here." He handed over a stack of purchase orders. "I spent the day making arrangements for this stuff to be shipped, and today I'm heading home."

Cody would have liked to insist that the man remain in town until they could check out the signatures on the purchase orders and confirm that he'd really occupied his time as he claimed, but with nothing to suggest he'd been involved in the murder, they had no reason to hold him. There wasn't a motive that Cody could see, not after all these years and so little contact between him and Dorothea.

"If you'd care to read about your relative, I believe there's an article in today's *Times*," Cody said on departing.

Follinger nodded. "Thanks for telling me. I'll take the paper home. The wife will want to know the details."

"A cold bloke, isn't 'e?" Cody commented. "He's shedding no tears over his lost stepdaughter. You'd think he'd at least ask about the children."

"His story bears checking," Yonkers said with a nod.

The two detectives spent the rest of the morning contacting the wholesale outlets Follinger had visited, only to gain confirmation that the man had indeed been on their premises, some distance from Greenwich Village, at the hour of the murder on the previous morning.

"We wasted our time on that one," Yonkers said.

"At least it beats reading that awful diary. The thing drips with passion. Why do women like to rave on about passion?"

"Beats me. Passion is great to feel, but it doesn't translate into words very well."

"You're so right about that," Cody said. "Descriptions of it are boring as hell, and I've had to read pages of 'em. If I fail as a detective, I can edit romance novels."

"Except you wouldn't want the job," Yonkers reminded him.

"You said it." Proud of his American colloquialism, he spoke emphatically.

They stopped for lunch at Chock Full o'Nuts and sat on stools eating cream-cheese and nut sandwiches on raisin bread. Cody sighed and admitted he felt frustrated at losing Carr Follinger. "Perfect suspect. He molested Dorothea, or so I hear. It's too late to get him for that, but to nail him for murder would be poetic justice."

"Yeah, too bad," Yonkers agreed.

"Daddy Szekely would have made a good suspect, too. He's so single-minded about helping his son become a concert pianist. I wonder if he forced the kid to practice, like Papa Mozart. I get the feeling that for him there's no alternative. He has a gifted son, and he intends—no matter what it takes—to push him to the top."

"Including murder?"

"He already tried to do away with his grandson, or at least with the unborn fetus that would have become his grandson. He's another shed-no-tears man."

"We sure got an odd mixture here: highly emotional women, unemotional men."

Wiping his lips and sipping coffee, Yonkers changed the subject to warn that they had a problem with the curtain rod that had been dismantled to provide the murder weapon. "I repeatedly took it apart, and even after three tries, I couldn't do it in the amount of time the murderer would have had to work on it. There almost had to have been an accomplice getting the fucking cord loose while Szekely faked leaving the house. Szekely couldn't have done everything himself in the allotted time. I figure one of two things had to have happened: either Maria Bini lied about how much time passed before she went back downstairs or Szekely had help with that cord."

"We don't have anyone else on the scene," Cody pointed out. "Unless you figure some neighbor ran over from next door, or that Maria Bini was really an accessory after all. Or the kid, Mama Falucci's teenager—what's her name, Leila? Oh, hell, it's all so bloody improbable."

"I know." Yonkers rubbed his forehead as if trying to ward off a mounting headache. "And the neighbors on the other side claim they just moved in and don't know anyone in the Falucci household. Same with the folks across the street—they've lived there for a while, and their kid has played with Marcello, but they never done more than say hello to any of the adults. There seems no way to tie them in."

"Well, let's interview them one more time and then see if we can find an expert who knows how to take drapery rods apart fast. There may be tricks you don't know. Also, we have to talk to Reggie Jackson, the fiancé, and Zoltan's estranged wife, Jill. And we need to track down other Juilliard instructors who knew Szekely well, especially his piano teacher—Dr. Gruenwald, wasn't it? Maybe Szekely confided in him."

Drapery experts proved hard to catch. While Cody checked his notes, Yonkers called several shops only to learn that the installers were out on jobs. When finally he located an available one, the man turned out to be new to his job and not much faster than Yonkers at dismantling drapery rods. The officers had to wait around for someone with greater expertise—and even for him, the dismantling proved a time-consuming procedure. No one seemed able to unstring the cord in less than four minutes, and if Maria was to be believed, Zoltan wouldn't have had four minutes. She'd have come downstairs before he finished.

"So why not just use his hands for the strangling?" Yonkers asked. "Strong pianist hands—he could easily—"

"Maybe he feared leaving bruises to match his fingers."

"Then why not cut the cord?"

"Nothing handy to cut it with? Ah, hell, I'm guessing."

"There were scissors in the desk drawer, if he'd thought to look."

"But he didn't, so he had help. As I say, we need to interview the estranged wife, Jill. She's a possibility."

Cody was forced to report to B.J. that the two men had mostly wasted the day. "We have to find an accomplice—or else juggle the timeline. Carr Follinger seemed a great prospect. Too bad he has an alibi."

B.J. said, "Stay with it, Cody. You have a good head on your shoulders; you've already figured out most of this thing. The cord's not a big deal. It'll come to you in the night how Szekely managed."

"So you agree he's guilty?" Cody asked. "You don't think we have to wait to find an accomplice?"

"Looks to me you have enough on him to go ahead and charge him," B.J. declared. "I'd do it first thing in the morning if I were you."

By now it was gone seven, or just past seven by American time-telling, and Cody's head was pounding from lack of sleep the night before. He decided to leave volume two of the diary in the drawer and go home to bed. There would be time enough tomorrow to read the erotica of Dorothea's passion for her new fiancé.

CHAPTER 13

◦◦◦

The Civilian World

—Kentucky, 1946

HAVING COME TO TERMS WITH a postwar visit to Kentucky, I vowed to mend some fences with my in-laws. Yet, once again, when we arrived, I found no opportunity to talk to the Szekelys of my home or my career plans.

By now I'd resigned myself to the fact that I wouldn't get to play honored daughter-in-law in the Szekely home, that my presence would be tolerated at best. I'd even faced and accepted that the shopping trip for civvies would proceed without me, as indeed it did. Zoltan came home looking a tad less dashing out of uniform than I'd anticipated, wearing dark gray instead of the blue I'd have picked out. I assumed my mood must have affected my view of him; I blamed the disappointment on what I took to be his rejection of my taste in clothes.

As before, Zoltan's time had been scheduled to the hilt with recitals, practice hours, and performances with Two-Piano. Allowed at least to share my spouse's room, where Kitty's bed had been added for my use, I had to be content with this sole acknowledgment of my status—that and the lecture on the need for a concert pianist's wife to dress well. The lectures puzzled me. After all, my gifted seamstress mother had made my clothes and I'd supposed I was properly attired already. Not even Kitty could compete with my mother. Her neat hand stitches outdid Lord and Taylor garments.

Criticized by both parents for not yet having regained fluency in his fingers, Zoltan was repeatedly reminded to practice more. At his recitals I was introduced to those who came backstage to meet him, but when people questioned me about my background and interests, I never managed to answer quickly enough. As if she didn't trust her gauche daughter-in-law to speak the right words, Annie piped up and answered for me—with frustrating inaccuracy. I'd plan what to say—hurriedly—the next time I faced that question, but next time never came. New occasions brought different questions and a new spate of my mother-in-law's ever-ready answers that had nothing to do with the truth about me. Clearly, she'd decided what her daughter-in-law ought to say in answer to every question, and fearing I would put my foot in it, she'd appointed herself my spokesperson.

Relegated again to the silent wallflower category, I overheard someone complain to Zoltan, "Your wife is hard to get to know."

After waiting almost two years for Zoltan's return, I found myself waiting again—for our month-long parental visit to end. I was consulted only when the time for my own parents' arrival neared. My in-laws quizzed me as to which tourist court, those rows of tiny, one-room cottages, should be rented for our visitors. They couldn't stay at a hotel, Janos argued, since they were coming by car and hotels of the day lacked parking facilities.

Suddenly I wanted very much for my parents' visit to go well. After all, it would set the stage for future relationships among my children's grandparents. If I couldn't be warmly welcomed into this household, at least I could let the Szekelys know I too belonged to a distinguished family, with accomplished parents and grandparents.

On the day of their arrival, Annie decided to bypass her tasty Hungarian cookery in favor of a soufflé for lunch. I couldn't bring myself to tell her that Dad was a meat-and-potatoes man who wouldn't like soufflé any better than he'd like goulash—probably less since it was meatless. He'd had enough meatless days during the war. Yet I knew he'd eat what was put before him. As he'd often told me, his mother had raised him to do that.

It turned out my parents had stopped at a restaurant en route and were not hungry. After a polite introduction and handshakes all around, I got a quick hug from my dad, while Zoltan received an enthusiastic hug from my mother. She raved, "I loved your letters and couldn't wait to meet you."

They opted to go to the tourist court to rest while we lunched. This turned out to be lucky because the soufflé would not have served seven people. It proved barely sufficient for five.

While we ate, Annie remarked, "Your folks are very nice people, Jill."

It seemed a tepid summing. I longed to declare that they were not quite so anonymous as all that, but, due to her hasty change of subject, I once again failed to get the words out fast enough. My mother had been a columnist for a newspaper. I was proud of her, especially since she was one of the few women of her generation who'd had a career and knew early on how to drive a car. My father worked as chief aircraft inspector at a naval base, with a pager to summon him for a final check whenever a plane was ready to fly. Like a doctor, he was always on call, and I suspected he'd had a hard time arranging even this brief vacation. The couple owned a charming home in the foothills, out toward Pasadena, and Mother wrote magazine articles about sharing her life with the local critters, such as rabbits, lizards, civet cats, and king snakes.

I doubted Annie and Janos would ever know any of this because they lacked interest in listening to what I had to say and I could never work up the courage to break through and communicate. My fault, my mother would say. "You make yourself hard to know, Jill. No wonder people complain."

When my parents returned in midafternoon, Zoltan performed for them. My father, a tall, lanky man, sitting with his legs crossed, his hand cradling his cheek, was clearly bored with the lengthy Bach chaconne—meaningless noise to him. At least, the boredom was clear to me, though he was trying hard to conceal it by twitching the muscles on his face occasionally, as if he were listening. Dad hated classical music.

I tried to imagine what Zoltan's parents were making of him. A self-proclaimed "practicing lowbrow," he was a longtime subscriber to the *Saturday Evening Post* and devoured popular fiction written by Clarence Buddington Kelland and Agatha Christie. I knew it wouldn't have entered his head to reach for one of the erudite books on politics and history languishing in the Szekely bookcase. His musical taste ran to songs like "The Daring Young Man on the Flying Trapeze." He loved to take long drives in the country with his family and get us to join him in singing as we trundled along. He was partial to his mother's favorite, "Billy Boy," and he knew all verses of "Hallelujah, I'm a Bum," which he belted out with gusto whenever he found himself behind the wheel of the car.

I knew he'd sorely missed those song-fest drives, so impossible to take during wartime years of gas rationing. He and my mother argued about which movies they would see. Mother loved Ronald Colman; Dad loved Bob Hope. They usually ended up seeing both.

The Szekelys, on the other hand, used the word Hollywood to define slick entertainment and second-rate art. "It's so Hollywood," they would say.

My father showed none of my reticence about speaking his thoughts to these people I'd tried so hard to impress. When the music ended and was duly applauded, he changed the subject as quickly as possible. He looked around approvingly and proclaimed that Janos had shown excellent sense in buying such a valuable piece of property, guaranteed to bring good money in a sale.

"Oh, I don't own this house," Janos informed him. "We're renting."

"Renting?" My father uncrossed his legs, planted his feet on the floor, and all but sprang out of his chair. "You've lived here what, fourteen years?"

"About that," Janos admitted.

"Do you know how much you've shelled out in all that time? You've paid for the place; you've bought your landlord a house!" Dad reached up to smooth brown hair, which flowed straight from his forehead toward the back of his head. He'd clearly suffered a jolt. I could understand his shock. In his family everyone had always owned property. Dad's grandfather had possessed one of the biggest farms in Michigan's Thumb district. No member of the Foster family had ever yet "enriched a landlord," as he put it.

Seeing his reaction, Janos winced and justified himself. "In Hungary, if Jews bought houses, the property was likely to be snatched from us in a pogrom, the money lost. We Jews learned to view property as a risky investment."

"You're in America now," my father argued.

Obviously embarrassed and rattled, raising a hand as if to wave away the offending truth, Janos conceded that he must now change his thinking and buy a house. Suddenly I felt a new sympathy for him. His words gave me insight into how frightened and insecure my in-laws really were. Their experiences in Europe must have led them to see all Christians, however friendly, as a potential threat. They must live, I theorized, in a constant state of tension between conforming to the Christian community and trying to retain their authentic selves. Their Unitarian daughter-in-law and their Catholic son-in-law, Barry Flannigan, were part of that frightening world out there, not to mention the two sets of Christian families they must now meet and relate to. I began to sense the awesome gap they had to bridge. New understanding led me to reassess their coolness toward me. Maybe, I speculated, they'd had to choose between distancing—to help them cope— and a complete loss of control.

Janos told us he'd had an offer to transfer to a company in Schenectady, New York, and thought that if he moved, he might buy a house there. He asked my father's advice about property values. He said, "I've always lived in town, but I wonder if I'd do better to seek a place in the suburbs."

"Definitely, the suburbs when you're buying," my dad said. "Best resale value these days."

Janos nodded and seemed ready to take his advice.

With my mother helping Annie in the kitchen, the women produced a tasty dinner sufficiently meat-and-potatoes oriented to please my father. My mother knew how to take control of the conversation in a way I did not. When Janos referred to her as "Christian," she at once defined for him the difference between Unitarians and conventional Christians. "We believe in the unity of all things, including God," she explained. "We believe that God is one, not three. That makes us Unitarians, as opposed to Trinitarians."

She also managed, as I never had, to not only talk during dinner, but keep the conversation focused on matters she could respond to rather than allowing it to drift off into descriptions of Zoltan's concerts and his performances with Two-Piano. She told how she and my father had built their home on Haddon's Hill, buying a little two-room cottage and gradually adding on rooms as they could afford them until they had exactly the home they wanted—on acreage with avocado and orange trees and a spectacular view of the distant mountains.

"The place had been empty for two years before we took over, and the wildlife had moved in." she said. "In the beginning we shared the house with a civet cat and a king snake—and our own cat, Peter, who learned the hard way not to tangle with either the snake or the civet." Now visitors raved over their beautiful home, onto which they planned to add a terrace room. "I write magazine articles about our place and our area." All the things I'd longed, but failed, to tell my in-laws, she managed to communicate effortlessly. I marveled how she commanded attention in this way, and wondered why I'd failed to do so.

I knew that in the Jewish culture it was considered acceptable and even desirable to brag on one's children. I'd learned about that when I'd accompanied my college friend Frieda Fishbein home for a visit one Christmas—or rather, for her, Hanukkah. Her presence was honored. Family members would exclaim as she entered a room, "Oh, look, here comes Frieda!" as if the Queen of England had just dropped in for a visit. But I did wonder what my parents, who lacked my experience in that regard, were thinking of Annie and Janos's raving about Kitty and Zoltan. In Dad's puritan culture, that sort of thing was not done. My dad was far more likely to say, in a teasing tone, "Jill's a nuisance, but we put up with her because she's decorative." I hoped he would not do that this time, as the remark would be sure to shock the Szekelys, who never kidded about family members.

Luckily, both my parents were sufficiently worldly and erudite to carry off this visit without undue tension. My mother chatted about the problems of building a house in wartime. "Since we couldn't buy lumber, we had to use leftovers from naval construction. Our house was built far beyond code yet with some aspects that fall short and now need upgrading."

My father suggested that Janos think about buying a lot and hiring a builder, thus guaranteeing that he would have exactly what he wanted. When Janos protested that he wouldn't know how to go about designing a house, my father offered his expertise, saying he'd learned a lot in the course of planning his own domain.

After dinner Zoltan performed again on the piano, and Dad managed to hide his boredom. We all expressed appreciation and somehow got through the visit amicably.

The next morning Zoltan and I jammed our bags into the trunk of my parents' car next to theirs, and with a wave of farewell to Annie, Janos, and Kitty, we drove off to see the glories of the West. I tried not to feel resentful at sharing this great experience with parents rather than spouse alone.

With midsummer weather too hot for the Grand Canyon, my parents suggested we visit the Ozarks and then, avoiding the heat of the day by staying in motels at midday while driving by night across Texas, explore the perennially chilly Carlsbad Caverns. Afterward, by planning our journey sensibly, with midday driving in the new air-conditioned car while sightseeing in the cool of morning and evening, they believed we could manage to "do" the cliff dwellings and pueblos. Mother seemed truly excited about traveling with us, and I felt guilty for wanting Zoltan all to myself.

In fact, despite my reluctance, it turned out to be a good trip. My career conflicts with my father were put aside now that I'd become the fair-haired daughter who captured a concert pianist for a husband. Around my folks, Zoltan proved fun and funny. He had a great sense of humor when he chose to display it. He seemed awed by the vast spaces of the West, and my parents were as proprietary in showing it off as if they owned an interest in it. Though Zoltan didn't care for my father's choice of songs, he good-naturedly sang with us as we drove. He told me he loved my folks. "Even though your mother and I exchanged so many letters, I had no idea you had such a wonderful family. What fun your parents are! I'm so glad we came!"

By all indications he enjoyed the trip, and I managed to conquer my resentment. I reminded myself it was important, after all, that he know something of my background. When we reached Pasadena, Zoltan raved over our house, saying it was every bit as beautiful as they'd described.

Approbation reigned. My mother adored Zoltan and approved of me for having snared him. I couldn't have chosen a more perfect mate, she assured me. While Zoltan practiced on the rented piano, she stood in the doorway listening. She raved to me about how gifted he was and how lucky I'd been in finding him. She threw parties just so he could perform, opening her home to neighbors and fellow church members and especially to my scoffing cousin, Babs. Babs had bypassed college to become, straight out of high school, a keypunch operator, and she and her mother had both treated Dad to a lot of taunting when they learned that I, a college graduate, earned at my library job just half what Babs did.

Things were different now. Mother wanted the whole world to hear her soon-to-be-famous son-in-law. While his fingers moved deftly over the keys, she stood glorying in his performance and basking in the guests'—and Babs's—awe of it.

Being an only child is both blessing and curse. You never have to share your toys, but it's not much fun playing alone. You're indulged by the adults, but you have to take all the blame when things go wrong. You receive all available attention from parents and grandparents, but you're never left to develop on your own, to find out who you might have been had you not been so thoroughly molded by older people. Siblings notoriously plot their naughtiness together, but an only child has no one to plot with. Rebellion requires awesome courage when there is no one to back you in it. You develop early on the tendency to accept rather than fight adult criticism. I believed what was told me about my awkwardness, my unruly hair, and my love of wearing colors wrong for me.

Now, as I basked in the sudden approval of my parents, I found myself playing again the role I'd played in their house when much younger—adored daughter who could do no wrong. My father didn't even object to my plans for graduate work; in fact, he celebrated my acceptance at NYU when it arrived by taking us all out to dinner. With Congress having recently voted to provide veterans money for college on the GI Bill, it appeared that Zoltan, with his fellowship, would receive both a paycheck and a government check while doing graduate work. It would be the first time that both of us Depression babies would not be forced to nickel-and-dime our way through life. We talked excitedly of the things we would do in New York, how I would study while Zoltan practiced, how we would meet for lunch at the Automat and would subscribe to concert series at Carnegie Hall and even—a big concession for Zoltan—attend some operas. Zoltan hated opera but smiled indulgently over my dreams of visiting the Met. My mother could make the clothes I'd need for these glamorous occasions.

It seemed too wonderful, too magical to be true. And so it proved. About a week before our departure to New York, we received a letter from Juilliard. Returning veterans, due to a change of policy, were not to be granted fellowships after all. To be equitable, fellowships would be assigned only to those students not eligible for monies under the GI Bill.

We were devastated. The GI money alone wouldn't have been adequate for two even in Ann Arbor, let alone in expensive New York. "I never dreamed this could happen," Zoltan wailed as he paced the den that pinch-hit as our bedroom. He wrung his hands. "My father warned me, but I'd been so sure. Juilliard promised. Now I feel I've let you down."

"I can always get a job," I said. "I do have a college degree." It was the only thing to be done under the circumstances. I felt tearful; I'd been excited about finishing my graduate work and qualifying as a psychiatric social worker.

"We'll really have to be careful now with birth control," Zoltan warned when we were alone. "A baby at this time would be a disaster. The dire poverty my father foresaw for us—it would come true for sure."

I agreed totally. Everything else in life had to be put on hold until he finished his studies.

He wrote to protest the decision and urge that Juilliard make an exception in our case; he pleaded that he'd married on the assumption he would have the promised fellowship and could support a wife. He pointed out that his military duties had already caused a serious disruption in his musical career, and he could brook no further delays. The school replied but remained adamant. Funds must be equitably divided; there must be no double-dippers. The GI money was meant for his education; his wife must fend for herself.

Zoltan paced, clutching his hair and repeating that the situation was shaping up exactly as his father had warned. My mother stood in the doorway and consoled him. "If things turn really bad, we can always help out."

Zoltan thanked her, saying there would undoubtedly be extra expenses—for one thing, his piano would need tuning after all these years—and he'd appreciate her help. But we both knew we'd require more than minimum aid. We faced grim economies on that limited income. We certainly couldn't ask for money for luxuries like Carnegie Hall concerts, my education, or all those wonderful things we'd dreamed of.

A few days later we boarded the bus for the East Coast, but not as triumphantly as we'd anticipated.

CHAPTER 14

La Vie Boheme

—*New York, 1946–1947*

IN THE FOLLOWING YEAR, AFTER things went so terribly wrong, I would look back and try to pinpoint the moment when the first signs of trouble showed themselves. I would remember and analyze, over and over, the events of earlier days and wonder, *Should I have known? When should I have known?*

Mostly, we were happy. There were problems but, once we adjusted to our limited income, nothing major, just life's small, nagging hurdles. First off, Zoltan's piano, which he sent for as soon as we'd settled into our tiny studio room on 124th Street, needed far more than the expected tuning. Its innards had deteriorated during more than four years in storage, and the small hammers that whacked out the notes needed to be replaced. We listened in horror to the tuner's estimate of nine hundred dollars—four hundred more than I'd managed to save during Zoltan's overseas deployment.

Zoltan asked me if I thought my parents would really give us a loan, as my mother had hinted. "I can't manage without my piano," he said. "I've never in my life borrowed money, and when your mom offered it, I had no intention of taking her up on the offer. Still, as long as we promise to repay every penny—I don't know—it's a compromise I hate to make, but with no collateral, I can't go to the bank."

Though I'd landed a job at Columbia University's Butler Library, I hadn't yet started work and wouldn't receive my first paycheck for more than two weeks. With my salary of thirty a week, it would take me years to pay off the other four hundred—if indeed I could save at all when I needed my income to live on.

Zoltan explained that his parents couldn't be asked for money, as they'd had to use their retirement savings for Kitty's education. "I feel badly about that, since the expense was rightly mine. I'd given my word to pay it."

I asked, "Couldn't you buy a used piano from Goodwill?"

"Professional quality," he insisted, "is essential in an instrument." He reminded me he meant to give private lessons and would need his Steinway to impress potential students.

As there seemed no help for it, I reluctantly—very reluctantly, given Dad's feelings about self-reliance—wrote to my mother. True to her word, she came through with the funds. Zoltan wrote to thank her profusely. I tried to share his gratitude even though it meant swallowing a leftover resentment. Why had similar funds not been available for my graduate work? I tried not to glower over the fact my mother was so ready to help someone else's offspring rather than her own. It wasn't just that he was male, I told myself. It was because she believed so passionately in his talents and his future.

I had to admit that Zoltan was no slacker; he justified my mother's faith in him. With the piano repaired, he practiced hard—so hard, in fact, that I anticipated complaints from other tenants. His foot whacked away at the pedal, and his hands and arms pounded the keys with enormous force. But apparently the neighbors were all music lovers. No one snarled, glared, or even frowned at us—though I knew they must hear every sound. The walls were so thin I could listen in on conversations from next door, where two homosexual men fought constantly. I'd hear the breadwinner urging his partner to get a job, while his partner countered with a few juicy epithets. "By God, Antoine, I keep busy every moment around here, cooking, washing, ironing, cleaning. What the hell do you want from me? Who'd iron your fucking shirts if I took a job? Who'd prepare these lovely dinners? You think I goddamn like slaving away in this tiny hellhole?"

Morning and night they argued, and more than once their disputes had left me forcing my mouth not to twitch into a smile. I knew from my college friends Frieda and Loren, who'd struggled in vain for years against being what was then called queer or limp-wristed, that it was impossible for them to change. Not even years of psychoanalysis and an awesome determination had done the job. Besides, Antoine's partner did prepare lovely dinners. The aromas emanating from their studio room were the most enticing I'd ever whiffed. I wished I could strike up a bargain with them: our music for a share of your food. Between a full-time job and keeping up with Zoltan's musical evenings at concerts around town, I found no time for fancy cookery—and I echoed my neighbor's assertions that, on a two-burner gas stove, the effort required all day. Zoltan and I survived on beans and tortillas, supplemented by leftover Automat food from Horn and Hardart's day-old store, where we could often buy delicious beef pies, chicken a la king, and even chocolate cake at a fraction of the restaurant price.

With the money saved by shopping at the day-old, we occasionally managed a fling at the Russian Tea Room, where, while dining on borscht and blinchiki, we rubbed elbows with the great and famous from Carnegie Hall. Eugene Ormandy ate there regularly, along with Leopold Stokowski when he was in town and the then-top maestro with the New York Philharmonic, Toscanini. Best of all to me, however, were the opera stars we spotted.

No, Zoltan would not have been happy seeing me devote my free hours to cooking as did my neighbor. Zoltan chose to assign every nonworking moment to showing me the sights of the great city. We spent much of each Saturday at either the Guggenheim or the Museum of Modern Art, and many evenings we sought out free concerts and recitals around town. At thirty cents to sit in the bleachers for an orchestra performance, Lewissohn Stadium provided an affordable outing. We also met interesting new people at Columbia and Juilliard and invited them to our tiny room to listen to music.

In time Zoltan and two other Juilliard students formed a trio—later to become a quartet—which met on weekend evenings to play Beethoven and Mozart. In our tiny studio, the group generated incredible excitement with their performances. We attracted music lovers from as far away as Greenwich Village, and they came bearing gifts of wine and exotic goodies to pass around. With nowhere to sit, they squatted on the bed and the floor. There were so many at times that they all but hung from the light fixtures.

Even crowded as we were, I loved hosting those musical soirees. In deference to the neighbors, we ended the performances at ten, but our conversations would go on until all hours. Among the faithful was red-haired Ingrid, a tall, bony young woman doing graduate work in philosophy at Columbia, and her friend Claire Beauchamp, an English major. The pair came every Friday and perched on our bed, hugging their knees while they listened to music and, later, talked of Kafka, Heidegger and Kierkegaard. There were those two poets, my friend from Ann Arbor, Frieda Fishbein, and her homosexual wannabe lover, Loren Altman, both still in analysis and struggling to turn straight. And there was the talented pianist and composer Leah Pearlman, who loved and hovered near Frieda in the perpetual hope that she'd come to terms with the lesbian lifestyle.

Being a musician's wife proved every bit as exciting as I'd anticipated. Yet I suffered acute disappointment over my dropped plans for college. There was simply no GI money left once Zoltan covered the cost of his tuition and college fees, bought his books and music, and paid our rent. All our living expenses had to come out of my paltry income. Whenever a monetary crisis arose, such as a dental bill we hadn't budgeted for, my parents were asked for a "loan," which they promptly supplied. Each time that ready check arrived from them, I squelched a sense of betrayal, fantasizing about how much more rewarding my life would be if they'd helped me earlier and I now had the income of the psychiatric social worker I'd hoped to become.

Zoltan always made note of the amount borrowed and assured me his first priority on graduation would be to pay back both sets of parents. He repeated that he owed his parents for Kitty's education; he wailed that he'd let them down badly, opting out of his promises. Now, with money owed to my parents, too, our indebtedness seemed to stretch to infinity.

Meanwhile, we economized. No new clothes, no Carnegie Hall concerts, no operas. No Macy's or Lord and Taylor. Our shopping center was the Goodwill store.

Zoltan's parents had moved to Schenectady, which meant we could take the Hudson River Day Line to nearby Albany and visit them. It was an all-day boat trip through some of the country's most beautiful scenery, such a thrill in itself that it transformed those visits into something to look forward to. Though I still felt like a foster child in the Szekely home, waiting politely while they ignored me and fussed over Zoltan, I'd learned not to let myself feel hurt. I seemed to have outgrown my need to please parents, and I wondered why Zoltan hadn't done so.

Zoltan's mother still bragged on her son to all who would listen, but his father withheld approval, and Zoltan, fretting, spent hours pondering what to say to justify himself to the man. On each visit he went prepared with a memorized script designed to win his father over—and each time nothing came of it. Sometimes he lost the courage to speak up; sometimes he spoke but not forcefully enough. He never seemed able to command the respect he longed for.

Instead, we heard again at each visit the monotonous list of things Zoltan must do to ensure the great future his parents visualized for him. Above all, they'd now grown impatient for us to move out of "that dreadful little room on 124th Street. Our son," they explained to me, "doesn't belong on the edge of Harlem. It's not a suitable setting for a pianist who needs to appear prosperous and successful."

Zoltan pointed out that his recitals for black audiences in Harlem, which he'd played before his army days and had recently resumed, always proved popular. "I'm proud of the fact I'm welcomed by blacks," he said. "I've even performed in their homes, and I consider that a great honor. They don't often trust white performers."

His parents argued that such a venue, besides bringing no income, wouldn't impress future pupils he might have. "And what about the agents and wealthy patrons likely to promote your career?"

"My career is best promoted by letting people enjoy my music."

"Yes, when the day comes that you can afford philanthropy. Right now you need to be selfish."

The Szekelys kept urging their New York relatives to remain on the lookout for housing for us. Finally, after almost two years of searching, Cousin Nadya learned of a big, six-room apartment on Manhattan Avenue that had hardwood floors, chandeliers, large windows, and the old-fashioned elegance befitting a budding concert pianist. Friends of hers were moving out of the place. Problem was, we had to "buy" the lease for five hundred dollars, and our rent would go from twenty dollars a month to seventy-five. The only way we could afford the increase would be to sublet some of the rooms.

I argued that we should stay on in the studio until Zoltan graduated and postpone extra expense until we had more income. Unfortunately, I was ignored. Annie and Janos continued writing to those friends, making the arrangements. I assumed, since they wanted this so much, that the five-hundred-dollar loan would this time come from them—but no, they took it for granted their son could manage to do whatever he needed to do to promote his career. After all, on marrying me he'd assured them he meant to be financially responsible. They took him at his word.

Once again he wrote to my parents, reminding them that if they could come up with the funds, we would owe them, as he was painfully aware, well over a thousand dollars. He assured them that he placed top priority on paying them back as quickly as possible after his graduation.

Three days later the check arrived in the mail, made out to him. He went straight to Manhattan Avenue and bought the lease. I ground my teeth and tried not to resent seeing Foster family money go to promote Zoltan's career. I kept reminding myself it was the way of the world. The man's career counted; the wife's didn't.

I began to wonder if I'd acquired a brother rather than a husband. I'd learned the hard way that men's careers were favored over women's. In college I'd had friends who dropped out because, as they'd explained, their parents could afford only one education—and that one had to be the son rather than the daughter. I'd been frustrated and annoyed when women expressed so little anger over the situation. In fact, far from mourning as they packed to head for home, more than one coed had shrugged it off saying, "Who cares? I didn't want to go to college anyway. I just came here to meet a man who'd support me well."

At that time I'd reacted with scorn, yet hadn't quite dared assert our right to an education, or to theorize that women shouldn't permit themselves to take a back seat to men. Now, as I watched my parents' money go to my husband's education, his piano, his fancy apartment, I felt even more strongly.

I suffered guilt about my own reaction. *Resentment doesn't become you, Jill*, I scolded myself. *It detracts from a woman's charm.*

I tried hard to cheer up. Both families insisted the move would prove good for us. A rent-controlled flat in Manhattan was a real prize.

We held one last celebratory concert in our tiny studio room, where we'd lived and loved and entertained for two happy though penurious years. Then a friend who owned a truck came and took away all that was ours—the piano, the typewriter, the small table and chairs, the bed and the dresser—and moved them into our new, sunny corner apartment on Manhattan Avenue, where they looked lost in the vast spaces. I faced the fact that once again I would not be free to quit my job and begin graduate studies. My income would be needed for upkeep of this new place. In order for us to take in renters, each of the rooms would have to be furnished with bed, dresser, and desk, not to mention sheets and blankets. For the kitchen, we would need dishes and cooking utensils, and every window would have to be curtained or draped.

There was a small room just off the living room, connecting to it with french doors and probably designed as a music room. As it would likely prove the least rentable—all the other rooms had solid wooden doors with locks—we put our bed and dresser in there and agreed to make it our bedroom. That left three large rooms to be prepared as rentals. As always, we went to Goodwill, where we bought a bed, a dresser, and draperies, all still in good condition, for what had once been the dining room. Once we assembled the furnishings and added a matching bedspread, the space looked warm and inviting. Zoltan gazed around happily. "With luck we may get as much as twenty dollars a month for it."

I didn't confess to him that I saw it—indeed, I dreamed of it—as a lovely child's room, big enough to be a playroom as well as a bedroom. I sat on the desk chair gazing around the newly decorated and curtained space, still smelling of fresh paint, and treated myself to a wild flight of imagination. I planned where I might put the crib, the toy chest, the bassinet, on that lovely day when I could at last anticipate the arrival of a child.

The other two rooms were smaller and would have to be rented more cheaply—but even so, once we got them furnished and decorated, my spouse thought we'd come close to getting our rent paid. Ever hopeful, he assured me, "We might even come out with a few extra bucks for a Carnegie Hall concert once in a while." He smiled at the prospect. Since I'd balked at bribing ushers to sneak us into Carnegie for a dollar, we hadn't gone there up to now.

Once again he proved overly optimistic. When the room didn't rent at twenty, we had to drop the price to seventeen. Finally, we located a Barnard student, new to the big city and timid about being on her own. On moving in, she treated us like substitute parents, apologizing profusely whenever she failed to make her bed or clean up after herself in the kitchen. We used her seventeen dollars to furnish one of the smaller rooms, which we rented for thirteen.

My mother had sent a packet of articles from *Sunset* magazine describing clever ways of painting and decorating cheaply, and working together in our free moments, Zoltan and I took the suggestions. We plastered the cracks with a product called Fix-All and then walloped the paintbrush over the walls, chatting and enjoying each other's company as we worked. Seeing the improvement in the place left us feeling well rewarded for our efforts. We decided to refinish the Goodwill furniture to make it more appealing.

We soon had three renters and collected more than half our next month's rent. However, there was still the bill for gas, electricity, and telephone, expenses we'd not faced in our tiny studio and had forgotten to budget for.

It took a while to come up with the money, eked out from my paycheck, to furnish the living room. Since all our furniture was Goodwill-drab, I made slipcovers for the couch and chairs to brighten them. In the end the place looked charming, and we took pride in showing it off when friends came for music sessions. Yet I hated the burden of debt, and I had moments when I confessed to Zoltan that a small Village apartment furnished with orange crates would have been more fun.

"It wouldn't impress piano students coming for lessons." He suppressed a smile as he added, "World-class musicians don't furnish their apartments with orange crates, dear."

Nor with Goodwill furniture, I almost blurted. But I didn't argue with him.

At least there was now room to squeeze everyone in for chamber music concerts. When the crowd expanded, we could open the french doors to our bedroom and allow people to sit on the bed. Still, things weren't the same. We were living beyond our means and kept having to borrow money from my parents. Besides, we had no privacy. With roomers frequently coming to sit in the living room and play our record player, we couldn't manage to feel alone even in bed. These renters were young students who, far from contributing an occasional meal for all of us, would ask hopefully if we could share our meal with them. If they did cook, they left the kitchen a mess and I had to clean it after work. When rent collection time came, they had a plethora of excuses why they couldn't come up with the full amount. Good-natured Zoltan sympathized with their financial problems.

The girl gave us no trouble, as her parents sent us her rent check each month, but the two boys were constantly behind in their payments. One of them, worried on overhearing our arguments about not keeping him on, solved his monetary problems by taking in a roommate. This gave me yet another person to clean up after. I steamed but tried to hide my annoyance. Zoltan seemed to enjoy the extra company. I would come home from work to find him happily involved in bull sessions with the renters when he should have been practicing.

Then three things happened at once to throw me into despair. The first seemed at the time a small matter. I began having sudden stomach upsets. One occurred as I worked in the stacks at the library. Out of the blue, I vomited onto the floor. The attack came on so suddenly that I couldn't make it to the restroom in time. My suspicious boss, assuming I'd been drinking, sent me to the infirmary to be checked out. The doctor inevitably ruled out alcohol—we couldn't afford even cheap wine now that we were keeping up the new apartment. After some probing and poking and testing, he decided I was suffering a blockage. He warned me that this sort of pathogen could before long close the passageways to the uterus. He consulted my chart and casually tossed off the remark that was to change my life. "You're twenty-eight? Are you aware your chances of having a first baby go way down after thirty? And with this added condition—well, I need to warn you, if you want children, it's now or never."

The statement threw me into a panic. I'd never thought of *not* having children. In fact, I'd looked forward to it. I'd postponed, not eliminated, the event.

To abandon forever all hope of offspring—I tried to imagine it and found it unthinkable. My only Foster cousin, Babs, was a confirmed spinster who showed no interest in men. I was the only one in my grandparents' family likely to produce a new generation. Without this, not only would Zoltan and I grow old alone, we would end the line at least on my side. Kitty'd had one child and was pregnant again, so the Szekelys could count on descendants, even if they were Catholic. My parents would have none at all. Facing the prospect of having no investment in the future of this planet, I found it at once scary and empty.

Yet I feared Zoltan would explode in anger if I told him we needed to get on with child-having at this time. Adamant about birth control, he never failed to assure himself I'd used the diaphragm. He'd repeatedly insisted, "There must be no babies until I graduate, give a Town Hall recital, launch my career, and pay your parents back."

I couldn't muster the courage to confess to him the doctor's ultimatum. At home I brought up the question casually, hinting about babies. How long, exactly, would he estimate it might be before I could consider becoming pregnant?

He confirmed my guess. "It'll be years yet. After graduation I'll try to get some sort of part-time job to repay your parents, but it can't be anything too time-consuming. For at least a year, I'll need to spend many hours each day practicing. It's so important to get good reviews at the Town Hall recital—it's the way concert careers are launched. Without good reviews, the expense of a recital is wasted. There'll be no agent, no promoter, nothing. Then, later, I'll need to do some concertizing—"

"Years!" I gazed at him, totally panicked now. "Did you say years?" My heart thudded. What to do? How to tell him?

He reached for my hand and consoled. "At least I won't be rushing off to class every day, dear. We can be together more." He had it all so carefully planned. I couldn't open my mouth to repeat the doctor's statement. But it kept playing itself over in my mind. "Children now or never." It sounded ever more ominous the more I thought about it.

And all of a sudden, I found myself thinking about it all the time. Worrying, I began to wonder if I ought to stay with Zoltan. Perhaps it was time for me to leave him and seek a man ready to be a father. We'd had a wonderful love affair, but, if it couldn't grow into a real marriage, it seemed destined to remain just that—an affair, however legal.

I'd wanted that once—it had seemed exciting—but it had lost its appeal.

CHAPTER 15

Intersecting the Past

—1947

THE SECOND DISASTER OCCURRED WHEN Cousin Nadya dropped off a large box of Zoltan's prewar belongings, explaining that it had been hidden at the back of the closet and overlooked when she returned his stuff to him. "Sorry it took me so long to get it to you."

She declined my offer of coffee and rushed off to do errands. Since Zoltan was on his way out the door for a Saturday morning class, he asked me to open the box and sort its contents. "I've forgotten what's in it. If it's clothing and hopelessly out of style, just put it out for Goodwill." With a wry smile, he added, "I get kidded enough for my long hair; I don't need to include old-fashioned suits in the mix."

I waved him away and began unpacking. On top I found a layer of sweaters. No style problems there; sweaters don't change much. Tucked beneath these lay a small notebook, and on flipping it open, I saw unfamiliar handwriting with female flourishes. Wondering how some other person's notebook had wandered into Zoltan's box, I began reading. I soon realized it was a diary, and it described an affair between two people, Zoltan and an unnamed "I." Though I knew it was not meant for my eyes, curiosity got the better of me. I fought guilt and thumbed through to seek a name to go with the pronoun. I soon found it.

"Zoltan and I had a terrible fight last night," I read. "He said, 'Dorothea, there's no way in the world I can marry you at this time.'" The diarist had added the pathetic statement, "If my darling means it, I may kill myself. I can't face another love affair gone wrong. I've been so good to him. I've cooked for him, slept with him, given him everything and asked for nothing. I thought I'd made myself indispensable." Further along, she wailed, "What's the matter with me, why can't I ever find a caring man? The world is full of women who manage it. Am I that bad looking? Mom always claimed I was awkward and ungainly, but surely I've conquered that since I learned to carry plates of food without dropping one. I took English courses, charm courses, even learned to dance—not that Zoltan cares a hoot about that."

I struggled with my conscience and told myself to put the diary aside. But I was hooked. Zoltan had mentioned a former girlfriend named Dorothea, who'd been a miner's daughter, and I'd known he was no novice at sex. After our marriage he'd instructed me in detail about my own body. Sex with him had always been great because he was so knowledgeable, so experienced.

Intrigued, I abandoned my scruples. I sat down, started reading, and soon found myself totally identified with the diarist. Dorothea had spelled out their relationship, from their first shared dinner to the final bitter outcome. "The Szekelys promised not to abandon me, but here I am, abandoned and alone." At the end she said she planned to tuck this book among his things so that he'd remember her when he came out of the military and realize she'd truly loved him.

There but for the grace of God go I, I told myself. The diary reflected my dilemma exactly. For weeks after that doctor visit, I'd wrestled nightly with indecision about whether to withhold the diaphragm and try for a child— even one unwanted by its father. And how easily, back in college, I might have given way to the temptation to say yes to that handsome soldier when he urged we spend the night together! So few men had shown an interest in me before that, and even those few had gone off to war. I well remembered the moment when Zoltan made the suggestion and the panic it inspired in me, the swirling emotions of temptation and fear. When I said no, I wanted to bite my tongue and change my answer. Now I knew what would have happened to me had I done so. Pregnancy would have happened. An illegitimate child would have happened. Loneliness, desolation, rejection by my family and his would have happened. I'd certainly have refused the offer of abortion, yet neither family would have welcomed the baby. Janos would have urged me to terminate the pregnancy, and when he failed, as he surely would have, I might have been abandoned as Dorothea was. We were sisters; we were twins. I longed to reach out and hold her hand.

Though I considered myself fully adult, had come to terms with many shockers, including a lesbian/homosexual couple among my best friends, had read, without blinking, Thomas Wolfe's best seller about the affair of a young man and an older woman, I couldn't deny to myself that I felt chagrined at finding this situation so close to home. After my years of struggle to become worldly, my puritan background had finally got the better of me. I'd never imagined this sort of thing might occur in my own family. A brief affair I could understand. But three years—and Zoltan never until toward the end enlightened Dorothea, never communicated his determination to remain single until he'd developed his concert career. Of course, she should have sensed it—his hesitance about introducing his parents spoke volumes—but she was struggling with her own demons. Her personal needs made her impervious to his signals, just as mine almost did after that doctor's warning: "Now or never." I still heard it echoing in my mind. *Now or never, Jill.* It hung in my thoughts like a malignant tumor I would have to deal with eventually.

Remembering what I'd gone through just getting fitted for a diaphragm, I sympathized with Dorothea, going off to that dreary room and having that baby flushed from her womb. I couldn't have faced it. The Szekely men had treated her abominably. True, she'd contrived the final denouement, but only after years of her life had been invested. Zoltan must have known she was desperate to make a home for her children, and he certainly knew he wouldn't marry her. So how could he stay with her all that time and never level with her about his true intentions? Never insist she look elsewhere for the family man she admittedly sought?

In her diary she'd been very clear about her hopes and dreams. To qualify as Zoltan's wife, she'd attended night school after her waitress shift ended and gotten a high school equivalency diploma. She'd learned to speak grammatical English so she could participate in conversations with Zoltan's educated friends and prepare herself to impress his family. She'd never meant to be an unwed mother; she desperately wanted to be married and have her youngsters with her. "I can't bear having no control over my children's lives," she'd written. "Why else does a woman have children but to feel she has a hand in the future, an opportunity to mold young people into fine adults? And to be remembered by them as a person of influence? Why has God chosen to deprive me of that privilege? Why did he give me children if I'm not meant to raise them?"

I tried to cling to my minimal sophistication. *Europeans take these relationships for granted*, I told myself. *This sort of older woman–younger man affair happens all the time in places like France and Hungary. Their literature and movies are full of it. Just such a film from Sweden,* Torment, *currently plays in New York, and I've seen it twice. Zoltan and Janos hadn't intended to be mean or uncaring, and obviously the relationship had to end. Why drag it on into a marriage and a sordid divorce? Why allow another foster care child to come into the world? Grow up*, I told myself. *This is life.*

Yet despite these self-chastisements, I saw myself as another Dorothea. True, Zoltan married me and not her, but that happened because he was going off to war. All soldiers felt the need of someone to wait at home, someone to write letters to them and count the days until their return. I also realized with chagrin how Janos and Annie must have perceived me when I first arrived at their home: just one more in the parade of predatory women who'd set a cap for their gifted son, one more duck to be knocked out of the row. No wonder they made no effort to get to know me; no wonder they devoted themselves to discouraging us from marrying. And no wonder Zoltan had been so eager for our marriage to become a fait accompli. After the humiliation he'd suffered in the Dorothea affair, watching helplessly as his father took charge of his life and dealt with his problems, he must have seen no other way to handle his parents.

And, of course, with our relationship starting off in that manner, his parents were unlikely to alter their attitude. I realized the fault was mine for failing in the beginning to demand respect from my in-laws. I should have made sure of my acceptance into the family. I should have refused to marry Zoltan until he won their blessing for our union. I'd made precisely the same mistake as Dorothea: I'd been too readily available. Now, as for her, it would be difficult, if not impossible, for me to change the pattern.

Zoltan was due back soon, but I hardly knew what I'd say to him. I warned myself to keep calm and listen to his side of the story. I had only Dorothea's side here, seen from her own bias.

When he came in, I coolly told him I'd found Dorothea's diary, which she'd tucked among his things to ensure that he'd remember her. He'd already, after walking in and giving me a quick kiss, picked up and begun thumbing through piano music. I doubted I had his full attention. Without even looking up, he said, "Really? How did that get there?"

"She claimed she put it there when she helped you pack. I gather she hoped you'd read it."

Still focused on the music, he showed little interest. He wasn't, as I'd anticipated, overcome with confusion and eager to justify himself.

"I feel sorry for her," I confessed.

He looked up at last and frowned. "I too felt sorry for her, Jill, but nothing could be done. Father was right. The relationship was impossible."

"It should have ended much sooner."

With a loud sigh, he put the music aside. He sat on the bed, rubbed his hands together, and reached out to take my hand. He seemed finally to grasp the fact I was upset about all this. "True, I should have broken up with her and insisted she look elsewhere. But I didn't know how to do that. She was so alone, so … abandoned by everyone, even her mother. She acted desolate when I tried to urge her to find a more suitable partner. I was young and inept about human relations; I couldn't figure out how to make my exit in a kindly way. If there *was* a kindly way. I'm not sure there was. Breaking up love affairs is always painful, and she was so vulnerable."

Recalling her threat of suicide, I felt concerned about Dorothea. I suggested we look her up to make sure she was okay. Zoltan frowned and shook his head. "Not a good idea, Jill. Best let sleeping dogs lie."

I insisted; I felt I needed to know. Dorothea had begun to seem a kind of alternate self. The things that might have happened to me had happened instead to her, allowing me to be forewarned of the outcome. Zoltan protested again. "I can't believe this. Why would you want me to get in touch with my former girlfriend? That's the last thing most wives want."

I thought about it. I supposed, a few weeks ago, I'd have felt that way— but the situation had changed in my marriage, and now I needed to learn exactly how problems of the past had impacted the participants. "I can't rest until I know she's okay," I said.

"You go by yourself, then. I'm out of it, and I want to stay out."

"Would you just call and make a date for me?"

He shrugged and reached for the phone book, where he found her name. On calling he learned she'd moved from the studio Janos had found for her and now shared a Greenwich Village house with friends. Keeping his voice impersonal, he informed her of our marriage.

After the call, he reported to me that she didn't seem upset at the news. She'd even invited us to visit. He'd told her that he couldn't spare the time, but his wife would like to meet her and learn how things were going with her. It seemed she promptly issued the invitation.

I went the following day. I found her in the Italian section of Greenwich Village, which always struck me as a charming area, with its red brick row houses, each with a set of steps and a wrought iron railing. This one had a boot scraper beside the front door, a treasure left over, no doubt, from days when the street was unpaved.

A brown-haired woman a bit older than I opened the door and greeted me with what seemed genuine warmth, offering a smile and a handshake. "So you're Zoltan's wife? I've heard about you—I still know some of the musicians Zoltan used to perform with, and they pass along the news. How kind of you to visit. I'm Dorothea. Come in, come in."

Both her poise and her friendliness surprised me. I studied her for any sign that her comment was made ironically. But no, she seemed a forthright sort of person, ready to speak her thoughts without subterfuge. She led me to a large, comfortably furnished studio room at the back of the house, saying she was free to use the whole downstairs, since the owner had her bedroom upstairs. I couldn't resist the impulse to stare. She was a tall woman, my height, thin and so large-boned that I thought of her as gaunt rather than slender. She had short, wavy hair and wore a full-skirted, sky blue dress. Everything about her seemed large: her brown eyes, her teeth with overbite, her prominent chin, her hands. Simple sandals encased generous-sized feet with long, prehensile toes and no toenail polish. I was reminded of the song "Clementine." The phrase "herring boxes without topses" crossed my mind.

I relaxed in Dorothea's company, partly because her manner put me at ease, partly because I too had large feet, felt most comfortable in sandals, and rarely bothered to polish my toenails. Just as I had while reading her diary, I saw us as sisters under the skin.

She offered me a chair, and seated herself on the many-pillowed bed serving as makeshift couch. "You've found a nice place to live," I commented. When she nodded, I politely added, "It's good to see you living so comfortably. Things must be going well for you."

"Things are great right now. My life has taken a turn for the better." She seemed happy; she kept smiling in an excited way that made her brown eyes sparkle. She confessed, somewhat breathlessly, "Up to now I've had rotten luck with men, but, at long last, I'm to be married."

"Married? Really?"

"Isn't it wonderful! The best part of all," she added, "is that I'll realize my longtime dream of getting my children back. The older kids have been in foster care for years. I can hardly wait for our grand reunion. It will be so wonderful to have them with me again." She leaned back and flung her hands up as she contemplated her future. She struck me as a naturally awkward person who'd taken a charm course, leaving her with a smooth overlay that didn't quite cover her jerky movements.

I saw no hint she was still carrying the torch for Zoltan. For that I felt relieved. Her manner when she inquired about him was friendly but formal; she seemed content to accept him as a man from her past. The very fact that she welcomed me without apparent jealousy suggested she no longer retained an emotional investment in my spouse. Leaning forward on bony elbows, she asked questions about his days in the army. Had he been overseas? Had he become involved in the fighting? She nodded and smiled when I assured her he'd studied German, played concerts in Asia and India, and gone on bivouacs. Though she asked when he'd been discharged, her interest seemed casual and conversational.

"As for me, I still work as a waitress at Mario's," she told me. "Been there for ages. I'll quit when I marry and concentrate on becoming a housewife and mother."

She studied me with friendly curiosity, as if waiting for me to tell her about my life, so I mentioned that I worked in the library at Columbia. She commented, "Libraries are fascinating places. And how do you like having a musician in the family?" When I said I loved it, she asked if she might attend one of Zoltan's concerts. "It'd be great to hear a performance of his again. I don't know a lot about classical music, but I enjoy it. Our friends used to gather to listen, and it was such fun entertaining people."

I told her Zoltan had no recital scheduled, but I'd call her if something came up. She requested our address and I gave it. I saw no reason not to. Her interest seemed casual and impersonal.

I turned down her offer of coffee and sweet rolls and left after a short visit. I'd only wanted to know she was all right. I had no plans to develop a lasting friendship.

Even though Dorothea showed no signs of harboring resentment, I still obsessed over what seemed to me Zoltan's less-than-noble role in the affair. The next day, wrestling with my doubts, I wrote to my mother about the situation, confessing my dismay at my spouse's behavior.

By return mail my mother argued, "A designing woman like that deserves what she gets." Dorothea had obviously, in her view, zeroed in on a naive young man and victimized him. "Boys are so vulnerable to women like that. His parents were right to get him away from such a predator by any means necessary. I'd have done the same if he were my son."

I squirmed over her portrait of Dorothea, which was not mine. I saw Dorothea as very much a victim of the position of women in our society, a woman desperately seeking to make a life for herself under almost impossible circumstances. I remembered reading in her diary that, forced out of her own home at a young age by a sexual predator, she'd been rejected by her mother and had lacked parental support and guidance. In relations with men, she'd had to learn by trial and error. In spite of that, she'd stayed off the streets and earned her living legitimately. For reward, she'd been forcibly and tragically separated from her children.

In my next letter, I pointed out to my mother that Zoltan was not a boy; he was nineteen when he met Dorothea, twenty-two at the end of the affair. Mother responded, "But innocent, obviously—and Dorothea saw her chance and took it. Zoltan is a loving, caring person who wouldn't know how to fight off that kind of manipulation. As I say, his dad did the only thing he could do."

I felt chastised; I again reminded myself I must achieve sophistication. I must not let this new knowledge alter my view of a husband I had to make a life with.

Yet the truth lay in front of me. I now knew what I could expect from the Szekelys when I announced my newfound dilemma, my wish to have a child "now or never."

I hadn't yet worked up the courage to discuss the offspring problem even with my mother, let alone with my spouse. I was amazed at my ongoing panic over this confrontation. I'd been prioritizing for so long, graduate school and then motherhood, that I hadn't become aware of my true feelings about children. I realized only now that the desire had been growing ever since wartime days, when I'd briefly worked as nanny to those adorable toddlers. Back then I'd packed my longings away in the "someday" closet. Now, forced by the doctor to bring them out and look at them, I faced an urgency I dared not admit to my career-oriented husband.

I did talk to Frieda, who, while agreeing with me about the Szekelys' mistreatment of Dorothea, claimed I need not share her fate. "It's different for you," she pointed out. "Zoltan married you; you're his wife. You've waited through a war and an education, and now no one can blame you if you pinprick the diaphragm."

But I was all too acutely aware of the outcome of Dorothea's pregnancy. I didn't want to be pregnant without spousal or parental support.

I paced, I debated, and I worried. My concentration at work fell off, leading my boss to complain. "Ever since the day of your illness in the stacks, you haven't been the same person."

He was so right. I certainly didn't feel like the same person. The one-time wannabe social worker had become a wannabe mother. A brand-new obsession had taken over my life, all the stronger for having arrived so late. I walked around in a permanent state of flitting butterflies. In those baby boom times, it seemed that everyone else in the world had acquired offspring. Kitty looked forward to her second, which was already "in the oven," as she laughingly put it. Suddenly, even for me, having children became a downright religious gesture, a promise that mankind was not destined to be wiped off this planet just yet, that life would continue in these postbomb years.

It struck me that perhaps I needed to let Zoltan off the hook and seek a man ready to raise children. But that was too drastic to contemplate. I put it out of my mind as quickly as it tiptoed in.

CHAPTER 16

<hr/>

The Last Straw

—Autumn, 1947

THE THIRD EVENT LEADING TO the collapse of my marriage masqueraded at first as triumph rather than tragedy. Yet it proved the proverbial straw that broke the camel's back. Zoltan, having entered a contest of which the prize was two evening performances with the Louisville Philharmonic, received a telegram notifying him he'd won. He'd receive a check for four hundred dollars.

Ecstatic, we celebrated with a meal at the Russian Tea Room. We dreamed of having, for the first time in either of our lives, a bank account. I began to hope that perhaps things would work out after all. If my spouse could win a few contests like this, our economic problems would lighten, and our future could at last begin.

He wanted me with him, of course. Together we made happy plans for our trip. Since he'd be needed in Louisville for two weeks of rehearsals with the orchestra, I arranged my vacation for that time. Zoltan's piano teacher, Dr. Gruenwald, knew of someone driving to California who could drop us off in Kentucky, saving us bus fare one way. By renting a room in a private home that offered kitchen privileges, we theorized we could do our own cooking and therefore manage to hang onto our money. I obtained copies of the Louisville paper, found a room advertised for rent by the week, and wrote to make the arrangements.

On arrival, we learned that this was not considered the proper lifestyle for the orchestra's solo performer. The Louisville sponsor who'd donated the money for this contest had done so to give the symphony a bit of much-needed advertising. Zoltan was to be wined, dined, feted, and photographed—and we were expected to stay in a decent hotel. We would also, obviously, for all this social life, require clothing far more elegant than any we currently owned.

Desperate, I wired my parents to send money. Our resources might cover our hotel, food, and taxi bill, but not the cost of a formal for me and a tux for Zoltan—not to mention that he'd need to rent tails for the two concerts.

My mother, as usual, came through with the money—and Zoltan, as usual, computed the additional loan and announced that we were now in debt to the tune of nineteen hundred dollars, a huge sum in those early postwar days. "We must try hard," he said, "not to need more, as we're already over our heads and will be years paying it off."

I bit my tongue and didn't answer.

We were the center of attention in Louisville; everyone wanted to meet us. Our phone rang constantly with invitations. People raved over Zoltan's playing and declared he was on the way to fame and fortune. "He knows how to make music exciting. I could hardly sit still." At his concerts the applause went on and on. I basked in his triumphs while women claimed to envy me. "How wonderful it must be to hear such great music all the time," they commented to me during postconcert receptions.

I smiled, nodded, and assured them it was dreamy and I loved it. That much was true. I did enjoy his playing, at least the Chopin, Liszt, and Beethoven pieces. I hadn't yet made the leap to Bach, who seemed to have put his notes together as a mathematical exercise rather than a melodious creation. An opera fan, I reveled in bel canto. I liked to hum along, and you can't hum a Bach chaconne.

We watched in distress as our expenses mounted. By the time we were ready to return home, we lacked money for tickets. Shaking his head, Zoltan said, "We can't wire your parents again. They've done too much for us already. We'll have to hitchhike, dear." He cast a sympathetic glance in my direction. "I hope you won't mind too terribly much."

I minded but could see no alternative. And so, the day after the last performance, the final moment of wildly enthusiastic applause, the last glamorous reception held in our honor, we packed our finery in suitcases and took the city bus to the highway at the edge of town. We stood by the road, an improbable pair of hitchhikers newly escaped from the world of galas. Zoltan seemed to regard thumbing a ride as no big deal. Indeed, he shrugged it off, saying, "I hitchhiked in army days, even took trips to Kentucky this way before I met you. It went all right. We'll be fine."

I couldn't bring myself to raise my trembling thumb. In time I squatted beside the suitcases with my arms crossed, hugging my shoulders. Zoltan stepped out alone to give the signal. Drivers ignored us; cars passed without stopping. Cold, shivery, and fearful, I rubbed my upper arms vigorously.

Zoltan noticed and suggested going into a nearby café for early lunch and hot coffee. I stood up, nodding. I'd have done anything to postpone this roadside hell.

We both ordered the blue plate special, which turned out to be a hot roast beef sandwich with gravy. A well-dressed man sat at the counter reading the newspaper, and I noticed him peeking from behind it to eye Zoltan with curiosity. He folded the paper so we could see it and remarked to us that Zoltan looked exactly like the musician whose picture was printed there. He passed the paper over. The article proved to be a flattering critique of Zoltan's performance of the previous night, complete with a photo of him in tails sitting at the piano. Luckily the camera had been pointed at a sideways angle, making it impossible to identify the performer with certainty. Even so, I squirmed with embarrassment; I knew the man must have seen us out there trying to hitchhike.

Zoltan pulled the whole thing off with aplomb. He said, "Isn't that a coincidence. What do you know—I have a double."

The man chuckled. "I felt sure you couldn't be performing with the orchestra. Those guys make big bucks and travel in luxury."

Zoltan nodded. "Don't I wish I were a successful concert pianist! That would be the life!"

I thought it lucky my picture hadn't been included. With the two of us, there could be no mistaking who we were. It would have been excruciatingly embarrassing.

The man introduced himself as Larry Ronan and then asked how far we were going. He explained, "I'm a traveling salesman headed for New York. I need a driver, and I'd be willing to take you if one of you has a current license. I just came from an all-night party, and I hope to snooze off the booze in the backseat."

Zoltan's prewar Kentucky license proved out of date, so I held up my still-current Michigan license and assured the man I was an experienced driver. He nodded. After eating, we climbed into his car, and I slid behind the wheel. While I drove, he watched from the backseat. Apparently deciding I passed muster, he finally curled up and went to sleep.

Mr. Ronan awoke around dinnertime and instructed me to stop at the next restaurant, where he bought us a meal. Afterward, tired and impatient to get home, I drove on. The sky had clouded over during the afternoon, and now the rain began. I clutched the wheel and peered past the wipers at wet pavement, batting heavy eyelids as I guided the car through the rainstorm while its owner slept and Zoltan chatted to help me stay awake. It was going to be a long night.

When an increase in bright lights hinted that we neared the coast, Zoltan too drifted off to sleep, and I found time to review my situation. I knew now the sad truth about concertizing, that the occasional performance would not bring us sufficient additional income—on the contrary, this one had increased our debt—and offered no means of escape from the financial hole we'd dug ourselves into. So what to do about my need to get on with childbearing? *Now or never, Jill,* I reminded myself.

I felt I had only to look in the mirror to see Dorothea. My problems were no less acute than hers.

One thing was clear: it was useless to confront Zoltan about the baby business. Now that we'd learned what a young concert pianist could expect in the way of financial remuneration, Zoltan would insist all the more vehemently that a baby at this moment was unthinkable.

I saw only one remaining solution.

During a brief stretch just before dawn, I made a hard decision. The artist's life was not for me. I'd waited long enough, and I didn't have more years to give to the project. Zoltan might well go on to become famous; I might be forced to watch a second wife enjoy the fruits of my sacrifices, be feted in my place, sit in the seat of honor that this one time had been mine, beside the conductor's spouse. Yet, heartbreaking though that would be, I needed to begin living my own life.

Part of my decision, of course, came from the grimly realistic picture of the concert pianist's life I'd just been exposed to. The biggest part, however, came from my fear of demanding the right to finish my studies and have a child in a family so intent on that musical career-to-be.

As Frieda had argued, I needed to start planning for raising a youngster, and that meant finding a man ready to share that adventure with me. I felt time slipping through my fingers, draining away and taking my future with it.

The hitchhiking incident gave me an excuse. When we reached home, I sadly, regretfully, informed Zoltan I couldn't go on any longer. I took all the blame; I admitted he'd been honest about how harsh, how lengthy and time consuming, the road to musical success might be. "I should have listened to you," I said. "I was overly optimistic."

This was to have been the great moment of triumph, when I finally told him of the doctor's warning. But we lacked the bank account we'd anticipated. I faced the possibility that if Zoltan learned of my predicament, he might break down and agree to take whatever job he could get to support a child. Afterward, devastated over his career loss, he would forever throw it up to me that I forced him to it. I didn't want that kind of marriage.

"I can't get on with my life right now," I added, rushing to fill the silence of his disbelief with words different from those I'd planned. While he stared at me, speechless, I struggled to explain. "I need to find a man who's already working, a man who can support children without paying the heavy price of a compromised career."

As I'd feared, after the first shock and lengthy silence, Zoltan reacted with fury. He shouted and hurled accusations. "And have you already found this alternate daddy? You've been out looking, haven't you! I've sensed that something was going on with you lately. You've been acting so damn weird. Have you met another guy? Come on, be honest now."

I gave way to the urge to act scornful. "Oh, don't be crass."

He shouted back what I'd just told him. "I've never hidden financial problems from you. I never promised you it would be easy. You knew what you were getting into."

I once again admitted it. "I just didn't know how long it would take. I didn't know it would drag on into an indefinite future—and that we'd end up owing my parents two thousand dollars we can't repay, and your parents thousands for Kitty's education that you'd agreed to pay."

He steamed in anger. He threw reminders at me, how I'd promised this and I'd promised that. I just kept shrugging and admitting it. Then suddenly he relaxed and began consoling. He took my hand. "Things will work out somehow, Jill. There must be some financial aid out there that we can get. I'll talk to the counselor at Juilliard."

Angry, Zoltan was hard to cope with. Conciliatory, he was impossible. I couldn't make him believe I wanted a separation. He went off at once to confer with a counselor. I wrote to my parents, forewarning them of my intentions of leaving the marriage.

I knew they'd be angry, and of course they were. Their accusatory letter came flying back. I read it a few days later, while Zoltan and I, in an armed truce, awaited the promised help from the school counselor. "What's the matter with you?" my mother asked. "You've got a great husband, who just triumphed at Louisville. Rejoice and knock off the nonsense."

My dad added a note of warning. "I'm peeved over your news. If you go through with this foolishness and walk away from your marriage, you needn't expect ever to receive another penny of financial help from me, not if you end up starving in the gutter."

In a second letter, my mother wrote to console Zoltan and assure him I was basically a good person who'd never before demonstrated such foolish behavior. She hinted to him that I must be suffering some sort of temporary aberration. "She's off the deep end now. Be patient with her, Zoltan, dear; I'm sure she'll snap out of this."

I was furious with her. I felt ready to snarl at both of them, Dad for his harshness, Mom for consoling Zoltan rather than me. I wailed to Frieda that, as my parents, they belonged on my side.

The Juilliard counselor did his research and came up with a grant we were eligible for. Zoltan's instructors all promised to give us glowing recommendations so we'd be sure to receive the money.

They were as good as their word, working hard at helping to plead our cause, and even getting the whole faculty involved. Each of Zoltan's instructors wrote a complimentary letter about us to the grant donor. Dr. Gruenwald, his piano teacher, assured us we couldn't lose. Any musical connoisseur, he said, could see that Zoltan was potentially a world-class pianist. He claimed Zoltan's talents vastly outshone those of the closest runner-up. "There's no comparison," he said. "Our boy is practically guaranteed to win."

We crossed our fingers. We paced the floor and waited for news. The grant would give us a year-long income so Zoltan could practice for his Town Hall recital and I could quit my job, finish my studies, and try for pregnancy.

It was not to be. Despite all efforts of the Juilliard staff, the donor decided the grant should go to a family who already had offspring. In the end, a far-less-promising candidate received the money because he was struggling to support his two children. Juilliard notified us in a letter, and we read it with tears, heartbreak, and disbelief. It seemed the winner, though less musically gifted, was needier. Devastated, I stormed around the room. "It's so unfair! They're penalizing us for being prudent, for not bringing into the world offspring we can't afford."

Sad-faced and woebegone, Zoltan nodded in agreement. "Everyone at Juilliard said it was in the bag for us. They promised."

We appealed the decision, but the donor was adamant: "Children already here must be cared for; that's the whole point of my gift." He wasn't interested, he said, in becoming a music patron; he simply wanted to aid the youngsters.

It was a final nail in my coffin. Everything turned to blackness. I lacked the money to live on my own; I was penniless once the rent and expenses on the apartment had been paid. I felt trapped forever in a job I now hated. It seemed that for the rest of my life I would get up and go to work, come home to cook dinner and iron shirts, and nothing would change. Both my career dreams and my hopes of being a mother receded into an unreachable distance. I felt all the pain of loss that Dorothea had so vividly described in her diary.

Despair overwhelmed me. I could scarcely remain in motion to go to work, come home, prepare meals. I couldn't eat. I lost weight. The apartment no longer shone with cleanliness. I longed to stay in bed all day and sleep my life away so I wouldn't hear that internal voice saying, *Now or never.*

Zoltan, his parents, and my parents all dealt with the problem in the same way—by scolding and urging me to snap out of it. Only Frieda remained supportive. She offered to share her tiny Village flat with me so I could leave Zoltan.

In those days, it seemed everyone in New York, including Frieda, was undergoing analysis. One day, I cashed my paycheck and, instead of putting the money into the kitty for next month's rent, brazenly took it to the office of a psychoanalyst. I told him about the problems in the marriage and asked what I should do.

He was a youngish man, midthirties, pleasant mannered and nice looking; his name was Moishe Aaron. He seemed baffled by my story. He confessed he couldn't understand why I hadn't fled the scene long ago. "You're what we Jews call a WASP—white Anglo-Saxon Protestant. This country belongs to you; you can have whatever you want. You don't have to put up with a man who fails to support you, who makes education and childbearing unthinkable for you."

It was shocking to hear my husband described as a potential wage earner. After hearing him referred to for so long, by both his family and mine, as a gifted musician who must have no financial burdens placed upon him, this was a new way of viewing matters. Dr. Aaron declared that a prudent man doesn't marry until he can support a wife. In response, I fell into the familiar pattern of justifying Zoltan's behavior, saying he'd expected to be able to support me; it was just that he'd been denied a promised fellowship and grant from the school.

"So he should find a job," Dr. Aaron said. "A grown man doesn't look to his wife and in-laws to solve his financial problems."

Unless he's a gifted musician or artist, I amended to myself. To him I explained, "He's behind in his practicing. He needs to regain fluency in his fingers after all those years in the military. I feel I have to let him do that. I mean, he'd already had his career disrupted in childhood by his flight from Hungary—and then again by the army. I can't add to his burdens."

"Hey, you people are not characters in the movie *Casablanca*," Dr. Aaron reminded me. "Zoltan was no freedom fighter interred by Nazis and needing special consideration. He was an ordinary soldier who endured no more hardship than the rest of us. We all had our careers disrupted by war and had to make the best of it on our return. Since he was in Special Services, his was less disrupted than most."

"But he's a musician."

"You don't owe him for that. A married man has a responsibility."

"Besides, his family has been through so much, having to leave their homeland and come here. I really can't—"

"Have they? From what you tell me, they saw the threat and removed themselves from it. I'm sure the six million Jews who died in gas chambers would have welcomed an opportunity to trade places with them. Offhand, I can name a few in my own family."

I'd run out of arguments. I could only repeat, "I feel so guilty. I feel downright anti-Semitic."

Dr. Aaron assured me he'd take me on for analysis, would even adjust his prices to what I could afford, but only on condition I move out. This marriage, he said, was probably not salvageable. There were too many people backing Zoltan in his failure to support me. He was too comfortable. No pressure had ever been put on him to change his thinking. "You need a life and a future—immediately. If Zoltan isn't ready to share it, you must find a man who wants what you want. There are men out there who will see things your way. So make the move to your friend's flat in the Village and start looking for that new someone."

This was just what I hadn't wanted to hear. I thought of the years I'd spent trying to impress the Szekelys. I admitted I'd tried before and hadn't had the courage to leave in the face of Zoltan's rage, my parents' rage, his parents' rage. "I'll be the villain in both families." I trembled at the prospect.

Dr. Aaron insisted the deed must be done, the inevitable step taken. "You can't live forever in this deep hollow of depression. You must be freed to get on with your life."

I left his office in a state of panic. Shaky, I went to the Automat for coffee and then headed toward home. As I walked I began working to organize the thoughts running through my head, prepping myself for the confrontation to come. So totally focused on my dilemma was I that I had little awareness of the blocks-long walk home. I later had a vague recall that it was raining, and that I was wet and chilly. I know I stopped at a corner drugstore to call Frieda and make sure her offer was still good. She sounded pleased. "I felt you needed to take this step," she said. "I'm so glad your analyst agrees with me."

On arriving home, I took a deep breath, clenched my fists, and walked into the front room, where music thundered from the piano. I touched Zoltan's shoulder and forced my mouth to say the words. "I'm moving out."

The explosion was predictable. Zoltan had taken it for granted the analyst would calm me down and make everything right for us. He jumped up from the piano and confronted me. "You can't go. It's out of the question!" He added, "Among other things we need your paycheck to pay the rent." When I refused to back down, he again accused me of being in love with some other man. He said, "I can psychoanalyze you myself, and I won't charge a thing for it. You don't need to go off and shell out money to that quack. I can tell you right now, you haven't outgrown your Electra complex; you're still looking for daddy—and I'm not daddy enough. I'm not tall and thin like Jerry Foster."

I'd already brought out my suitcase and started packing, but I paused to stare at him. *Where*, I asked, *does he get these strange ideas?* "What on earth put such a thought into your mind?"

"I got that from observing you," he said. "When other men visit, you're very quick to offer them danish and coffee—but you expect me to get my own. You're always more attentive to the other men than you are to your own husband. It's the psychopathology of everyday life, just as Freud says."

I became frustrated when he quoted Freud, since I didn't know the man's work well enough to argue back. We didn't study Freud in social work classes; our psychology courses were of a less-theoretical nature. I snapped, "You're not a guest, you can get your own coffee."

I was tempted to add that if I had an Electra complex, Zoltan suffered an Oedipus complex. As mama's boy, he would never upset his mother by asking for monetary aid. "It's always my parents, not yours, who have to bail us out when an emergency arises," I reminded him. "You'll have to get in touch with yours this time or collect from those deadbeat renters—or better, throw the renters out and find tenants who can actually shell out for their pad. I'll need my paychecks to buy my own groceries and help with Frieda's rent." And pay the analyst, but I didn't mention that.

He wasted another five minutes going through a song-and-dance about how this wasn't me. "You're suffering some kind of breakdown and will rethink your situation in the morning." After offering more psychological analysis, he sat again at the piano. Putting on a show of indifference, he shrugged. "Go then, if you must." He started to play.

With my typewriter in one hand, my suitcase in the other, and my winter coat slung over my shoulders, I left the apartment accompanied by a shower of notes from Rachmaninoff's Second Concerto. I closed the door against it. I took the subway to the Village and arrived, a tremulous refugee, at Frieda's tiny cold-water flat.

The place sported a single large room plus two tiny, six-by-eight bedrooms, a miniscule kitchen, and a bathroom contrived from an old closet—so narrow that a woman had to back into it in order to sit on the stool. But at least the fourth-floor walk-up was bright and sunny.

Frieda welcomed me with a warm hug and assured me I'd been right to leave. She'd cleared out the second bedroom for me. It had no closet, only a curtain hiding a clothes hanger stand, but I owned few outfits anyway. There'd never been enough money for me to buy clothes.

I unpacked, put my underwear and hose into the empty dresser drawers, and thanked my hostess for accepting me. I knew she'd had to cramp herself in order to make this bedroom available to me.

She made coffee for both of us and then we sat talking. She pointed out that though Zoltan was indeed a top-notch musician, there was far too much competition in the music field these days. "All the great musicians of Europe fled to New York," she reminded me. "They're competing to give concerts. Under the circumstances, I doubt that either Zoltan or our friend Leah is destined for a great performing career."

Leah, the pianist and composer from our college days, currently worked as a waitress to keep body and soul together. Frieda confessed that while I'd agonized with Zoltan, she'd agonized with Leah, helping to pay her bills, consoling her in her struggle to find grants and fellowships. "I finally faced reality about a situation which neither Zoltan nor Leah seems ready to recognize: there's simply not a sufficient audience out there to support so much musical talent. But you and I can't change their thinking, Jill; we have to disengage ourselves." She sipped her coffee and reached across the table to touch my hand. "You've taken the first step in leaving Zoltan and entering analysis. I'm sure you needed to do that. You haven't seemed truly happy since you moved from your studio room."

I explained that our big apartment lacked privacy and had proved a grave financial burden. "I'm solely responsible for the rent when the tenants don't pay—and they often don't." I poured out all my problems; it seemed good to talk. I described how I'd felt the dollar bills being ripped from my fingertips, a useless struggle to make the rental rooms more enticing so that we might get better renters and collect more money. "We keep borrowing from my mother. Our debts are horrendous, and there seems no possibility of Zoltan taking financial responsibility anytime soon." I added that the GI money would end at his graduation next month. "He has one pupil, who pays him two dollars a lesson—when she shows up, which is about every other week. If I stay, I'll have to support him as well as myself."

My mother never seemed to agree with my view of Zoltan. When I wrote to complain of his failure to help out with finances, she reminded me that I'd chosen to marry a musician and should have anticipated this.

Clearly, I could seek no sympathy there. In Mother's eyes I was to blame for all that went wrong, and I needed to straighten up and fly right. Since I didn't intend to do that, at least not according to her definition of what was right (staying put and keeping my job), I could only sigh and comment to Frieda that I hoped the two-piano girl, Betty Ann or whatever her name was, still awaited Zoltan in Kentucky. With a giggle, I added, "Too bad Dorothea's marrying; she might have come back to him."

I was soon to look back in horror and wonder how I ever found that idea funny.

My tiny bedroom in Frieda's apartment opened onto a light well with windows of other apartments around it. Some tenant had a night-light in the form of a tiny lighthouse with a beacon that circled our outdoor space and periodically swung its beam across my ceiling. That first night, feeling twittery and jittery and unable to sleep, I lay there counting the seconds between sweeps. So much of Dr. Aaron's reaction had come as a surprise to me. I could still hear those unwelcome words, "This marriage isn't salvageable." Yet I knew the truth of them. I couldn't begin to guess what Zoltan might say if I insisted on having a child. It had always been taken for granted in both families that he must first succeed as a concert pianist.

Night after night I watched that fake lighthouse beam circle my ceiling. I reviewed every moment of my marriage and tried to think when it was that things went so terribly wrong. Was it at Zoltan's disappointing return from overseas, when I discovered he didn't mean to share with me those sacred rites, buying civvies or taking a belated honeymoon? Undoubtedly, a certain mystique had fled at that moment. But now, since reading Dorothea's diary and assessing her mistakes, I suspected I should have been alerted even earlier. I should have been warned off by the Szekelys' nonacceptance of our marriage.

I stayed with Frieda and continued to see Dr. Aaron, while my parents pleaded with me to return to my spouse. I ignored them. I wrote to Ann Arbor to say I needed to finish my graduate studies and wished to apply for a teaching assistantship. Assured they would welcome me as both student and instructor—it seemed all my professors had endorsed me—I believed that after two more semesters of study, I'd at last earn my social work credentials.

Though my heart wasn't in it, I still put in an appearance at my job and went through the motions. I even managed to show up at Zoltan's graduation ceremony, to stand by his side and force a smile while his parents gave me the cold shoulder and hardly spoke. At night I thrashed and berated myself for failing to anticipate what now appeared to be an inevitable outcome of past situations and events. I worried about how Zoltan's parents were handling the news of my departure. I wondered if my parents would disown me altogether. The villain role was new to me, and I couldn't come to terms with it.

"My marriage could be so great," I wailed to Frieda while we dunked biscotti into our breakfast coffee at the corner cafe. "We really love each other. If only things had worked out so Zoltan could earn a little money. I never minded economizing for his career, but I can't give up living my life for it."

She sighed. "Life is full of might-have-beens, Jill. I've had oceans of them. Loren and I really loved each other, but we just couldn't manage the transition into the straight lifestyle—at least he couldn't. I struggled to make it with Leah, but we both felt guilty about our lesbian life. It wasn't fun hiding from our families. Now Leah's gone back to playing the tease with men, leading them on but refusing to sleep with them, while I'm trying to come to terms with being Frieda Fishbein, soloist, for the rest of my life."

I gazed at my housemate in sympathy and realized she had problems every bit as severe as mine. It was high time I stopped feeling sorry for myself and got on with my life. She was right, I needed to cease mourning the might-have-beens and begin to plan for what had to be, a life without my musician husband.

Then, just three days after Zoltan's graduation, I received that improbable, unbelievable call from my spouse notifying me that he'd been picked up by the police. At once, I had to rethink everything.

CHAPTER 17

Death in the Morning

—1948

Arriving at work early, Cody poured a cup of coffee and forced himself to bring out volume two of the diary. The time had come to wallow in drippy romance. He needed a clear picture of the Reggie Jackson relationship before interviewing the murder victim's fiancé.

There appeared to be a gap of four or five years between the volumes. Here, as in the earlier volume, Dorothea started off writing well. She asserted that a bright future was shaping up for her—and all because she'd made the hard decision to settle for Reggie Jackson, a kind though not sexy man who claimed to love her and promised to care for her and her children. She'd finally come to terms, she claimed, with the fact that romance was the stuff of novels and movies. In life, you gave thanks for good companionship, for heartfelt caring, and asked for no more.

Then, three days before the scheduled wedding, she received startling news. Her first love, Joel Fisk, turned up again. She received a note from him saying he planned a visit to New York and needed to talk to her. Excitement shot through her; she believed he'd broken up with his wife back in Peoria—or was it North Carolina?—and wanted her back. While agreeing to see him, she promised herself she wouldn't accept him until he spoke the word marriage. It would be all or nothing this time. No more living together with her fingers crossed, hoping for something that never materialized.

It seemed that, while writing, she heard voices in the hall. That, she noted, would be Leila, taking Marcie to preschool. She explained that Sophia Falucci normally dropped the child off on her way to the shop, but right now, with the older woman laid up in the hospital, the younger woman, whose shift at the shop started later, had offered to give the child his breakfast and get him ready for school. "Leila's not the rebellious teenager she used to be," Dorothea wrote. "I don't know what happened to change her, but she acts nicer and more helpful lately. Maybe she's impressed by the fact her housemate will soon be a bride. I'm impressed myself. A bride—the word sounds lovely, even with Reggie as groom. I say it over and over to myself. It would be far lovelier with Joel as groom, but I'd need to hear a very emphatic promise about that."

The next entry must have been made later, as it was in a different shade of ink.

"This morning as I lay in bed gazing at a gray window the sun hadn't yet got around to, I heard in my mind Mother's voice speaking lovingly and calling me Dodie. It's such a long time since I've heard that name or that loving tone. I wanted to weep. Ever since she learned of the Carr incidents, Mother's tone has been angry, calling me Dorothea, accusing me of something I'd never dream of doing. Why would I choose to steal the love of that awful guy who leered and pawed? He's nauseating. How in the world could Mother have thought I wanted that sort of thing or encouraged it? Actually, I even wondered what my mother saw in the monster. For myself, I only wanted Carr out of the house. To be accused of setting my cap for him was hurtful and grossly unfair."

The diary became repetitive along these lines. Cody flipped pages. Dorothea wished things could be different with her mother. She longed to write a nice, normal letter and say, "Joel is coming to visit me, Mom. I hope to win my first love back and not find myself stuck marrying Reggie after all." But these days, she claimed, her mother refused to accept her letters and wrote "Return to sender" on them. She had only Aunt Belle as a substitute, Aunt Belle who tried to act as go-between, keeping her tenuously connected to her family—more and more ineffectually as the gap widened.

"Maybe, once I actually marry, Mom will stop viewing me as a threat and begin to love me again. She might become a real grandmother to the boys." Dorothea rehearsed her planned speech for Joel. "First love is best," she'd tell him. "I've always dreamed of us getting together again."

Snuggling deeper into a soft mattress and pillow—she loved describing sensual experiences—she lay in bed wondering if she should cancel her wedding plans with Reggie. But no, that might jinx things. She could, however, postpone. She could claim she wasn't feeling up to par. She and Reggie were to honeymoon at Niagara Falls, and Reggie would understand that she needed to feel great and enjoy the trip.

She opted to wait until she talked to Joel, since what she had to say to Reggie might prove to be farewell forever. But what if things weren't all that clear with Joel? What if he merely wanted to "have a try at reconciliation," as so many of her friends were doing? She could refuse to sleep with him, but that was her only weapon. So what should she do about Reggie? How could she keep him waiting in the wings while she tried to work things out with Mr. Handsome?

Whatever she said, she recognized that she'd need to say it soon. Reggie had arranged his vacation starting on the fourth. He had tickets for the two of them on the Hudson Day Line and reservations at a hotel. He'd need to change everything—and quickly.

"This is the first time in my life I've been free to choose between two men," she wrote. She confessed that she luxuriated in the feeling; she'd feared it would never happen to her. She described how she took out Joel's note from under her pillow and read it again and again. It was short. "I'll be in New York for the next three or four days, and I want to talk to you. I'll drop in at Mario's around noon and take you somewhere for lunch. See you soon."

Even though he'd signed it *Joel* instead of *J,* as formerly, it surely meant he'd left his wife. She'd often fantasized that he would someday remember his first love fondly. She'd daydreamed that he'd come back to her—or Zoltan would. In her daydreams, the two men alternated. First it was Joel, and then Zoltan, who abandoned his wife in favor of a more-romantic past love. She'd long ago decided to accept either one if he came. She wouldn't waste time in foolish recriminations, but would rise above her anger over the past.

She recorded that just then she heard the hall phone ringing. Leila answered and called out to her. "Dot, you awake?" Then louder, "Telephone."

Cody could picture her getting up, flinging on a robe, and asking, "Who is it?"

It was her Aunt Belle. She recorded that Leila had left the wall-phone receiver dangling and said, "I'm off; I'll see you later."

"I waved good-bye to Marcie, who followed Leila out of the house," she wrote. "I went to the phone reluctantly and said, 'Hi, Aunt Belle.' It was a bad moment to have to talk to my aunt, just when I was feeling indecisive about the wedding. I wasn't ready to confide in her because I didn't yet know what was up with Joel. Luckily, Belle didn't sense my hesitance; she only worried about her sewing. She said, 'Dot, I need you to come over for another fitting of this wedding dress. I'm having trouble with the waistline. I'm afraid I've made it too small.'"

"I felt an impulse to giggle and promise not to eat for the next three days," she wrote. But of course that wouldn't work. She'd need to stall her aunt some way. She improvised. "Maybe we should hold off a bit, Auntie. I've been thinking and I—"

"Don't tell me you're about to back out of this wedding!" Aunt Belle shouted.

"Well, no, but I … I might need to postpone—"

"Dotty, I'm at my wit's end with you." Aunt Belle always doubled the volume when she spoke on the phone, and right now she tripled or quadrupled it. Dorothea was forced to hold the receiver away from her ear as her aunt ranted on. "You drive me out of my cotton-picking mind. I've tried to help you for the boys' sake, but you keep waffling, and I can't think why. You know Reggie's the best. He'll care for you and the kids." She took a deep breath, audible over the phone. "Do you know how hard it is to find a man willing to commit to raising children? Do you know how many women have to trick their husbands into having kids? I've heard at least fifty women admit they were forced to 'forget' the diaphragm, as their husbands would never agree to a child. You've lucked out with a guy who *wants* your youngsters."

"Auntie, I don't love him!" Dorothea wailed.

"Oh, for heaven's sake. Love him! That's Hollywood stuff, designed for naive virgins. Grown women—especially those who already have children—plan a life with a man who chooses to share his life with them. They don't howl about love."

Hear, hear! Cody thought. *You tell her, Aunt Belle. I'm with you.*

Predictably, Dorothea argued the point. "But, Auntie, think what you're asking. I can't just go to bed with any old—"

"You managed to go to bed with three or four other men that I know of," her aunt snapped. "It can't be as bad as all that." Her tone grew angry. "This is nonsense. If you cancel, Reggie will be furious and so will I." She raised the volume to top level. "You get over here for the fitting before you go to work, Dorothea Granger, or I'm finished with you!"

"I don't think it's unreasonable to want to love the man you plan to spend the rest of your life with."

"You'll learn to love him, girl. Stop romanticizing."

With a sigh, Dorothea backed down. "All right, all right, I'll come."

She described how she hung up and drooped her way to the kitchen, where she put Marcie and Leila's breakfast dishes in the sink and poured a cup of coffee from the still-warm pot. On checking the calendar, she straightened up. Today was the day. She could spare Aunt Belle twenty or thirty minutes. By lunchtime she'd be with Joel again. She'd arranged for Leila to pick up Marcie after school and take him to the park; she'd even asked to have the afternoon off at work. If she and Joel hit it off after all these years, they could have hours together to renew their relationship. By evening they'd be back to old times, holding hands and laughing together the way they used to. Perhaps he'd even suggest they go to a hotel for the night and pick up Randy tomorrow for a picnic at Coney. Just Randy by himself. She'd let Joel enjoy his own little family for a few days before introducing stepchildren into the mix.

She went on: "I dressed more carefully than usual for work, with more makeup, more attention to my hair. It's at least ten years since Joel last saw me. He lived close by for a while after we separated, before he moved to North Carolina, and we used to run into each other occasionally. I know I can't hope to look exactly as I did back then, but my figure is still good, my hair still brown and curly, and makeup will hide those lines I've been noticing lately."

Later, with the marginal comment, "How wrong I was!" she'd recorded every moment of that day, the day before her murder. She'd stopped by Aunt Belle's and dutifully stood still, avoiding further arguments, while the wedding dress was fitted. Then she'd gone on to work.

The morning had passed slowly. She watched the clock. Joel arrived at twelve on the dot. She recognized him at once when he stepped through the doorway. She felt an initial shock on noticing that his once-dark hair had gone salt-and-pepper, but it was still a thick mane like that of her oldest son, Randy, and he shared with their son a triangular face, with a broad forehead, a narrow chin, and a prominent dimple. She saw that his midriff now sported a slight pot. Well, that was to be expected. He'd had those years, too, and probably a stint in the army during the war.

She smiled warmly—but not too warmly. She reminded herself to play it cool. *Don't overwhelm him, Dot.* She was prone to come across too needy. "Joel, how wonderful … I mean … how nice to see you."

He spoke brusquely. "Shall we go to lunch?" he asked. "Can you get away?"

"My boss offered us the use of the private room here," she told him. "It's not reserved today—it'll give me more time." When he nodded, she added, "I'll go get Cook to dish us up some food. I remember how you loved the veal parmigiana here." He smiled and admitted that sounded good. She said, "Back in a sec."

He seemed polite and remote, not as eager and excited as she'd hoped. She decided this reunion might take a bit more patience and effort on her part than at first appeared. But that was all right. Whatever it took, she'd handle it. She went to the kitchen. The cook dished up fettuccini for her and veal parmigiana for him, along with a bit of salad and some rolls. She carried the plates out and led the way to the private room. Another waitress brought their drinks and then left the couple alone.

"So how've you been, Dorothea?" Joel asked. "You're looking good."

"I'm fine." She resisted the temptation to begin telling him about her life. "This time I'm determined to remain a mystery woman," she'd noted in the diary. She asked, "How about you, Joel?"

The question was meant to provide an opening for his confession that he'd left his wife. She confidently waited to hear the words. Instead, to her surprise and confusion, he responded, "Things are going great," and then began describing in detail the resort he ran in North Carolina. "It's on a lake—beautiful country—I own a dozen cabins, each with its own kitchenette. People come there for boating and fishing. I'm doing fine with it."

"I'm so pleased to hear it." She wondered what it had to do with her. Was she to be invited to join him there, to see if she could take the isolation? Of course she could take the isolation; she grew up in a small town in Pennsylvania, didn't she? She prepared to say, "Oh, I'm used to that sort of thing. It won't bother me at all." She awaited the invitation.

Instead of asking her to pack her belongings, he began talking about Randy. He said, "Only problem, we never had children. I really need Randy, and it would be such a great life for the kid. He could learn to run the boat and take tourists out on the lake. He could serve as guide on hikes."

But of course they'd have Randy with them; that went without saying. So why was he saying it?

"Dorothea, I've visited with Randy several times," he confessed.

"Have you? I'm delighted to hear it. I always felt that you two would hit it off."

"He's a fine kid. He's the spitting image of me."

"Yes, he is," she agreed. "It's really sad that you didn't connect sooner—but it's never too late. He particularly needs his dad now that he's a teenager."

"I'm so glad you see it that way. I was very wrong to refuse to recognize him as my son. I've worried you might hold it against me."

"Oh, you should know me better than that. I never hold things against people. The past is the past." She held her smile in place, but the conversation was making her nervous. He was beginning to sound a little too focused on Randy alone. She'd hoped to see more interest in herself. She patted her hair, gazed at him appealingly, and asked him how he liked the veal.

"Good as ever," he said. "This place doesn't change." After tossing off the comment, he reverted to the subject. "It would be such a great lifestyle for the kid." He frowned and added, "You can't deny him that, Dotty, after so many years in foster care. You really must let me have him."

Suddenly, with an icy shock, it sank in. He wanted Randy but not her. She sputtered as if doused with cold water. He calmly went on to explain, to plead, but she could hardly concentrate on the words. They seemed to float in the air around her. "Mary Jean and I wanted a child so badly. We waited, hoped, even prayed, but no baby arrived. It would mean the world to us to have a son and heir. I hired a private eye to find the youngster. One look at Randy and I knew he was mine. He's a younger version of me, Dotty. I've been very wrong to deny it. I want you to know I'm terribly sorry for the way I accused you of infidelity that time."

"Whoring," she said.

"What?"

"You accused me of whoring. You said Randy had to be some other man's bastard."

"Oh, Dorothea, I'm so sorry. What can I say to make it up to you? I was upset; I hardly knew what was coming out of my mouth. Of course I realized you weren't the wandering type. I hope you can forgive me, Dotty, and say yes to my request. I want us to remain friends, so I can write to you about Randy."

She gazed at him in speechless horror. He wanted to take Randy from her and give him to some woman named Mary Jean. Randy, her firstborn!

She burst out, "You want my kid but not me!"

He looked baffled. "Dotty, I'm married. I've been married for eight years. I can't invite you down there. I mean, occasional visits, maybe—I wouldn't want to cut you off."

She stood up and pushed away her untouched plate of food. "Then you can't invite my son! What are you thinking?"

He remained calm. "I'm thinking you'll be unselfish and agree to do what's best for the boy. He'll have a wonderful life with us, and he'll be my sole heir. He'll inherit a valuable piece of resort property when Mary Jean and I are gone. You can't ask for better than that for our son."

"And in return I'm to give him up!"

He frowned. "You've already given him up, Dot. I've investigated; I know you see him once a month at best. He tells me you won't release him for adoption, that he hasn't ever had a life or a family. He's been shuffled from one foster home to another for years. He resents it, and not without justification." He reached out a hand to her. "Sit down and be reasonable. I'm not blaming you. You wanted the kid; you wanted to make a home for him—and I wasn't ready for that at the time. I was at fault, I admit it. You did the only thing you could do; you placed him in foster care. Now I'm offering you the opportunity to give him a good home with his birth father. You can't deny him that."

"I can," she said. "I do. I didn't wait and work and struggle these fourteen years for a home just to have some Mary Jean person snatch my son from me."

He frowned deeply. She remembered how she used to tremble at his anger, and felt relieved to find she didn't fear him any longer. He said, "You're not thinking of the kid's interests at all. You're just thinking of your own selfish—"

She picked up a saltshaker and raised it threateningly. "Just get out of here, Joel Fisk, and don't ever let me hear from you again!"

He got up, turned away from his half-eaten veal portion, and headed for the door. Over his shoulder, he said, "I'll do the first but not the second." With his hand on the doorknob, he swung back and faced her. "I want Randy, Dorothea, and I'll hire a lawyer if I have to. Dammit, I'll sue you. I'll say you're an unfit mother who dumped your child in foster care and never took him out again."

He went out and slammed the door. She sat down and burst into tears. She wept for a long time, struggling to come to terms with the grim fact that she wasn't to be rescued. Her future would include Mr. Short-n-fat after all—and lucky she hadn't canceled the wedding.

Drying her tears, she took the plates of mostly untouched food and returned them to the kitchen. She told her boss, "You won't be shorthanded this afternoon, Mario; I'm not going out. I changed my mind."

Back at work, she couldn't focus on people's orders. She fumed inwardly, arguing with Joel in her mind. "How dare you, after all these years—and you never showed the slightest interest in the kid. You denied he was yours. You called me a whore. How dare you come along now and try to take him away!"

The afternoon passed in a fog of anger and worry. She wondered what he could really do. How many rights might a father have after years of neglect? If he went to court, how would she afford the legal fees to fight him?

Yet for all her inability to concentrate, in the end it turned out to be lucky she'd stayed. At dinnertime, through her welter of feelings, she became conscious of the gossip at a table she was waiting on. She wrote, "It came from a group of artsy-fartsy lesbian types wearing those 'new look' outfits, narrow skirts almost ankle length, with stretch tights just barely showing below. This crowd often eats at Mario's, and in listening to them, I learn the news of the music and art colony here in the Village."

On this particular day, she'd been too shaken up and preoccupied to pay attention to their conversation, but she came back with a jolt to the present when one of them said, "I hear Jill Szekely has left her husband and moved in with Frieda Fishbein." The speaker smiled and looked around the table. "Good old Jill, I guess she got tired of the straight life and decided to visit Lesbos for a while."

Nobody at the table seemed shocked by this statement. Greenwich Villagers were used to lesbians and homosexuals; the Village was full of them, and they were open about their sexual orientation. Dorothea had learned to take them in stride.

It was the news about Jill and Zoltan that registered. The fog lifted and the dark clouds vanished. Zoltan, free again! That was what Dorothea needed, a man she cared for who was free, who wouldn't foist a Mary Jean on her to steal her son away. She'd wondered why Jill had wanted to meet her. She told herself Jill's abandoned spouse would need consoling and that she should get in touch at once. She'd lost round one with Joel, but she would win round two with Zoltan.

While serving dinner she planned what she would say to him. She had a real shocker to announce, one she knew would bring him running. The only question was, should she bring out her big guns at once or move more gradually?

By the time her shift ended, she'd decided on the big guns. Go for broke. Gamble her whole future on one big boom. Win or lose.

On leaving Mario's she went to the drugstore and bought a card with a blank interior. She stopped off at the Automat for pie and coffee and, while seated there, jotted her memorized note. Cody knew what it said, as she'd dropped it off at the Manhattan Avenue apartment, where he'd found and read it. It was part of the reason he'd felt so confident about arresting the musician.

> *Zoltan, there's something you need to know. I wasn't planning to tell you, but I hear you're separated, so I've changed my mind. The fact is you have a son. That abortion your dad arranged for me turned out to be a botched job. Six months after I last saw you, I had Marcello. He's five years old now, a darling blonde like your sister Kitty. I know you'll love him. You were always good with kids.*
>
> *We need to talk about this before you meet the boy, so we can arrange a meeting that won't upset him. I don't want to shock him by suddenly presenting him with a daddy. So please, let's get together for a chat in the morning while he's at preschool, and I'll tell you about him.*
>
> *I still work the eleven-to-seven shift at Mario's, same as always, so if you could come to my place before ten, that would be good.*

After signing her name, she took from her wallet her picture of Marcie and inserted it into the card. She opened her address book, where she'd jotted Zoltan's address on the day Jill visited her. Then she decided this message was too important to trust to the post. She would take it uptown herself and deposit it in his mailbox. She wanted to see the apartment house where, if she knew her Zoltan, she might soon be living.

She rode the bus instead of the subway so she could assess the neighborhood as she went. She had no trouble finding the building. It was just the kind of place she'd always dreamed of living in—large and impressive, with bay windows and an elevator. She entered the well-lit lobby, popped the envelope into the Szekely mailbox, and paused to admire her surroundings. *Thank you, Jill, for returning my true love to me,* she said in her mind.

She thrashed all night wondering if he'd found the note and how he'd taken it. She jumped to the phone when it rang at 8:30 the next morning. It was Zoltan, who promised, "I'll be with you in an hour." He was brusque; his voice shook, and he seemed impatient to end the conversation. But of course, it was natural, inevitable even, that he'd be upset. She'd known she'd distress him by bringing this fact to light.

No matter, he'd get over it. He owed her. Three long years of her life, not to mention that nightmare clinic!

She dressed as carefully next morning as she had the day before, with generous makeup to cover those midlife lines. She soon discovered that Zoltan had not dressed carefully at all. He arrived looking wrinkled, as if he'd slept in his clothes and forgotten to brush his hair or even shave. That was fine with her; it showed how much he cared. She was reminded of the tumbled way his hair looked back in the days when he awoke each morning in her bed. "I loved every brown curl on his body, not only those on his head, but the ones on his chest, and even the ones surrounding that member which was the source of so much of our joy," she wrote. "Amazing what a little extra skin and muscle can produce by way of happiness."

His coloring was lovely; all the fine brown hairs of his body matched his eyes. Oh, it would be great to have him in her bed once again. She was a keeper, the faithful type; she didn't jump easily from man to man and hadn't looked forward to sleeping with Reggie. She'd once loved Joel, but no longer, not after yesterday—now she loved only Zoltan.

At this point Cody struggled against the impulse to flip pages. He needed to know this stuff. "Zoltan has matured, but otherwise he looks the same. I led him into my room, where I hadn't bothered to hide the toys. He studied the trucks, the crayons, the coloring books, and frowned. The hand he held out to me shook. It reminded me of the time I sprang the news of my pregnancy on him. I felt a pang at distressing him so badly. But I had to get his attention, didn't I? Right now, he was surely focused on recapturing his wandering wife, Jill, and was not thinking about renewing a past relationship with me. I had to open the door to a world long lost to him."

He frowned at her. "Dorothea, is this the truth?"

"I wouldn't have told you if it wasn't the truth," she said. "You think it's easy for me to make a confession like this? I know you don't want the child. At least you didn't in the past."

"Frankly, I can't believe this and don't know what to think."

"I expect you'd like to see pictures of him?" She took the album from the shelf and flipped through it. "There he is as a baby. Here are his first steps—and here he's a toddler in the park. A darling, isn't he? You should be proud."

Dorothea recorded everything, including the fact she heard footsteps in the hall and wondered if that curious teenager, Leila, might be listening at the door. "Well, let her. She'll know soon anyway."

Zoltan ran his hands through his hair and repeated, "I don't know what to say. What do you want from me, Dotty?"

"I want what I always wanted—for us to be a family."

"Too late for that now. Too much water under the bridge."

"It's never too late when we have a connection like this. Especially now that you're separated from Jill."

"How do you know about that?"

"I have my ways. Let me tell you about your son." She displayed Marcie's crayon drawings and talked about his preschool and what he was learning. She gave the address and suggested Zoltan go by at 10:30, when the class had their outdoor play and he could catch a glimpse of the boy. "You'll know him because there aren't any other blonde kids in that Italian school." She told him Marcie resembled his sister Kitty. "I never met Kitty," she said, "but I used to see her in the hall when she came to visit you along with your parents. I remember her long blonde hair. I wasn't surprised when Marcie turned out so fair."

She offered him coffee, but he refused, saying he needed to give thought to her news. He shuffled his feet, ran his hands through his hair, and seemed impatient to be off. She was reminded of those long-ago days after her pregnancy announcement, when he walked by himself for hours on end or sat silently in the park thinking.

"He took down the address of the preschool and promised to be in touch after he'd had time to absorb the news and plan what to do. The minute he left, I sat down at my desk to describe the visit in this diary. I have to get every word of this down; it's a great story, and I just know someone will publish it someday. My one-time lover seems upset at the moment, but if I know my Zoltan, he'll be back.

"The outer door closed, but I just heard it open again. I couldn't help smiling to myself. I was right; he's returning. This time I'll play it cool.

Pretend I expected him. Sit tight. Don't even turn." There's silence while, she supposes, he's debating. "And now—ah, now I hear his footsteps behind me. Yes! He's come to terms with the situation; he's made up his mind to face the music. I speak. 'I knew you'd come back, dear. You were always such a caring man.'

"A cord drops over my head. He's teasing, but—."

It must have been then that she dropped the pen, grabbed at her throat so desperately her fingernails left bloody marks, and kicked the desk so hard her shoe left a scratch on the crossbar.

When Yonkers came in, Cody closed the book and told him, "It's time to charge Szekely. And we also have to interview Joel Fisk and Reggie Jackson— and, of course, Jill Szekely. We'll need to talk to Dorothea's Aunt Belle, too. Make the appointments, will you?"

Yonkers nodded. "Okay, C.C." Cyril Cody smiled; he'd graduated to being addressed by his initials, just like the lieutenant.

CHAPTER 18

Jill Faces a Grim Decision

—1948

I FOUND IT EARTH-SHATTERING READING the story on an inner page of the *Times*. It made real something I'd up to now assumed to be an error soon to be corrected. Even when I read through it, I at first didn't take it in. Finding articles in the morning paper with your spouse's name in them is just not something your mind is eager to accept. The words stabbed at me, and I swiveled my gaze back and started over. On second reading, the article still made the same unwelcome statement. Dorothea Granger had been murdered the previous day, with Zoltan Szekely taken into police custody as a person of interest. Yesterday, the words "person of interest" had suggested an observer. Now, in print, they carried the ominous implication of suspect.

What is this magic in words, especially the printed word? Somehow, when it's in black and white, an event takes on reality. I scanned the story. "Found dead in her room ... well known to Villagers ... longtime waitress at Mario's Restaurant ... Colleagues confirm that she and Mr. Szekely had once been an item but insist those days are long past, and she planned to marry someone else. Yet for reasons unknown, Szekely went to visit her. Her housemate, Leila Falucci, expressed bafflement as to why the two would have chosen to get together again. Police refused to speculate about motive."

"At least they're shielding the kid from publicity." I pulled myself together and shoved the paper across the table to Frieda, my breakfast companion. "Poor Dorothea, what a tragic outcome of a sad life—and just before a wedding, too. I'd almost forgotten she was to be married." Then, as jolt followed jolt, I said, "But they're out of their minds to suspect my spouse. Zoltan may not be a prince among men, but he's no killer."

"Unless he's desperate now that he's on his own," Frieda speculated.

"He couldn't be desperate enough to change so completely so quickly. It's unthinkable. Impossible." I ran my hands through my hair. "It's like hearing that Chopin or … or Beethoven committed a murder."

"Jill, I wonder if you ever really knew Zoltan." Frieda studied me and shook her head thoughtfully. "You see him as a man who lives and breathes music, and I'm not at all sure that's the person he is. Granted, he's a gifted pianist—he's top-notch, even world-class. But I sense that he's doing what his parents want rather than what he wants. They chose his profession back when he was a child—and without knowing if he had that spark, that special something that sets genius apart. I suspect you've been glamorizing him all these years, putting him up where he doesn't belong. It's possible that at last the pressure of everyone's expectations became too much for him."

I frowned, bit my lip, and wondered if she could be right. *Did I overglamorize? Did I see a great musician who never really existed?*

"What on earth should I do?" I wrung my hands, not asking for answers so much as hoping to assemble my own thoughts. "Should I go try to bail him out?" Jittery and disoriented, I felt impatient to take action but saw no sensible pathway opening ahead.

Frieda shrugged. "Daddy Szekely is probably doing that right now. *If* Zoltan's been charged. You can't talk about bail until you've been charged, and even then—well, I doubt they grant bail in murder cases."

I winced. Of course Zoltan would turn to his father rather than to me in this disastrous situation. Whatever made me think that, as his wife, I would be the one asked to come to his aid? The girl who couldn't be trusted to help pick out his civvies would hardly be relied upon to rescue him in a crisis.

"You can be sure his daddy will get him a good lawyer," Frieda added. "No need to involve yourself."

I paced, convinced I ought to rush out and take action yet having no idea what to do. My first impulse was to go to the police to insist they'd gotten the wrong man. Zoltan was no killer. Of course, they wouldn't listen to me, especially now that I'd become the estranged wife. *It sounds so dead-end dreary: "the estranged wife." How on earth did I arrive at this point?*

But was I right about him? Did I really know what Zoltan might do in a state of desperation after I'd left him? Or was it true, as Frieda theorized, that I never really knew him? In all those years I'd spent trying to make him happy, had I blinded myself to the essence of his character? I'd never witnessed a serious outbreak of bad temper, but I'd never done anything to cause one. I'd walked cautiously out of fear of deep feelings I'd sensed simmering below the surface. Had I seen the man I wanted to be married to rather than the man Zoltan truly was?

I read the offending article in more detail. Dorothea Granger was "strangled in her studio room," as the newspaper expressed it. Her housemate claimed she'd had a visitor just prior to discovery of the body, and this visitor had been identified as Zoltan Szekely. Police not only offered no motive, but also refused to speculate as to whether the Juilliard graduate would be charged with her murder.

I fell to pondering why Zoltan had chosen to visit Dorothea. I thought perhaps the Manhattan Avenue apartment might provide answers. "I'd better go home," I said.

"Home?" Frieda frowned. "This is home now, Toots. You've moved out."

"Legally, I share responsibility for that apartment. I cosigned the lease. Someone needs to run the place and check on the tenants." I pulled myself together and began to muster my thoughts. "Right now, I guess I'm elected." I reached for my sweater.

"I'll go with you," Frieda offered.

"Thanks. I'll be glad of your company."

I still felt the sense of unreality that accompanies shock. It was Frieda who remembered to call the library and tell them I wasn't feeling well and wouldn't be in that day. As for her own work, she was a salesgirl at Macy's, a store that didn't open until ten. She had two hours yet.

Together, we left her apartment and rode the subway uptown. I tried to still my trembling hands, to force myself to relax. I felt like a zombie, doing what seemed the only thing to do under the circumstances. As we approached the station, a sudden panicky doubt assailed me. *Did I still have a key to the apartment?* I fumbled in my purse and sighed with relief when my probe encountered metal. With shaking fingers, I retrieved it.

As it turned out, I didn't need a key. One of our tenants, George Lawton, a divorced man who worked night shift as a waiter and took classes at Columbia during the day, had left the door unlocked behind him when he entered. I locked it behind me. We found the tenant in the kitchen eating the meal he called his dinner. George was one of the less deadbeat of our tenants; he'd only once failed to pay his rent, a month when he'd lost his job for attacking an obnoxious patron at his restaurant. On locating another job, he'd started catching up at a dollar or two a week, his debt now almost paid off.

Fork in hand, he glanced up and waved. In his early twenties, he'd already gone partly bald. Thin, lanky, and almost gaunt, he looked much older than his years. "Jill, I'm so glad you came," he said. "I've been wondering how to get in touch. Did you see the morning paper?"

"You mean the article about Zoltan still being held by the cops? I assume—I hope—he's just being questioned as a friend of the deceased."

"I understand he's a suspect. Clarence was here when the cops came yesterday, and he claims Zoltan acted surprised and shocked—didn't seem to know Dorothea was dead, let alone grasp the fact he might be accused of involvement. But the cops took away something from his desk they seemed to think was evidence."

Oh, Lord. The diary! They'd find out about all that past garbage and connect it to the present. Zoltan would have some heavy-duty explaining to do. "I can imagine his shock." I was just saying words. In truth, I couldn't imagine any of it, not even why Zoltan would have been in touch with Dorothea in the first place. I'd have said she was the last person he'd turn to in his distress. He'd told me he always found her too needy, claimed his attraction to her was already dead the last year or two that he lived with her and he simply hadn't known how to break up.

"Clarence was in a dither," George went on. "He said Zoltan kept insisting on his innocence, claiming the officers must have him mixed up with someone else." Clarence was the worst of our deadbeat tenants. He owed three months' rent and lacked a job or a means of paying. If I took over the running of this place, he was the first person I'd need to evict.

In a moment of cynicism, I scoffed. "Clarence worries about losing a good landlord."

"Well, of course there's that," George defended. "I mean, it's a scare for all of us. We live here, we need our rooms. But that doesn't mean we don't—you know—sympathize with a friend hauled off to jail."

I introduced George to Frieda and then asked, "Do you know if Zoltan's been seeing Dorothea?"

Our tenant seemed reluctant to answer. He avoided my eyes, studying the curtains as if fascinated by their multicolored stripes. Finally he confessed. "Well, the cops claimed he had, anyway. Seems she found out somehow that you and Zoltan had split up, and she contacted him—I suppose to offer her condolences or something. The cops must have had a search warrant when they went through Zoltan's stuff here."

"They must have been very sure of themselves, to seek a warrant."

"Clarence says he heard one officer tell the other he'd found a note from Miss Granger addressed to Zoltan."

"She wrote to Zoltan?" I frowned in surprise. When I'd visited, I hadn't at all gained the impression that Dorothea might take advantage of our separation. Quite the contrary, I'd felt sure she had something of her own on the cooker. In fact, I recalled she'd said something along those lines, something about things working out for her at last with some other guy. She'd seemed excited and happy—had even mentioned that forthcoming wedding—and it had nothing to do with Zoltan.

George confessed that he knew about the note. "I was here when Zoltan opened his mail. He was royally pissed. I asked if anything was wrong. He said his former girlfriend wanted him to come and visit her, but he knew he shouldn't go. I can't think why he capitulated and went—but it seems he did. Anyway, that's what the police claim." He shuffled his feet uneasily. He pointed to the coffee pot. "Why don't you sit down and have coffee with me? There's plenty."

I usually make a point of not socializing with the tenants. Friendliness had caused Zoltan no end of problems, making it difficult to act businesslike at that crucial moment when it was time to deny his "friend" another rent-free month. But right now I really needed to learn what George knew about this situation. So I sat, waving Frieda to another chair. George poured coffee and passed the cups over. Frieda perched on the edge of her seat, tipping cream into her beverage. I sipped mine black.

"Were you here when he came home from meeting Dorothea?" I asked.

"Yeah, I was eating, like now. It was morning."

"Did he give you a hint of what went on?"

"He didn't say."

"Did he still seem upset?"

George shrugged. "Definitely, the guy was edgy, but not—you know—not murdering violent. Not a spitfire. Just kind of—I don't know—bewildered—disbelieving—ghost-ridden. Like, whatever she'd told him, he couldn't take it in."

I thought I knew what it was he'd been told—that he had a child. He certainly would be bewildered and ghost-ridden over that. A lifetime of struggling over the economic problems of becoming a concert pianist—and then he learns he owes child support that he can't possibly afford at the moment. He must have been devastated.

George pushed his plate aside and excused himself, saying it was time he hit the sack. Frieda and I sat on, pondering the situation. I knew the Szekelys would be frantic right now. *I* was frantic. My midriff churned. I couldn't begin to imagine how Zoltan would feel, and how his parents would feel, over the prospect of a trial, the scary possibility of a guilty verdict. The event would destroy his career. It might well kill his mother. I couldn't even guess what it would mean for me. What complications would arise from having a spouse in prison? Could the divorce proceed? Would I still be accepted for university teaching, or would there be a cloud over me? And if things dragged on, what should I do with this apartment? Should I sell the lease and put the furniture in storage? If I did so, where would Zoltan live if the charges were later dropped, or if, on appeal, he were acquitted? It wouldn't be easy to find another rent-controlled flat.

If he's found guilty, my parents and his will blame me, I thought. *They'll say he was heartbroken over my departure and didn't know what he was doing. The situation will be my fault.*

I felt shaky; I didn't know what to do. Everything was at sixes and sevens. "I need to talk to Zoltan," I said. "I wonder if they'd let me visit him."

"You're incredible," Frieda said. "You've left the guy; he's a man from your past. You're supposed to wash your hands of his problems."

"I wonder if a man you've lived with for years ever becomes a man from your past," I said.

"I'd think you'd be furious with the crumb. You should be cussing him out, not offering to visit him."

I thought about it. "I'm not furious with Zoltan. He is what he is—a man who doesn't know when to quit, a man unable to step off the path he's laid out for himself. I'm furious with myself for not seeing that about him in time to avoid this train wreck. Now I'm involved whether I like it or not."

She shrugged. I washed out our cups and replaced them in the cupboard and then wandered through the apartment. It still seemed very much my own—as if I'd never left. I noticed a tear in one of the living room slipcovers and instinctively reached to a closet shelf for my sewing kit. Watching me, Frieda frowned and shook her head. "Let it go, you ninny. It's not your worry anymore."

I winced at her disapproval. "In a way I suppose you're right. I ought to disengage from all this—but right now I can't organize my thoughts."

I worked on. I'd only just mended the tear and was still holding my sewing basket when I heard a key inserted into the front door. Curious, I stood up and peered down the hall. This was not an hour when tenants were likely to show up. Mornings, they were either in class or at work—except for George, who'd gone to bed. Just for an instant, I fancied Zoltan had been released and was coming home.

I was astonished to see Zoltan's mom and dad walk—or rather shuffle, for they were suddenly moving like old people—into the apartment. Apparently, they echoed my surprise. For several seconds they stared at me where I stood, rooted in the hall with my hands full. I suffered a wave of embarrassment and wondered how they must now feel about the daughter-in-law who'd abandoned the family. I searched their faces for signs of anger but saw only distress.

Finally, Janos remembered to close the door. After a long moment while I inched backward and managed to mouth a greeting, the couple made their way down the hall. They followed me into the living room, Janos guiding his wife, who was clearly in a state of shock.

"Jill, I'm glad you're here. We were planning to get in touch." Janos sounded as weary as he looked. His voice was ragged. "We need to talk."

"Yes, I guess we do." I tried to regain my poise; I reminded myself this was still my apartment. I clung to the sewing basket, which seemed to give me authority, to put me in charge. Then I noticed that my guests were disheveled, her hat awry, his tie loosened. Her eyes didn't seem to focus, and he acted distraught and uncertain. I waved them to the couch and gestured toward Frieda. "This is my housemate, Frieda Fishbein. Mr. and Mrs. Szekely."

Almost inaudibly, as if it were an effort, Frieda said, "Pleased to meet you."

Annie, as she sank onto the couch, managed to mutter, "How do you do." Janos merely nodded and perched beside his wife.

Frieda glanced at her watch and announced it was time for her to go to work. "I'll see you later, Jill. I hope you can work things out."

I thanked her. Janos nodded again. She waved and left.

When I heard the apartment door close, I said, "We just learned that Zoltan is still in custody. It was in the morning paper."

Annie moaned. Janos said, "This is unbelievable. It can't be happening. I keep hoping to awake from the nightmare."

"I'll do anything I can," I said. "Tell me what's going on."

Annie leaned her head back and flung her hand over her eyes. Janos inched backward on the couch, repositioning himself. "How much do you know about Zoltan and Dorothea, Jill?"

I shrugged. "I know they lived together. I confess I was shocked when I learned of their relationship, but I … I realize now I was being naive. Those things happen. They were young."

"Did you know she got pregnant?"

"Yes—and that she had an abortion." I refrained from accusing Janos of having engineered it, or explaining how it failed. It seemed my restraint was unnecessary; they already knew the latter fact.

"We learned Dorothea got in touch with Zoltan and gave him the news that the abortion didn't work. She had the baby. She showed him a picture of her five-year-old child and claimed Zoltan is the father. He had to believe her—the timing and all. The youngster's age is right."

"Oh my God." Panic hit me. Concerned for my spouse and sorrowing over the murder of a woman who'd gone before me in many ways, I'd given little thought to the child. Suddenly the implications seemed enormous. I realized I had a stepson and his mother was dead. Zoltan was now his only parent. As his wife, I might be next in line to care for the boy while Zoltan was in prison. I wanted a child, but not this way, not instantaneously and already partly grown. "Where is the youngster now?"

"He's staying with the people Dorothea lived with." Janos rubbed his forehead. "Things look bad. The police are convinced Tanni killed Dorothea when he learned of the boy. After all, he'd have to support him—just at this moment, when he needs more than ever to establish a career. Of course he wouldn't commit murder, not even with that kind of provocation—but how are we to convince the police of that? He has no alibi. He went to see her when he learned the news; he left just moments before her death. Even the lawyer shows little hope of getting him off from this."

"You've hired a lawyer already?"

"We phoned from Schenectady yesterday, made the appointment, and talked to the lawyer first thing this morning. It was horrible, Jill; the man kept shaking his head and asking questions as if even he believed Zoltan guilty."

I bit my lip and echoed his statement. "Zoltan couldn't commit a murder." I spoke without thinking and then had to ask myself if I could be sure of that. As Frieda had pointed out, circumstances like these might have driven him to desperation. Newly graduated, he lacked a job or income, and his wife had opted out of helping him financially. What had Dorothea demanded of him? Child support? A live-in father for her children? Facing such demands at a moment when his life was falling apart, might he not have experienced an overwhelming temptation to rid himself of this pesky woman before she could announce the child's parentage to the world? Under the circumstances, even a nonkiller might become desperate—and Zoltan had a long history of problems with Dorothea.

Surely, given sufficient cause, anyone, even Zoltan, was capable of murder.

As if the same thought had occurred to him, Janos winced and squeezed the skin of his forehead above his eye. I asked, "Would you like an aspirin?"

"I'd be most grateful, Jill." He sounded humble. I wouldn't have believed anything could humble Janos, the man in charge, the man who could never be denied the right to choose his son's clothing, criticize his performances, and run his life. Yet here he was, clearly a broken soul. Life had at last become too much for him.

I put my sewing kit away, went to the bathroom, and, after pawing through the medicine cabinet, found the aspirin. My hands were shaking. While I filled a glass with water, I wondered what I could say to the Szekelys. No words seemed sufficient consolation for this mess, and anyway, how could I console when I was involved? I was already responsible for the apartment. Would I now be asked to care for the youngster? Obviously the grandparents were in no condition to do it, and since Dorothea's parents had more or less written their daughter off, they would probably not agree to raise her child.

Janos suggested his wife lie down and rest for a while, and when she nodded, he helped her into the bedroom. While he laid her hat aside and removed her shoes, I closed the draperies. With the room darkened, we left her, and the two of us returned to the living room. He swallowed the aspirin while I pondered what we might do to persuade a judge that Zoltan was no murderer.

"If he didn't kill her, someone else did," I said.

"Precisely. And the police aren't even looking. They're convinced they've got their man. 'Open and shut case,' they said. I talked to the cop last night."

I ran a comb through my hair. I still felt an urge to go somewhere, to do something, though I couldn't imagine where or what.

Neither of us suspected we were destined soon to make a startling discovery.

CHAPTER 19

More Shocking News

—1948

It was one thing to resolve to play detective; it was another to know how to go about it. We pondered our next step. Janos suggested we search and see if Dorothea had written him other letters to provide leads. Doubting she'd done that, I urged a visit to the house where Dorothea lived, to talk to her other housemate, the one we hadn't yet interviewed. In the end, we decided to do both.

When, as I'd anticipated, our search of the apartment turned up no secret love letters hidden away, we checked on Annie and found her dozing. Janos explained that she'd taken a tranquilizer and would probably sleep for a while. She'd stayed awake all night. "She was writing, writing, writing," he said. "She must have written letters to everyone we know."

After jotting a note telling her where we'd gone, we slipped out.

Janos seemed eager to view the scene of the crime. It was almost as if he felt that by looking at it, he could intuit what happened. I led the way down to the subway station, and we headed for Dorothea's place in Greenwich Village. On the brief trip, Janos talked about Zoltan, about how he was no killer and couldn't possibly have done this thing. I told him, "You're preaching to the choir here. I agree with you."

This time we were admitted to the house by the teenager Maria Bini had spoken of: a short, dark-haired, olive-skinned young woman of eighteen or nineteen, in a full-skirted, yellow dress, vivid against her long black hair. She was accompanied by a boy of five or so, barefoot and dressed in shorts and T-shirt. This, of course, would be the survivor of the botched abortion. On seeing Janos eye his putative grandson and wince, I tried to get a glimpse of the child's face. A shy kid, he hid behind the young woman's voluminous skirt.

I explained to the girl that we were friends of both Dorothea and Zoltan and would like to see the place where the crime happened. She frowned and looked dubious. "I don't know if the police want me to—"

Janos pulled himself together and tilted his chin to its most authoritative level. "Did they tell you not to let anyone in?"

"Well, no."

"Then it's okay." He managed his take-charge manner long enough to push past her and enter. She shrugged and allowed the door to be flung wide. I followed him. As we stepped into the inner hall, the boy emerged from his hiding place, and I studied him. He was blonde and blue-eyed. I didn't think he resembled my brown-eyed, brown-haired husband at all. He had a prominent, well-defined nose, which, unlike Zoltan's straight nose, sported a Roman curve. Doubt flooded through me. Was he really Zoltan's child? He was the right age, and he was Dorothea's—and she surely lived with Zoltan at the time. Unless she got pregnant immediately after the abortion—but her diary accounts gave no hint of another man in her life. This had to be Janos's grandson.

I noticed my father-in-law sneaking uneasy glances at the boy. I guessed he must be thinking similar thoughts.

The child quickly retreated from our scrutiny, hiding again behind the full skirt. That was understandable, of course; he'd certainly suffered trauma in losing his mother and would probably for some time fear strangers. I forced my gaze away from him and turned to the young woman.

"I'm Leila," she said. "And this is Marcie." She reached behind her and rumpled the child's hair.

"You were Dorothea's housemate?" I asked.

"Well, I guess, technically, she was *my* housemate. And Mother's." She explained. "My mother owns this place. She felt sorry for Dorothea and invited her to live here. She's been with us since Marcie was born. We've watched him grow up … helped take care of him."

"It was good of you both to take her in," I said. "She must have been in great distress, with a child and no husband." Zoltan would have been away in the army when the baby arrived, and of course Dorothea would not have dared to appeal to Annie and Janos for help, lest they take the child away and place him for adoption.

"Yes, she was pretty desperate. Suicidal even. Mother offered as much aid as possible."

She led the way down the hall to Dorothea's room. Though it was sunny, I shuddered and thought, *A woman was murdered here.*

It hadn't changed since I was here before, except that now, as a kind of gruesome addition, there were toys on the floor—trucks, blocks, a tractor. There had been no hint of a child during my earlier visit, and I found it hard to imagine that Marcie would be allowed to play at the scene of the crime. Of course, the room was bright now, with a window opening onto the backyard. I'd previously stayed for only fifteen minutes or so, but obviously Dorothea had carefully hidden all evidence of the boy. I'd gained the impression she planned at that time to get on with her life with her new man; I'd seen no hint she longed to reinvolve herself with Zoltan. Things must have changed for her since then.

Leila offered us a seat on the studio couch. Though she told the child to go play with the cat, saying, "I think he's upstairs in the front bedroom," he only burrowed deeper into her skirt. She tried to push him away. When he persisted, she gave up and let him stay. She turned back to me and pointed to the desk. "We found Dotty right there with a cord around her neck. She'd been sitting and writing in her diary when someone came up behind her and choked her to death." She spoke like an informant, uninvolved. That was for Marcie's benefit, I supposed, to avoid causing him further trauma with an emotional account.

In view of her consideration, I stifled the impulse to say, "Poor Dorothea." Janos said, "And you discovered her?"

"No, our upstairs tenant, Maria Bini, did. She came down to borrow sugar or something, and noticed Dorothea slumped at her desk. I was in the bathroom, shampooing, getting ready to go visit my mom in the hospital. I heard nothing, no yelling or anything. It all happened so quietly. That is—until Maria screamed." She shuddered. "It's eerie. To think I was alone downstairs with this horror. My God, the monster might have come after me! I hadn't even locked the bathroom door. I mean, we generally don't—we're just four women in this house."

"The boy wasn't here?"

She shook her head. "No, he goes to nursery school every morning now." She patted his arm.

"And you believe Zoltan did it?"

She shrugged. "Zoltan was visiting and pretended to leave—but he came back. His prints are on the doorknob. The police claim it's obvious he went out and came in again. They assume—well, he was the only visitor Dorothea had that day. What else can they think?"

Janos clenched his fists and then visibly forced himself to relax and open his hands. He asked, "Did the boy witness anything at all?"

"Luckily, he was in preschool the whole time. I'm so relieved about that— we'd almost decided to keep him home that day to go visit the hospital. My mom is there, you see; she had an operation three days ago. They don't allow children to visit, but he likes to wave to her from below the window. Marcie adores my mother. She … you know … helped to raise him. She's sort of an alternate parent. That's how I managed to convince the social worker not to put him in foster care now that his mother's gone. This has been his home all his life, and he's used to us. I said, 'He lost one mother, don't make him lose another.' Luckily, she agreed to leave him with us for the time being."

She sat on a loveseat opposite us, and the child scrunched himself up close to her and again hid his face. I wanted to comment that blonde hair wasn't a Szekely feature, but then I remembered that Kitty had blonde hair. I said instead, "I always thought Marcie was a girl's name."

"It's really Marcello," Leila said.

Marcello. Italian. Dorothea was not Italian, so why did she name her child Marcello? I couldn't help voicing my surprise.

"Well, I guess," Leila flushed, embarrassed, "we're Italian, Mother and I. Maybe she wanted to show her gratitude. We did stand by at the birth and all. We were the only ones at the hospital with her. Or maybe … maybe she just liked the name."

I nodded but was puzzled. I studied the child more carefully. I couldn't see his face, which was hidden against Leila's dress, but since he was barefoot, I observed his toes. I remembered noticing Dorothea's long, prehensile toes. I recalled thinking she could swing from trees with those appendages. This child, quite the opposite, had very short toes. His second toe almost wasn't there at all; it was like the bud of a toe that hadn't ever grown out. Zoltan had normal-length toes, as did both his parents. So where, genetically, did this short toe come from?

Without consciously planning to, I switched my gaze to the floor and studied Leila's toes, encased in sandals but thrust out slightly from the forward strap. Short. Very short. Almost no second toe at all. Like Marcello's.

I didn't think what I was saying. If I'd thought about it, I may have lacked the courage to create a confrontation. It just burst out of me. "Marcello isn't really Dorothea's kid, is he? He's some way related to you." The moment I spoke, I winced. I feared I'd come up with a shocker, that Leila probably didn't know the child's true parentage. Leila looked like a child herself, sitting there with her long, skinny legs jutting out of what I now realized were yellow culottes. *Little brother and big sister*, I thought. Aware it was a rude question but one I had to know the answer to, I asked, "Is he your mom's kid?"

She went snow-white. I wouldn't have thought an olive complexion could turn so white. She stared at me, her eyes bugging out, her lip trembling. She reached out to Marcie and clutched him tight against her. After a long moment, she breathed, "My God. How did you know? He doesn't look anything like our family."

"The toes," I said. "You and he have twin feet."

She thrust a foot across the carpet and looked down at it. "Oh my God, we do, don't we? I never thought about it." She turned her gaze to me and then to Janos, who'd also gone white with shock. "Don't tell anyone! Please! Please don't! Mother doesn't want the rest of the family and the neighbors to know. She half-died of embarrassment when she got … you know … in the family way. It was well after Dad went to prison, which made it … questionable." She put her hands over Marcie's ears. He ignored the gesture and buried his face more fully in the abundant, flaring, yellow culottes.

I felt enormous relief. Zoltan was off the hook. Janos had no illegitimate grandson. I had no stepson.

I saw Janos gape, open-mouthed. I asked, "So that's why you claim he's Dorothea's?"

She released Marcie to thrust a hand in her pocket and bring out a handkerchief. She wiped her eyes. "We're Catholic, you see. Mom had been raped by a man who pretended to be a customer at her shop, and she couldn't bear for the neighbors to know—or Dad's family. An illegitimate kid—hey, we're not *that* kind of Greenwich Villagers. You hear a lot about wild artist types living in sin here, but basically the Village is an Italian immigrant town, pretty religious. Mom hid out in the house for the last three months of her pregnancy and had me help the hired woman run the shop. We claimed she was suffering from migraines. We'd met Dorothea when she was lonely and unhappy—well, you know, the loss of her lover and kid. When she talked of suicide, Mother offered to let her live with us free in return for caring for Marcie and claiming he was hers. That way, Mom could go back to work with no embarrassment, and we could keep Marcie with us. It seemed the perfect arrangement all around." She pressed the child against her and gazed pleadingly at both of us. "It will kill my mother if all this comes out. This is such a tight neighborhood—you have no idea. Even though it's New York, it's like a small town; everyone knows my mother. She has a shop on Fourteenth Street—Mama Falucci's—and sells homemade sauces and imported Italian stuff. All her customers are from around here." She flung her free hand to her forehead. "Oh, she'd die."

"Hopefully, no neighbors will need to know," I said, "but I'm afraid the police must be told."

Janos had gone from wide-eyed shock to frown. He nodded sternly. "By all means. We must go to them at once."

Still ghostly white, Leila urged, "I suppose you must, but please ask them to keep it to themselves." She wailed, "Mom would … oh, I can't think what she'd do. She'll blame me. She'll say I told."

She looked downright pitiful. She'd run her hands through her hair until it was awry. With her arm tight around him, the child had burrowed against her skirt and almost buried his head. I hoped he didn't know what we were talking about. I said, "I'll do what I can."

"I'm grateful to Dorothea, and I certainly want to see her killer brought justice," she added. "She steered us through a terrible time. Without her to play Marcie's mother, we couldn't have handled the humiliation." She leaned back, ran her hands through her hair again, and confessed, "Dorothea made it possible for us to hide the scandal, and for me to graduate high school and even finish a year of business school. Thanks to her, I've become a good business woman; I've helped my mother expand into imports and make money. But Mother has a standing in this community. She's a popular merchant, and if people knew the truth, it would be a disaster. Oh, I'm not exaggerating. It would kill Mother to have all this stuff come out. I mean, she's had embarrassment enough already with my dad in prison. He was framed and didn't do anything wrong, but he's a convict, and for that we still face humiliation."

Actually, now that I thought about it, I saw no way this information would be of help to the police. It changed a great deal, yet it really changed nothing as far as the investigation was concerned. Obviously, Dorothea had official custody of Marcello and used him to lure Zoltan back—and pulled it off so convincingly that Zoltan believed her. This was the only thing the police would be interested in. The true parentage of the child wouldn't alter those grim facts.

Janos asked what Leila's father was in prison for. Leila shrugged. "He assisted in a bank robbery. As I say, it wasn't his fault; he was a hired driver. The firm was bogus—but how was he to know? He was only doing what he was hired to do, chauffeuring."

I'd heard that criminals rarely considered their crimes their own fault, but I didn't comment aloud. Leila had enough on her plate. Janos said, "That must have been hard on your mother." He glanced at his watch, reached for his sweater, and remarked to me that it was time for us to leave.

Leila disengaged from Marcie and got up, offering to see us to the door. I told her not to bother. "We can find our way. You look after the boy." I doubted he'd understood much of what we said, but still, he must feel like an orphan now, coping with the trauma of losing the woman he thought of as his mother. Luckily, he seemed to have a good relationship with Leila, and also, apparently, with Mrs. Falucci, whom he would probably in time accept as his mom—assuming she could work out a way to cope with the neighbors and stop worrying about those lifted eyebrows.

As we left the house, I noticed my father-in-law breathing heavily. I asked, "Are you all right?"

He shook his head and put his hand on his chest. On the front steps, I reached out to him, fearing he might stumble. Instead, he suddenly burst into wild laughter. He laughed until he cried. On the bottom step he sat down. It struck me he was hysterical. I wondered what I could do for him. Run back into house and get him some water? Ask Leila for hot coffee?

Like Leila, earlier, he kept repeating, "Oh my God. Oh my God." He looked up at me with tears in his eyes. Finally, he found his voice and told me what was going on with him. "When we first got here, I kept studying the boy to see if he'd been damaged in any way by that failed abortion. I felt so guilty. I guess I thought he'd be lame or mentally deficient or something. And to think—no abortion ever happened to him! And he's not ours!" He laughed again, but by now his laughter was more like a sob.

I looked down and studied his thinning, whitening hair, his head held in his shaking hands as he struggled to regain control. This was the man who'd been through nightmares in Hungary. I recalled things I'd heard him say in the past about the conditions of his earlier life: "When the government forced us to wear armbands labeling us as Jews, I knew they had something horrible in mind for us and we must leave our homeland … We feared to buy property lest it make us more vulnerable to pogroms." He'd survived all that horror in Europe—and now this! His son in jail for a murder he may or may not have committed, after being tricked into thinking he had a child who wasn't really his. And I had to add the sad thought that had earlier occurred to me. "You don't have a grandson, Janos, and I don't have a stepson—thank God for that. But it doesn't help Zoltan's situation at all. It's what Zoltan *believed* that counts with the cops and the court."

He managed a nod. "I know, I know." He rumpled what was left of his thinning hair and added, in a shaky voice, "You're the only one who can help us now, Jill."

"I?" I stared at him. "What can I do?"

"As you said, if Zoltan didn't do it, someone else did. The police won't be looking for that person; they think they have an open-and-shut case. Someone needs to talk to Dorothea's friends and find out what was going on in her life—and it can't be me. I'm the enemy. Her friends won't chat with me. But you could do it."

I shook my head. "Janos, I have no idea how to conduct an investigation. You need a private eye for a job like this."

A forlorn expression settled on his face. "Our lawyer called one. He was on the job for less than an hour—phoned me the moment I got back to the hotel. Seems his contact at the police department gave him the scoop. The cops found Dorothea's diary detailing her affair with Tanni."

I winced. "My fault. I left it in the desk. I never thought—"

"They also have the note she wrote, telling Tanni about the child. It's all pretty damning." He paused for a long moment, holding his head in his hands. "They have Tanni's prints on the doorknob, on top of Maria's, to confirm her story that he returned to the house. They have a neighbor who saw Tanni leave the house the first time and then turn around and start back in. Then there's the girl Leila, the chief witness—she let him in the first time and was in the bathroom when he returned. She claims she heard his footsteps in the hall. And they have Dorothea's diary, where she recorded his return and all but described her own murder."

By now I was biting my lip. "God, it does look bad!"

"I can tell you word for word what the private investigator said. It's burned into my mind. 'Ain't nothing an eye can do when the fuzz got *that* kind of evidence. I can't change the facts, mister. I'm good but not that good.'" Janos grimaced as he imitated the man's fractured English. Despite a faint lingering accent, Janos's own English was flawless, the bookish language of a man who'd learned the language in school rather than as a native speaker.

He shook his head despairingly and looked up. "You're our only hope, Jill." His brown eyes made a desperate appeal.

"But, Janos, if a trained investigator can't do anything, what do you expect me to come up with? I have no idea how to—"

"Someone needs to talk to Dorothea's friends and see who else might have wanted her dead. Tanni claims he started to go back into the house but changed his mind and walked away. So someone else went in and committed the murder. We need to investigate and find out who it was." As I still hesitated, he added, more forcefully, "It has to be done, and the police are clearly not planning to do it."

This was exactly what I'd been thinking, yet when Janos suggested it, I found myself annoyed. I remembered all the times I'd been snubbed by the Szekelys. I remembered how left out I'd felt on visits to their house. I remembered how Annie used to subtly communicate that she'd have preferred Two-Piano as a daughter-in-law. I wanted to shout, *You think I'd take a risk like that for you? Whoever killed Dorothea could come after me for threatening to expose him. Why should I involve myself? What did you people ever do for me? When did you show that you cared about me?*

I couldn't speak the words. I saw my father-in-law's hands trembling and wondered how I was to get him home in this condition. The events of the day had obviously been too much for a man of seventy who'd already been exposed to abundant trauma in his life. I leaned against the wall and stood waiting for him to calm down. I wondered what I should say.

"All these years I felt guilty about that abortion," he confessed. "My own grandson, deprived of life! And now it's caught up with our family."

He glanced up. "I'm sorry, Jill," he said. "I'll pull myself together in a minute." He closed his eyes. He still shook uncontrollably. I saw that he'd aged since I last saw him; he looked elderly and feeble.

Finally he held out a hand. "Help me up, and let's go get coffee or something. I believe I saw a café on the corner. A hot drink will put me back on my feet."

I reached out a hand to draw him up from the step where he'd been sitting and held his elbow to steady him. I realized he'd grown shorter lately; I found myself looking down on the top of his head as I'd never done before. Unsteady, he held on rather longer than normal to the railing beside the steps. Then he swallowed hard, visibly pulled himself together, and headed for the corner café three doors down.

As I walked beside him, words came out of me that I hadn't planned to say. "We'll survive this, Janos. Things will work out. I'll talk to Dorothea's friends—she had a pal named … uh … it'll come back to me. We'll find the killer."

"Thank you, Jill, for standing by. It means so much to me that you're here."

I supposed it was as near to an apology as I would ever get. If he'd learned at last to appreciate me, that spelled improvement to our relationship.

CHAPTER 20

Grilled

—*1948*

I finally got Janos onto the subway, and we returned to Manhattan Avenue. With Annie still sleeping, Janos insisted on calling the lawyer at once to tell him the child was not Zoltan's. I heard him say into the phone, "Do, please, pass that along to Tanni and the police. And tell my son Jill promised to help me find the real killer. We all know Tanni didn't do this."

Rueful, I bit my lip over the fact that Janos should begin including me in the family just when I'd finally decided to get out of it.

The call completed, I managed, by persuading him he needed a rest after a wild morning, to get him settled down for a nap on the couch. I made a list of names and places recalled from the diary. First, there was Mario's, the restaurant where Dorothea worked. I could talk to her colleagues there. Joel Fisk, her first boyfriend, came to mind—and John Whatever, her second, along with Randy and Denny, her sons, now eight and fourteen. Lastly, I searched my memory for the name of her closest friend, a name I seemed to recall being the same as that of my maternal cousin, Ray. Norma Ray, wasn't it?

I hunted up Mario's Restaurant in the telephone book and jotted down the address. Then I looked up Norma Ray—and found her still living on 125th Street, just a couple of blocks from our own former studio, where we'd held those memorable music salons.

I immediately gave her a call. As it was half an hour past noon, I didn't really expect an answer, but surprisingly, I got one. A female voice said, "Norma Ray here."

I identified myself. "I'm Zoltan Szekely's wife, Jill. I know you were a friend of Dorothea Granger, so I guess you know Zoltan." The moment the words were out, I wondered if I should have been so outspoken. By now this woman might well perceive Zoltan as the killer of her friend. That would put me in the enemy category, along with Janos. I should have sought a more subtle way of introducing myself.

But she sounded friendly. "Dorothea told me about you, Jill. She said you and Zoltan were separated. I was surprised; I always thought Zoltan would be a loyal and faithful spouse once he married and settled down. He was so sincere. You know, the forthright type."

I wondered how Dorothea had learned of our separation. Had Zoltan rushed straight to her when I left him? I'd seen no hint that he still cared for her. Yet she'd found out somehow. "Then you don't think Zoltan is guilty?" I asked. "Of the murder, I mean. You *had* heard that Dorothea is dead, hadn't you?"

"Yes, the police interviewed me. I took off from work today because I hope to find out who really killed my old pal. Zoltan wouldn't have done it. I feel sure the cops have the wrong man."

I couldn't hold back a sigh of relief. "My thought exactly." I added a quick explanation. "It's no easy matter to be the wife of a dedicated musician, and it's true I was bowing out of the role, but I can't for a moment believe the man's a killer. The idea is absurd."

"Of course it is. He's not the type. It isn't in him to be mean or violent. At worst he was just neglectful. If he goes to prison, the real killer goes free."

"Do you have thoughts about how to investigate?" I asked.

"I'm on it already." At these words, I felt instantly hopeful of acquiring a colleague. However, my hopes were dashed when she added, "I have a friend who's a medium, and I've invited Dorothea's aunt, son, lover, and ex-lover for a séance tomorrow night. I expect—at least I hope—Dorothea herself will name her killer for us. Through the medium, you know. Why don't you come on over and join us?"

"Oh, I—" It was on the tip of my tongue to say I didn't believe in that hocus-pocus. Talk about absurd. I considered séances the ultimate foolishness, but I caught my breath and swallowed my words. It hit me that a gathering of Dorothea's circle was exactly what I needed. I would meet them all and hear their thoughts about this situation. I'd learn something of Dorothea's recent life. I'd line up viable suspects for further questioning. And who knew? Perhaps I'd even find a killer among them.

"Thank you, of course I'll come," I said. "I appreciate the invitation. I've never attended a séance before, but I'll—" I'll what? Submerse my doubts? Not likely. I floundered and sought words to complete the sentence.

She didn't wait for them. She asked, "Do you know how to get here?"

"Oh, yes, I'm familiar with your neighborhood; I lived nearby for two years."

"We'll see you about eight tomorrow then."

I hung up, relieved that I didn't have to confess my views on séances.

I spent the rest of that day trying to make sure my in-laws were all right, coaxing them to eat when they had no appetite, and helping them back to their hotel as night came on. I assumed that sooner or later I'd be grilled by the police, and I uneasily awaited the moment.

It came toward lunch time the next day. I'd searched for food in the fridge to have ready for Annie and Janos when they joined me again at the apartment. On Zoltan's shelf I saw only snacks and kielbasa. I did find canned tomatoes, onions, and rice in his section of cupboard, and decided that, by borrowing a few stalks of celery from George, I could put together a one-dish casserole, what my mother always called Spanish rice. Mother made the mixture with hamburger, but I thought it might be good with kielbasa. I cut up the onions and celery and began to brown them, and then I sliced the sausage into the pan. The concoction sizzled and gave out a tempting aroma, which I hoped might lure even my very upset guests to the kitchen when they arrived. I opened the can of tomatoes, started the rice cooking, and sought out the rosemary and basil, along with some garlic powder, from a spice collection untouched since I moved out.

I'd planned to head down to Mario's in midafternoon, when, hopefully, between lunch and dinner, the waitresses might have time to talk. But before I'd even finished preparing the food, the detectives arrived—at least, I assumed they were the detectives, as I expected no one else. I opened the door to their ring. The two men who stood there gave their names, which I was far too shaken to remember, and held up their badges. They asked if I was Mrs. Zoltan Szekely, and when I nodded, the tall one announced that they wished to talk to me. I felt a stab of uneasiness, fearing I'd say the wrong thing. But how could I? I knew nothing.

"It'll have to be in the kitchen," I said. "I'm cooking rice, and I need to time it."

"Kitchen's fine," the taller one said. He followed me, and I noticed he had a slight limp. He folded himself into the chair George had earlier vacated, while his shorter, balding companion slid into a second chair, his back to the stove. That left me, if I sat down, facing a window glaring with sunlight. I chose to avoid sitting. I didn't want my eyes dazzled when I had to cope with cops.

"We understood you were staying in Greenwich Village." Limpy Tall

Man spoke in an English accent. I like an English accent, but it didn't sound so great coming from an accusatory detective.

"I am. I'm just … just here cooking lunch for my in-laws." Why, I wondered, was I acting apologetic? This was my apartment. I had a right to be here.

"Where were you two mornings ago at gone nine?" Mr. Tall Man asked. "I mean, at just past nine."

I stared in astonishment. "Why? You think I helped Zoltan commit murder?"

"Just answer the question."

"I was at work."

"Where's work?"

"Columbia University Butler Library, journalism department."

"You were there all day?"

"Nine to five."

"And lunch?"

"In the student cafeteria."

"Someone saw you there?"

"Well, of course. I ate with my colleagues."

"So you didn't leave the campus at all? You didn't come here to consult with your husband?"

"I did not." I almost added, *I didn't go to the Village to help commit murder, either.* But I thought better of it.

The baldy suddenly shot a question at me. "Why are you two living separately, Mrs. Szekely?" I shrugged; it was too complicated to explain. When I didn't answer, he went on, "We were told we'd find you in Greenwich Village. We checked there but found no one home. A neighbor suggested you might have come here. Kind of back and forth, are you? Not really separated?"

His tone sounded even more hostile than Limpy's. I had the feeling these two didn't believe a word I was saying. I felt tempted to snap, *None of your business,* but I stifled it and answered, "No, I live in the Village now. We … uh … didn't get along."

"Why? Was he abusive?"

I could barely control a snort of laughter. Unless you counted those quotes from Freud as mental abuse, I couldn't picture Zoltan as abusive. I answered, "Certainly not."

"Perhaps he cheated on you with his former girlfriend?" Mr. Limpy Tall Man suggested.

So that was the way their thinking went! This thing with Dorothea had been going on all along and had driven me to leave Zoltan, providing him with motive to murder the former mistress who'd destroyed his marriage. I should have known. People always assume breakups involve a third party.

I fumed. I felt like snarling, but I kept my voice calm. "It had nothing to do with cheating. Neither of us cheated. I—" I tried to think how to explain about the money shortages of a musician's life. While I hesitated, pondering, the rice boiled over. I rushed to turn it off and snatch the pan from the stove. Of course the handle was hot, so I dropped it. Cursing under my breath, I turned on the faucet and held my burned palm under the running water until the pain eased. "I even urged him to get in touch with Dorothea," I blurted. "I wanted to make sure she was all right."

"Oh, yes—that visit to Dorothea. Tell us about that. Why would a wife contact a man's former girlfriend unless she was jealous? Did you go there to make a threat?" Limpy sounded highly skeptical. I started to answer, but, on the verge of speaking, I realized that the true explanation, "I worried because she'd spoken of suicide," would get me more deeply involved. He'd only demand to know why I cared. While he finger-combed his thick, brown hair, I wondered if he might then envision a ménage à trois. Who could know what twisted minds these cops had?

I decided I'd best say no more. I shrugged the question off and tried to calm my trembling fingers. I scooped the rice into the large fry pan with the browned vegetables and kielbasa.

Baldy waited for an answer, got none, and finally ventured, "Or did you maybe want to case the premises where she was living?"

The words *You have to be kidding* came to mind, but I squelched them. He was twisting everything. I bit my lip and kept still. Maybe I should consult Zoltan's lawyer.

Limpy Tall Man seemed to sense that I'd decided to clam up. He tipped his chair back and relaxed. He glanced around the room and made a comment to his colleague, whom he called Yonkers. Then suddenly he turned back, gave me a piercing look, and tried to act sympathetic. "I hear Mr. Szekely recently lost out on a promising grant. That must have been upsetting to you."

So they even knew about the lost grant. They'd talked to Zoltan's instructors at Juilliard. That must have been a gruesome experience for those classical musicians, being questioned about a murder. The police must believe they had an airtight case: loss of anticipated income, recent departure of wife, sudden addition of a child support demand, career on hold or maybe down the tubes. Those were motives galore for a rash impulse to kill, especially given Zoltan's devotion to his music.

I maintained my determination to keep silent until I talked to that lawyer. I tried not to let my hand shake as I stirred the casserole. The two detectives consulted with each other, and I heard Yonkers refer to Limpy Tall Man as Cody. He turned to me and said, "I gather you just moved out. Is most of your stuff still here?"

Surprised at the turn of the questioning, I answered readily. "Well, of course. I have only a tiny room in the Village, and it's temporary."

"Mind if we have a look through your desk?"

"I thought you already searched."

"His stuff, not yours."

I shrugged. I had nothing incriminating in there. Bills, letters from my mother—all they would prove was what the police already knew, that we faced financial problems. Assuming they had a warrant anyway, I said, "Go ahead, but you won't find anything. There's nothing to find."

As they went down the hall, I heard fragments of Yonkers's statement to Cody. "Crucial to prove … and planning, Cody … collaboration." His partner answered, "Can't prove what isn't there." It dawned on me they were looking for signs of premeditation. Probably they hoped to go for murder one, and to rope me in as an accessory.

Clearly, I had no choice but to pursue my own investigation. As Zoltan's wife, I was involved whether I wanted to be or not. Though my hand still burned, I took out my anger and frustration on the Spanish rice casserole by stirring it so vigorously that grains of rice flew out and I had to search for a dishcloth to clean the stove.

The detectives soon came back down the hall. They paused at the kitchen door. Detective Cody said, "That will be all for now, Mrs. Szekely, but we may have more questions later." Yonkers jotted hastily in a notebook. I suppose he took note of the fact Zoltan's wife could give no adequate reason for the separation. That would leave the two of them free to speculate about all sorts of kinky triangles involving Dorothea. No doubt they also wanted to add to the financial motivations they'd already found. I winced as I imagined their thoughts.

When my in-laws arrived, I was still shaking. I decided not to worry them with the bad news about the freaky case the detectives were building and the difference they'd defined between premeditated and impulse murder.

At least I was able to provide Zoltan's folks with a late lunch, which they seemed to enjoy and even complimented me on—a first for them. But for myself, I'd lost my appetite. I picked at my food while they ate and worried that I might have said the wrong thing to the cops.

We'd only just washed the dishes and put away the leftovers when the lawyer, Mr. Reitman, called. He asked to speak to Janos. I handed the phone to my father-in-law. After a brief conversation, he hung up and turned to us, looking gray with fatigue.

"Zoltan's been booked." He trembled, speaking in a shaky voice like an aged man.

"Murder one?" I asked.

"Mr. Reitman didn't say. He just said, 'They're charging him.'"

I bit my lip and wondered if I'd contributed to this disaster. I'd tried so hard to avoid saying anything to add to the case against Zoltan, but perhaps some inadvertent comment had given the cops the final piece of evidence they needed. I reviewed the conversation but could find no hint.

My father-in-law collapsed into a chair. Clearly he was falling apart. Everything was up to me now.

In late afternoon I made a quick trip to the Village, where, on Fourteenth Street, I located Mario's restaurant. I pretty much knew where it was; I'd passed the place often enough. I think I'd even once or twice enjoyed a cappuccino at the sidewalk café, though I'd never gone inside. This time I did—and breathed the warm odors of onion, garlic, and pesto. I saw that I'd chosen a good moment, too early for the dinner crowd. There were only two couples in booths, one single diner at a small table near the window, and a waitress idling near the coffee pot. I went over to her and asked if she could spare a few minutes to talk to me about the death of Dorothea. She assured me she'd already told the cops all she knew.

"I'm a private investigator," I lied. "I don't have access to what the cops know. I need to learn about it for myself."

She was a short, slim woman with black hair swept back from her face in a neat french twist. She looked around the room, assessed her customers, and told me she could take her break as soon as the other waitress came back. "Why don't you sit down and have a Coke or something, and I'll join you when I can."

I nodded, slid into a booth, and looked around. There was a pinball machine in one corner and one of those iron claw contraptions in another corner. The iron claw hung over a container filled with mostly jelly beans, with objects scattered among them such as billfolds, powder puffs, lipsticks, compacts, and stuffed animals, all designed to fool people into thinking they might get something for their money when, in fact, the claw would probably only pick up jelly beans. I wondered why people fell for those things.

The waitress brought me a Coke, and I waited while she went to inquire if her customers wanted dessert. It seemed they didn't; in fact, one couple and the single man left immediately. With just one couple remaining, she tallied and presented their bill, and then, after pouring another Coke, came to join me, carrying her drink in the familiar narrow-waist glass. She placed the glass opposite me and held out her hand. "Janet Cummerlin."

"Hi, Janet. I'm … Gillian Foster." I remembered at the last moment not to give the name Szekely, which, as a colleague of Dorothea's, she might well recognize.

She sighed, sat down, and loosened the top button of her uniform, studying me with interest. "A private investigator," she marveled. "I didn't know women did that sort of work. It sounds exciting."

I improvised. "Sometimes women can find out things that men can't, things one woman would only confide to another."

"I expect. So what did you want to know?"

"Whatever you can tell me about what happened to Dorothea recently. Did she say anything to you about her life or her situation?"

"Well, it was strange." She bit her lip and gazed toward the window. "She'd been planning her wedding, you know, and then all of a sudden she started talking a lot about her former boyfriend. I mean, not Zoltan or her fiance, her *other* former boyfriend, a guy named Fisk … Uh, Joe Fisk, maybe? He'd come to town, and it seems he wrote to say he wanted to lunch with her." She frowned and shook her head. "She grew wildly excited, which I thought was odd, since she was scheduled to marry this other guy in three days—a guy named Reggie. We were all invited to the wedding. Anyhow, she decided to buy this Joe guy a lunch right here at Mario's. They went into the private room to eat. It was creepy, you know? I got the feeling she hoped he might suggest they get together again, though, as I say, I can't imagine why under the circumstances. I mean, she had Reggie, didn't she? Why would a bride become excited about an old boy friend?"

"Perhaps she'd been carrying the torch all those years."

"In any case, it didn't happen. We couldn't hear everything, but they had a terrible argument, loud yelling, and when he left, he threatened to sue her and have her declared an unfit mother."

"Do you have any idea what it was all about?"

"I gathered he wanted to adopt one of her kids. Dorothea was determined to keep them. She was crazy about those youngsters. Even those two in foster care—she always said she would never, ever give them up for adoption."

I couldn't help raising my eyebrows. This quarrel, her former lover demanding his child while she angrily refused, sounded like a lovely motive for murder, and I'd uncovered it on my first try. Maybe I'd turn out to be a good investigator after all. If I could somehow prove that this Fisk went to Dorothea's house, I'd have evidence for the cops.

Janet went on to describe Dorothea—what a hard worker she was, how reliable, how much they'd miss her. None of it seemed particularly relative to the attack on her. Anyway, I already had the plum I'd sought. When she swallowed the last of her Coke and announced she had to get back to work, I thanked her and left.

I went home but didn't tell Janos what I'd learned. I needed to think about this Fisk situation for a while. It seemed promising indeed.

CHAPTER 21

The Séance

—1948

Before I left for the séance, Annie complained of chest pains. While we both stood over her anxiously, Janos pleaded about taking her to the emergency room. Annie shook her head over the suggestion. I offered to stay, but Janos urged me to go. "I've called Cousin Nadya and asked her to come and help out here. We need you to find out what's going on with Dorothea's friends and what they may have told the police. That's something I can't do."

I worried about that séance. I feared I'd be tempted to scoff, to giggle, maybe even to burst out in one of those uncontrollable snorts of laughter and spoil everyone's fun. But I had to learn more about Mr. Fisk. I nodded, gave Annie one more anxious glance, and raised a hand in farewell when she waved me away.

Norma's place was just two stops away by subway, and within fifteen minutes I was ringing her doorbell and being buzzed in. She had a third floor walk-up in an older building, and she awaited me in the doorway.

Like Dorothea, she was tall and bony-slim, with mouse-colored hair drawn back from her face. She wore a basic black dress, unadorned except for a single strand of pearls, and she seemed more understated than the usual flamboyant New Yorker. She held out a hand to me in a forthright manner seldom seen in women of that era. I hid my surprise and responded in kind to her masculine handshake. She said, "You must be Jill. I'm Norma. I knew your husband years ago—had the room next to his. Used to lie in bed and listen to his playing."

I smiled. "Was that a luxury or an annoyance?"

"Oh, luxury, definitely. He's a great pianist. Dorothea and I both loved being part of that musical ambiance."

She ushered me inside. The room I entered was large, with crown molding, an old-fashioned center chandelier, and a large window showing, through a gap in the heavy, flowered draperies, a gleam of twilight. Glancing around, I saw, against a cluttered background of shelves of ceramics, six other people in the room: three men I didn't know, two women, one of whom I recognized as Leila, and a teenage boy. I waved to Leila and guessed the teenage boy to be Dorothea's oldest son, Randy. The salt-and-pepper haired man who stood beside him—and looked so strikingly like the boy—must be his father and the man who'd fought with Dorothea at the restaurant, Joel Fisk. As with Leila and Marcie, who shared that toe anomaly, their relationship was not just an assumption. The resemblance was unmistakable. The dimple on both faces looked as if some taller person had grasped it between his fingers and twisted it upward in order to show it off better.

My hostess said, "We were so glad you could join us, Jill. I believe you know Leila, and this young man is her boyfriend, Carlo Capetto."

I wanted to study Joel Fisk further, but I reminded myself I needed to view all these people as suspects. I smiled and nodded at Carlo, a darkly handsome, brooding twenty-something, who took Leila's hand protectively. Norma went on to introduce the other female, an older woman whose pink cheeks and salt-and-pepper hair pulled back in a neat bun might have qualified her to be a spokesperson for homemade cookies or fudge. "This is Belle Granger, Dorothea's aunt and her only relative in New York. Belle was the first person the police notified of this terrible event."

"So tragic. I was just finishing the hem on her wedding dress when the cops came," the woman said. "We were in the midst of planning a wedding. Poor Reggie, I can't bear it for him." She squeezed the arm of the pudgy man beside her, and his expression turned duly tragic.

Norma added, "Belle called to notify me, and I got in touch with the others."

"How nice to meet you, Jill." Belle offered her hand, which I took. She added, a tad overtragically I thought, "My poor, poor niece. She tried so hard to make a good life for herself. This is all so sad."

She didn't sound sad so much as—what? Annoyed? Sorry for herself? I had the feeling she was just saying the proper words for the occasion. Had there been bad blood between her and Dorothea? I'd seen no mention of her in the diary. Apparently she hadn't come forward to console when Dorothea suffered the post-Zoltan loneliness and despair that set her to contemplating suicide and drove her, finally, to Mama Falucci and the desperate lie about Marcello's parentage.

The man thrust out his hand and confirmed my guess about him. "I'm Joel Fisk, and this is my son—and Dorothea's son—Randy. I don't know how much you know about Dorothea—"

"I know she had two boys by former lovers." I didn't confess my surprise at seeing these two together. I wondered how the man had so quickly gained permission to take the boy from his foster home. The diary claimed that Joel Fisk not only rejected fatherhood but moved out and eventually disappeared after Dorothea got pregnant with Randy. Obviously he must have changed his mind at some point along the way, decided he wanted the boy after all, and come to New York to talk Dorothea into giving him up. And when she'd refused—then what? Had he followed her home and sneaked into the apartment when Zoltan departed, planning to dispose of her?

He certainly proved attentive to the boy now, keeping a hand on the youngster's left arm. Randy held a glass of brown liquid, probably cola, in his right hand. Everyone else seemed to be drinking wine.

The other man, who was short and even balder than my erstwhile nosey detective, was introduced as Reggie Jackson. "Dorothea's fiancé," Norma explained. The man's tragic expression had faded. He didn't offer to shake my hand, but gave a curt nod in response to the introduction. Then he frowned and studied me with distaste, as if in his book I'd become a prime suspect.

"We're waiting for Madame Lili Aya, the famous medium," Norma said. "Meanwhile, can I get you a glass of wine or a soda? I don't have any hard liquor because Madame Aya said it would interfere with … uh … you know how much concentration a séance takes, right? Well, anyway, we can't afford to have anyone smashed. She did say she'd allow a small glass of Burgundy but nothing stronger."

"A glass of Burgundy would be fine." I had no interest in getting smashed, either. I needed my wits about me to probe the motives of these people. I believed Dorothea's murderer was in this room, and I intended to investigate all leads.

Norma indicated a seat on the couch for me, and I went over and sat down. While the others resumed sipping from the glasses they held, my hostess poured wind for me. As she handed me the stemware, she said, "We've all been wondering how you felt about this situation. I mean, since you left Zoltan and all. Well, it isn't quite like having a beloved husband under arrest, but it still must be upsetting, being drawn into something like this after you've severed the ties."

Wishing to be the questioner rather than the questioned, I tried to turn the conversation away from me. "Of course it is, but I confess, I'm puzzled how Dorothea learned that I'd left Zoltan. Did he get in touch with her instantly or what?"

Norma winced in embarrassment. "Well, you know how it is down there. They don't call that the Village for nothing. It's a small town within a city; everyone knows everyone. Dorothea kept up with the wannabe musicians she and Zoltan used to hang out with. She knew when Leah and Frieda broke up. So when she heard you moved in with Frieda, she figured … you know … she figured you realized you were a lesbian and couldn't go on living with a man." She bit her lip and looked rueful. "It happens so often in Greenwich Village, doesn't it? I mean, the homos fake it for a while and then all of a sudden realize they have to accept who they are, even if it spells trouble with the family and employers." She blushed and waved her hands as if she didn't quite know what to do with them. "I hope I'm not embarrassing you. I just—well, that story was going the rounds."

I felt my face flame. I hadn't supposed anyone even suspected about Leah and Frieda's lesbian relationship, let alone adding me to the mix. But, as she'd said, Villagers were canny about such matters—in this case, too canny.

"I don't *live* with Frieda," I burst out. "I rent a room in her apartment."

They all looked surprised. I hunched my shoulders in chagrin. Norma reddened even more and said, "Sorry, we just assumed. So, uh, why *did* you leave Zoltan, then?"

I relaxed, looked around at baffled expressions, and realized they'd all been in on this assumption. Everyone but Randy stared at me. Dorothea's son occupied himself with brushing off a dusty spot on his pants, either teenage embarrassed or naively unaware of the implications of the Bloomsbury lifestyle these folks projected onto me, with males and females freely shifting lovers back and forth.

I couldn't think how to explain my true reason for leaving. Would they believe me if I said there was no other man, no woman, just money shortages and a lack of a future for me? The faces that I gazed at were neither hostile nor caring, just puzzled. How could I communicate to such people my longing to have a child and a career, my frustration that neither seemed possible with Zoltan? For them, that wouldn't present a compelling enough motive to break up a marriage.

I realized I didn't owe them an explanation. In the end I simply shrugged and said, "We weren't getting along."

"Zoltan always seemed an easy man to get along with." Norma's face still registered puzzlement.

"Yes, up to a point—the point where his music interfered with what his wife wanted." I shuffled my feet but then fought my tendency to grow nervous when in the spotlight. I again reminded myself I was here to learn, not to answer questions. "Concert pianists are dedicated people." I paused and then added, "I mean, dedicated to music, not to marriage."

After a polite silence, during which I sensed that no one's curiosity had been satisfied, I turned to Joel Fisk, hoping to get acquainted. "I'm surprised to find you here, Mr. Fisk. I understood that you and Dorothea had broken up long ago, and that—" I glanced uneasily at Randy and didn't finish the sentence. I didn't want to remind the boy that his father hadn't wanted him.

Joel answered the question I didn't ask. "Actually, I'm hoping to adopt Randy—or rather, for my wife to adopt him. She and I have no children together, you see. We own a lake resort, with fishing, boating, water skiing, and that sort of thing. We need an heir to help out now and take over later. Randy loves sports, my wife wants to adopt him—it seems a perfect arrangement."

Except that Dorothea must have objected violently. I knew from the diary that she lived and breathed for the day she could have her sons with her. She must have been devastated over the threat of losing this boy she'd waited so long to be reunited with.

As if thinking along the same lines, Joel justified himself. "Dotty still had Denny and Marcello. And Randy really wants to come with me." He patted his son's knee. "He'd written her a note begging her to give him permission. Of course, she never received it; she died that morning before the mail came."

I recalled what I'd heard somewhere: "You can't replace one child with another." Marcello wasn't even hers. And Randy was her firstborn. That made him special. No, Dorothea would not have been happy about this proposal. The great question was, just how badly did Joel want Randy? Badly enough to commit murder for him?

"Dorothea never seemed to know what was good for her—or good for her kids," her aunt commented. I glanced at the woman and tried to recall her name. Belle, wasn't it? I wondered why Dorothea never mentioned an aunt in her diary. In her lonely state, I'd have thought a relative would be a precious asset.

"You and Dorothea were close?" I asked.

"Not really," she admitted. "Actually I'm only a relative by marriage. Dorothea didn't get along with any of the family. She was—" The woman bit her lip and fell silent, but she blushed so violently, I could guess the criticism she'd started to offer. *She was the mother of illegitimate children.* Of course, she'd stifled that statement in Randy's presence, but the fact was there, a fact which would embarrass the relatives if they were social-climbers—and something about this woman, perhaps her phony-expensive paisley dress and fake pearls, told me she might be that type. Her dress looked like a Lerner's trying to mimic Lord and Taylor, its fluff and ruffles carefully removed to achieve high class simplicity, yet lacking the quality material and excellent fit of the genuine article.

"None of the Granger family seemed willing to have anything to do with Dorothea until you happened along," Norma remarked. "I often wondered why no relative ever came forward to help her. Poor girl, she had it rough."

"There wasn't much anyone could do," Belle defended. "She just couldn't seem to straighten out her life. Her mom thought she'd managed it with Zoltan, but then it all fell apart and—"

"I'd have straightened out her life." Baldy spoke up aggressively. "You all didn't understand her. She was a loving person who gave her love freely, no obsessing about legalities. And she trusted people. She wasn't wrong to trust; others were wrong to betray her." Again he frowned at the room's occupants as if to designate each of us guilty, as if he saw a vast conspiracy against Dorothea with present company complicit in it.

"Yes, you were good for her, Reggie. You knew how to handle her," Norma cooed. "It's sad that things didn't work out for you two, such a short time before your wedding. I'm sure she'd still be here if she'd only—"

"We'd be safely married and on our honeymoon now." He sounded wistful, but his next words came out angrily. "We had no problems until Zoltan came along." I squirmed and bit my lip, knowing Zoltan wouldn't have visited Dorothea if I'd still been with him. Everything seemed to focus on me.

The room grew silent. Before anyone could gather thoughts for further comment, the doorbell rang. Norma said, "Here's the medium, at last. We can hold the séance now."

A minute later, Madame Aya, huffing a bit from the stairs, was among us. She was a small, plump woman, swathed in multicolored scarves and playing to the hilt her role as psychic. I struggled not to giggle. This all seemed so silly; I wished I could leave at once. I'd already gleaned at least three motives for murder. Joel Fisk wanted his son while Dorothea refused to give the boy up. Belle hated having a niece with questionable morals. Old Baldy, Reggie Jackson, had loved a woman who didn't truly reciprocate his feelings—not surprisingly, since he was too short for her, not to mention his morbid obesity and his lack of masculine attractions.

Short men are a problem for us tall girls. In dancing school I'd felt silly shuffling around the floor with one while looking over his head at the other dancers, as if I were dancing with a little brother. I could sympathize with Dorothea. She was tall. She'd found a loyal man in Reggie, but she undoubtedly felt gigantic and conspicuous in his company. If he didn't understand, if he felt rejected by her, that was a third motive for murder.

Madame Aya, still huffing, addressed the group. "I need to warn you all that it won't be easy to get through to Dorothea so soon after her death—if indeed it's possible at all. The newly dead require time to adapt, and often they're unable to communicate for a week or so after their demise. In fact, most mediums would refuse to attempt contact this soon. I agreed to it because I know it's important to get through to her and learn the name of her killer. I want to remind you, you'll need to be patient and give her time to orient herself." She leaned back in her chair and closed her eyes. When her breathing calmed, she went on, "Luckily, I have a contact named Theron, who lived in eighteenth-century New England. We'll call on him if we have to—but I'd far rather reach Dorothea directly. We'll try that first. I mean, since her son is here, as well as her fiancé and her best friend, I believe she'll make a major effort."

Randy stirred restlessly and shuffled his feet.

Everyone gathered around the table, where two extensions had been added to make it big enough. I reluctantly took the place assigned to me. Silly or not, I knew I had to see this through. Norma drew the draperies tighter, dimmed the lights, and joined us. The room grew quiet. We all held hands. I clasped Joel's hand on my left and Norma's on my right. Randy hung his head, shuffled his feet, and surrendered his hands reluctantly. Leila and Carlo, side by side opposite me, glanced at one another uneasily; no doubt they feared ghosts. Reggie Jackson still frowned. Belle looked dreamy, as if she'd gone off into a world of her own.

Madame Aya closed her eyes and pretended—at least I suspected pretense—to go into a trance. I looked around and saw that the others, except for Reggie, had also closed their eyes. Reggie smoothed away his frown and pursed his lips.

I thought, *Everyone but me believes this nonsense. I must not giggle. Think about something else, Jill.*

For a while we all listened to our own breathing and the sound of cars on the street below. Then Madame Aya said, "Is anyone there?"

A kind of electric jolt seemed to pass from one to another around the table. I assumed it had been caused by an impulse for everyone to move at once.

"Is this Dorothea?" the medium asked.

Nothing, no response. She said, "We need to talk to Dorothea. Dorothea, dear, if you're here in the room, we need to know. It's hard the first time you come through, dear, but keep trying. We're all your friends. Send us a signal. Stir a curtain. You can do it if you work at it."

All heads swiveled toward the draperies. We waited. After a few moments, the bottom section stirred slightly. I assumed the window was open a crack. Again I had that overwhelming urge to giggle. I swallowed hard to stifle it.

"Thank you, dear." She took a deep breath. "Dorothea, we're here because we want to find out the name of your killer. Only you can tell us. I intend to sink deep into a trance, and I'm going to let you talk through me. I know it's hard, but I trust you to find the way to do it."

She opened her eyes and announced that Dorothea's son, as her closest relative, should handle the questioning. Randy looked alarmed and protested that he couldn't do it. "I wouldn't know what to ask."

Madame Aya looked at Reggie. "Mr. Jackson? As her fiancé, you—"

Still scowling, Reggie shook his head. "Not me. I'm not into this stuff. I'm willing to listen in, but I don't talk to ghosts."

"She's not a ghost, she's an entity. If you're a doubter, you'll throw a spanner in the works."

"I didn't say I was a doubter, I said I don't participate in this sort of thing."

Madame Aya turned to Norma. "I guess it'll be up to you to do the questioning, Miss Ray. As her best friend, you're the other person she's most likely to communicate with. If she doesn't answer, call on Theron and ask him to help. He always comes. He's probably here already."

Norma nodded. Madame Aya warned us not to break the circle. Then she closed her eyes and let silence settle over the group. The curtain again stirred lightly. Traffic sounds came from the street, and down the block the train rumbled into the station, stopped, and pulled out again. Norma said, "Dorothea, can you hear me? This is your old friend, Norma. Remember?"

Still silence. Again we waited. Leila frowned, and her face contorted as if she were biting the side of her cheek. I wondered if anything would really happen—and how long we would keep up this farce with no response.

Norma urged, "You must remember, Dotty. We shopped and had lunch together a week ago—at Macy's tearoom. We talked about your upcoming wedding to Reggie."

More silence. Norma said, "Your son is here, Dorothea. You want to contact Randy, don't you? And Reggie's here, too."

We were so quiet we could hear everyone's breathing. Norma said, "Theron, are you there? Can you help?"

"I'm here," Madame Aya said in a growly voice not her own, "but you must give Dorothea a chance. She's trying very hard."

"Dorothea, you do remember me, don't you?" Norma said. "I'm Norma, your friend for all the years you lived in New York."

"She wishes her mother were here," Madame Aya's deep Theron voice growled. "She wants to talk to her mother."

"Maybe in the future we can bring your mother," Norma said.

"She wants to remind her mother that the children need looking after," the Theron voice said. "She wants to know they'll be safe."

"Your children are safe, but we'll try to get in touch with your mom,"

Norma responded. "Meanwhile, it's just me, Norma, and your son and fiancé. I'm sure you recall, Dorothea, our lunch in the tearoom just days ago."

After another silence, and in a voice deeper than natural, but not quite as deep as Theron's, Madame Aya said, "Yes, tearoom. I remember the tearoom."

"And do you recall what happened a few days later? Do you know you got in touch with Zoltan? Just days before your wedding to Reggie Jackson, remember?'

"Where am I?" the voice said. "I don't know where I am."

"You're in my apartment. You've been here many times, Dotty. You used to visit me often. Tell me, do you remember getting in touch with—"

"Zoltan. Yes, yes, I remember. The note. I sent a note. He came. He called on me."

"And that morning you were attacked."

"Throat. Something tight around my throat. Someone standing behind me." The medium's hands, still grasping others, scrabbled toward her neck as if to massage it. "I couldn't breathe, everything went black." Madame Aya screamed. Everyone tensed and looked around restlessly. Hands tightened, holding on, keeping the circle intact. After a few nervous moments, we all settled down and there was silence again.

"We want you to tell us who your killer was. Can you do that?"

"It was … it was …"

"Yes? Dorothea, we're all listening."

"It was Zoltan!"

"Are you sure?"

Louder and more distinctly, the voice repeated, "It was Zoltan!"

A sharp jolt went around the circle, separating our hands. Madame Aya slid forward until her head rested on the table, and Belle rushed to bring her a pillow. Norma flipped on a light and went for water; Joel rubbed the medium's hands. After a moment she rallied and asked what happened.

"Dorothea accused Zoltan," Norma said, bringing the glass of water. "I find it hard to believe he could have done it, but Dorothea seemed very sure. She said it twice: 'Zoltan. It was Zoltan.'"

"The dead know their killers," Madame Aya intoned. "You can trust them absolutely." She frowned and looked around, her gaze piercing each one of us as if she dared us to suggest she hadn't really contacted Dorothea.

CHAPTER 22

❦

Jail

—1948

I DIDN'T FALL FOR THAT stuff for a minute. I went home convinced that Norma, for reasons unknown, had cooked up that dramatic scene with the medium. In reviewing the evening, I tried to imagine her motive for trying to convince everyone, contrary to her own assertions, of Zoltan's guilt. I couldn't see what was in it for her beyond the thrill of being involved.

I didn't believe Dorothea had come through from the Great Beyond to name Zoltan as her killer. I've never bought the idea that we could contact the dead. I wished we could; I'd love to tell dear old Gramps, who was always so fascinated by astronomy, about recent discoveries in our universe. He'd have gone wild over the first photograph of the Andromeda galaxy. But I knew that sort of thing didn't happen. Wherever the dead were, they were gone from us, and no phony medium could convince me otherwise.

I returned to the Manhattan Avenue apartment to find an ambulance at the curb. Worried, I rushed into the lobby to see Annie being carried out on a stretcher. She looked pale and helpless.

I importuned Janos, who accompanied her, "What happened?"

"More severe chest pains. I thought we ought to check." Janos explained that he also feared she might be having another nervous breakdown. She couldn't stop weeping. "A half hour ago, Nadya left me alone with her, and George has gone to work—I decided to take no chances."

I asked if he wanted me to accompany him to the hospital. He shook his head. "You get some rest, Jill. We need you alert, on the job. I'll meet you here in the morning."

I nodded. As the stretcher passed, I grasped Annie's hand and told her not to worry. "I have good leads, Annie. I'll find the killer. I promise."

Her eyes opened and patted my hand. "Thanks, Jill." She murmured something else I couldn't quite catch, but it sounded like, "Appreciate it."

Not having brought my overnight things, I decided to go back to Frieda's. I locked the front door, headed for the subway, and twenty minutes later, let myself into the apartment. I found my housemate curled up on the couch in her pajamas listening to the radio.

Looking up at me, she said, "There'll be an arraignment in the morning."

"Yes, I know. The lawyer called."

To lighten the mood, I thought I'd laughingly tell her of those accusations of lesbianism, but I decided she might not find them funny. Actually, I didn't find them funny myself. I'd never thought it was anyone's business how others managed their sex lives, and when people had nudged me and winked, pointing to Leah and Frieda, I'd shrugged it off or ignored them. This had only happened twice, and not with close friends. We didn't have that kind of friends.

"I've been listening to the radio, but I've heard nothing more," Frieda said. "They just blathered out that one statement and then went on to other news."

"Be glad they're not harping on it," I said. "Zoltan doesn't need that kind of publicity."

I told her about the séance at Norma's, about the three viable murder suspects I'd found there. She seemed surprised that I flat out rejected the verdict of the medium. "It hasn't even occurred to you that Zoltan could be guilty, has it, Jill?"

I shook my head. "I've been married to the man for five years. It's not in him to grab a cord and choke the life out of someone."

"Easier than grabbing a knife and dealing with all that blood. They say everyone has it in them to commit murder if the motivation is strong enough."

"Nonsense. I don't see myself committing a murder. Nor you. Nor Zoltan."

"You're very loyal, Jill," Frieda said. "I hope you're not too loyal."

"I'm a realist. I know some of us are killers, and some are not."

All the same, I didn't sleep that night. I tossed and turned, watching the flashing night-light and wondering if I could be wrong about the man I married. Frieda had forced me to confront the question, was I indeed too loyal, too trusting?

After midnight, I finally ordered myself to stop worrying and get some sleep. All I had to do was keep looking for the killer. If I didn't find one, it would at least prove the police right, and I'd go ahead with the divorce as planned. If I did find one, I'd need to rethink my involvement with the Szekely family and decide if, by chance, I'd made too quick a decision about leaving.

In the morning, I checked with Janos about Annie and learned that she'd been kept in the hospital overnight, with probable discharge soon. Over coffee, I made a list of things to do. I planned to interview each of the people at the séance, including Randy if possible—and I'd want to talk again to those two witnesses, Leila and Maria, to seek holes in their stories.

I'd only just finished my list and copied down all the addresses and phone numbers when Janos called back. The lawyer, he told me, had succeeded in arranging a jail visit with Zoltan for the two of us, wife and parent, at eleven o'clock this morning, right after the arraignment.

Never before having had a relative or friend in jail, I felt uneasy about the experience, but it was essential to talk to Zoltan and hear his side of the story. I needed to be clear about what had happened, and his attitude would tell me much. I knew him so well. A lifted eyebrow or twitching facial muscle could speak volumes.

"Have you eaten breakfast yet?" Janos asked.

"No, I'm just having coffee."

"Why don't you come to our hotel and let me buy you breakfast? Then we'll go from here."

"Good plan. Give me a few minutes."

"Meet me in the coffee shop. I'll go on down and order. What would you like?"

"Pancakes sound good," I told him. "Or I guess they call them hotcakes in New York."

The few minutes I'd asked for were to be spent putting on makeup and doing my hair. As I worked, at my bureau mirror since Frieda's bathroom was too tiny for grooming chores, I wondered what I was doing. Who would I see in that jail who needed impressing? Theoretically, I was finished with both my husband and my father-in-law. It was just habit, attempting to impress the Szekelys. I never succeeded, and yet I never stopped trying. I gave a final pat to my nose with the powder puff, grabbed my purse, left the apartment, and hurriedly clattered down the stairs.

Within minutes I was on the subway, trying to think how one talks to an estranged husband in jail. *Attentively, even sympathetically, but not too lovingly,* I counseled myself—so as not to hint at a reunion, which was probably not in the cards for us.

I found Janos in a booth in the coffee shop. The two plates of food must have just been delivered, as both looked steamy hot. His was ham and eggs, mine, pancakes with a side of ham. Abashed, drawing his own plate closer, he explained that he always ordered ham and eggs in restaurants because he never got them at home. The daughter of a rabbi, Annika wouldn't have dreamed of having ham in the house—or bacon.

"Plain old pork I can live without, but ham and bacon are something else." He cut into the ham and let a hint of a smile play on his lips. "I sneak them in whenever I'm on a business trip. Don't tell on me, will you?"

I smiled in return. He was human after all. I'd wondered sometimes. In the past I'd tended to think of him as Mr. Always Right. "I promise to restrain my tattling impulses."

"So tell me, Jill, what happened at this so-called séance?" I knew my father-in-law didn't believe in that spiritualist stuff any more than I did. *We share much in common*, I thought. *Why can't we communicate better? Why can't we be friends?*

"The medium pretended to speak for Dorothea—I'm convinced it was a pretense—and claimed Zoltan murdered her. I'd have sworn Norma believed in his innocence, but maybe not. It's weird—she hired the medium, and they must have cooked up that nonsense between them. I need to talk to her alone and find out what's going on."

"Sometimes people are afraid to express their convictions directly to the relatives, and so they hide behind tricks like that," Janos theorized.

"Anyhow, I intend to interview each of them. I feel I've turned up three good motives for murder." I explained that a man named Joel Fisk had been Dorothea's lover before Zoltan, and the couple had a child named Randy, who'd been in foster care all these years. "I gather that Joel first denied the youngster was his but now, for some reason, has changed his mind and wants him—badly, I'd say. He brought the kid to the séance last night and seemed very possessive, with his hand on the boy's shoulder all evening. There's no question of the relationship: the kid looks just like him. Yet I hear Dorothea refused to give the youngster up. Seems Joel and Dorothea were warring over custody the day before she died."

Janos dipped into his scrambled eggs and then, with a nod, held his fork aloft with a mouthful impaled on it. "That's a good lead, Jill. Custody's a motive."

"Yes, there's something there. I mean, why would he care so much, after all these years?"

"Good question. Sounds like one of those Gothic mysteries where the neglected young person is suddenly in line to inherit a fortune from an unknown relative, and everyone wants to claim him or her." He gazed off as he chewed, savoring his guilty indulgence. "What about the other people?"

I poured syrup on my pancakes. "There's a man named Reggie Jackson.

He planned to marry Dorothea and glowered at all of us for not being sufficiently sympathetic to his true love. And there's an aunt who seems to have found Dorothea's lifestyle distasteful—too many illegitimate kids. Neither one shapes up as a likely murderer, at least not with a strong motive like Joel's. But again, there may be more than meets the eye."

Janos agreed, "They're all worth looking into. I seem to have read somewhere that this Reggie Jackson is a Texas oil man. If so, he might have suffered paranoid suspicions that Dorothea was after him for his money. He may have experienced a moment of murderous anger on learning of her shenanigans with other men—and now he's playing the devoted fiancé to put us off the track."

I agreed. "Someone isn't telling the truth."

While we ate he talked about Annie. She hadn't had the heart attack he'd feared; that was the good news. The bad news: the doctor wanted him to put her in a private psychiatric facility for rest and recuperation. He speculated that she might be suffering from chronic depression due to the many stresses in her life, the separation from loved ones in Europe, the worry over relatives currently at risk. He went on, with a sigh, "Those places are expensive, Jill. I keep trying to save for my retirement, but things keep coming up. Your dad was so right—I made a bad mistake when I shelled out money for rent all those years in Kentucky. I could have sold the place for top price if I'd had the good sense to purchase."

He'd never before been candid like this about his money problems. Touched that he trusted me, I consoled. "We all act on what the past has taught us." I added, "We may get lucky and solve this murder. My bet's on Joel as the perp, and I plan to zero in on him."

He nodded. "I hope you're right and can prove it. Unfortunately, there's still Kitty. Things haven't been going well in that arena, Jill. Kitty is pregnant again, and I guess you heard she turned Catholic. She'll be raising her children in the Christian faith. Her mother's very upset about that. And then there's—" He hesitated, but I guessed what he meant to say. *There's the breakup of your marriage.*

Though I realized he and Annie had had a lot to deal with lately, I couldn't honestly promise him a happy outcome on that score, much as I was tempted to do so. The reality of our money problems had not gone away. I glanced at my watch. "It's almost ten. I suppose we should get started."

He'd already finished his ham and was using his toast as a scooper to clean his plate of egg. While I ate the last of my pancakes, he checked the bill and drew out his wallet. I walked ahead toward the door while he counted out money and, I'm sure, added a generous tip. I knew he always tipped generously.

On the subway my stomach churned. I couldn't imagine what one said to a husband in jail for such a heinous crime. I could see that Janos was nervous, too, but he tried to stay focused. He talked about the questions we needed to ask in order to pursue an investigation. "It all revolves around what happened in those few minutes when Tanni was out of the house and someone else must have gone in. If he saw someone approaching, then we're in business for sure. We just need to find that someone."

"Will there be a glass between him and us?" I asked.

"I think that's only in prisons."

When we arrived at the jail, we were ushered into a bleak cubicle furnished only with a table and chairs. We waited, and soon Zoltan was brought in by a uniformed guard. He didn't look well; in fact, he looked gray and bloodless, as his father had looked the day before. *The light, maybe?* I tried to tell myself it was only that, but I immediately felt anxious about him. He was not his normal self. Standing near me, he hesitated and seemed unsure of his next move. Perhaps he wondered, as I did, whether we were allowed a hug. We both opted not to test the waters in that regard, even though the impulse to embrace and console him almost overwhelmed me. I still loved this man. It was no lack of caring that had driven me from him. I had to remind myself of my determination to convey no wrong impressions.

We sat down at the table, and the guard told us, before retreating, that we had ten minutes. Through the glass wall we could see him waiting, just outside the door.

"It's great to see you both," Zoltan spoke in a haunted voice, as if he too struggled with what to say in these circumstances. "I really appreciate you finding out about Marcello, Jill. I felt such relief knowing he wasn't related to me."

"Yes, thank God for that," Janos said.

"It's horrible in jail. They put you in with hardened criminals. I don't dare say I'm a musician—the guys here already resent and distrust me as a foreigner. They feel I'm not one of them. I can't imagine what prison must be like; surely a person could be lost and forgotten for years … for a lifetime."

Janos looked pained. "Don't worry, son, we won't forget you, and we won't stop trying to get you out. We'll persist until we succeed. You can count on that."

"Thanks, Dad, I'm grateful for your help. Yours too, Jill. It means so much to me to know you're willing to do what you can."

"Tell us everything that happened," I said.

"I guess you heard they decided at the arraignment that they had sufficient evidence to charge me—and worse, to deny bail." He shook his head. "It's all so crazy; I didn't even know Dorothea was dead. She was fine when I left her.

When the detectives came to the apartment and asked to search it, I let them do it—I felt I had nothing to hide. I didn't realize they'd use Dorothea's note and diary as evidence against me."

"Yes, we know all that," Janos said. "Let's waste no time. We're investigating, and we need to pinpoint exactly what happened on the day of the murder. Start from the beginning, when you went to Dorothea's house."

"She claimed the kid was hers … ours, I mean. Mine. The abortion was botched. I owed her. When I arrived she acted as if this were a great romantic moment; she seemed to have some weird idea that now, since Jill and I had broken up, I'd miraculously find myself in love with her. As usual with Dorothea, I didn't know what to say. She lived in a dream world and cast me as lead in her romantic Hollywood drama. I never did know how to deal with that stuff. I'd just come there to find out if the kid was really mine and if I'd owe child support. When I saw how the wind was blowing, I couldn't think what to say, how to disabuse her of her crazy notions. So I told her I'd get back to her and I left."

With a loud sigh, he ran his fingers through his hair and then clutched his head. "I did notice in passing the living room that someone had taken down the draperies while I was talking to Dorothea, but I didn't stop to check them. It wasn't my concern what the Faluccis did with their curtains. Now the cops say I took them down to get the cord and use it to strangle Dotty. It's not true! I've put up draperies in our apartment, but the cords were already strung. I'd have no idea how to take one of those things apart."

"You just passed them by and went on?" Janos asked.

He nodded. "I went outside and stood on the front stoop while I debated what to do. Right away I realized I should make it clear to Dorothea that I wouldn't get together with her in any case." He looked up at his father appealingly. "You know, Dad, that was my big mistake before. I didn't communicate forcefully; I didn't let her know for sure there could be nothing permanent between us. I meant to do better this time."

"It was a good thought, anyway," Janos said.

"I stood there working it out. I'd go back into the apartment and inform Dotty that the most she could hope for was child support. The kid didn't know me as a father, and I meant to leave it at that. Why introduce him to an unavailable dad? Better she should marry someone else and let the boy relate to that person as a father. Spare him from double loyalties."

Janos nodded. "Good thinking. That makes sense."

Zoltan rubbed his palms together and then ran his hands again through his hair. He closed his eyes and remained silent for a long moment, as if working out his thoughts. "While I hesitated, some woman passed me and entered the house. She closed the door behind her, and I reached out and opened it again. I planned to enter but changed my mind. I didn't put a foot inside. I decided it would be better to go first to the school and have a look at the boy, see if I felt he was really mine. I mean, there had to be some sort of genetic connection. I thought, once I knew about that, I could plan more clearly; I could come back and tell Dorothea exactly what I would do.

"I went down the steps, headed toward the school, and then decided I felt too upset right then to look at the kid. I needed to be calm and rational when I did that. So I went on home—and forgot to go back and check the door. I must have left it ajar, and someone else must have entered behind me without touching the knob. The cops claim that my prints cover all the others."

"Someone could have elbowed their way in through a partially opened door," Janos said. "Did you see anyone on the sidewalk? Did anyone else approach the house?"

"That's the thing. I don't remember seeing a soul. I keep telling myself there must have been someone, but I don't remember. I admit I wasn't looking; I was … I was distraught."

"If no one came along, then someone was already in the house," Janos said. "Someone hid in a closet or another bedroom."

"Yes—unless one of those women did it," Zoltan said. "I understand there were two women in the house."

"Oh, yes, the two witnesses. One's a mere girl, but the other one—Maria something—she'd bear investigating. We need to interview her."

Zoltan sighed and rumpled his hair again. "The lawyer urged me to plead guilty and try for a plea bargain, claiming Dorothea tricked and upset me so badly that I was of unsound mind. That way there'd be hope for a lighter sentence. I told him I wouldn't go along with that. I didn't kill her, of unsound mind or otherwise, and I'm not going to have a murder on my record."

Janos agreed. "There has to be another explanation, and Jill and I will find it."

Zoltan asked, "How's Mother? Is she okay?"

"Doc wants her to go into a psychiatric facility for a rest," Janos said. "I'm trying to figure out how I'll afford it. Those private places are expensive."

At that moment the guard stepped in and announced, "Time's up." We all stood. I found it hard not to give Zoltan a hug. He looked so forlorn I could hardly bear to leave him.

CHAPTER 23

Losing a Suspect

—*1948*

WHEN WE ARRIVED HOME, ANNIE had been discharged from the hospital. We found her sitting at the kitchen table drinking coffee. I was relieved to see she looked stronger, with more color in her face. She said, "Nadya offered to stay, but I sent her home. I'm all right."

She told me Norma had called and wanted to talk to me. I at once returned the call. Currently at work at a restaurant near her home, Norma suggested we meet for lunch. "I only have a half hour, so it would have to be here—and it would have to be soon. I'm scheduled for a lunch break from two to two thirty."

I glanced at the clock. One forty. "I'll come right over." I'd wanted to talk to her anyway.

"It's the Dutch Kitchen, West End Avenue near Juilliard."

"I know where it is." She'd already told me where she worked. I was familiar with the restaurant; Zoltan and I treated ourselves to lunch there on those rare occasions when we could afford more elegance than the Automat.

I slung on my sweater, grabbed my purse, and promised my in-laws I'd return soon. I almost ran the few blocks to Broadway, where I caught a passing bus. At five minutes past two, I walked into the Dutch Kitchen. There were few customers at this late hour, and I easily spotted Norma in a back booth and hurried over to her. Her lunch consisted of a large bowl of tomato soup, into which she was breaking crackers, and half a sandwich, on a plate at her elbow. She wore a bluish green uniform that heightened her hair color, making it less mousy. The uniform looked a great deal better on her than had that basic black; it brought out the flecks of blue and green in her eyes as well as enhanced the coppery sheen of her hair. Though at our previous meeting I'd thought her plain, she now looked almost pretty.

"Hi, Jill," she said. "Want some lunch?"

I nodded. My pancake breakfast had been burned off long ago. "Soup and salad would be nice."

She nodded and waved. Another waitress came to the booth and listed off the variety of soups available. "Vegetable beef, chicken noodle, cream of tomato, cream of broccoli." None of it sounded Dutch, but then I'd never been to Holland and didn't know what they served in restaurants there. I chose chicken noodle. She asked, "House dressing on the salad?" When Norma assured me the house dressing was good, I nodded.

When we were alone again, Norma broke more crackers into her soup and confessed, "I'm worried about last night. I wanted to talk to you."

Not wishing to confess to her my skepticism about that medium's act, I merely commented, "What a surprise. Did you believe it?"

"I believe Dorothea thinks Zoltan was the killer—but I feel sure she's mistaken."

"I just talked to Zoltan," I told her. "He denies doing it. He denies even going back into the house as the witnesses claim he did. He's so vehement about his innocence that he won't even consider a plea bargain. His lawyer suggested he might get a lighter sentence if he, you know, pleads guilty of committing the murder while of unsound mind. That would count as manslaughter. He flat out rejects the idea."

Norma gulped down a couple of quick spoonfuls of her soup. She shook her head thoughtfully. "Dorothea and I have been friends since she came to New York. For years we worked together at Mario's in the Village. I was fond of her, but I've known her to do foolish things in her day. This took the cake, telling a guy he had a son when he didn't. You could hardly blame Zoltan if he *had* killed her."

"But you don't think he did?"

"Jill, I knew the man for the whole three years he was with Dorothea. Had a room down the hall from them for a while when I was living with my own first boyfriend, Ronnie Boltman. We used to attend their musical salons." I winced over a stab of chagrin that I wasn't the first woman to host Zoltan's salons, but I reminded myself that of course Dorothea had preceded me in that department, as in others. She was my mirror image, after all. If I'd stayed with Zoltan and punctured the diaphragm, as I'd thought of doing, I'd have echoed those later experiences of hers as well.

Norma went on. "Zoltan's such a good-hearted guy that he couldn't even bring himself to tell Dotty he'd grown tired of her—though it was obvious to all of us that he had. I mean, I think in the beginning it was exciting for him, sort of sophisticated and Bohemian, but in the end it grew scary. He began to feel stuck with this older woman who already had children. I believe I was aware of that fact before he was. I sensed he felt trapped and wanted out. Dot was the only one who couldn't see it. She was so focused on getting a father for her boys that she couldn't admit she'd lost that battle. She refused to hear what Zoltan was telling her; she kept insisting his only problem was his worry about his parents' reaction."

"And you couldn't explain?" I asked. "Offer a little friendly counsel, suggest she back off?"

"God knows I tried." She sighed. "She didn't listen, and at the time I thought maybe that was a good trait, admirable. She remained loyal to her men and tried hard to make a go of things. No man has ever walked out on me—if things weren't working, I took off before he did. Dotty stayed and tried to mend the relationship. I almost envied her the ability to persist—but look where her persistence got her!"

"Yes, she persisted too hard with someone," I agreed. "The question is, who? If you don't think it could be Zoltan, then how about those other two guys she lived with?"

"Johnny's in Peoria," Norma said. "Far as I know, he went back to his wife and kids and never left again. I suspect Dorothea was only a convenience for him, someone to cook his meals and share his bed while he put in his time in New York. He warned Dot from the start that his assignment here was temporary. He had two years to help his firm start up a New York office, and he'd be sent back to Peoria as soon as things were up and running. During all that time, he kept his own place and they never actually lived together. When Dot asked to go to Peoria with him, he admitted he was married and explained that his wife had stayed at home to be near her family. He didn't even feel guilty about finding a substitute woman for those two years. He was such a user."

Norma leaned back and sighed. "When she learned about the wife, Dotty convinced herself his marriage must be falling apart. That was Dot, always inventing a tale of woe for her guys. She came up with the naive argument that she could make Johnny happier than his wife had. Dotty could always convince herself that things would work out the way she wanted them to. He disabused her of the idea, so she pulled the same trick she later pulled with Zoltan—she got pregnant and had a kid. She thought little Denny would tip the balance and make Johnny want to stay with her. Didn't work, of course, and the poor kid ended up in foster care along with Randy. Dot would never release those boys for adoption; she wanted them so badly. At least the social workers managed to keep the two brothers together up until recently. You may have noticed that Randy seems mature beyond his years. He had to look after his kid brother all that time."

I nodded but didn't admit that I'd talked very little to Randy. Just then the other waitress brought out my soup and salad, and my stomach, more empty than I'd realized, rumbled loudly. The soup was the homemade type and smelled wonderful. I broke a couple of crackers into the bowl, stirred, and sampled. Savoring it, I asked her, "What about Joel? I was told that he and Dorothea had a big fight on the morning before the murder. It seems Joel asked to adopt Randy, and Dorothea wasn't having it. That sounds to me like a good motive for murder."

"Again, he doesn't seem the type. I knew him well, too. As I say, I've known Dotty ever since she came to New York. She and Joel were together for ages. Granted, it was a stormy relationship. At that time, he refused to believe Randy was his, even though Randy looked like him. Now, of course, he makes a big deal of the fact Randy is the spitting image of him."

"If it was stormy, why are you so sure he's not a killer?"

"Well, I mean, if he had killer urges, why wait until now? He had a lot more opportunity when he lived with her, not to mention bundles— armloads—of provocation."

"There's a tipping point," I said. "We put up with things for a long time and then—whammo. Maybe this custody thing was his tipping point. Her death worked out well for him. He wants the kid, and now there's no one to say he can't have him."

She shrugged. "That's true. I was surprised that the authorities so readily released Randy to his father. I don't know. I guess there've been custody battle motives in the past and they're used to it."

"At the moment, Joel stands out in my mind as suspect number one," I said. "Do you have his address?"

"Sure thing." She fumbled in her purse and drew out her address book. "But if you're planning to confront and accuse him, please don't mention my name. I don't want to take him on, and you shouldn't, either. The man has a temper—I've seen it in action."

"I'll be subtle," I promised.

She wrote out his address on a separate sheet torn from her book. I suggested she give me the other addresses while she was at it. "There's Reggie Jackson. He can't have been happy to have his bride using all these shenanigans to capture another man—and on the eve of his wedding, too. I mean, assuming he knew about it."

"Oh, he must have known about it. How could he not? She'd been putting him off, coming up with excuses." She thumbed through the book to look him up.

While she wrote, I added, "I'd like to talk to the aunt, too."

"I don't have her address, but I'll jot down the phone number. It's dubious, though. Dotty didn't see Belle very often. The family wasn't close. They were down on her because of her illegitimate children. Except for Belle, they mostly refused to acknowledge her at all. I thought that was stinking of them, since it was, after all, because of her family that she got into that predicament. If her mother had been a decent parent, she'd have protected her daughter from that awful stepfather, and Dotty wouldn't have run away to New York in the first place." She looked up at me suddenly, and I gazed into intensely focused brown eyes. "Do you have any idea what it's like coming to New York with no money and no job skills? It's not a fun place to be, I guarantee it."

"It must have been traumatic for her," I agreed.

"Traumatic, hell. Tepid word. She was scared to death of men when I first met her. Scared and attracted at the same time. She used to be what men call a tease. Lure them and then run from them. I recall at least two of her guys coming to me practically in tears, wanting to know what they'd done wrong to make Dorothea drop them just when they thought they were about to score with her."

"She did have problems." Clearly she'd needed analysis more than I did. Too bad it wasn't available to her.

"It took three years before she was able to calm down enough to move in with Joel and begin to work out a real relationship—and as I said, even that was stormy."

"She was lucky to have such a good friend."

"We met the day she arrived here. She took a waitress job at the place where I was working but got fired the first day for dropping dishes. I found her weeping in the restroom. She told me she desperately needed the job; she had no place to stay and had been sleeping on a park bench, so she lied on her application and claimed to be experienced. But how could she become experienced if no one would hire her when inexperienced? That's always the big problem. I got experience by volunteering in my uncle's restaurant. Dotty was just sixteen, and you're not legally permitted to work before that age. So I offered to show her the ropes. I was only a couple years older; I'd come to New York after my parents were killed in a car crash, and lived with my aunt and uncle until I could afford my own place.

"Well, Dot moved in with me, and I risked my own dishes—they were only from Goodwill, but I needed them—letting her practice carrying plates to customers. You have to be able to carry four at a time, two on your arm and two in your hands. She finally got the hang of it, and Mario took her back. We roomed together until she moved in with Joel."

She did all that at sixteen, and with no adult guidance. Small wonder that she made some bad decisions. I decided I ought to be more grateful to my parents, who stood by and taught me how to handle myself in the world.

While Norma and I finished our lunch, she told me a little about her own life and more about Dorothea. Dorothea, she said, had been determined to impress and capture a good man, and so she'd settled down to finish high school at night and then to attend a charm school where she could learn how to speak and dress properly. She knew she came across as a hick. "At seventeen, she was supporting herself and attending night school," she said. "You have to hand it to Dotty; she tried hard. I feel so bad for her. I wish the murder could be undone and we could have her back."

I agreed. "For Zoltan's sake as well as hers." I still worried about Zoltan. He'd looked so gray and wan. I didn't know how much more of this he could take. I hadn't learned anything today that would help me pinpoint a murderer.

"This must be terrible for him," Norma said.

"Then you didn't believe last night's accusation against him?"

"Certainly not. Poor Dorothea, she faced the other way, writing in her diary. She didn't know who was behind her; she just assumed it was Zoltan. Now I don't know how we'll find out the truth, but if you think of something, let me know. I'll help any way I can." She glanced at her watch. "I have to get back to work, but you needn't rush. I've paid for your meal. Take your time."

"Thanks, I appreciate it."

"Keep in touch," she said, "and remember to approach with caution when you go questioning people."

"I'll hold your warnings in mind."

"Good luck." She gathered up her empty dishes and my soup bowl. While I finished my salad and roll, I gazed out the window at pedestrians walking by and thought about Dorothea and her unfulfilled longing to create a family—the story of so many women's lives during wartime years. It was sad: the men came home longing for travel and adventure, to be shared with their girl, but the women longed only for children. I'm sure Dorothea was far from the only one who forgot the diaphragm.

I pushed my plate aside and studied the scrap of paper with the phone numbers. I tried to decide which one to contact first. I still thought Joel sounded the most promising. He could so easily have entered that house in the Village and hidden there until opportunity presented itself to commit murder. Clearly, the front door was unlocked, since Zoltan had started to go back in. With Dorothea in her room and Leila in the bathroom, it would be a cinch for Joel to grab the rope from the draperies and creep down the hall. Naturally, Leila and Dorothea would assume it was Zoltan.

How do you talk to a murderer without arousing suspicion and anger? I pondered that question as I walked home from the Dutch Kitchen. I didn't want to stir up hostility, and I certainly didn't want to focus attention on myself. I scuffed along, looking at nothing but the lines in the sidewalk retreating beneath my feet. I was so preoccupied I didn't even notice an old friend from our musical salons, Claire Beauchamp, until she called out to me. She was a Columbia student I'd met at my library job, one of those who'd sat up late with us discussing Kafka, Heidegger, and Kierkegaard. She fell into step beside me and wanted to know what was going on.

"I've tried to call you, but I get no answer," she said. "I read the news in the paper, and I feel sure Zoltan isn't guilty. There's not a violent bone in his body. He has to have been framed."

"I'm sure of it, too." I'd been so worried about Zoltan and his parents that I hadn't stopped to consider what our friends must think of this situation. Of course they'd read about it. Embarrassment flooded over me; I hadn't planned what to say to our circle of acquaintances. Even the Juilliard faculty—Zoltan's professors, not to mention his fellow students—would have seen the news in the papers. My colleagues at the Columbia library would have read it. Suddenly I wished I could grow small like those ants in the cracks of the sidewalk and crawl into their mound with them.

I started to blurt out that I was working on finding a way to prove his innocence, but I stifled myself. I didn't want word to get around that I was acting as private investigator. Someone might tell my two chief suspects, Joel and Reggie. I played the clueless wife. "I don't know, Claire. The police don't tell me anything. I can only hope they're still looking for the real killer."

"If you need a character witness, you can count on me. I'll tell them—a man who plays Bach and reads Kafka is no killer."

"Thanks, Claire. I appreciate your support." I couldn't muster the courage to ask if she'd been notified about our breakup. She might yet have second thoughts and conclude that a man who'd just split from his wife was no longer the contented music student she'd known.

She walked with me for a short distance asking questions. I kept shaking my head, claiming I didn't know anything. Finally she turned off, saying, "I'm headed for Butler Library."

"I'll be back at work soon," I told her. "I'll see you around campus."

"Good luck." She waved and departed. Biting my lip, I walked on, wondering what our other friends from salon days were thinking.

When I reached home, Annie and Janos informed me that Kitty planned to come down from Schenectady. "We told her she shouldn't be traveling in her condition—she's six months along—but she insisted she had to be with us. She's catching the early train at five in the morning."

"A train trip shouldn't hurt her," I consoled. "She can have our room, and I'll stay on in Frieda's apartment in the Village."

"Then there's the problem of what all these upsets may do to her healthwise. I appreciate her desire to help, but I fear it would be better for her to keep out of it at this time." Annie was sounding stronger and more forceful. I thought that, in spite of her protests, it was good for her to have Kitty take enough interest to come. I hoped Kitty's presence might perk her up.

"But of course she'd want to be with her parents at a time like this," I said. "I would, too. Any daughter would."

Janos eased himself into an overstuffed chair slipcovered with a blue and yellow fabric. I recalled the tedious effort of making the slipcover. Knowing very little about sewing, I'd had to cut out each piece separately and fit it to the right section of the chair. The process had taken days.

"So tell me what you learned," Janos said.

"Not much," I confessed, "but I did get the address of the three prime suspects." I managed a faint smile as I spoke. "I guess you know who they are—Joel, Reggie, and Belle. As to Joel, he could well have gone to the house, maybe not planning murder, maybe planning to talk to Dorothea again, to plead with her to give him the kid or face a lawsuit. But when Zoltan arrived, he saw his golden opportunity to get rid of Dotty and frame Zoltan. Possibly he was hiding in a closet. It's a big, empty house, with only two women at home and plenty of room to hide."

"Yes, that's logical, that could have happened," Janos agreed. "Good thinking. You have an investigator's mind, Jill. But I don't want you talking to him. A man like that—well, let me do the interviewing this time."

"Oh, I've already planned what to say. I'll just be a concerned friend of the family, wanting to make sure Randy is happily situated."

"He'll be suspicious. He knows you're Zoltan's wife."

"Estranged wife. And student social worker. I'll play the role—disgusted with Dorothea for not jumping at the chance to accept a great future for Randy, hopeful that now at last things will work out for the kid. I'll find out indirectly what Joel was doing at the time of the murder. I'll look for alibis."

"At least let me come with you. Two are safer than one."

"That sounds good. I'll give him a call."

Joel was staying at a hotel with weekly rates. When I called and was put through to his room, a boy answered. I asked to speak with Joel, and he responded, "Dad's in the shower. Can you call back in fifteen minutes or so?"

"Sure thing. Is this Randy?"

"Yes. Who are you?" He sounded puzzled.

"Jill. I'm a friend of your mom's. I met you at the séance." I decided to come right out and ask what I wanted to know. "Why are you there? Has your dad got custody of you now?"

"Not officially, not until the judge okays it," Randy admitted. "They're letting us have a little time to get acquainted before they decide. I'm told they'll ask me what I want—but hey, who wouldn't choose to live at a resort on a lake? I can't wait. Dad promised to teach me to run the boat."

Everything was working out smoothly for Joel. A few days ago he was anticipating a lawsuit to get Randy. Now his opposition had died and he had the kid, just like that. I was astonished at the speed of it.

"As a friend of your mom's, I'd like to talk to the social worker," I said. "Can you give me her name?"

He readily gave the name and said he had the phone number handy. I heard him fumbling with something, and then he read it off. I jotted the number on a piece of paper and told him, "I won't bother to call back; I'll just stop by your hotel in a half hour."

"Well, Dad and I were going to the zoo." He sounded hesitant.

"I won't keep you," I said. "I'll just be a minute." I couldn't spare much more than a minute anyway; I needed to replenish my empty refrigerator and plan some family meals. There'd be Kitty as well as the Szekelys. All the same, I felt I had to find out how Joel had gotten Randy so quickly. It seemed the sort of thing that should have dragged on, with many hearings.

When we arrived at Joel's hotel, we met him and Randy in the lobby, just leaving. That was good, I thought. There were people around, guests coming and going, bellhops bringing in luggage. I didn't want to be found dead in a lonely hotel room.

Joel recognized me and admitted they'd given up waiting for us and decided to take off for the zoo. I apologized for being late and introduced my father-in-law. We all sat down, reluctantly and uneasily, on chairs grouped in a cluster in one corner. The small lobby was neat but not luxurious, clearly a businessman's headquarters.

I turned to the father-son pair and was struck again by their strong resemblance to one another. That odd twist of the chin, that showing off of the dimple—it had to be genetic. "You may not believe this, but I always felt sorry for Dorothea," I said. "She was treated shabbily. I want to be sure Randy's okay." I smiled at the wary, unsmiling man. To avoid arousing hostility, I said to Randy, "I guess you're lucky to have your dad here at this moment."

"I sure am," he agreed.

Joel relaxed a bit. "I was here for almost a month in the spring," he said. "It's taken a lot of time to convince the court I'm really Randy's dad. I couldn't locate our old landlady. I had to get Norma to swear I'd lived with Dorothea for years. God knows why—you can see to look at us we're related. The judge even sent someone to check out Gull's Nest. That's our resort in North Carolina."

"I guess you didn't approach Dorothea until all was settled then?"

"That's right, I didn't. No point in asking her for something the court wouldn't let me have. As it turned out, I should have contacted her sooner and given her time to get used to the idea of my having Randy. I thought she'd jump at the chance to get the kid out of foster care. Why would a mother want her child stuck living with strangers when his own dad was offering to raise him?"

"Mom always hoped to get me out of there," Randy said. "You'd think she'd have celebrated."

"She wanted you with her," I pointed out.

"But things never worked out. And poor Denny—his foster family wants to adopt him, and she wouldn't let that happen, either." Joel shook his head. "I can't figure her out. Those folks love Denny and are good to him. Just like me with Randy. What was her objection?"

This suspect wasn't panning out very well. Joel seemed not the violent type.

"Well, she planned to get married," I said. "I expect—"

"When *didn't* Mom plan to get married?" Randy burst out. "That's all I ever heard from her. 'One of these days, I'll get married and have a real home, and then you boys and I can be a family.' It never happened."

"Randy's whole childhood was spent waiting for that mythical marriage," Joel said. "My fault, too; I admit it." He put both hands on the chair arms and lifted himself up. "Well, if you people will excuse us, we ought to get going. The zoo closes around five, so we'll only have a couple of hours." He turned to Randy, who jumped up.

I nodded and thanked him for his time. After they left, Janos looked at me and shook his head. "An unlikely murderer," he said.

"I suppose so." All the same, I wanted to talk to the social worker. I called her from the phone booth in the hotel lobby. She seemed unforthcoming about why Randy had been released to his father. She said, "Well, we felt he had trauma enough in his life with that murder. He lived with his mother during his early years, so there had to be a strong bonding. It seemed a good idea for him to be with a blood relative at this time."

"Aren't you worried about the possibility the father could be the killer?"

"What, Mr. Fisk?" She chuckled. "My dear, Mr. Fisk was with the lawyer the morning Miss Granger was killed. He'd found a lawyer who specializes in custody cases, and the two of them breakfasted together and spent much of the morning head to head, seeking a loophole for him to gain custody. They only separated when they learned of the murder."

Reeling with shock and disappointment, I managed to thank her for the information and then hung up. I must have returned looking droopy and discouraged, as Janos asked what was wrong.

"We just lost our prime suspect." I flopped onto a chair beside him and put my hand to my forehead. "Joel Fisk spent that morning with a custody lawyer." I sprawled backward and sighed. "I'd been so sure we'd found our murderer. What do we do now?"

"We go after number two and three on our list." Janos patted my hand and added, "Cheer up, Jill. It's bad to lose Fisk as a suspect, but I'm relieved for Randy. What a terrible thing that would have been for the child—his mother dead, his father in prison for the murder."

"There's that," I admitted. "I guess that's the silver lining, saving Randy."

CHAPTER 24

Kitty Joins the Search

—1948

ON THE FOURTH MORNING, I received an urgent phone call from my father-in-law. He'd discovered, to his horror, that the tabloids had printed the Dorothea story in their usual juicy fashion, skewing the truth. In a shaky voice, he read me the sensational headline. "'Love Triangle Killing.' It gets worse, Jill." And he went on: "'She worked as a waitress, so her murder was relegated to the back pages of the newspapers. Hardly noted by anyone was the fact that she was about to marry into a family of wealth, her fiancé an oil man. Did a former lover of Dorothea Granger resurface to commit murder on the eve of her marriage to his rival? Police deny the rumors with suspicious vehemence.' There's a lot of nonsense about how Reggie owns oil wells—and that she was destined for high living after she married him. Zoltan proved wildly jealous, of course. He couldn't endure seeing her triumph. Not a word of truth in it. How can they be allowed to do this?"

"That's awful," I agreed. "How's Annie taking it?"

"I hardly need to tell you she's prostrate. The whole experience has been such a nightmare—and now this. Jill, I hate to ask it, but as you know, Kitty's on her way down here, and someone needs to meet the train. I know you planned to return to work this morning, but I can't leave Annie, and I wondered if you might meet her."

I promptly agreed to go. This was something new, my father-in-law actually requesting favors of me. It seemed good to finally be needed. I asked, "When does the train arrive?"

"Two hours and ten minutes from now," he said.

"I'll call the library and request another day or two off." I still had people to interview anyway.

Two hours later, I was in Grand Central awaiting the arrival of the train from Upstate New York. I wasn't sure just how Kitty would feel about having only me as her greeter; we'd never been the best of friends. That is, we weren't enemies, but more like rivals, with Annie always raving about how accomplished her daughter was, how academically gifted yet also proficient at those homemaking talents that eluded me, such as making her own clothing.

Kitty and her husband, Barry, lived in Troy, close to Schenectady, so I usually saw her when we visited Zoltan's folks. We never seemed to find much to say to each other. I admired the baby, Robin, now almost two, while Kitty smiled at my praise and claimed to love being a mother. That was about the extent of our common interests. Kitty usually went on to ask about her brother's progress on the piano, wanting to know how his most recent recital went. The conversation thereafter focused on Zoltan. Inevitably, when I left my husband, I pretty much cut off communication with my sister-in-law.

I was surprised when, lumbering toward me with a bulging stomach, she smiled warmly and held out her hand.

"Jill, how nice of you to come and meet me," she said.

I marveled at how Zoltan's arrest had changed the family dynamics. I do believe that was the first genuine smile Kitty ever offered me. It faded quickly when she looked around and realized that her parents were not with me.

"The folks okay?" she asked.

"They're upset about that tabloid article. You heard about it?"

"I was the one who told them about it. Barry saw the headline last night on his way home from swing shift and bought the paper. He woke me up to read it. It convinced me I needed to come here today and be with my mother; I felt sure she wouldn't take it well."

"No one could take that stuff well," I said.

"Not much I can do but hold her hand. Hopefully, that may help."

When I asked, "How is Robin?" she assured me he was chubby and happy. I inquired about her health. "I heard your pregnancy wasn't going well."

"I had a lot of spotting and worried about a miscarriage, but that seems to have ended now." She pointed to the baggage check. "I just brought one suitcase. I don't plan to stay long."

I got the suitcase and carried it for her. She suggested we stop off at a café and grab a late breakfast. "I left before dawn and didn't eat on the train. I've always suffered from motion sickness. Coming to America—I'll never forget that nightmare boat trip."

I suggested the Automat, but she chose a quieter spot with high-backed booths for privacy, a place that served breakfast all day. When we were settled, with cups of coffee in front of us and her eggs and toast on order, she said, "Barry and the folks didn't want me to take this trip at this time, but I had to know what's going on. So tell me the whole story. What's it all about?"

I related everything I knew. She frowned. "I just keep wondering why in hell—excuse my language, but it's needed in this situation—why in hell Tanni went to see the woman in the first place. I'd think she'd be the last person in the world he'd want to visit after all he went through with her. Father had to rescue him from her clutches, you know."

"Yes, I do know—and I know he didn't want to see her. Earlier, he refused to go with me. It's just that—"

"Just that he needed solace because you left him, I suppose." She sounded disgusted.

"No, it had to do with a child. Dorothea was raising a kid and claimed it was his. She said the abortion failed."

Kitty's mouth formed an astonished O. "Heavy. Poor Tanni, he must have felt trapped—again." She shook her head and bit her lip. "Even so, he should have stayed away and hired a lawyer to handle the situation."

"That would certainly have been best," I agreed. "But Zoltan hasn't a grain of cynicism in his makeup. It never occurs to him that people might dupe him. Apparently he never doubted the kid was his—though of course it was not."

"Thank God for that," she said fervently.

Her breakfast arrived, and she piled scrambled eggs on toast and took a bite. "Speaking of God, Jill, there's something I need to discuss with you."

I nodded; I suspected what it was. Her recent conversion to Catholicism had caused major distress in the family. Zoltan had been writing consoling letters to his parents about it.

Sure enough, she said, "I guess you know my folks are having kittens about the Catholicism business." When I nodded, she went on. "What is it with them, anyway? They've spent a lifetime trying to convince people we weren't Jewish. I have to call myself Kitty instead of Katya, and when asked my religion, I'm to say Presbyterian. Even my sorority sisters didn't know I was Jewish. They didn't accept Jews in my sorority at the time I joined. Yet now that I'm safely ensconced in the Catholic Church, you'd think I went in for devil worship for all the fuss they've made."

"I guess the conversion is really a sore point with them. Doesn't make sense, does it?"

"I'm supposed to remain Jewish forever but keep the fact hidden," she glumly remarked. Then, straightening up and lifting her chin, she added, "Well, the children have to be raised with something. Barry wants it to be Catholicism, and that's good enough for me. Barry's a good man who loves his family, and I love him. I never felt truly Presbyterian anyway. I wasn't told I was Jewish until I was six—and even then I didn't know what it meant."

"Stick to your guns," I said. I appreciated the fact that she confided all this to me. "I'll back you up if I'm needed."

"Thanks, Jill. It's good to talk to you."

She scooped the last of her eggs onto toast, an action that reminded me of her father. "I've hated to face the folks because of this tension, but it's got to be done, so I'd best finish this meal and get on with it."

"And then perhaps you can help with some interviewing," I said. "Your dad and I have been inquiring on our own. The cops don't seem open to alternate possibilities, so it looks like it'll be up to us to find the real killer."

"I'll do anything I can," Kitty said. "Zoltan's been stupid about Dorothea from the beginning, but I'm certain he's no murderer." She took a few more bites of her food and then said, "Let's get to it. What's this nonsense about a love triangle? Had Tanni agreed to go back to Dorothea?"

"Don't you believe it. That stuff's just media hype. Someone else is involved here." I listed off the other people I thought might have had motive for murder. Kitty listened carefully.

"Could the youngster's mom have killed Dorothea?" she asked. "I mean, maybe Dorothea refused to return the child. Well, after all, she *was* using the kid to manipulate Tanni, so it's logical she'd hang onto him and drive the mother to commit murder."

"Good thought. Unfortunately, Marcello's mom has the world's best alibi. She's in the hospital, recovering from an operation. Wasn't even able to get out of bed that first day, let alone sneak home and commit a murder."

Kitty winced. "Too bad. So how about this guy who was marrying Dorothea? Isn't it generally the fiancé or husband who does the killing?"

"He's our last hope." I agreed I needed to talk to him. "Keep your fingers crossed that he has no cast-iron alibi. There's an aunt who was pretty frustrated with Dorothea, but frustration is hardly a motive for murder. I'd hate to try to prove her guilty. She's a possibility, of course, but a remote one."

"Unless the frustration has been ongoing," Kitty ventured. "There may have been something in the past. Does anyone know anything about Dorothea's family?"

"Just a few basic details, but nothing that would drive someone to commit murder. For the most part, Dorothea'd lost touch with her relatives."

"Still sounds like a good spot to check out. If there's anger, estrangement, hard feelings, maybe one family member finally blew his stack and eliminated her."

"How in the world would we investigate? We'd have to go to Pennsylvania and look them up—and then figure out how to get them to talk to us." I shook my head in despair; I'd already thought about this and dismissed it as impossible.

"Could some crazy man just sneak in off the street and kill her?"

I admitted that that sort of random killing could happen in New York and no one would be the wiser. "I wouldn't know how to look into that kind of murder. That takes police expertise." I sighed. "Poor Zoltan. For his sake, I hope we can find a hint of something less senseless."

Kitty finished her breakfast and insisted on paying for my coffee. I took the suitcase, and we made our way to the IRT.

As we stood waiting on the platform for the northbound express, we became aware of a commotion behind us and swung around. A short, portly, balding man hurried toward us, waving frantically and frowning. "You!" he shouted. "You, Jill Szekely, you wait there. I have a bone to pick with you." He charged up to us, his face contorted in an expression of fury. "Were you the one who told the reporters all those horrible things about my poor darling Dorothea?"

It was Reggie Jackson. I instinctively flung hand to face and tried to calm him. "I told the reporters nothing, not one word, Mr. Jackson."

The man didn't soften his glare. He stood like a banty rooster, confronting us as if he meant to take us both on for a fight. Short as he was, he managed to appear threatening; he seemed ready to push us off the platform in front of an oncoming train. I grasped Kitty's arm to protect her. In her present state, she was both awkward and vulnerable. She hitched her purse up to her shoulder, backed up against a post, and locked her hands around it. I grasped the suitcase, ready to thrust it at Jackson if he came any closer.

The man ranted on. "You damn well must have told them something. Dorothea was a good Christian woman, and she didn't have children out of wedlock or ... or pretend to be the mother of children who weren't hers. And she wouldn't have sent for a former lover. None of that newspaper poppycock is true. Furthermore, I'd like to know who put my name in the papers without my authorization. Love triangle, indeed!"

"I wouldn't know about that, Mr. Jackson," I said. "I only know that my husband has been arrested for a crime he didn't commit."

"What makes you so sure about that?" Reginald Jackson demanded. "Were you a witness?"

"No, but, as I understand it, neither were you." I gathered my courage and asked, "Where were you the day she was murdered?"

"Me? You're accusing me?" he almost screamed. "I was at work at the post office, where I belong. If your husband had been at a job, there'd have been no murder." The banty rooster puffed up and tilted his chin even higher. Then he abruptly collapsed into the little man he was, as if all muscles had given way at once. A tragic expression replaced the anger on his face. "We'd have been married yesterday, Dot and I. We'd be honeymooning at Niagara now."

"I'm very sorry about that, but I'm sure my spouse had no role in it." I took Kitty's arm to guide her as the train rolled in. We stepped aboard quickly, and I was relieved to see the door shut behind us. The train started up, leaving Jackson on the platform, still frowning at us.

Kitty let out a sigh of relief. "I thought he was going to push us in front of the train."

"I planned to bash him with the suitcase if he tried anything," I said.

"What's this 'good Christian woman' stuff? Who'd describe Dorothea that way?"

I couldn't answer that, but I reminded her, "Unfortunately, we've just lost our last viable suspect. He was at work, or so he says."

"God, you're right. I hadn't thought of that."

I confessed, "I hardly know where else to look. There's only Aunt Belle, and she's a long shot. I could quiz Norma again and see if she can think of anyone else in Dorothea's past. Maybe you could come with me, Kitty. Two heads are better than one. You might pick up a clue."

"A murder investigation," Kitty said, "will be a breeze compared to dealing with my mother about the Catholicism business."

When we arrived at the Manhattan Avenue apartment, Annie waited in the kitchen, ready with sandwiches and lemonade she'd prepared for us. Kitty nervously confessed that she'd just stopped for a late breakfast. Annie said the sandwiches would keep and then gave Kitty a hug and a kiss.

"How are you, Mom?"

"I'm bearing up, in spite of that awful tabloid."

As mother and daughter struggled to move past the awkwardness of not knowing what to expect from the other, I jumped into the tale of our scary encounter with Reggie. Annie gasped and said, "You girls shouldn't wander around town alone without Janos. Anything could happen. Tempers are out of control."

Nothing was said about the conversion to Catholicism. I wondered if possibly the folks had come to terms with it. Perhaps Kitty worried for nothing.

"The police have released Dorothea's body, and it's to be buried tomorrow," Annie said. "There'll be graveside services."

"I think Kitty and I should go," I said. "We're on the hunt for suspects, and maybe we'll spot someone there."

Annie and Kitty agreed that it was a good idea.

"We'll finally get to meet Marcello's real mom," I added. "I hear she's to be released from the hospital tomorrow. She may be able to tell us something we don't know about Dorothea's life. They lived together during the war."

"Let's hope so," Annie replied. "We need to learn something helpful to get Tanni out of that jail. His fingers will stiffen if he can't practice."

Kitty made a face, and I could guess her thought. Her mother was still focused on music, still fancying her Zoltan destined for a great concert career. I wondered myself if she would ever face reality about that. I'd become convinced Frieda was right, that even assuming Tanni had the talent to be a world-class pianist, the times weren't serendipitous for creating young Mozarts. There was enormous competition, with most famous European musicians now living in New York.

"I think I'll give Norma a call and see if we can talk to her again this afternoon," I said. "We really need to find a better suspect. I was so sure the murder had to be done by either Joel Fisk or Reggie Jackson, but alibis are coming at us thick and fast."

"Unless those guys hired someone else to do the job," Kitty said. "And how would we ever prove that?"

"I guess we dig in and learn to be private investigators," I said.

CHAPTER 25

◦○◦

Annie's World Crumbles

—1948

Annie's memoirs:

While Kitty napped and Jill and Janos sat in the kitchen going over the list of suspects, I lay on the living room couch, staring at the ceiling and pondering the question likely asked by distraught mothers since the beginning of time: what did I do wrong?

How do you raise a gifted child? How do you keep up with the constant curiosity, the nonstop demands for learning, practicing, growing? How much attention is enough, and how much is too much? At what point do you become a hovering mother? I'd struggled with those questions for eighteen years until Tanni went off to Juilliard—and I thought that even with the added complications of emigrating from Hungary, I'd handled things well. Yet since he left home, Tanni has faced nothing but chaos in his life.

Worse, there's now a distancing between Kitty and me—not to mention a chasm between myself and a daughter-in-law who may or may not still count herself member of the family.

I'm well aware that Kitty felt left out all those years in which my focus had been on my musician son, and that her flight to Barry Flannigan's family and Catholicism represented a search for belonging. I watched with heartbreak as my daughter plunged deeper and deeper into that world so alien to me, the world of Irish Catholicism. Not even sensing the vast gap she'd bridged, Kitty once quipped, "I'm not Abie's Irish rose, so I must be Barry's Jewish thorn." It broke my heart.

But what could I have done? At age four, Zoltan began giving recitals. At five, he toured towns in Austria and Hungary playing two-piano pieces with his pregnant mother. At eight, he was one of three gifted children, the others a violinist and a cellist, chosen to perform with the Budapest Symphony Orchestra. Three-year-old Kitty had to be left with Grandmama while I took Zoltan to rehearsals. Afterward, for months, the three musically gifted children played trios together around town and had to be escorted to practice sessions and performances. Kitty was literally raised by Grandmama, next door while I hovered over my son, guiding him in music, trying to hold him back from playing pieces far ahead of his age range or helping him finish his homework quickly so he could return to his beloved piano.

That all ended as the pogroms escalated, one occurring right in the neighborhood where we lived. We hid behind boxes in the attic. The government did nothing about it except restrict the activities of the Jews under the fiction of keeping us safe. Suddenly, the children were taken out of their school and sent to a synagogue school. Zoltan was denied, allegedly for his own safety, the privilege of performing in public. We were ordered to wear armbands. Kitty had only just started first grade three months before, and already she had won a prize for her linguistic abilities. Even that wasn't enough to keep her in her school. When we applied to emigrate to America, we learned we were on a long wait list and it would be as much as four or five years before our name came up.

Janos appealed to the New York cousins to find a way. Nadya and Lazlo dutifully took action. They found Janos a job with a New York firm developing television. They convinced the employer to request Jan's immediate presence. It worked. Our family moved to the head of the immigrant list, and all went well—until that moment of terror on arrival at Ellis Island, when Kitty refused to speak to the inspector.

Looking back, I know very well why that incident happened. Kitty had bonded to Grandmama and didn't want to leave her. She'd cried a lot on the voyage and dramatized her seasickness as worse than it was. With no real grasp of the horrors developing in her homeland, she didn't understand why she'd been snatched from her beloved caregiver and brought to a strange land where she had no grandmother on her side in her competition with her brother. She pleaded to go home.

The rift never truly healed, as I found no way to express what I needed to say: "I'm sorry I didn't know how to do what I had to do, raise two very different children and give each one all the attention needed. I kept trying to figure it out. Perhaps I was wrong to focus so much on Tanni; perhaps I failed you both."

How can I say it now, with Kitty an adult with a family of her own? There seems no way. And so we skirt all the issues between us and talk of how Tanni is holding up, of how this situation is affecting him. And all the while I worry, recalling the coolness of the hug Kitty gave me on arrival and the memory of the warmth she'd shown toward her mother-in-law, Bridey Flannigan, at her wedding, as if she'd come home at last to Grandmama.

It's just one more anxiety to add to my growing burden of problems with my children and my terror about what's to happen to my son.

CHAPTER 26

Norma Tries to Help

—*1948*

WHILE WE ATE SANDWICHES AND sipped lemonade, Janos and I brought Kitty up to date on the investigation. Kitty said, "Reggie Jackson just has to be guilty. I mean, why attack us otherwise? You attack others in order to cover your own guilt, right?"

We heard Annie coming down the hall. In the doorway she paused to ask, "Is his alibi unbreakable? Has anyone checked to see if he was really at work that day?"

"I'm sure the police would have done that," Janos said. "No, I think we have to look elsewhere. Much as I'd like for Jackson to be guilty, I fear he wouldn't claim an alibi like that if it weren't true."

"He was like a strutting rooster standing on that platform," I said. "Like a stage figure. He was frightening, and yet I wanted to giggle."

"'Beware the Jubjub bird, and shun the frumious Bandersnatch,'" Kitty quoted.

I nodded. "Reggie Jackson's a Bandersnatch if ever I saw one."

Kitty managed a wispy smile. "I see you read my favorite author, Jill. Tanni and I used to quote Lewis Carroll by the hour."

Annie poured herself lemonade and sat down. I talked about the séance. "I feel as if there was something there I should have noticed. I keep going over it in my mind. It was a perfect gathering of suspects."

The doorbell rang. I stood and called through the speaker, "Who is it?"

The tube sputtered, "Norma Ray."

Surprised, I pressed the buzzer and then went to the door and waited. When Norma stepped off the elevator, she said, "I'm relieved to find you at home, Jill."

I led her into the kitchen and made the introductions. "My in-laws, Mr. and Mrs. Szekely, and my sister-in-law, Kitty. This is Norma Ray, Dorothea's friend."

"I've been hoping to talk to you about the séance," Norma said to me. "I thought I'd run over for a few minutes while everything is quiet at the restaurant. But if you're busy—"

"No, we were just discussing the murder. Please do join us. I'll get a chair from the living room."

"I'll get it." Janos stood. "You take mine, Miss Ray."

"I don't want to interrupt your lunch," Norma protested.

"No problem," I said. "Have you eaten? We have extra sandwiches."

"I grabbed a bite before I left."

I poured her a glass of lemonade. Our guest sipped it and looked around the table. "I read that awful article in the tabloid this morning, and I want you to know there's not a word of truth in it. Zoltan never cared enough about Dorothea to kill her out of jealousy. I roomed in a shared apartment with the couple, back when they were breaking up, and it was clear to all of us that Zoltan wasn't in love with Dorothea. He even confessed as much to me. I recall clearly what he said: 'It's hard for a man to tell a woman he loves her, but it's almost impossible to tell her he *doesn't*. I lie awake nights thinking how to confess to Dorothea that I want to leave her.' I remember trying to help him find a way to break the news. I even tried to tip Dotty off in advance by pointing out that Zoltan showed no signs of being a man in love. Poor Dot was just so lost in her dream world you couldn't get through to her. She'd deny every word; she'd describe some thoughtful gesture of his to prove he really cared."

"What about that trick, her pretending the child Marcello was hers?" Janos asked. "You do know she lied about that?"

"Unfortunately, I was out of town when Marce was born," Norma said. "I'd gone home to take care of a dying father. When I returned eight months later, there was the baby in Dot's arms, and she insisted the abortion didn't work. Yet I always doubted Marcie really belonged to her. She didn't seem attached to him the way she was to Randy and Denny. I mean, she lived and breathed to get back custody of those two boys, while around Marcie she was only dutiful. As for Marce being Zoltan's—utterly unbelievable. There's nothing of Zoltan about him."

"We finally got the girl Leila to admit that Mrs. Falucci was the kid's mother," Janos said. "But keep that under your hat. We promised Leila we wouldn't let word get around in the Village."

"I always suspected it," Norma admitted. "Dorothea used to say, 'There's a secret I have to tell you about Marcie, but I can't tell you yet.' She was very mysterious about him. She kept promising, 'Someday I'll reveal all.'"

"She certainly gave Zoltan a scare. Not enough to turn him into a killer, though. I doubt anything could do that." Janos sounded positive on that score.

Norma swallowed more lemonade and glanced at her watch. "I really have to get back to the restaurant. I just wanted to let you know I'm willing to help any way I can. I hate to see Zoltan in a pickle like this, and I doubt Dorothea would have wanted it—at least not if she knew the truth."

"What do you believe the truth is?" Annie asked. "Who do you think really killed her?"

Norma frowned. "I wish I knew. The problem is, she was what the guys call a tease—when she was between lovers, that is. She put on an act of being available, but actually she wasn't free and easy at all. She remained faithful to her lovers while she was with them, and fussy about whom she'd sleep with between times. She had to be wildly attracted before she'd let the man into her bed. But she flirted—to widen the playing field, as she used to put it. She called it finding that rare jewel in the sand. 'To do that,' she claimed, 'you have to spend a lot of time in the sand.' I warned her it was a dangerous game to play. Men don't like to be manipulated in that way."

She spilled a few drops of lemonade on the table and ran her finger through the wet spot, idly drawing faces with the liquid while she talked about her friend. "She was planning to bite the bullet and marry Reggie so she could have a home and get her children back, but it wasn't an easy decision for her. She kept saying it would be the first time she ever slept with a man she felt no passion for, and she didn't know if she could bring herself to face a lifetime of it."

"So you think Reggie learned about that? But he claims he was working at the post office when she—"

"More likely there may have been some other rejected guy that we don't know about. Some guy who didn't put up with her tease game." Norma swallowed the last of her lemonade and stood up. "I really have to run. I just wanted to tell you. I hope I haven't said anything that sounds like a putdown of Dotty. I don't mean to criticize. She was a good soul, just not the smartest person about men. There was that accusation she made against Zoltan at the séance—but of course she didn't know the truth."

In the face of that comment, Janos managed somehow to keep a straight face. "We'll keep in mind what you said," he told her. "Thank you so much for coming."

"Thanks for the lemonade." She waved farewell and left the apartment.

"Well! What do you think about that?" Janos asked.

"I think we have to go looking for another suspect, and we haven't a clue where to look," I said.

Janos agreed. "That certainly seems to be the case."

"I'd like to go and walk around the Village," Kitty said. "Just to get a sense of Dorothea's life. Maybe something will occur to me."

I nodded. "Good plan. We could visit Mama Falucci's and maybe drop in again at the restaurant where Dorothea worked. And there's Belle to talk to. I'll give her a call."

"Won't we see her tomorrow at the funeral?" Kitty asked.

"Probably, but that's not a great time for an interview. Better to drop by her place after she gets out of work tonight. We need to learn more about Dorothea's family." I searched my purse for the number and went to the hall phone to call. I came back to report that Belle would be available at six. "She lives near Columbus Circle—that's on our way. We could bring home Chinese takeout for dinner afterward."

"We'll get the Chinese takeout," Annie said. "You two concentrate on the interviews. And be careful! Watch your step."

I turned to Kitty. "Shall we go, then?"

Annie shoved her chair back and spoke up. "I want to thank you girls for all you're doing. I know how much it means to Zoltan, too—but I'll let him speak for himself when he's free and available. For myself, I doubt I could have survived all this if I hadn't had you two helping out."

Kitty got up and went to hug her mother. "It's okay, Mom, we're family. We want to help."

Annie hugged back. "Do take care of yourself, dear. You, too, Jill. Don't let weird characters accost you in the subway."

"We'll ride the bus if that'll make you feel better," I said. "On surface roads it's easier to call for help."

"Good plan." Annie got up and hugged me, too, a genuine clasp and not the pallid, token hug she'd always before offered. "I can't thank you enough, Jill, for all you're doing. I haven't been fair to you, I can see that. I used to think you couldn't possibly understand our problems, our lives—you couldn't know what we Jews have been through. I believe I was wrong about that."

"I doubt if anyone fully knows what the other guy has been through," I said, "but I can at least sympathize." I returned the hug. "I'll do what I can, Mother Annie."

CHAPTER 27

The Search for a Mystery Man

—1948

I'd NEVER IMAGINED ANNIE COULD change so much. I'd assumed the wall she'd built against me was airtight for a lifetime. I was gratified to see the barrier crash down. Too bad it couldn't have happened under happier circumstances. Just a year before, I'd have welcomed it as a wondrous improvement, but now, having arranged another life for myself with studies in Michigan, I feared it was too little, too late. I choked up at her sudden warmth and, on leaving the apartment, wiped away a furtive tear. Why, I wondered, do people wait too long to learn to care for one another? I'd felt a high regard for Annie when I first climbed off the bus in Kentucky; I'd longed for her response. Yet it had taken her all this time to finally return the feeling.

Kitty and I kept our promise and rode the bus downtown. Slower than the subway, it was scenic, a good way to see the town, especially from the upper deck, where we made our way to the front.

Seated beside me, Kitty talked about her distress in turning her child over to her sister-in-law. "Robin seemed happy when he toddled off to play with his cousins, but I felt weepy. It's my first trip without him. I try not to farm him out to sitters because you never know what will happen. I was farmed out to Grandmama while Mother worked with Tanni. The two of them were always at the piano together or going to his recitals and rehearsals. I made Grandmama my special person and then, when we came to America, had to part with her. It was terrible, wrenching. I rebelled. I expect you heard how I almost prevented the family from getting into this country."

"Your mom told me the story," I said.

"I don't want Robin to bond that way to Barry's mother or sister."

I assured Kitty I understood her dilemma. "I envy you; I hope to have a child, too, someday."

"You, Jill?" Kitty looked at me in surprise. "I thought you were the ultimate career woman."

"I'd like to be both." I confessed I hadn't dared to suggest to Zoltan that I get pregnant, since I needed my job and couldn't stay home to care for a baby. "It must be terribly hard to turn a child over to strangers to raise. You at least have relatives handy. I don't, unfortunately."

"Is that why you and Zoltan separated?" Kitty asked. "I wondered."

"That's the main reason. He claims it will be years before he can develop his concert career, and I don't have years. Doc says it's now or never."

Kitty winced. "That's rough, Jill. Zoltan feels he has to please our parents because they put their own lives aside for us—for him. Especially Mom. As I've said, she devoted her life to his career. He can't seem to pull himself out of guilt mode and organize his world realistically for his own future."

"That's what my housemate, Frieda Fishbein, claims."

"Maybe this disaster will be a wakeup call for him," Kitty speculated. "I hate to see you two break up."

I said, "Yes, maybe," but privately I felt I didn't want to be in the position of having sabotaged that great musical career. *Let Zoltan go on pursuing his dream of concert work, and let me start looking for a man ready to be a father now.* It seemed the sensible thing to do.

When we arrived in the Village, we walked along Fourteenth Street until we came to Mama Falucci's. Kitty peered in the window. When we'd passed, she hesitated, turned back, and said, "Let's go in. I'm curious."

I feared becoming conspicuous at this moment when we ought to keep a low profile. "What excuse will we use? Shouldn't we be looking for something?" Just as I noticed the banner under the shop name—*Everything you need for Italian cooking*—Kitty said, "How about a cookbook? I love Italian. I could use recipes."

I nodded. We entered a dark, hole-in-the-wall shop smelling of garlic and spices. Bunches of garlic hung from the ceiling, and wheels of cheese and lengths of sausage filled the display cases. The walls were lined with jars of olives, varieties of mustard, and sauces. Offhand, I saw no cookbooks. There was little room to move about, as there were already two groups of customers ahead of us. A short, chubby, thirty-something woman with dark hair in a bun waited on a pair of them. Another chubby woman leaned on the counter awaiting a turn, while her thin, white-haired companion turned away to explore the jars on the wall. I watched her take them down, read labels, and replace them. Kitty and I stood behind the waiting customer, who moved along the counter when her predecessors left. The plump woman smiled at us and said, "I'll be with you in a minute."

It was an interesting shop, and we had no trouble entertaining ourselves studying the merchandise. Besides mozzarella, there were cheeses I'd never heard of: pecorino romano, grana padano, parmigiano reggiano. There were pizza sauces, spaghetti sauces, parmigiana sauces, Alfredo sauces. Kitty pulled a jar of spaghetti sauce off the shelf and declared she meant to give Italian cooking her best shot.

We had a lengthy wait as customer number two proved uncertain what to buy. She consulted with the salesperson, who seemed knowledgeable about the proper ingredients for all sorts of exotic dishes. When finally the customer left and our turn came, the plump woman apologized. "Sorry for the long wait. I'm here by myself. It's ironic, this is the first time in the whole eight years I've worked here that I've had to run the shop alone—and wouldn't you know, we've tripled our volume of sales the last few days. There's nothing like getting mentioned in the newspaper for luring in customers."

"Oh, did you get mentioned in the newspaper?" Kitty played ignorant as she handed over the sauce. "I didn't know."

"You must be from out of town," the woman said.

"Just came down this morning from Upstate New York," Kitty said.

"I expect you haven't heard about the murder, then, at the boss's house. She wasn't involved, luckily. She was in the hospital having an operation—thank God for that. She's had a hard life, poor woman. Her husband went to prison soon after she opened this shop. She manages the business all on her own, with very little help from that snip of a kid she raised as a single mom. She doesn't need to be a suspect in a murder."

"So her name got in the paper and brought everyone rushing to her shop out of curiosity?"

"Precisely. I've been deluged."

"Is there no other help besides you?" I asked. It seemed odd that this woman should claim that she never before, in eight years, ran the shop by herself. What about that time five years ago, when Mama Falucci stayed at home hiding her pregnancy from the neighbors? Leila was only a kid then, so this woman must have been alone here. I almost blurted out the question but stifled it at the last minute, remembering my promise to Leila not to mention the subject in the Village.

The woman conceded, "There's her daughter, Leila. She helped out after she graduated high school. Just lately she's been busy minding the child and visiting the hospital. The dead woman had a child, you see."

"Oh, how sad." I quickly computed the passing years. Leila would have been thirteen when Marcello was born—old enough for babysitting, but not much help in the shop.

"Yes, indeed, a tragic situation—and rough on me. I've been run off my feet."

"Couldn't they call back some former employee temporarily?"

"There is no former employee. We three have run the shop between us ever since it opened."

"Did you know the dead woman well?"

She shook her head. "I've talked to her, of course. She worked nearby and used to drop in here occasionally. She had that kid to look after when she wasn't at her own job."

"Then you don't know anything about her private life or her men friends?"

"Oh, she had men friends. They came in with her sometimes. But I never talked to any of them, not even her fiancé. She was about to be married."

Another customer entered the shop at that moment, effectively ending the conversation. Kitty asked for a cookbook, and when one was produced from behind the counter, she paid and we left. I confessed as we walked on, "I'm puzzled. Leila said there was a three-month period when her mother stayed in the house to hide her pregnancy from neighbors, and yet the shop assistant denies she ever ran the place by herself. Someone's lying."

"She may have forgotten," Kitty speculated. "Right now she's dramatizing her situation."

"Yes, that may be it." But it seemed strange the two stories didn't jibe. I frowned as I pondered it, remembering Leila's insistence that her mother had remained imprisoned at home for three months to hide her pregnancy. It was a very different story from the one we just heard.

We walked on along my favorite shopping street, its fascinating boutiques featuring everything from handmade jewelry to custom pottery—one shop even featured a potter in the window. People had gathered to watch as the woman worked, spinning the wheel and forming shapeless clay into graceful pot. We paused and then moved on.

After peering at window displays and admiring artistic creations, we soon came to Mario's, the restaurant where Dorothea had worked. I pointed it out to Kitty.

On entering, we sniffed the same Italian fragrances we'd noticed in Mama Falucci's shop. I commented that I could distinguish an Italian, a Mexican, or even a Hungarian restaurant by its smell alone. "If someone were to lead me, blindfolded, into any one of those, I could name its nationality—just as I could pinpoint an Indian restaurant by its strong smell of curry. But not," I added, puzzling over the fact, "a French or a Russian restaurant. Those seem less identifiable by aroma."

"I can only be certain of fish places," Kitty admitted. "Well, maybe Hungarian—I never tried, but I suppose I could manage."

I saw Janet and waved to her. Today she'd opted for an upsweep instead of a French twist, and had piled all her hair forward on her head so that it ballooned upward from her forehead and made her look taller. When I slid into a booth facing the machines, pinball and iron claw, she came over and smiled at us. She reached out a hand to touch Kitty's elbow and assist her into the booth. "Hi, there. It's the lady private investigator, right? And—"

"And sister-in-law," I said. "Mrs. Kitty Flannigan."

"Have you made any progress with your inquiries?"

"Still working on it," I said. "Do you have a minute, Janet?"

"Just about." She glanced at her watch. "We'll need to get ready for dinner, so it can't be much more than a minute. Shall I get us Cokes?"

"Sounds good," I said.

"Vernors ginger ale for me if you have it," Kitty said. "I'm supposed to avoid caffeine."

Janet soon returned with two Coca-Colas and a Vernors and slid into our booth. "So what can I tell you? Not that I know anything."

"You can tell me about Dorothea," I said. "We're looking for someone who had it in for her."

"I can't think of a soul," Janet said. "We all liked her, all of the staff."

"And the customers?"

"Customers, too. She even had special ones who always asked for her."

"How'd she act with the men? Was she flirty?"

Janet drew three straws from her uniform pocket, tossed two on the table, and tore the paper from the third. She jabbed it her into her glass. While we reached for ours and unwrapped them, she stirred thoughtfully and gazed down as if into a crystal ball. "Truth is we're all flirty with our regular customers. You know—it passes the time—you kid around. 'What're you up to these days, Joe Blow? Keeping out of trouble?' They come back at you: 'Why would I want to keep out of trouble? That'd be boring as hell.' Then they grab your arm and say, 'Trouble would be great fun if I could have it with you, baby. How about it? Shall we make trouble together?' You break loose and say, 'Joe Blow, quit your kidding. You don't need me, you're rolling in girlfriends.' He says, 'I can always use one more.' It's back and forth. 'Forget it; you wouldn't know what to do with another one.' 'Hell, I grant you this is my busy season with the women.' Then the punch line: 'Come on, stud, all your seasons are busy seasons. Admit it, Joe Blow.' Everyone laughs and no one takes it seriously."

"Dorothea did a lot of that sort of kidding around?"

"Sure. We all do—with the guys we know, the regulars who eat here every day."

"But what if one person *did* take it seriously? What if one guy believed he really had a girlfriend? And then he came in one day and learned of her planned marriage and felt betrayed?"

"Ooh, I don't know. I hadn't thought of it. I suppose it could happen. I remember there was a guy who won a silver compact out of that claw machine back there in the corner. He kept feeding in dimes by the fistful until the claw finally picked up the compact. He polished the thing on his sleeve and presented it to Dorothea, very solemn and formal. It had a powder compartment, rouge compartment, eye shadow, the works. He made a ceremony of presenting it. She tried to refuse it—management doesn't like us to accept gifts—but he insisted and wouldn't leave until he'd handed it over. It was kind of creepy. I suppose that type might take you seriously—and then if he heard that Dotty was to be married, he'd freak."

"Do you recall who he is?"

"No, as far as I know, he hasn't been in since her engagement was announced. He may have got his nose out of joint. I have no idea where you'd find him."

I wrote down my phone number and gave it to Janet. "If he comes in, would you let me know?"

"Sure thing. I'll even try to find out his name."

I remembered Norma's comment that Dorothea was playing a dangerous teasing game. "If you think of any other men who might have grown serious about her, let me know of them, too." As she nodded, I added, "Kitty and I both have reason to believe the man who's now in custody isn't guilty—and so someone else must be, and we need to follow up every lead."

"I'll keep an eye out for the guy," Janet promised.

We left shortly after and wandered through the boutiques killing time. Kitty soon complained of weariness, so I suggested we go to my apartment and rest up until it was time for our interview with Belle. When I warned Kitty that she'd have to cope with a fourth-floor walk-up, she suggested we sit in the park instead. Washington Square was close by. We wandered over and located an empty bench with no students perched on it. All around us on benches and on the grass, people bent over books. With NYU close by, the park tended to double as a college campus.

Kitty sighed as she sat and slid her feet out of her shoes. I noticed her ankles were swollen, and asked. "Are you okay?"

"I guess so. Doc says exercise is good for me."

We relaxed and watched people—walking their dogs, heading for the subway, carrying armloads of books. The Greenwich Village women were easily distinguished, as they all wore "new look" outfits, with tight skirts to their ankles, while students still sported the standard coed garb—sweaters with knee-length skirts. Kitty remarked that the minute the new baby arrived, she meant to upgrade her wardrobe with new look outfits. She studied me curiously and asked, "So tell me, Jill—is it over? Are you finished with my brother?"

"I'm afraid so," I said. "It's not that I don't love him, Kitty, or that I haven't been happy listening to his music—actually I had fun holding those musical salons. But there's no future in it for me. I can't get on with my social work studies, and we can't have children. His income doesn't promise to be good enough, not for years to come. I feel dead-ended."

"It's not easy being part of a gifted family like mine," Kitty said. "Mom has expectations for me, too, and I've let her down. She expected I'd go on to get my PhD and become a professor of languages—but I only want to stay home and raise children. Mom just can't take it in that anyone in our family would actually choose to be a housewife or marry a factory worker like Barry."

"I admire your courage in going your own way," I told her. "I wish Zoltan were like you."

Kitty sighed. "Zoltan bears the heavy burden of Mother's devotion. When I think of my childhood, what comes to mind is a picture of Mother and Tanni at the piano together, with me wondering how I'd ever manage to break into that tight twosome."

"I can't break in either. I know his music means everything to her— and to your dad. I just can't figure out how to have a life for myself in the situation."

She turned to study my face. "Have you found someone else?"

"Not yet. My immediate plan is to finish work on my master's and find a job. After that, I'll worry about meeting guys."

I checked the time. It was five thirty. "We should get started. The buses will be crowded at this hour, and it may take time to get to Columbus Circle."

She nodded and replaced her shoes. I carried her package for her. We wandered to the bus stop and saw that, sure enough, there was a line. We had to let one bus go without us. It worked out well, however, as we were first in line to get on the next one, and had no trouble finding a seat for Kitty. I stood in the aisle and grasped the overhead strap for the ride to Columbus Circle.

Even with many stops along the way, by five minutes of six, we'd left the bus and located Belle's apartment building. We debated over whether it would be gauche to arrive early. Since this wasn't a formal visit, we decided it didn't matter, and I rang the bell. Buzzed in, we rode the elevator to the seventh floor. In the upper hall, Belle poked her head out of her apartment looking for us.

"Down here," she called. "I'm in the corner."

We entered a light, pleasant apartment with a picture window. The late sun slanted across a large living room. I introduced Kitty, and Belle ushered us to the couch.

As before, Belle brought to my mind an ad for a baked good or something sweet. When I looked at her, I couldn't imagine her as a killer. Dorothea's aunt could serve as the prototype for aunts everywhere. She seemed the epitome of auntness. I'd put her on the suspect list only because she was a member of a family that rejected Dorothea and her lifestyle.

Belle offered coffee. "I don't have it ready, as I just got home from work about ten minutes ago. Wouldn't take me long to make some."

"We stopped for drinks at Mario's." Trying not to sound too curious, I asked, "Where do you work, Belle?"

"I'm the office girl at the dental clinic down the street. I do appointments, billing, bookkeeping, that sort of thing. It generally means a good deal of overtime—that's how I manage to afford this classy apartment. Luckily, today I got off at five thirty, the time I'm supposed to be free. That's rare; I'm usually stuck with some last-minute customer with an emergency."

"I don't suppose you get much time off?"

"We close the office for two weeks a year for summer vacation—that's in August—but otherwise we keep going."

There went my third suspect. She was at work. I shuffled my feet on the thick carpet and wondered what else I could ask her. She'd already stated that she saw little of her niece, so presumably she wouldn't know anything about the mysterious iron claw man.

"So you're still hot on the trail?" She smiled. "The séance didn't convince you?"

"I'm not much of a believer in that kind of stuff," I confessed.

"Neither am I. Madame Aya puts on a good show, but when you look back on it, it seems all smoke and mirrors."

"We're trying to find out more about Dorothea's life," Kitty said.

"I doubt I'm the one to tell you." Improbably, Belle lit a cigarette. I'd have pinpointed her as the last person in the world to be a smoker. I watched the smoke from her mouth and nose curl above her head and drift toward the kitchen. "She and I weren't close. I felt sorry for her because her mother rejected her. I don't hold with that sort of thing. You bring a child into this world, you're responsible for it. But I couldn't change her mind; I'm an in-law."

I couldn't think how to ask my question subtly, so I blurted it out. "Could her mother or any other relative have hated her enough to kill her? What about that stepdad?"

Belle shrugged. "He'd bear investigating, I suppose. Who knows what a guy like that could do. The man's always pawing some woman. But hell, he lives in Pennsylvania."

"Pennsylvania's not that far away."

Belle shrugged. "Why now, after all these years?"

"Well, she was planning to marry. He might have resented it."

"It seems doubtful, but I can't say it's impossible. He's such a crumb. I'll give you their address if you like, and you can go there and ask if he's been out of town lately—just don't involve me." She jotted an address on a piece of paper and handed it over. I popped it in my purse, thanked her, and sought a different line of questioning. I agreed with her that the stepfather seemed an unlikely suspect—a long shot.

"I understand Dorothea had her children taken away because she hired an eight-year-old baby-sitter," I said.

"That's right. Eight or nine."

"What I'm wondering is, couldn't she have gone on welfare and stayed home, so she could get custody?"

Belle shrugged. "Probably she could if she'd wanted to. But that would have forever ended all hope of contact with her mother. The woman's view of welfare recipients is so low it can't even be put into polite language."

"So Dorothea believed that in marrying Reggie Jackson, she'd create a family that her mother would accept?"

"That was the idea. She wasn't in love with Reggie. Her problem was she never seemed to fall in love with the marrying kind of men." She sighed. "I guess that's pretty universal among women. It's my problem, too. I was always attracted to lovable rogues."

Me, too, I thought—though I couldn't quite define Zoltan as a lovable rogue, just a lovable nonpartner.

Belle went on to talk of Dorothea's problems with men. She added nothing to my knowledge. I asked if she recalled Dorothea mentioning an admirer who'd recently given her a silver compact at her workplace. Belle shook her head. "But of course she wouldn't have told me because I'd have yelled at her. I tended to lose patience with her insistence that she be wildly attracted to the men she slept with. A woman has to settle for something less than perfection when she has children. Not every man is eager to take on a ready-made family."

I stood and told her I needed to get my sister-in-law home. "I'm sure you're anxious to prepare your dinner after a long day at work."

Belle thanked us for stopping by. We promised to see her at the funeral the next day.

CHAPTER 28

Cody's Dilemma

—1948

CODY HAD HIS EVIDENCE LINED up, ready to go to court—but there was still one glitch. That time gap of two or three minutes remained unaccounted for. Mrs. Bini insisted there could have been no more than four minutes—five if you stretched it, but she didn't see how you could. She'd timed her movements repeatedly—everything she'd done between the time she went upstairs and the time she came down again and found the body. Yet the dismantling of the drapery cord had to have taken at least four minutes, and the garroting required an equal amount of time. That added up to eight minutes, not allowing for the walk down the hall and back, which required a couple seconds.

Cody'd felt sure there must have been a co-conspirator helping to dismantle the drapery cord, and who more likely than Jill, for whom Dorothea represented major competition? She seemed the only logical person. He felt frustrated over her unbreakable alibi. Yet her colleagues all swore she hadn't left the library that day except for a five-minute phone call.

He'd found no one else who qualified as an accessory to this murder. Yonkers had speculated that the breakup of a marriage usually implied a third person, an accessory, but none had turned up.

"I cannot believe in the theory of someone hiding outside the house, magically available at the right moment to rush in and murder Miss Granger," Cody told Yonkers. "For one thing, there's nowhere to hide on a street of row houses, no convenient areaways between buildings. No, it had to have been Szekely—but given the timeline, he needed help."

Yonkers, whose hair growth all seemed concentrated on his face, thrust forth his darkening chin and drew his heavy brows together. "Could someone have been hiding inside the house, in one of the upstairs bedrooms, maybe?"

"Too convenient. That mythical someone had to have arrived with Szekely or just a few minutes ahead of him. And how would this hypothetical person know the musician was coming? The visit involved a private agreement between Granger and Szekely." Cody shook his head. He was at his wit's end. One great puzzle remained: Why didn't Zoltan just cut the cord instead of unraveling it? Unraveling was a hellish chore. The drapery expert who'd agreed to demonstrate the dismantling had proved that the record for unraveling the cord in that particular type of frame was four minutes two seconds. That after several practice sessions. Zoltan would have had no practice at all. And to top it off, it was not your standard type of cord. It required a specialized knowledge.

"We need to talk to Mrs. Bini again," Cody said. "Her time upstairs has to have been longer than she claims. There's something she's forgotten. She must have got a phone call or—"

"Ma Bell has no record of a phone call," Yonkers reminded.

"Or a letter, and she paused to read it. Or maybe she spent a couple minutes feeding the cat. Hell—who knows?—she could even have stopped to comb her hair or write out a grocery list. We need to jog her memory."

They returned for a third go-around with Maria Bini. Her top-floor apartment, usually a sunny place, was gloomy on this cloudy day. Mrs. Bini sat opposite them shaking her head. "I don't get much mail, Officer. The household bills and ads go to Mrs. Falucci, and my friends all live in town and use the phone when they want to talk to me. I do have a sister in Illinois, but we only exchange letters four or five times a year—and nothing has come recently."

"You must have done something when you came in that day. Fed the cat?"

"It's not my cat, I don't feed it. It's Mama Falucci's. Leila's been feeding it while Sophie's in the hospital."

"You combed your hair?"

"Hey, I'd come home. At home you relax, you don't spiff yourself up."

"You studied a recipe book?"

She shook her head. "I have that recipe memorized. I rarely need a cookbook anymore for anything, and certainly not for cookies."

"Maybe you picked up a magazine and read an article."

She waved an arm around a room with no visible magazines. "I do subscribe to *Redbook*, but I keep it by my bed for nighttime reading when I can't sleep."

"Sat and listened to the radio?"

She shook her head again more emphatically. "I remember that day, Officer. Finding a corpse fixes the moment in memory. I recall seeing the cat on my couch and giving him a few pats on the head, washing my hands, going to the kitchen, opening my sugar canister, finding it empty, looking in the cupboard, and heading straight downstairs. That's all that happened. I assure you it didn't take eight minutes. Not even half that."

"Were the draperies down when you came in?" Yonkers asked.

"I don't know, I didn't look. I focused on this Szekely guy. He was frowning—no, he was glowering—obviously very upset. I pondered about what happened. I didn't peer into the living room or notice the curtains."

When the officers walked away from the house, Cody again shook his head. "Something had to have delayed the woman," he said. "It's the only scenario that makes sense. And we have to find that something. The man has been charged and the court date set. The defense will focus on those missing minutes and blather about reasonable doubt."

"I've heard that hypnotists can help in cases like this," Yonkers said. "They seem to be pretty successful at jogging people's memories."

Cody shook his head and let out a curse under his breath. He'd hoped to be able to report to B.J. that the missing minutes had been accounted for. He couldn't imagine what the lieutenant would say to a suggestion of hypnotism.

"Just three bloody minutes between me and a great court case." He sighed. "Hell, there has to be a way to account for those minutes. We'll just have to keep looking."

"Szekely must have had help with that cord," Yonkers said.

"No sign of a mate."

"Marriage breaking up, and no one seems to know why—I keep coming back to the possibility that our man has a secret girlfriend. We need to churchee la femme."

"I believe that's cherchez. But you're right, it's blooming weird the way no one seems to know the reason why the Szekelys split. Maybe there *is* another femme in the picture. I felt certain Jill must have helped him, but her alibi's solid. She was at work."

"We gotta find the woman," Yonkers said. "Maybe grill those friends that used to attend their musical gatherings. I have a list. There's a Claire somebody, an Ingrid somebody, and that Frieda Fishbein woman Jill Szekely lives with." He fumbled in his pocket, drew out his notebook, and flipped it open. "Loren, Leah—I have about ten people here who attended the salons faithfully. Maybe some of them can tell us who our boy was seeing. Them university folks, they hate to gossip. It's hell, you gotta trick 'em—but it can be done."

Cody agreed. "We better get right on it. If we go to trial and can't account for the missing minutes, our man will get off scot-free and the DA will have our hides." He sighed deeply. "That's a bloody … I mean it's one hell of an outcome to my first case." He reminded himself not to use the word *bloody*, which proved ineffective around Yanks. In Britain it worked, but here it got no reaction.

"Yup, it's rotten luck all around." Yonkers shoved his hands in his pockets, glared at the sidewalk, and let out some Anglo-Saxon. "So fucking near and yet so far."

"We shouldn't have charged the bloke until we'd accounted for those minutes." Cody sighed. "Too late to be looking for another suspect."

"There is no other suspect. We've leaned on everyone remotely involved in this case. They all have airtight alibis."

"You're so bloody right." He decided right then and there to use the word anyway, because saying it made him feel better.

"Is there any chance one of the two women in the house could be our missing accomplice?" Yonkers asked. "Well, not Maria. She has a married sister she spends all her time with, seems scarcely involved in the Falucci household at all, and helps out with the sister's kids. Hardly ever stays home alone, they say. It don't seem likely she'd be feuding with Dorothea. How about the Leila kid? She could have had a fight with her housemate and helped with the murder for revenge."

"Or she could have taken the draperies down for some other reason, and hesitates to say so now for fear she'll get in trouble," Cody speculated. "Let's go to the hospital and talk to Mrs. Falucci. See if we can discover any strains between the women or any plans to change the draperies."

They found Mrs. Falucci sitting up in bed. At their approach, she drew her hospital gown together and nodded a greeting. She seemed on the road to recovery. A small but solidly built woman with dark hair to her shoulders, olive complexion, and a Roman nose, she smiled and acted cooperative, holding out a hand when Cody introduced himself. "Leila told me what happened, but I just can't believe it. Such a tragedy. Poor Dorothea. How could anyone do such a thing? She was trying hard to get her life together— and she'd found love at last. I'm so glad you've caught the culprit. I want you to know that Leila and I will look after Marcello. We've had him with us from babyhood; we've helped to raise him, and we love him like our own."

"All the same, I expect he'll have to go into foster care temporarily." Cody spoke formally; he disliked participating in family lies. "I'm surprised they haven't already taken him. It's possible the fiancé may want him." He tried to hint to Mrs. Falucci that her secret about Marcie's parentage would now have to be revealed if the family hoped to keep him.

"Foster care? The fiancé?" Agitated, Mrs. Falucci frowned and waved her hands. "You can't mean it! We're Marcello's family; our house is his home. Why would they want to rip the child away from everything he's known—especially at a time like this?"

"They'll look into possible near relatives, their backgrounds and financial stability, that sort of thing. Well, we know the fiancé has more than enough money to care for the boy, but that doesn't necessarily mean he'll want to. But if he does, he'd certainly stand a good chance of getting custody. You women can also apply to be foster parents, of course." He gave her a sharp look that tried to suggest there was another alternative—the truth about Marce—but, despite her agitation, she failed to pick up on it.

"But, Officer, this is no time to disrupt his life. Dorothea's relatives didn't even want her, let alone him. They were awful to her; they literally disowned her. And the fiancé hardly knows the kid."

"That will be up to the social worker. I'm sure she'll be happy to have your input." Cody tried to speak soothingly. He didn't want to get into the question of what was to happen to Marcello. He changed the subject. "We've come to ask you about your daughter."

"Leila? What does she have to do with it?"

"We were just wondering if there'd ever been strains or conflict between her and Dorothea?"

"Oh, not at all," Mrs. Falucci said. "They got along great. Leila has helped out a lot with the boy, especially lately, since Dot has been so involved with her wedding plans. Dot appreciated it. Why do you ask?"

"We need information about everybody involved in the case," Cody said. "Does Leila have a close friend or confidante who could confirm what you say about her?"

"Of course she does. She went to Stella Maris Academy, you know. She has a pal from there, Beulah Dominici. We used to call them the twins, Leila and Beulah. They were inseparable."

"Can you give me her address?"

"I have her phone number here in my book." When Mrs. Falucci reached for her purse, Yonkers jumped up and handed it to her. She fumbled for an address book, read off the phone number, and waited while Cody jotted it down. She added, "I'm sure she'll tell you Leila was fond of Dot. Leila's been excited about the wedding. She was to be bridesmaid, you know."

"Just one other question," Cody said. "Did you have any plans to change your living room draperies?"

"Change my draperies?" She chuckled. "At a time like this? I'll be lucky if I pay off all my medical bills. My draperies are destined to hang there for years to come."

On leaving, Yonkers sighed. "We've got our work cut out for us. How in the world are we to get all these women to reveal girlie secrets about their chums? We have Claire and Ingrid and Frieda to interview, and now Beulah."

"You go in first," Cody suggested. "I'll follow. Limpy guys are not intimidating."

"Neither are shorties."

"Well, then, I guess we'll have to tell them they need to tell the exact truth in order to get their chum off the hook. Remind them we have to be able to check out their story. Let's start with Jill Szekely's friends. I still find Jill the most likely candidate for accessory."

"I'm with you there," Yonkers said.

CHAPTER 29

Jill Faces Danger

—1948

UNANNOUNCED TO THE PUBLIC, THE funeral drew no curiosity-hounds. It proved to be a small graveside gathering, at which all but a few mourners were familiar to me. Maria and Leila had come bringing Marcello, solemn and gentlemanly in his best Sunday suit. They arrived by taxi just behind us. Leila explained to Kitty and me that her mother, newly arrived from the hospital, hadn't felt up to the trip but was prepared to greet us all when we came to the house for a postfuneral reception.

The sun had gone under a cloud, and a cool breeze swirled grass cuttings across the lawn, recalling to me the smell of new-mown hay. I hastily drew on my sweater. This was a modern cemetery, with plaques flat in the ground—no ancient, mossy tombstones leaning precariously backward, no flowery inscriptions, just names and dates. A robin eyed us from a safe distance.

Kitty leaned against a tree to catch her breath. I paused for a private moment of farewell to the woman I'd seen as my mirror reflection, the woman who'd gone before me in so many ways, including the most important one, pregnancy with Zoltan's child. Then I fixed my mind in investigator mode. I glanced up and wondered aloud if there'd be rain. Beside Kitty, I strolled on across the grass to the open grave.

Randy and his father were already there, as were all the people from the séance with the exception of Madame Aya. Belle and Norma nodded to me. Belle was with two tall, skinny people that I took to be relatives of Dorothea, as they sported that same lanky, bony build. The woman, in fact, rather resembled Dorothea. I wondered if it was possible the parents had had a change of heart and decided to show up. These people were the right age, sixtyish, with salt-and-pepper hair. *Sad,* I thought, *to have this epiphany too late for Dorothea, who'd so much longed for contact with her mother.*

A slim, handsome, swarthy young man, whom I recognized as Leila's boyfriend, Carlo, broke away from the crowd and went to join Leila. He bent to give her a kiss and then clasped her hand and positioned himself at her side, placing Marcello in front of the two of them. There was something proprietary about his actions. I thought, *She's done well for herself,* and then scolded myself for my bitchiness and forced my gaze away.

Janet, the waitress from Mario's, was there with an older man and another young woman. Since they stood grouped together, I assumed they must be Dorothea's colleagues from the restaurant. A tall woman in a black coat had brought a boy of about nine, who I guessed to be Dorothea's younger son, Denny. If so, the woman would be his foster mother. She kept a consoling hand on his shoulder. The grandparents, if that's what they were, eyed the boy, as did Reggie Jackson, who stood frowning, looking broody. Jackson was flanked by an older couple, probably his own parents, since they resembled him in short and portly build. The woman reached out and squeezed his arm in sympathy. Wearing a black suit with black tie and a flower in his buttonhole, he'd positioned himself close to the grave, conspicuous as the principal mourner.

Following a prayer, the minister began to speak. The departed, he said, had had a tragic life and tragic death. "Her sons were taken from her at an early age to be placed in foster care, and after that she never realized her dream of getting her small family back together. Though she lived for the great day, it wasn't destined to happen. Yet she worked hard always; she refused assistance from the government. Sadly, she died with the anticipated wedding, the love of a husband, the joy of a family, just days away. God had promised her happiness at last, but her murderer saw fit to interfere with God's plan."

A big bird flew overhead, its shadow darkening the ground. The timing was a perfect symbol, I thought, of life departing. In my mind, I said, *Goodbye, Dorothea. I wish I'd known you better.*

"Though she'd kept her children in foster care," the minister went on, "she never gave them up for adoption. She loved them and wanted them, and she left them a legacy of strength, of persistence in seeking to do the right thing, of trying to make life work out."

Reggie Jackson wiped his eyes, as did the bony woman. As far as I could see, no one else grew teary, not even the boys. Randy watched a squirrel on the lawn and Denny shuffled impatiently, as if he longed to make his getaway. Marcello stood, dutifully polite, between Leila and Maria. I looked around at the crowd and noticed that most people had dressed, as Kitty and I had, in black or at least dark clothing—all but Leila, who wore a blue sundress with straps in place of sleeves, a dress that showed off her slim figure and smooth shoulders. She'd selected her clothing, clearly, in honor of her boyfriend rather than the deceased.

I glanced toward the road hoping for the late arrival of a mystery mourner, hoping the man of the iron claw gift would appear and provide a new lead. But no one came. I looked out over the crowd while my mind echoed Macbeth's question on the appearance of Banquo's ghost at the feast: "Which of you has done this thing?" I still felt it had to be either Joel, who desperately wanted his kid, or Reggie, who might somehow have learned of his fiancée's interest in Zoltan and taken revenge by framing his nemesis.

They have alibis, I reminded myself. And promptly answered, *Alibis can be disproven.*

The minister droned on, growing less personal and more theological, quoting the Bible. I couldn't focus. It dawned on me that at funerals one tends to think about oneself, one's own mortality. Dorothea hadn't been my true mirror image. I'd succeeded where she failed: I'd married Zoltan. She'd wanted Zoltan so badly she was willing to keep her job just so she could be with him. This thought led to my feeling I'd been selfish to wish for him to give up his career dreams and support me, support our future child. If I longed for such a thing, I should have done what Kitty did—married a man who was ready and willing to offer me that opportunity. You don't marry a budding concert pianist if you want a home and family. What was I thinking?

I wasn't thinking, I reminded myself. In wartime, you don't think past the immediate moment, the chance to experience life as it flies by you. The prospect of a future is too dim and uncertain; it may never come to a wartime bride and groom. It never even came to Dorothea, and she'd preceded me by years.

The minister asked us to bow our heads once again in memory of the dear departed. We dutifully did so, but I peeked behind me to see if a late mourner might yet arrive. None did.

When the prayer ended, the minister asked Randy, as the nearest relative and oldest son, to come forward and pour dirt into the grave. It seemed a heavy duty to place on a child, but Randy didn't seem to grasp its significance. He performed the task in a matter-of-fact way and then stepped back. Before long we were all hurrying, trying to beat the threatened rainstorm, back to the parking area, where taxis had gathered in anticipation of customers. Leila urged everyone to come to the Village later for a memorial reception. Kitty and I hadn't planned to go, but I remarked that perhaps we should, after all.

"No mystery man turned up at the graveside. Maybe we'll get lucky and he'll come to the reception."

Kitty nodded and took my arm. As the persons least concerned with mourning, we left first and walked back toward the line of waiting taxis. Belle and the two lanky people came behind us, and I overheard from them snippets of conversation confirming my guess that these were Dorothea's parents. The woman said, "Such delightful children. I had no idea. I'm afraid I've been guilty of assuming that illegitimate meant delinquent. Single mother who couldn't handle the kids and had to place them in foster care—it seemed they would surely be wild youngsters. Now I wish I'd been in touch all these years. Carr, are you sure there's no chance we can get custody?"

The man muttered something, his words too quiet to be overheard, and Belle interjected a comment. Then the man demanded in a loud voice, "You mean to say it's a done deal? All settled already? Hell, why didn't they give us a chance to have some input? We're the grandparents, after all."

I didn't hear Belle's response to that, as we were already climbing into one of the waiting taxis. I watched the couple move on to the next car, apparently arguing with one another.

While we rode to the nearest subway entrance, Kitty sighed. "Poor Dorothea, she really had it rough, didn't she? No family support in all she went through."

I agreed. "It couldn't have been easy, living in New York by herself during the Depression. She recorded in her diary how hard it was to keep a job and how nebulous the tips were in those days. Someone once left her a dime, and she didn't realize it was a tip. She'd had so few. I faulted Zoltan for taking advantage of her personal tragedy, yet I don't suppose her life would have been that great if he'd walked away from her. Who knows, maybe he gave her three years of happiness she wouldn't otherwise have had."

While we waited on the platform, Kitty confessed, "I felt edgy during the service. I feared that everyone saw my brother as the person who destroyed Dorothea's future."

I confessed I didn't pay all that much attention. "I kept an eye out hoping the man of the iron claw would show up. He's the only viable suspect we have left, and we need to find him."

Kitty said, "I worry that Zoltan could be locked away for years just because the real murderer can't be found. He could even get the death penalty. That would kill my parents. I can't even imagine anything so horrible." Her hands massaged her cheeks. "Dear God, don't let it be!"

I tried to console her. "It won't happen, Kitty. We'll persist until we find our man. Someone has to know something. There's that oil inheritance. If that's real, it could have inspired someone's anger against Dorothea. People in line to inherit money don't eagerly welcome newcomers to the family. Some relative of Reggie's may have wanted to stop the wedding."

"But how on earth can you look into a thing like that?"

I shrugged. "I've come this far; I guess I'll find a way to keep going."

"I don't know what we'd do without you, Jill," Kitty said. "I believe you've saved my parents' sanity."

It was raining when we left the subway. Since we hadn't brought umbrellas and Kitty wasn't up to running, we huddled in a doorway waiting for the downpour to subside. As a result, we arrived late and found everyone sitting around eating. With the draperies restored to the front window and a loaded buffet table set up along one wall, the large living room seemed crowded. Maria Bini was behind the table, serving. The two older boys and their caregivers had not come, nor had their grandparents. Marcello played alone in a corner, stacking blocks. I saw several women and one elderly couple who hadn't attended the funeral. Leila, resplendent in her light blue sundress, her skirt swirling as she whipped around the room as hostess, introduced them one by one, saying they were neighbors who'd known Dorothea.

She also introduced her mother, a smallish, dark-haired woman with a chubby face that must have been beautiful before it became ravaged by aging and the difficulties of raising children alone and earning a living while her husband languished in prison. She wore a flowered dress and white sandals. Seated in an overstuffed chair, she didn't rise for the introduction. She apologized, holding out her hand. "I'm just home from the hospital and don't have much energy yet. I'm Sophia Falucci. I guess you've heard about me?"

"Only good things. We visited your store and were very impressed. It must be one of the most interesting shops in the Village."

"I'm going home and learning Italian cooking," Kitty told her. "My husband loves it."

"The store has been gratifyingly successful." Mrs. Falucci smiled; she had an overbite just pronounced enough to be charming. I felt an instinctive liking for her and rejoiced that she needn't be placed on my suspect list. She added, "I understand you girls don't believe our young pianist is guilty."

"Well, you see," I said, "it would have been easy for someone else to have sneaked into the house. I'm told the door was unlocked."

"But it's such a coincidence," she said. "Who would know that the house had been left unsecured at that very moment?"

I suggested answers. "Someone who had it in for Dorothea for some reason and was watching the place. Someone who'd been waiting to find the door ajar."

"I can't imagine that Dorothea had an enemy who hated her that much. She was a lovely person, kind to everyone, not the type to ruffle feathers."

"I've wondered if there might have been cause for blackmail," Kitty said.

"Could Dorothea possibly have seen or known something? I mean, she was desperate for money to hire a proper babysitter and get her children back, so if she'd learned of a crime that she thought might pay off, she probably wouldn't hesitate to pressure the person."

Mrs. Falucci smiled. "It sounds far-fetched, but who knows?" She turned to Norma, who'd come up behind her. "How about it, my dear? You've known Dorothea for ages. Can you think of anyone who might blackmail her?"

Norma bit her lip, frowned, and shook her head. ""I wish I could." Zoltan seems such an unlikely suspect. I've racked my brains trying to think who might have wanted Dorothea dead, and I can't come up with a soul."

"Nor can I," Mrs. Falucci agreed. "But you girls feel free to ask around. I'm sure we all want to learn the truth. And do help yourselves to the cold cuts over there."

We thanked her and moved past a window almost opaque with raindrops to the refreshment table, where we filled our plates. Carlo came to carry Kitty's plate for her and help her to a seat. She'd refused both wine and coffee, so I got her a drink of water from the kitchen. When I returned with it, Belle had plunked down beside her and was telling her about the séance. I moved among the newcomers and asked them how well they'd known Dorothea. Not well, it seemed. They all claimed to have only a speaking acquaintance. One or two said they'd played cards with her. "She was fond of canasta, you know. We had a neighborhood card club that got together every Thursday evening."

I talked briefly to Maria and learned that she too had been no closer to Dorothea than to participate with her in the neighborhood game sessions. She shook her head when I asked if she could think of anyone who had it in for the murdered woman for any reason.

As for the blackmail notion, Norma, when quizzed, theorized that Dorothea would have told her if anything unusual was going on in her life, if she'd been witness to a crime or anything of that nature.

"What if her stepfather got in touch with her?" I asked.

"Oh, she certainly would have mentioned that. We were like sisters; we shared that sort of thing," she said.

No mystery guest arrived. When people began drifting away, we gave up and, since the rain had slowed to a drizzle, prepared to leave. Mrs. Falucci promised to be in touch if anything new came up. "I know how you girls must feel, having someone so close to you involved in a murder. It's been a terrible shock for us, too."

We wished her a speedy recovery, waved to Leila, who was now standing in the corner talking to Mr. Handsome, and left.

Though the rain had dwindled, a cold wind had followed on the storm's tail. Waiting at the bus stop, I felt the chill piercing through me. I buttoned my sweater all the way to my throat and asked Kitty, "Aren't you cold?" She wore a long-sleeved dress but had brought no wrap. She shivered and admitted she felt chilly. "There's not much I can do about it except get home quickly," she said. "Perhaps we should take the subway again."

"That'll be the second time today," I reminded. "Your dad said—"

She shrugged. "If you want to go to Brooklyn, you take the BMT."

"Still, we promised your parents."

We waited at the bus stop. There were few vehicles on the road in the rain. No bus appeared. The wind blew Kitty's long hair, and she shivered again. "Come on, Jill. There's no wind on the subway platform. And who'd be after us? We haven't yet found out anything."

I agreed it was silly to stand here in the cold, so we hurried to the nearest subway entrance and, with relief, escaped the wind. A crowd awaited the train. Realizing it was near rush hour, I estimated we might have to miss two or three trains before we'd be on our way home. When the local pulled in, a lot of people boarded, allowing us to move up until we stood beside the tracks to await the express. The crowds closed in behind us.

The next train was coming. I could see the light down the tunnel, could hear and feel the rumble. Suddenly there was a hard thump against my back, and I found myself plummeting forward. I instinctively reached out with both hands, scrabbling frantically for something to grab onto. For a moment I teetered on the edge. I saw only empty air in front of me, and below me, the tracks, where I'd be meat in an instant when the train pulled in. Terror shot through me. Time stopped as I flailed and hung there, staring down at the tracks so hard that my eyes seemed to bug out.

Then someone must have caught my sweater. It pulled tight against me, choking but righting me. When the pressure was released, I grabbed a breath of air, grasped my neck, and glanced behind me. There were several men back there, two of whom frowned at me in concern. One of these must have been the sweater-grabber. Beside one of them, I thought I caught a glimpse of Mr. Handsome, Leila's Carlo. My hand flew to my chest as my heart pounded. *Did he push me or save me?*

The train rushed at us and moved along just inches from my face. The breeze from it swirled around me, so close it left me breathless. Kitty said, "My God, Jill, what happened there? I thought you were about to fall right in front of the train."

"I thought so, too," I admitted. By now I was shaking all over. "Thank God I'd buttoned my sweater. It could have slipped off when my rescuer yanked on it. I'd have flown on down to the tracks."

Kitty asked if I was all right. I nodded and glanced behind me again, but this time I saw no familiar face. No one in the crowd was looking at me now; everyone was watching the arriving train.

The train slowed to a stop, and we stepped aboard. Shaking, I grabbed a hand strap and turned around, hoping to find and thank my rescuer. When that failed, I began searching for Mr. Handsome among the passengers who boarded behind us. There was no sign of him. I didn't know if he'd really been there or if I'd imagined him. And if he was there, I still didn't know if he pushed me—or if he was the one who pulled me back. It all happened so fast I couldn't tell. All I knew for sure was that I'd escaped death by a mere instant.

"Pop was right, we should have stayed off the subway," Kitty said. "From now on, I'll carry along a wrap so we can ride the bus."

Still shaking, I slid onto a seat. My legs trembled, and my knees bumped together.

"We must be getting closer to the truth than we know," I said, when I got my breath back. "Someone doesn't want us investigating. I thought I saw Leila's boyfriend back there."

"We'd better tell the cops about this."

"They'll think it was an accident. Even I can't be sure it wasn't."

At home, we apprised the elder Szekelys of our problems and failures. I told them we'd spotted no new suspects, no mystery mourner—and yet someone must have thought we'd learned something. Kitty told them how someone had tried to push me onto the train tracks in front of an oncoming train. Annie gazed at me in horror and exclaimed, "Oh, Jill!"

Janos said, "That's it; I can't let you girls go on investigating in this way. Someone is getting nervous."

"Not necessarily," I said. "There's no proof the gesture was deliberate. It may have been accidental. I'm just awfully glad I'd buttoned my sweater."

"Tell them who you think did it," Kitty said. "Tell them about Leila's boyfriend."

I thought back. That whole event seemed to have occurred in slow motion, with me falling forward in a lengthy, dreamlike way, being yanked back so hard it choked me, and then looking around and seeing, in a single, freeze-frame instant, that familiar handsome face. "I'm not even certain it was him."

"Who's this *him*?" Annie asked. "What *him* are we talking about?"

I told her his name was Carlo. I'd dismissed him as a possible suspect because he seemed too young to be involved with Dorothea. He was a kid, like Leila. "I mean, Dorothea would have had to be a cradle robber to go after him," I said. "He can't be more than twenty at most."

"People can be involved in other ways than sexually," Annie said. "What if he committed a crime, and she found out about it and threatened to tell? That might be grounds for murder."

I admitted it. "I guess I shouldn't have dismissed him so readily. I wonder if there's some way we can learn more about him."

"I shall try to learn more about him," Janos said. "You've done enough, and I don't want you involved any longer. You've come up with good leads, and I'll follow through."

"I don't recall his last name," I wailed. "I was told once, at the séance, but I … I just can't remember what it was."

"I'll quiz the salesgirl at Mama Falucci's," Janos said. "She may know the last name of the man Leila is dating. Then I'll track him down in the city directory, find out where he lives, and go talk to him. I'll talk to Mr. Jackson, too. He must know something more about Dorothea's life that we've just not uncovered yet."

"Couldn't we just tell the police about this subway incident and get them to follow up on it?" Annie asked.

Janos reached out to squeeze her hand. "We might if we were sure the gesture was deliberate. But people on subway platforms do jostle one another and push toward the train. Sergeant Cody knows we're searching for an alternate suspect, and he may think we're making a mountain out of a molehill. Jill says she isn't even certain she saw this Carl or Carlo."

"Not a hundred percent certain," I admitted. "As I said, it all happened so fast."

I went to bed that night discouraged, down in the dumps. Still feeling shaky, I couldn't sleep. I kept going over and over that subway incident in my mind, rerunning the event in slow motion—feeling again the hard shove against my back, sensing the rush of the oncoming train, seeing the tracks below me, feeling my hands claw the air and finding nothing to grab onto. The event could imply that we were getting painfully close to the truth, and someone wanted to stop us—or it could simply have been an accident. I had no way of knowing. As Janos had said, people do jostle one another in the subway station. If someone had pushed me when I wasn't standing on the edge, I'd have thought nothing of it. In the past I'd been pushed a lot harder in the press of people getting onto trains. Luckily, I hadn't then been close to the tracks.

It was late when I fell asleep. Then, toward morning, I suddenly sat up in bed, picturing in my mind Mrs. Falucci's feet in those sandals. Normal-length toes. I perceived a new lead. In fact, it hit me so strongly I couldn't go back to sleep. I got up, paced about the small apartment—quietly so as not to wake Frieda—and made myself cocoa. I sat by the window sipping it and gazing out at the pink dawn as the early birds headed for work along a sidewalk that sported puddles from yesterday's rain. The moment I saw a shaft of sun, I called Janos at the hotel. He answered sleepily.

"Sorry to wake you so early," I said, "but I just realized something."

"Yes, Jill, what is it?"

"The person we have to find is Mr. Falucci."

"Mr. Falucci?" He sounded disbelieving. "He's been in prison for years. What had he to do with Dorothea?"

"Nothing, probably," I said. "It's his toes that I'm concerned with. We have to get a look at his toes."

"Jill, are you kidding me?"

"No, I'm not. I was told he was accessory to an armed robbery—I seem to have heard he drove the getaway car. We're going to have to enlist Cody's help here. Do you think we can do that?"

"We'll need an awfully good reason."

"I might have an awfully good reason."

"I'll meet you at the Automat near your house in half an hour," Janos said.

CHAPTER 30

The Whole Truth

—1948

CODY MUST HAVE BEEN DESPERATE. Though he'd interviewed my friends and my housemate, he apparently found nothing suspicious. When I approached him, he assured me he welcomed input from the public. I confessed I needed to know the length of Mr. Falucci's second toe. "Don't laugh," I said.

He sighed. "I'm not amused by any aspect of this case, Mrs. Szekely. We Brits knew before you lot did what Hitler got up to with Jews. Believe me, I get no joy from 'assling a refugee Jewish family. It's just … it's a puzzler how I'm to worm out this information. We can order prisoners as to where they'll go and what they'll do, but when it comes to personal matters like peeking at their toes—well, I don't know."

"Surely someone has seen him in the shower," I suggested.

"Bloody 'ell," he said. "I've run out of leads, so I'm ready to try anything. So, I guess it's off to the prison for me."

He told us afterward how he contrived to gain a look at the toes. He offered a prize of a carton of cigarettes to the person with the shortest second toe. Everyone scrambled to remove shoes. Sure enough, Mr. Falucci won the prize. He even, as winner, allowed his feet to be photographed, providing Cody with evidence for the court. Just as I'd suspected, that nontoe proved genetic in the Falucci family. "Smooth-looking bloke, 'e is. A real pretty boy. Claims he hadn't a clue he was being hired to drive a getaway car involved in a crime."

So now I knew why Mrs. Falucci hadn't really missed three months of work at her shop, and why Leila had lied when describing her mother's absence. I even knew why Dorothea had been killed. It only wanted final proof. I made my second suggestion timidly, fearing Cody might resent my interference. Luckily, he seemed willing to test out my theory. He checked out the Stella Maris Academy, near the Falucci home in Greenwich Village; he even agreed to accompany us—Janos and Kitty and me, that is—to call on Mama Falucci and Leila later in the day. *Our visit won't exactly be according to protocol, but then Cody's an English cop, and the English seem a tad more willing to bend the law than our New York police are.* Or maybe it was just that this was his first case of his own, and he really longed to win it.

I wasn't exactly sure how I'd manage this visit. Ushered in by Leila, we all sat in the Falucci living room, with Kitty on the couch beside me, and Janos and Cody in chairs opposite. Detective Larramie sat at the desk with his notebook. Mrs. Falucci, in a fluffy-ruffled pink bathrobe with matching slippers, her hair done up in a clasp, relaxed again in the overstuffed chair. Leila, wearing a pale green business suit, perched on the edge of her seat as if impatient for us to leave so she could get on with whatever she meant to do. She explained that she'd just returned from taking Marcello to nursery school and needed to hurry off to the shop. Obviously unhappy about being detained, she said she hoped we'd be quick about what she frowningly defined as "this routine questioning."

Mrs. Falucci seemed nervous and kept folding and unfolding her handkerchief, leaning her head against a pillow at her back and sending her upsweep hairdo into disarray. Leila showed no sign of nervousness, but merely impatience, drumming her fingers on the chair arm.

"I've been puzzled about a couple of minor points in this case," I said. "I sensed a good deal of confusion in people's stories about that period five years ago when Mrs. Falucci did or didn't miss a couple of months of work at her shop because of pregnancy."

Mrs. Falucci looked astonished. "I? Five years ago? I never … I wasn't … Marcello was born five years ago, but …" She frowned in bafflement at her daughter. "Who's been talking about that? What has that to do with anything?" Swiveling back to me, she added, "Marcello was Dorothea's child. It had nothing to do with our family."

"I don't think so. There's the toe problem, you see, a genetic anomaly that runs in families. I understand Mr. Falucci has it, too—an almost nonexistent second toe. Dorothea had long, prehensile toes, and I noticed that your toes are normal."

Mrs. Falucci gasped, slid off a slipper to eye her toes, and paled. Leila suddenly busied herself with picking cat hairs off her suit collar and tried to look detached. I added, "I believe that both Leila and Marcello are direct descendants of Mr. Falucci. I suspect it was Leila, not you, who got pregnant."

Leila's head snapped up, and her face contorted into an angry frown. "That's a damned lie! You can't prove it!"

"I checked your school records at Stella Maris," Cody told her. "You were the one who went absent for almost three months that spring, not your mother."

She backed down. "Well, I … I did visit my aunt for a while."

"To hide a pregnancy?"

"Of course not. I was only thirteen."

"All the more reason."

"It's a lie. Mother, tell them!"

Mrs. Falucci looked ready to faint. She leaned back so suddenly that her hair loosened from its clip and fell over her shoulders, swirling black against her pink robe. Hand to forehead, she spoke in a quivering voice. "I'm afraid the truth must come out now, dear. We're going to have to correct the records on Marcello, or we won't be granted custody. We're no kin of Dorothea. The social workers are talking of placement elsewhere, with his supposed grandparents, and we … we wouldn't want that, would we?"

"You care more about Marcello than me!" Leila flared. "I've always suspected it."

"I care about keeping my family together. I can't do that if we lie to police officers. There are hospital records. They'll find out."

Leila folded her arms and turned belligerent. She glared at me. "So okay, I admit he's my kid, so what?"

"I tried so hard to protect my daughter and still keep the child." Mrs. Falucci rallied, sighed, and rubbed her forehead. "My grandchild—we'd meant to have him adopted out, but Leila didn't want to. She pleaded with me to keep him, but I thought it was best for her, for both of them. But the moment I looked at that baby in the hospital, I knew I couldn't go through with it. I couldn't turn my flesh and blood over to strangers. Yet neither could I think what to tell the relatives and neighbors. How would we explain him without creating a scandal?

"When I met Dorothea in the park, sobbing her heart out, I came up with an inspiration. I'd offer her free room and board, along with a small salary, to become Marcello's nanny and claim she was the mother. That way, Marcello could stay with us." She bit her lip and shook her head. "The setup worked well for years. Dot served as his nanny for three years until he started preschool. Then she went back to work at Mario's, and we agreed on a new arrangement: free room in return for passing as his mom."

"And what were you planning to do about Marcello after Dorothea's marriage?"

"Oh, Dorothea didn't want Marcello, at least not until she suddenly reconnected with this Zoltan guy and saw the advantage of the relationship. She had two boys of her own, so we agreed she'd simply leave Marcello with us. Marcello wouldn't mind; he was more bonded to us than to Dorothea anyway. People would get used to him living with us, and in time we'd claim to have adopted him." She fumbled for the hair clip on her shoulder and struggled to restore her hairdo, but stray locks kept escaping. Finally she gave up and let her hair fall around her shoulders. With a pitiful expression, she asked, "Does all this have to come out? I'd hoped to protect both children from scandal."

"Our problem," I pointed out, "isn't with the parentage of Marcello, but with who killed Dorothea. I mean, assuming Zoltan didn't—and those of us who know him well can't believe he turned killer."

Mrs. Falucci squirmed in her seat and frowned at her daughter. I went on. "There's another detail that doesn't quite fit. Your door was unlocked for a short time that morning after Zoltan left, but as you yourself remarked, Mrs. Falucci, it would be an unbelievable coincidence that a killer should come along at that precise moment to zero in on Dorothea. That leaves us with the two people who were already in the house, Leila and Maria Bini. Maria is a hard-working widow lady with a life of her own and little interest in this household. Leila, on the other hand, seems to have had a long history of bitter competition with Dorothea."

I looked from one to the other of the Falucci women and saw that I had their full attention. Two pairs of brown eyes, one pair angry, one puzzled, stared in my direction. Mrs. Falucci said, "You're wrong. They got along fine, I told you."

Addressing myself to her, I went on, "I doubt that. Think about it from Leila's point of view. Her child was snatched from her and given to a woman who'd been installed in the house like another daughter, while she herself was sent back to a hated school and—"

"I wanted to go back to school!" Leila seemed ready to burst. "Like I said, I was grateful to Dorothea. She made it possible for me to graduate."

"That's not what your friend Beulah recalls," Cody told her. "I talked to her this morning, and she claims you boasted of your pregnancy. You were happy about it; you celebrated the fact you'd get to stay home and care for the baby."

"You told?" Mrs. Falucci gazed at her daughter in horror. "Beulah knew? I was doing everything in the world to protect your reputation—and you told?"

"She was my best friend," Leila defended. "We shared everything."

"If she's to be believed," Cody said, "you looked forward to raising the baby. And then your mother snatched him from you at birth and gave him to Dorothea—and invited her into your home to care for him. Meanwhile, you were sent back to a school that I'm told you rebelled against."

Leila tossed her head defiantly. "I had good reason. The nuns hated me. They suspected I was pregnant and accused me of being fast. It was a lie. I wasn't fast, I'd been—"

"Let's not talk about that," her mother snapped. "That isn't police business."

I believed I knew what it was Mama Falucci wouldn't talk about. I believed her husband had been a molester and fathered her daughter's child. But nothing could be done about that unless Leila chose to press charges, as so far she apparently had not.

I went on, speaking mostly to Leila. "So now you assumed Dorothea was to be married and gone, out of your hair at last—until that final day, when you overheard a conversation that led you to believe she was using Marcello as a lure to win Zoltan. You fancied she was about to take off with your child, claiming him as hers. You snapped and—"

"I knew nothing about that!" Leila rose from her chair, shouting out her denial. "I was in the shower. I've already told the police—"

"There's one more time gap that's puzzling here." In the face of her fury, Cody lifted a hand and held it palm out to stop her from talking over him. "Mrs. Bini insists it was no more than five minutes after she went upstairs before she came down again. She washed her hands, went to the kitchen to get out the ingredients for the cookies she planned to bake—and found she was out of sugar. She says she searched, hoping she had an unopened pack somewhere, but the search took only seconds in her small cupboard. That means Dorothea was killed in that brief time period.

"It takes even an expert about four minutes to undo that drapery cord, which has to be unfastened from several hooks and then unwoven through complicated openings. So why not cut the cord? Because the person who unraveled it planned to replace it and leave no hint it had been used as a murder weapon. This person had to work slowly and carefully in order to avoid damage to the cord, and had expected to have the leisure for that—but, due to the unexpected return of Mrs. Bini, the project had to be hastened. Count at least four minutes for the strangled woman to die—that doesn't leave time enough for Szekely to reenter the house, unfasten the drapery cord, strangle Miss Granger, and depart. The diary also shows that the time was brief, since Miss Granger managed to write only a couple of sentences."

Cody paused, looked around at us all, and then focused again on Leila.

"The time lag indicates to me that someone in the house had overheard the conversation in that studio room and prepared the cord in advance—and was ready to rush in and do the deed the minute Mr. Szekely left." He frowned at the now uneasy, lip-biting young woman. "Mrs. Bini came downstairs unexpectedly and gave you no time to replace the cord. Did you quickly fling it aside on hearing footsteps on the stairs, Miss Falucci? Did you then rush to the shower to wet yourself and establish an alibi?"

Leila retreated behind her chair and grasped the back of it. "Certainly not. You can't pin this on me. I was washing my hair, like I said."

"Or wetting it, anyway. Our assumption that someone came in and walked down the hall is based on your testimony. No one else heard footsteps."

Her mother shook her head vigorously. "She's only a kid; she wouldn't have the strength to strangle anyone."

"Oh, I think she would; I understand she's quite a gymnast. Her friend told me she has a life membership at the local health club. She swims and jogs every morning in addition to working out. Miss Granger, on the other hand, didn't exercise, as she was on her feet all day waiting tables. Also, she got caught by surprise in a seated position offering little opportunity to fight back. She could kick and squirm, but she couldn't touch her attacker."

"I didn't do it," Leila repeated. "You're making that up."

"And then there's the fact that I was assaulted in the subway yesterday by your boyfriend, Carlo," I said. "He tried to push me into the path of an oncoming train. He wanted to protect his true love from my investigation. Why would he do that if he didn't suspect—or know—she was guilty?"

Mrs. Falucci turned to her daughter with a frown. "Leila, I can't believe this of you. Could I be wrong? Tell the truth now. We've been living with lies for too many years. Did you do this terrible thing, as they say?"

Suddenly Leila was sobbing. "It's your fault, Mother. Like she says, you brought Dorothea into the family and made *her* your daughter. You let *her* be the mother of your grandchild. I became just the hired help, good enough to run the shop after school so you could go home and be with your precious Marcello. I didn't even get to raise my own kid. I had to push off to that stupid academy every day and then mind the shop."

She took a deep, sobbing breath and then rushed on. "Now you say, 'Don't let's talk about Marcello!' He's exactly what we need to talk about! How do you think I felt, living with my own kid for five years and never getting to act as his mother or even admit I *am* his mother?" She pranced across the room waving her arms, shouting it out. "I'm his mother! I'm Marcello's mother! I want the whole world to know!"

"Hush, hush." Mrs. Falucci grimaced. "Leila, dear, you know I did the best I could under the circumstances. We couldn't announce to the world that—"

"What, Mother, that your husband forced his own daughter to—"

"Leila, keep still, don't say it!"

Leila caught her breath. There was a moment's silence and then Cody said, "Miss Leila Falucci, you're under arrest for the murder of Dorothea Granger."

"What a sad case," I commented to Janos later. We three had left the house right behind the two detectives and Leila and headed for the subway. We hadn't wanted to stay around to find out what Mama Falucci thought of us for exposing her daughter's guilt. I'm sure she took no joy in it.

"Leila will surely get a light sentence if she and her mother can bring themselves to speak the truth about the father," Janos said. "She's more victim than perpetrator. The pressures on that young girl all these years must have been terrible."

"I can't even imagine it," I said. "Living with your own child and not being free to claim him—it sounds like hell on earth. You couldn't hug him, you couldn't discipline him, you couldn't protest if his fake mother disciplined too much." I shook my head in sympathy. "Will they let Zoltan out right away?"

"I should think so. They have no cause to hold him any longer."

We went down to the subway, but I stayed well back from the edge of the platform. Somebody might still resent my interference. Janos, beside me, asked how I'd figured things out. I told him about the Lizzie Borden case. "I've been hearing about it all my life. As kids, we used to sing about it: 'Lizzie Borden took an ax and gave her mother forty whacks.' The Bordens' door was unlocked that morning, too, but the police found no evidence of an outsider having entered, and there were two people in the house, including Lizzie. I don't know why I didn't think of that case and make the connection sooner. It was obvious once I thought about it. Two women in the house, one a person not really involved in what had been occurring there, the other a daughter very much at the heart of things."

"Of course, you didn't know that at the time."

"The truth is, I haven't been thinking straight. It's all been so scary."

"I don't believe I've got back to thinking straight even yet," Kitty said. "I still have that fluttery-midriff feeling of being involved in something totally out of control."

When we arrived at the Manhattan Avenue apartment, word had come that Zoltan would be released at two o'clock, when the judge would return and issue the court order. Annie was waiting in the hall to hug us and rejoice in our success. She'd prepared soup and sandwiches, and while we ate, we talked about Dorothea and Leila—rather, Janos talked about them, telling the others the whole tragic story, praising me as the heroine who rescued their son.

I smiled dutifully but didn't have much to add to the tale. I was busy worrying about what I would say to Zoltan. Everyone seemed to assume that I was now happily reinstated in the family, but that was not my plan at all. I cared about this family; I'd wanted to help them and had done that. But my own problem remained. I needed to get on with my life. I didn't need to be married to a penniless musician. True, I didn't believe he should be penniless; I considered it unfair that he'd been screwed out of his fellowship and a grant. But my beliefs didn't alter the facts: we were too broke to get on with child-raising. I had to abandon one or the other—my dream of a career and children, or my status as a musician's wife.

The family kept probing, wanting me to describe my role in the Dorothea mystery. Kitty asked, "How did you work it all out, Jill?"

I thought back over recent events. "It started with the toe business. I saw those two kids sitting there on the couch together, both with an almost nonexistent second toe. They looked like brother and sister. And then I remembered that Dorothea had had prehensile toes. That was when it struck me that Dorothea was not the mother of Marcello, that the child was a Falucci. From then on it was a question of family dynamics, wondering what went on between mother and daughter that drove them to pretend Dorothea had borne that child. What might they be so desperate to conceal? It had to be something more terrible than just an illegitimate child. Illegitimate children are an embarrassment, but they happen. People either accept them or adopt them out and get on with their lives. But not in this case. In this case they kept the child close to them by manipulating someone else to claim motherhood. I kept wondering about that."

I smiled, remembering my sudden revelation. "At the crack of dawn, it all came together, and I saw the total picture, including the fact that the absent Mr. Falucci had to be involved in the Marcello business. I got Cody to check, and sure enough—those two kids *are* brother and sister. They're also mother and son."

"Thank God you saw it," Annie said. "We're eternally grateful to you, Jill."

"We'll never forget what you did for us," Janos added.

"And thank God Cody was willing to listen to me and help out," I said. "I guessed the truth, but he found the evidence the court needs for a conviction—the timing of the murder versus the time it takes to unravel that cord. I wouldn't have known to test all that."

"He also managed to get information from the academy in a way that would have been difficult for us," Janos said. "They'll open their records to the police but not to casual visitors. And he located and interviewed Leila's friend, Beulah Dominici."

"I wonder how he got this Beulah to spill the beans about Leila being pregnant and wanting to keep the baby. I'd think, as a friend, she'd have clammed up."

"She may have believed she was saving Leila from involvement in the murder," Annie speculated.

"Or maybe she panicked when cops came inquiring," Kitty suggested.

"Lucky for us Cody's English," Kitty said. "I doubt the regular New York cops would be so agreeable about helping you. I hear they resent amateur assistance and are suspicious of everyone. "

"Especially me, because I'm married to Zoltan," I said. And at once I remembered that I *was* married to Zoltan and that my real problem hadn't gone away.

The time had come to go to the jail and meet Zoltan on his release. And I hadn't decided what I'd say to him. I looked at the faces around the table—Annie's still ravished with weariness and worry; Kitty's looking relieved, its down-lines all lifted so that she almost smiled; Janos's still with the thoughtful frown of a man reviewing the recent past. It struck me that if I insisted on leaving, I'd be divorcing all these people—and Barry and Robin, too. I would no longer be Kitty and Barry's sister-in-law or Robin's aunt. The realization was devastating. I cared about them all. Barry was a fun sort of guy, and Robin, a delightful child. On our visits to Upstate New York, I'd enjoyed them both.

Walking away from a marriage, I'd discovered, was not as easy as it seemed. The thought occurred to me that money-shortages were not worth breaking up a family for. I argued with myself. It was not money-shortage I'd walked away from, but freedom to have a child of my own and a career of my own. Those were the things I needed to focus on. And those were the things we still had no answers for.

While Janos went to make a quick call to Cousin Nadya and give her the news, I sat biting my lip and trying to think what to do.

CHAPTER 31

❧

Planning the Future

—1948

Zoltan, thin and worn, his green sweater and brown slacks hanging loosely on his frame, had been released and stood waiting outside the jail when we arrived. He rushed to me at once and flung out his arms for a bear hug. "Jill, I can never thank you enough for your help. The lawyer told me what happened. I am so grateful!"

As Zoltan made the rounds, hugging his mother, his father, his sister, and me again, everyone was teary-eyed. Janos announced that he planned to take the whole family to the Russian Tea Room for dinner to celebrate. "It'll have to be an early dinner, though; we want to catch the seven o'clock train for Schenectady."

"I can't wait to have a good meal after that dreadful jail food," Zoltan said. "For five horrible days, I hardly ate anything. The soup was watery, the bread was stale, and the meat, what little there was of it, was unchewable." He winced. "I hope I never have to go through an experience like that again."

"It must have been bad," Janos said. "You've lost weight."

"It's horrible. I tried to tell the exact truth so that the cops could investigate and find the real killer. Instead they twisted my words to make me look guilty."

"They're masters at that," I said.

"It seemed every word I said just got me in deeper. I should have taken them up on their offer to let me remain silent. If I'm ever in that position again, I'll do that."

"At least Cody helped in the end," Janos said as he hailed a taxi. "We need to go check out of our hotel. We'll take our suitcases to the apartment, and then I'll call our friends and let them know you're off the hook."

"They'll read about it in the paper," Zoltan said. "The reporters bombarded me when I was released, wanting a statement. I told them I knew nothing except that, since I wasn't guilty, obviously someone else had to be. They asked a lot of silly questions I refused to answer, such as how I felt about Dorothea's death. No doubt they'll come out with some crazy story they've invented."

"How do you feel about her now?" Kitty asked, turning to look at her brother from the front seat of the taxi. "Even though she's dead, I'd think you'd be furious with her."

"Not much use in fury. Actually, I feel sorry for her and wish things could have gone differently in her life—but of course I resent the trick she pulled on me. She scared me to death, hitting me with the prospect of child support at a moment when I have no way even to support myself."

"Such a manipulator," Annie said. "The woman always was. I'm convinced it was no accident, her getting pregnant at the exact moment you tried to break up with her."

I silently congratulated myself for not having done likewise. Dorothea and I had gone down the same road, but I'd managed to avoid the pitfall she fell into, partly because I'd seen what happened to her when she plunged into it.

It was a short trip to the hotel. There we waited in the lobby while Annie and Janos packed their bags and checked out. From there we squeezed into another taxi and rode to the Manhattan Avenue apartment, where Kitty packed her things and put her bag with those of her parents.

With everyone packed and ready to head home, we still had an hour until the Tea Room would begin serving dinner. Zoltan decided to shower and change into a suit, and then we killed time rehashing the events of the murder.

"The great problem for the cops seemed to be that drapery cord," Zoltan said. "A dozen times they made me unstring it, and it always took me five minutes, even after I'd figured out how it worked. The darn thing was complicated; it has to be unwoven through many holes. There weren't five minutes available for the task, since the murder required time. It seems a person doesn't die the instant the cord tightens around the neck; it has to be held tight until the brain dies from oxygen deprivation. I wouldn't have known that. I wonder how the girl realized it."

"She had a lot of years to hate Dorothea and figure out a way to eliminate her," I reminded him. "The plan had probably occurred to her before."

"Anyhow, I understand that Mrs. Bini insisted she was upstairs no more than five minutes. Since I couldn't have undone that cord and strangled Dorothea in that time, it was clear I couldn't have managed the murder. But

Cody didn't seem to want to admit the fact. Instead of looking for another suspect, he kept trying to force the time to fit. He kept repeating that, with my nimble, pianist fingers, I could surely work faster at the cord. He claimed I was faking when I said I didn't know how."

"He must have been ready to abandon that notion," I said. "We had no trouble convincing him to take a closer look at Leila and her father. He even agreed to check with her school—not to mention that he interviewed her girlfriend and learned Leila'd wanted to have a baby. With no real conception of the problems of motherhood, she may have seen the baby as an excuse to get out of school. Anyhow, I knew she had to feel a lot of resentment toward Dorothea, despite her sanctimonious claims of being grateful."

Zoltan reached out and squeezed my hand. "Lucky you saw through the girl. Everyone else dismissed her as a mere child."

"She must have lived for years eaten up with bitterness against Dorothea," Annie said.

"I'll never know how Jill guessed." Zoltan still held my hand, and I didn't attempt to remove it. His hand felt warm and pleasant. "How did you, Jill?"

I told him about the toes. "Both of those kids had short buds rather than a real second toe. I knew it must be genetic. The thought came to me in the middle of the night: Mrs. Falucci had normal toes, so Leila must be the mother of the kid and her dad the father. That was the horrible truth the family was concealing. If so, I could immediately see what it must have been like for Leila, living with that secret all those years, watching another woman acting as mother of her child. When she heard what she thought was Dorothea's plan to take the kid away to form a new family, she must have gone off the deep end. She sneaked into the living room, took down the draperies, and dismantled that cord to be ready the moment you left. After she strangled Dorothea, she must have jumped into the shower to establish her alibi, and Mrs. Bini must have come downstairs the moment she got in there."

"Why not just grab a kitchen knife? Do you think she had the smarts to realize a knife would hold fingerprints?"

"Who knows? Maybe she has an instinctive revulsion to blood. Lots of people do."

Kitty glanced at her watch and remarked that we'd better get started. We needed to check the bags before we ate. Janos called another taxi, and we went to the station where we women waited while the men attended to the bags. Then we drove on to the Russian Tea Room.

The restaurant was not crowded at this early hour, and the waiter came at once. We ordered beef stroganoff all around and talked nonstop while we ate. There were so many things to wonder about, such as what might happen to the younger children. Would the Falucci family get to keep Marcie? And what about little Denny? Would his foster family finally get their wish and be allowed to adopt him, now that there was no one to nix the plan?

I added that I suspected the grandmother had belatedly come around to appreciating her descendants and might choose to be there for them in the future. "Kitty and I heard some mea culpas from her at the funeral," I said. "As for Marcello, presumably there must be records somewhere to show his true parentage."

We'd almost finished eating when suddenly everyone turned to me. It was as if they'd all simultaneously recalled their unfinished business with me. I felt myself blushing. I looked around the table at curious, attentive faces, including that of my spouse. I knew what they were wondering, and I knew I had no good answer.

Janos spoke up. "We don't want to lose you from the family, Jill. We've grown very fond of you. Is there any chance you'll change your mind and move back in with Zoltan?"

I felt instantly teary. I squirmed and cleared my throat. "My problem isn't with Zoltan; it's with the musician's lifestyle." I worked up my courage to confess my dilemma. "I was horrified to discover how little money he actually earned at the Louisville concert. In fact, he didn't earn anything. We had to borrow money for that trip, and even then we came home broke. There seems little prospect of an adequate income in the near future. And I must confess that I'm no different from Kitty and Dorothea: I want a child. The doctor says it's now or never." I gazed around at worried faces and added, a bit lamely, "I have a condition, you see, which will make conception more improbable as time goes on. Unfortunately, Zoltan isn't ready for a child. He has no income and no immediate prospects, and he claims he needs a year of practice to regain fluency in his fingers and work up some show pieces."

"Maybe not a whole year," Zoltan said. "Honey, if you could just give me a little time." Zoltan reached for my hand again. "I've graduated now, and I'm willing to look for something … some teaching job, so I could manage to … to support you at least for a few months until you … until we …"

I could see he was struggling desperately to find answers in a situation that offered no answers. I shook my head. "No, you need to focus on your concert work now. If you sacrifice your career plans, you'll resent me later. It won't make for a happy lifetime partnership. You'll always be thinking of what you might have done if only your wife hadn't saddled you with responsibilities."

"I'm afraid this is my fault," Annie said. "I've made Zoltan feel that he has to be a concert pianist at any cost. I confess it never occurred to either of us, Jan or me, to assure our children we'll still love them even if they don't win success in their careers. But of course we will. A person shouldn't have to choose between career and baby. We had no business putting you two in a position like that. I just—I hadn't realized that the issue would arise so soon—or be so pressing."

"Certainly, you shouldn't have to break up your marriage over that," Janos agreed. "I just wish we were in a position to help. If only we hadn't had to leave everything behind in Europe—"

"But you did," I said. "And now we have to face facts. I don't want to deprive Zoltan of his chance at a concert career—but I also can't deprive myself of the chance to raise a child."

"Do you have someone else in mind?" Janos asked.

I shook my head. "I plan to go to Michigan, where I have a teaching assistantship lined up while I finish work on my master's degree, and then I'll find a job. It's possible that may pay well enough that I can afford to have a child without financial help from Zoltan. If so, we can get together again later. I can't make any promises—but I'm hoping for the best."

"I'll come with you to Ann Arbor." Zoltan reached for my hand. "Something may turn up in my field there. Things may work out. I don't want to lose you, Jill."

"If you really feel that way," I said, "I would welcome your company." I squeezed his hand, batted away tears, and managed a smile. "On one condition: you don't quote Freud to me anymore. I hate it when you accuse me of Freudian slips."

"I'll try to remember," he promised. "I admit I'm overly devoted to Freud."

I asked what he would do about the apartment. He said he'd advertise at Columbia and Juilliard for someone to sublet the place. "In these days of housing shortage, it ought to be easy to arrange a sublet."

It all seemed overwhelming to me. He would need his piano in Ann Arbor. I couldn't imagine how we would afford, on my small prospective teaching income, an apartment big enough to accommodate a piano—not to mention the shipping cost of a heavy instrument like that. And I'd vowed to borrow no more money from my parents, who'd surely claim I was out of my mind for insisting on more education. Whenever I mentioned the idea, they reminded me of Babs' success with no college at all.

I didn't want to speak up and spoil the happy mood of the day. This was the moment to celebrate Zoltan's freedom and not allow the gloom of an uncertain future to overshadow our happiness. I squeezed his hand again and said no more.

When we returned to the apartment, after seeing the elder Szekelys and Kitty off on the train, we found a note from George. Zoltan's piano teacher from Juilliard had called and requested that Zoltan call him back. When Zoltan did so, he learned that the Juilliard staff had been working on his behalf to arrange a tour for him as part of a quartet. The group was booked through the south and the midwest during the last three months of the year, and though he would earn only an honorarium, at least all expenses would be paid. He still had his tux, so this time it appeared he could really save what he earned. With my fellowship income, it might prove possible for us to have a life.

We agreed that we would try our best to stay together and make do with this minimal income. To celebrate our decision, we went for a walk along Riverside Drive, where we held hands and admired the lights from Palisades Park on the Jersey shore. Zoltan had plunged back into his optimistic mood and kept insisting things would work out. "I just wish you'd told me about the baby problem," he said, swinging my arm along with his. "At least you could have given me the chance to decide."

"It didn't occur to me you might opt for having a child," I admitted. "Or rather—it occurred to me that if you said yes, I'd be forever the villain of the family. I'd be the girl who ruined Zoltan's career."

A smile played on his lips. "Having a child can be a great thing when you love its mother."

I asserted my conviction that no man should have unwanted parenthood thrust upon him, especially not a man like Zoltan, who'd taken all possible precautions.

"In the future, let me decide about that. Don't just disappear out of my life and leave me assuming you love someone else. I can't take it."

"It was your Freud fetish that led you to that conclusion," I said. "That and *The Psychopathology of Everyday Life*. I admit that when I forget to pour your coffee, it means I have something else on my mind, but the something else isn't necessarily another man."

He'd dropped behind, looking at the view, so I stopped and turned to assure myself he was listening. In the dark he crashed into me, and his arms went around me. I liked the feel of him through my thin summer dress. I reveled in his closeness and pressed closer, smelling his aftershave.

"Not every cigar is a phallus," I whispered in his ear, "and not every forgetting means a secret lover. It could be a toothache or an overdue library book. Don't make a thing of it."

His arms encircled my waist, and he hugged me tight. Then he raised his right hand. "I hereby vow to put Freud behind me forever."

"Good. If there's another man, I'll tell you."

"The important thing," he said, "is that we love each other." He drew me into the shadows of a nearby elm tree and lowered his head. His lips sought mine, and we kissed passionately.

Then we headed for home.